5/18

The Designs of Lord Randolph Cavanaugh

This Large Print Book carries the
Seal of Approval of N.A.V.H.

THE DESIGNS OF LORD RANDOLPH CAVANAUGH

STEPHANIE LAURENS

THORNDIKE PRESS
A part of Gale, a Cengage Company

Farmington Hills, Mich • San Francisco • New York • Waterville, Maine
Meriden, Conn • Mason, Ohio • Chicago

Copyright © 2018 by Savdek Management Proprietary Limited.
The Cavanaughs.
Thorndike Press, a part of Gale, a Cengage Company.

Thorndike Press® Large Print Romance.
The text of this Large Print edition is unabridged.
Other aspects of the book may vary from the original edition.
Set in 16 pt. Plantin.

LIBRARY OF CONGRESS CIP DATA ON FILE.
CATALOGUING IN PUBLICATION FOR THIS BOOK
IS AVAILABLE FROM THE LIBRARY OF CONGRESS.

ISBN-13: 978-1-4328-5200-9 (hardcover)

Published in 2018 by arrangement with Harlequin Books S. A.

Printed in Mexico
1 2 3 4 5 6 7 22 21 20 19 18

THE DESIGNS OF LORD RANDOLPH CAVANAUGH

PROLOGUE

"I'm prepared to pay off all your debts provided that you complete a particular task for me."

The pale-faced, neatly dressed gentleman elegantly seated in one of the Antium Club's armchairs blinked, then stared through the fug of the smoking room at the older gentleman in the armchair opposite — his uncle. "What — *all* of them?" His tone suggested he was having difficulty believing his ears.

His uncle nodded portentously. "Indeed. And yes, I comprehend that's a significant sum. I also understand that you owe most if not all of that amount to . . . Shall we say a somewhat notorious lender-of-last-resort?" The older gentleman paused, then continued, "I assume you appealed to me because you're desperate, and you know your

7

brother and brothers-in-law won't lend you a sou regardless of any threats to your continuing good health."

The younger gentleman's lips tightened. "Just so." He hesitated, then asked, "What task do you need attended to?"

What could possibly be worth that much to you? The unvoiced question hung in the smoky air between them.

The older man's expression eased, and he waved a manicured hand. "Nothing too onerous." He paused as if ordering his thoughts, then went on, "You're aware that I invest in various projects, that I lead syndicates who fund enterprises such as railways and gas companies and the like. All very much above board. Unfortunately, these days, there's a welter of upstart inventors pushing wild ideas and making a lot of noise." He frowned. "Steering investors away from such ideas — ideas that will never amount to anything — isn't always easy. Men with money but little sense often behave like children — they get excited over the latest new thing. At present, there's a great deal of talk about improvements to steam engines, the sort that might make steam-powered horseless carriages into a commercial reality. All balderdash, of course, but it's making my life much harder." His frown darkened to a scowl.

After several moments of, apparently, dwelling on the iniquities of any situation that dared to make his life more difficult, his voice lowering, the older man said, "There's one particular invention that I've heard is nearing completion. It's due to be unveiled at the exhibition to be held in Birmingham on the twenty-second of July."

The older man's eyes, their expression shrewd and hard, cut to his nephew's face. "I need to be assured that that invention will fail — or at the very least, that it will not be successfully demonstrated at the exhibition, which will be attended by Prince Albert. I need to be able to hold that failure up to my investors as an example of the dangers of putting their money into such ill-envisioned, poorly designed projects. Projects that are not simply speculative but that have next to no chance of success."

The younger gentleman steepled his fingers before his face. He studied his uncle for several long moments, then murmured, "I assume you're asking me to interfere with — to sabotage — this invention." When his uncle's jaw set, and he returned the younger man's gaze levelly, the younger man asked with patently sincere curiosity, "How do you imagine I might do that?"

His uncle sat back and fussily straightened his trouser legs. "As to that . . . I can tell you where the inventor lives. His workshop is at his house. As to how you gain access or exactly how to . . . thrust a spoke in the invention's wheels, I will leave that to you to decide." The older gentleman met the younger man's eyes. "You are, apparently, a creative person — I'm sure you'll think of a way."

Despite his current situation, the younger gentleman was no fool. The sum of money his uncle was offering was substantial. To pay so much for tampering with a piece of machinery seemed a poor deal. Yet his uncle was known as a shrewd, ostentatiously rigid businessman, one who held on to his coin with a tight grip, and although he was a childless widower, he'd never previously shown any mellowness or warmth toward the members of his wider family.

The younger man leaned forward, his gaze on his uncle's face. "What is it about this particular invention that makes it so" — *threatening* — "undesirable?"

His uncle's face hardened. Anger flared, readily discernible in his brown eyes, yet it was not directed at his nephew but, apparently, at the invention in question. "It's . . . a *travesty* of an investment project. It

10

shouldn't be allowed — not as a syndicated investment. We don't need bally horseless carriages — we have perfectly good horses, and there's nothing wrong with the carriages they pull. These machines — these newfangled engines — are full of not just cogs and gears but valves and tubing and gauges and pistons. How they work is incomprehensible — for my money, deliberately so."

He drew in a breath. "Steam locomotives were one thing. Even steam-powered looms were straightforward enough. But this latest round of contraptions!" He flung up his hands in a gesture of either incomprehension or defeat — or perhaps both. Although he kept his voice low, he was all but ranting as he continued, "How am I supposed to deal with my investors? They rattle on about pressures and inclines, and because I can't explain why it's wrong, they won't listen to my advice that we — all of society — don't need these things, and they shouldn't invest in them."

Aha. You're losing investors to those who are running the syndicates for these new inventions. You're a Luddite, and you don't understand, so . . . . The younger man hid a smile. Now he understood that, the deal seemed much more even-handed. His life

11

and his livelihood were under threat from his principal creditor, and this invention, the success of it, threatened his uncle's livelihood — his uncle's reason for being.

He might be about to undertake to do something not entirely above board, but at least, to his way of thinking, the exchange seemed fair enough.

His gaze still on his uncle's now-distinctly choleric face, the younger man slowly nodded. "I see." He paused, then quietly said, "Very well. I'll do it. I'll take care of this matter for you, and you will take care of my debts for me." He held out his hand.

His uncle studied his eyes, then grasped his hand, and they shook.

Retrieving his hand, the younger man said, "You'd better tell me all you can about this invention."

His uncle complied, revealing the invention's location, the inventor's name, and that the invention was some sort of steam engine purported to incorporate several improvements on Russell's reworking of Trevithick's original of 1803.

The younger man had less notion of what that description meant than, he suspected, his uncle did. However, he nodded. After rapidly replaying their earlier conversation, he asked, "Am I correct in thinking that, regardless of whether this engine actually runs or not, as long as it's not unveiled to any fanfare at the exhibition in Birmingham, you will be satisfied?"

His uncle frowned slightly. "That should suffice. If the invention isn't successfully demonstrated there" — he smiled tightly, coldly — "no one will believe it works." After a second, he nodded decisively. "Yes. That will be enough."

"Good-oh." The younger gentleman pushed to his feet.

His uncle looked up at him. "I will, of course, be attending the exhibition myself, so I'll be present to view the outcome of your efforts first-hand."

The younger man inclined his head. "I'll endeavor to please. And now, I'd best be on my way."

His uncle murmured a farewell, and the younger gentleman made for the Antium's main door.

He paused on the club's front steps and looked up at the cloudless summer sky.

How hard could it be to rearrange a lever or two, or unscrew a few bolts, or swipe the notes of some absentminded inventor?

He suspected he could satisfy his uncle easily enough, after which his life and his future would be his again.

Yet as he descended the steps and set out for his lodgings, he could feel uneasiness over what he'd agreed to do swirling inside. *But . . .*

When it came down to it, he was desperate. Truly desperate. And at least, this way, no one would die.

ONE

Lord Randolph Cavanaugh — Rand to his family, friends, and associates — tooled his curricle down the leafy lanes and reveled in the fresh country air. After spending the past four months in London, he was more than ready for a change, and a long-scheduled visit to Raventhorne Abbey to catch up with his brother and sister-in-law and their children had provided the perfect excuse to leave the steadily escalating heat of the capital behind.

However, as matters had fallen out, the trip to the Abbey in Wiltshire had coincided with an unexpected need to check up on one of the projects Rand's firm, Cavanaugh Investments, had underwritten. For the past five years, ever since he'd reached twenty-five and come into his full inheritance, Rand had worked steadily and diligently to carve out a place — a life and a purpose — for himself. He wasn't content to simply be Raventhorne's half brother. He'd wanted something more — some enterprise to call his own.

Through Ryder — Rand's older half brother, now the Marquess of Raventhorne — and Ryder's marchioness, Mary, Rand had come to know the Cynsters. Gabriel Cynster, one of Mary's older cousins, had long been a renowned figure in investment circles. Rand had shamelessly apprenticed himself, albeit informally, to Gabriel. After several years of learning from the master, Rand had struck out on his own. He'd made managing investments in the latest inventions his particular area of expertise.

One of his syndicate's current investments was an exclusive stake in the Throgmorton Steam-Powered Horseless Carriage. There'd been steam-powered horseless carriages before — Trevithick had demonstrated the principle in 1803 — but none had solved the various issues that had kept such inventions from becoming widely adopted. William Throgmorton had made his name through a spate of steam-powered inventions that had refined the machines of earlier inventors, making the modified engines much more commercially attractive.

When it came to inventions, Throgmorton was a known and established name. Investing in his latest project, while still ranking as definitely speculative, had seemed a good wager, one with possibly very high returns.

Rand had known William Throgmorton for several years. Through his syndicated investment fund, Rand had supported several of Throgmorton's earlier projects, all of which had delivered satisfactorily. Rand was entirely comfortable with his current investment in Throgmorton's latest project.

What he wasn't so comfortable with — what had necessitated this side trip into deepest Berkshire — was Throgmorton's recent silence. The last report Rand had received had been over three months ago. Until March, Throgmorton had reported more or less every month.

Rand trusted Throgmorton. More, he knew that inventors sometimes became so caught up in the actual work that they lost track of time, and all other responsibilities faded from their minds. Yet over the years Rand had worked with him, Throgmorton hadn't missed reporting before.

What was even more troubling was that Throgmorton had failed to respond to not one but two letters Rand had subsequently sent. That wasn't like Throgmorton at any time, but now, with the Birmingham exhibition — at which the presentation and demonstration of the Throgmorton engine had already been widely touted — less than a month away, Rand needed reassurance that all was progressing smoothly with the invention, not just for himself but for all his syndicate's investors.

The cream of British inventing would be at the exhibition. Prince Albert was scheduled to open it, and the Prince could be relied on to take a keen interest in the inventions on show. Success at the exhibition was crucial for the future of Throgmorton's engine and also for Rand's status in the investment community. If Throgmorton failed to deliver . . .

Rand pushed the thought from his mind. Throgmorton hadn't failed him yet.

Nevertheless, Rand needed to know what was going on at Throgmorton Hall. He needed to hear of progress from Throgmorton himself, and as the man wasn't answering his letters, Rand had decided to call in person.

He hadn't visited Throgmorton Hall before; he'd always met William in the City. All he knew of the Hall was that it lay close to the village of Hampstead Norreys, buried in the depths of Berkshire. Aside from all else, Rand would admit he was curious to see Throgmorton's workshop.

So instead of continuing west out of Reading and thus to Raventhorne Abbey, on reaching Reading, Rand had taken the Wantage road. He'd stopped at an inn in Pangbourne for lunch, and his groom, Shields, had consulted with the ostlers. Armed with the information Shields had gained, Rand had elected to drive on to Basildon before turning off the highway onto the narrower country lanes and steering his horses first to the west, then the southwest. He'd passed through Ashampstead some time ago. According to the signposts, the village of Hampstead Norreys lay just a mile or so on.

Rand held his bays to a steady trot. After calling on Throgmorton and reviewing his progress and receiving the assurances Rand and his investors required, Rand would have plenty of time to drive on to the Abbey. With any luck, he would arrive before his eldest nephew and his niece had been put to bed. His youngest nephew was just two years old; Rand wasn't sure what time he would be tucked in.

Rand had discovered he enjoyed being an

uncle; he and his two younger brothers, Christopher — Kit — and Godfrey, openly vied for the title of favorite uncle to Ryder and Mary's three offspring. Rand grinned to himself; he was looking forward to spending the next few days — perhaps the next week — with Ryder, Mary, and their noisy brood.

An arched gray-stone bridge appeared along the lane; Rand slowed his horses and let them walk up and over. A small sign at the crest of the bridge informed him he was crossing the Pang, presumably the upper reaches of the same river he'd earlier crossed at Pangbourne.

"Looks like the village we want just ahead," Shields said from his perch behind Rand. "Seems it stretches away to the right."

Rand nodded and shook the reins. The horses picked up their pace, and the curricle bowled smoothly on.

To the left, the lane was bordered by trees, with more trees behind them — a thick forest of oaks and beeches, much like the old outliers of the Savernake that still lingered near Raventhorne.

The trees thinned to the right, where the village stretched parallel to the stream; Rand glimpsed roofs of thatch and lead through breaks in the canopies.

A sign by the road declared they'd reached the village of Hampstead Norreys. As Shields had predicted, the village street lay to the right, stretching northward, with shops and houses on either side. An inn — the Norreys Arms — squatted at the nearest corner.

Rand drew up in the lane opposite the inn. The lane led on, heading west through an avenue of trees before curving to the left — to the southwest.

Shields dropped to the lane. "I'll go and ask."

Rand merely nodded. He watched as Shields strode into the inn yard and spoke with the stable lad sweeping the cobbles by the inn's side door.

Then Shields passed the boy a coin and hurried back. The curricle tipped as he clambered up behind Rand. "We follow the lane on," Shields reported. "Apparently, the drive to the Hall lies just around that curve ahead, and there's no way we'll miss it. There are stone gateposts with eagles atop, but no gate."

Rand dipped his head in acknowledgment and gave his pair the office. They obediently stepped out, and he guided them on.

Sure enough, just yards around the curve to the southwest, a pair of stone gateposts

21

marked the entrance to a well-tended drive. Rand slowed the horses and turned them onto the smooth, beaten earth. As the carriage bowled along, he glanced around, taking in the cool shade cast by the surrounding trees and the shafts of sunlight that filtered through, dispelling the gloom. The drive was bordered by woodland — primarily beech and oak, but with occasional poplars with their shimmering leaves randomly interspersed here and there. After the warmth of the summer day, the tree-lined drive formed a pleasant avenue; indeed, all he'd seen of the area suggested it was one of those pockets of quietly contented, lush and green, rural countryside that could still be found dotted about southern England.

No house or building had been visible from the lane. Eventually, the drive emerged from the woodland into a large clearing in which Throgmorton Hall stood front and center, dominating the space between the trees.

The Hall was a three-storied block clad in the local pale-gray stone. Rand suspected the house's Palladian façade had been added to an older building, yet the remodeling had been well done; Throgmorton Hall projected the image of a comfortable gentleman's residence. The house faced west, and the long-paned white-framed windows of the lower two stories and the dormer windows of the upper story overlooked a wide swath of lawn. More lawn ran away to the south, dotted with several large old trees and ultimately bordered by the woodlands, which, as far as Rand could see, completely encircled the house.

He'd slowed the horses to a walk. As they drew nearer the house, to his left, he spotted a shrubbery backing into the woodland, with a decent-sized stable tucked tidily beyond it.

The drive ended in a large oval forecourt before the steps leading up to a semicircular porch shielding the large front door. A small, circular fountain stood in the center of the forecourt, directly opposite the door.

Rand drove his curricle into the forecourt and around the fountain and drew up beside the edge of the lawn opposite the front steps. He set the brake, then handed the reins to Shields and stepped down. "I don't know how long I'll be." He spotted a lad coming from the stables. "Perhaps an hour — maybe two. Do what you think is best."

Shields grunted.

Rand left him to deal with the horses and

carriage and set off across the forecourt.

He'd taken only two paces when a muffled *boom!* fractured the slumbering silence.

The sound came from inside the house.

Rand checked, then his face set, and he ran toward the house.

Wisps of vapor seeped out from around the door, then the door was wrenched open, and people — maids, footmen, and others — came streaming out, along with billowing clouds of steam.

Even as he raced toward them, Rand registered that none of those coughing and waving aside the steamy clouds seemed the least bit panic-stricken. He slowed as he neared the steps. Those escaping from the house looked at him curiously — then an older lady came tottering out, one hand clutched to her impressive bosom.

Rand leapt up the steps. "Here — take my arm."

The lady blinked at him, then smiled. "Thank you. No matter how often it happens, it's always a shock." The rest of those who had emerged from the house had gathered around the fountain and stood looking expectantly at the door. The matronly lady pointed down the steps to a bench set before the flowerbed along the front of the house. "I usually sit there and catch my breath."

Swallowing the many questions leaping to his tongue, Rand assisted the lady down the steps and guided her to the bench.

She sat with a heartfelt sigh, then looked up at him. "I don't believe we've been introduced, but thank you." She looked past him at his curricle, then raised her gaze — now openly curious — to his face. "I take it you've just arrived."

"Indeed." Before Rand could give his name, a commotion in the open doorway drew his and the lady's attention.

Someone was attempting to propel a slender gentleman outside. He was clad in a long, gray inventor's coat and sported a pair of goggles, now hanging about his neck. The coat was smudged in several places, the gentleman's dark-brown hair was sticking out from his head in tufts, and he appeared rather dazed.

The person behind him prodded more violently, and staggering somewhat, the gentleman stumbled out of the steamy interior onto the front porch.

He was followed by a young lady. Scowling ferociously, she planted her hands on her hips and glared at the hapless gentleman.

Rand blinked, then looked again.

Slender, of middling height, with a pale complexion and fine features, clad in a sky-blue gown and all but vibrating with reined emotion, courtesy of her stance, the young lady looked every inch a virago with rose-gold hair.

Rand had never seen a more fascinating creature.

"That's it!" the virago declared. Her voice was pleasingly low, yet presently carried the razor-sharp edge of frustrated ire. "Enough!" she continued, still addressing the gentleman, who was shaking his head as if to clear smothering clouds from his brain. "You have to stop! You can't keep blowing the wretched contraption up!"

The gentleman frowned into the distance. "I think I know what went wrong." He turned toward the virago, clearly intending to argue her point. "It was the feed —"

As the gentleman swung to face the young lady, his gaze landed on Rand, and his words died.

The virago followed the gentleman's gaze. She saw Rand and stiffened. Her expression blanked, and she lowered her arms to her sides. Along with the apparently dumb-founded gentleman, she stared at Rand.

The gentleman faintly frowned. "Good afternoon. Can we help you?" His gaze flicked across the forecourt, and he took in Rand's curricle — an expensive equipage drawn by top-of-the-line horseflesh. The gentleman's eyes widened, and he looked back at Rand.

With a murmur of "Excuse me" to the older lady, Rand left her on the bench and climbed the steps to the porch. He halted a yard from the younger lady and the gentleman. Now he was on the same level, he realized the gentleman was nearly as tall as he was, although of slighter build. By the cast of the gentleman's features and his bright hazel eyes, he was plainly William Throgmorton's son. As for the young lady . . . despite her eyes being more green than hazel and her wonderful hair a tumbling mass of rose-gold curls, judging by the set of her lips and chin, Rand rather thought she must be William's daughter. He inclined his head to her, then focused on the gentleman. "My name is Lord Randolph Cavanaugh. I'm here to see Mr. William Throgmorton." He paused, then added, "I assume he's your father."

Silence greeted his announcement.

The gentleman continued to stare even as he paled; Rand had little doubt he'd recognized Rand's name.

Rand glanced at the virago. Her eyes had

27

widened in what had to be shock; as Rand looked, she paled, too.

Then her green eyes narrowed, her lips and chin firmed, and she looked at the young gentleman. "William John . . . ?" Her tone was both questioning and demanding.

Judging by William John's expression, all sorts of unwelcome thoughts were tumbling through his brain; they left him looking faintly terrified. He glanced at his sister, and guilt was added to the mix.

What is going on here?

Rand laid a firm hand on the reins of his own temper. He glanced past the pair into the house; the steamy haze was evaporating. Evenly, he asked, "Is Mr. William Throgmorton at home?"

He looked back at the younger man, apparently William John Throgmorton.

Finally, William John focused on Rand's face and somewhat sheepishly said, "Ah. As to that . . ."

When, apparently lost for words, William John fell silent again, Rand looked to the virago.

Briefly, she raised her eyes to his, then dipped in a curtsy. "Lord Cavanaugh. I'm Miss Throgmorton, and, as you've no doubt guessed, this is my brother, William John Throgmorton." She paused, then clasped

28

her hands before her, tipped up her chin, and met Rand's eyes. "As for our father, I regret to inform you that he passed away in January."

It was Rand's turn to stare. In his case, unseeing, while his thoughts turned cartwheels in his head. Eventually, his accents clipped and curt, he stated, as much for himself as anyone else, "William Throgmorton is dead."

It wasn't a question, and no one replied.

Rand blinked and refocused on William John. "In *January*?" Despite his hold on his temper, incensed incredulity underscored his words.

Helplessly, William John stared back.

From the corner of his eye, Rand saw Miss Throgmorton, her gaze fixed on her brother, her expression close to an open accusation, confirm that telling detail with a decisive nod.

Rand returned his attention to the pale and blinking William John. If William Throgmorton was dead, then presumably William John was his heir — legally and financially. The question burning in Rand's brain was whether William John was his father's successor intellectually as well.

If he was, then . . .

There might — just possibly — be a way

out of the fire William Throgmorton's death, his son's failure to tell Rand of it, and the rapidly approaching exhibition in Birmingham had landed Rand in.

The three of them remained staring at each other, weighing each other up in various ways. Then Rand drew in a long, deep breath and looked past the open door. "Perhaps," he said, his tone crisp and rigidly even, "assuming it's safe, we might take the discussion of our dilemma — the business arrangement my investment syndicate had with your father — inside."

The virago glanced into the hall, then looked out at the staff and called, "All's clear." Then she glanced at Rand; he was perfectly certain he saw wariness in her eyes. "If you will follow me, my lord."

She led the way inside.

With an awkward wave, William John gestured for Rand to precede him.

As Rand crossed the threshold into the well-appointed front hall and the telltale scent of overheated metal reached him, he counseled himself that his first step in sorting out this mess had to be to learn all he could about the true situation at Throgmorton Hall.

"The boiler exploded, you see." Trailing behind Rand, William John apparently thought that part of his explanation was the most critical.

Following Miss Throgmorton across the hall tiles toward the door of what Rand assumed would be the drawing room, he glanced back to see William John deviating toward a plain wooden door — the sort usually found at the bottom of tower steps — that was set into the wall to the right of the front door and presently stood ajar.

Rand halted. Beyond the door, he glimpsed stone steps spiraling down. The metallic scent was emanating from there.

"Oh no." Miss Throgmorton brushed past him. "You are not disappearing down there." She clamped her hands about her brother's arm and forcibly dragged him away from the partially open door. "The drawing room, William John." Her tone was stern. She didn't look at Rand as she towed her brother past him. "You need to explain what's happened to Lord Cavanaugh." She uttered a small humph. "I'd like to hear your version of that as well."

Rand felt his brows rise. He fell in behind the Throgmorton siblings, inwardly reflecting that the next hour was bidding fair to being significantly more fraught than he'd anticipated.

The drawing room possessed a similar

ambiance to the front hall — well lit, comfortable, and unostentatious. Unfussy, yet feminine — or at least bearing the imprint of some female hand. The armchairs and long sofa were well stuffed and covered in flowery chintz. The walls were a very pale green, and the white painted woodwork gleamed. Long windows opened onto a flagstone terrace that overlooked the long south lawn and allowed slanting summer sunlight to illuminate the room.

Miss Throgmorton all but pushed her brother down to sit on the sofa, then moved to claim one of the chintz-covered armchairs — the one that faced the door. With a wave significantly more graceful than her brother's, she invited Rand to take the armchair that faced the sofa across a low table.

Rand sat, strangely aware that he was dressed informally, wearing breeches, riding jacket, and top boots, rather than his customary trousers and well-cut coat. Why the thought popped into his mind, he had no idea. As matters stood, he had far more to worry about than the figure he cut in the Throgmortons' eyes, and he seriously doubted William John would notice.

He focused on the younger man. He judged William John to be in his mid-twenties. Having siblings of his own, after watching the interaction between brother and sister, he would wager Miss Throgmorton was about a year younger than her transparently exasperating brother.

At present, William John was sitting upright, with his hands clasped between his knees and a slight frown on his face. His gaze was fixed on his hands.

After taking in that sight, Miss Throgmorton cleared her throat and glanced at Rand. "I apprehend you had business dealings with my father, my lord. If you would explain what those were, perhaps we might" — she gestured vaguely and rather weakly concluded — "be able to assist you."

Rand studied her for a moment, then looked at William John. "I suspect your brother knows very well what my dealings with your father were, Miss Throgmorton. William John — it might be easier for us all if I use that name — certainly recognized my name."

William John raised his eyes, met Rand's, then grimaced. He looked at Miss Throgmorton. "Lord Cavanaugh is the principal investor in the syndicate that funded Papa's steam engine."

Felicia Throgmorton stared at her brother. "The one you just blew up? Yet again." A sensation of coldness was welling inside her.

33

Gloomily, William John nodded.

The cold was dread, and it continued to spread. Felicia glanced at Lord Cavanaugh, then looked again at William John. "What, exactly, do you mean by 'funded'?"

William John shifted on the sofa in a way that only chilled Felicia more. "Lord Randolph" — William John glanced at the lord sitting unmovingly and projecting all the menace of a crouching tiger — "or more accurately, he and the investors who band together with him in his investing syndicate, advanced Papa the funds to finish the engine and present it at the exhibition in return for a two-thirds share of the rights in the invention."

Felicia compressed her lips into a tight line, holding back any too-aggressive response. As the daughter of a longtime inventor, she understood enough about rights and funding to comprehend the situation. But in the circumstances . . . Without looking at Lord Cavanaugh, she nodded crisply. "I see. So where are these funds as of this moment? How does the account stand?"

"Well, we're only three weeks from the exhibition, you know." William John cast an apologetic look at Lord Cavanaugh. "Most of the money's been spent."

She frowned. "Spent on what? Other than

two replacement boilers and a few valves, you haven't bought much since Papa died." She glanced at Lord Cavanaugh; he was watching their exchange with an entirely unreadable — but by no means encouraging — expression on his handsome, autocratic face. Her nerves twitched, and she hurried to say, "I'm sure we can repay his lordship whatever sum was left at the time Papa died —"

Frantic gestures from William John had her looking back at him.

The cold inside coalesced into an icy knot and sank to the pit of her stomach. "What?" She heard her voice rise. "We can't?"

William John stared at her, then warily said, "The money you've been using to pay the bills . . ."

"What?" Even to her own ears, her voice sounded shrill. "But . . ." She stared at her brother. "You — and Papa — told me that money was royalties from his earlier inventions."

"Yes, well." William John squirmed more definitely. "We knew you wouldn't understand, so . . ."

"So you lied to me." She felt as if the bottom had dropped out of her world. More quietly, she added, "Both of you."

When William John grimaced and looked

down at his clasped hands, she forced herself to draw in a shuddering breath and, seizing the reins of her temper in an iron grip and banishing the pain of what felt perilously like betrayal from her mind, with rigid calm, she stated, "You encouraged me to use investors' funds for the household."

William John blinked, then frowned and met her eyes. "We had to live."

The presence in the armchair opposite the sofa uncrossed his long, well-muscled legs.

The graceful and controlled movement immediately drew her eyes.

Rand had been waiting; he caught Miss Throgmorton's gaze. "To clarify, Miss Throgmorton, the terms of our investment in your father's work included a stipend for living expenses for your father and his assistant." With a dip of his head, Rand indicated William John. "The arrangement also included funds for the upkeep of the laboratory-workshop and so on. Consequently, that the funds were used for household expenses isn't an issue. I assure you neither I nor the investors I represent will be in any way concerned about that."

It was, however, telling that she had known enough to be concerned. In this particular case, it didn't matter; in many cases, it would have.

"However" — he transferred his gaze to her brother — "as William John has pointed out, the exhibition at which it was agreed that your father would demonstrate the success of his improved steam engine is now a mere three weeks away." He met William John's hazel eyes. "At this point, my principal concern — mine and that of the investors I represent — is whether the Throgmorton steam engine will be operational and fit to be unveiled at the exhibition as planned."

So much was riding on that outcome; until now, he hadn't realized how much — inside, he was still grappling with the full scope of the impending threat.

He kept his gaze steady on William John's face — refusing to give in to the impulse to glance at Miss Throgmorton to see how she was coping with what had clearly been a painful revelation — and suggested, "Why don't you outline for me where the invention stands at present?"

To any inventor, such a request was an invitation to be seized, and William John proved he was as single-minded as his father; he eagerly complied and rattled on. Several times, when his descriptions became too technical, Rand halted the flow and asked for clarification. Nevertheless, within a few minutes, any doubts that William John was his father's son had been laid to rest.

Whether he could accomplish what his father had not managed to achieve prior to his death was another matter.

While William John related all he had done since their father's death, Miss Throgmorton, Rand noticed, sat back in her chair and listened intently. Her mind did not wander; judging by the steady focus of her gaze, she was able to understand William John's explanation, possibly as well as Rand could.

Eventually, William John reached the present. "So, you see, now that we've finally got the flow adjusted and the mechanisms properly aligned, it's purely a matter of getting the controls correctly reset to allow for the increased power." He grimaced. "That's why the boiler blew. I still haven't got the settings right."

Miss Throgmorton made a disapproving sound. "That was the third boiler in as many weeks."

William John shrugged. "The adjustments to the controls are . . . complicated. If they're not correct, then the pressure in the boiler continues to increase, and if we can't release it or shut down the engine quickly enough . . ." He raised his hands in a helpless gesture.

Miss Throgmorton sniffed.

Rand studied the younger man. "I have a question." The point was puzzling. "Your father died in January, yet I continued to receive reports on his — your — progress until the end of March. From what you've told me, those reports were accurate, yet they were in your father's hand . . ." He realized. "But they weren't, were they?"

William John shook his head. "I've been writing the reports for Papa for years. I just . . . continued."

Rand nodded. "Very well. My last question. When your father died, why didn't you inform me and the syndicate of his death?"

William John compressed his lips and stared levelly back at Rand.

Rand waited. He was grateful that Miss Throgmorton also remained silent.

Eventually, without shifting his gaze from Rand's face, William John said, "I worked alongside Papa on this invention from its inception. From an inventor's perspective, I have just as much invested in it as he. It was and still is my hope — my very real ambition — to complete the engine and take it to the exhibition. I knew that I would meet you and perhaps some of the other investors there. I thought I could explain what had happened then and, in so doing, establish myself as an inventor in my own right." He glanced briefly at his sister, then looked back at Rand. "As my father's heir invention-wise, so to speak."

Rand knew that answer was the unvarnished truth. William John was like many inventors — incapable of guile, at least when it came to inventions and inventing. In that field, they spent so much time focused unrelentingly on facts that dissembling did not come easily; indeed, most saw any form of lie as a waste of time.

Moreover, Rand could understand William John's position. The son would need to prove himself to move out of the shadow of an established personality. Indeed, Rand's own quest for recognition separate from the large presence of Ryder and the marquessate was what had led him to the Throgmortons' drawing room. As much as William John, Rand needed this invention to work. He'd staked a great deal more than mere money on it; his reputation as a leader of investment syndicates was riding on this project. If he failed . . . his chances of attracting investors to any future syndicate would dim considerably.

While not strictly correct, William John's approach to the situation was entirely understandable, at least to Rand.

Slowly, he nodded. "Very well. We now know where we stand." His personal strength lay in evaluating options and finding the best way out of any difficulty. He straightened in his chair. "What we need to do next is to define the problems facing us."

Still reeling from the impact of successive revelations, Felicia felt that defining their problems was a very good idea. That both her father and her brother had been so duplicitous, at least in her eyes, deeply troubled her; the scope of what had been going on under her nose while she'd remained entirely unaware had shaken her to her foundations. She'd always believed she had been the one steering the ship of their household, while in reality, she hadn't even known in which direction they'd been headed.

She focused on Lord Cavanaugh as, with a slight frown — one of concentration — drawing down his dark brows, he stated, "With only three weeks to go before the exhibition, we cannot withdraw from the event — not without sustaining considerable damage to all our reputations. A withdrawal at this stage would signal to everyone that the invention had failed. That, of course, is the one result we would all prefer to avoid."

His lordship's gaze rested on William John. Felicia had already noticed that Cavanaugh had eyes of the warmest mid brown she'd ever seen — like heated caramel or melted toffee.

"I believe," he continued, "that in the circumstances, we must hold to our goal of getting the steam engine working per your father's plans and successfully unveil the Throgmorton Steam-Powered Horseless Carriage at the exhibition. If we fail to do so" — he shot Felicia a glance, then returned his gaze to William John — "William John's future as an inventor will be ruined before he truly starts. You will become an investment pariah" — again, Cavanaugh glanced Felicia's way — "and as I understand it, you don't have the capital to undertake further inventing of this nature on your own."

William John grimaced. "All you say is true. That's why I've forged on so doggedly — I *have* to get the engine working perfectly and present it at the exhibition."

Cavanaugh inclined his head. "But there's more at stake than just your future."

Felicia nearly laughed — humorlessly — at the surprise that showed in William John's face. As she well knew, inventors

42

never thought beyond the invention. Beyond their work.

She felt Cavanaugh's gaze touch her face again, then he said, "Forgive me if I mistook the implications of your earlier exchange, but it seemed to me that absent the funds advanced to support this latest invention, this household would not be solvent."

Felicia met Cavanaugh's eyes and grimly nodded. "No need to apologize — you're quite correct." For an instant, she allowed herself to hold to the steady warmth in his gaze while she rapidly reviewed the household accounts. "Put simply" — she looked at William John — "if this latest invention isn't a success, the family will be financially ruined. We do not have sufficient income from other sources to continue the upkeep of the Hall." She allowed her gaze to weigh on her brother. "We would be forced to sell up."

William John flinched. "Really?" He met her eyes as if willing her to say she was joking.

"Yes." It was past time he faced the truth of the dire straits to which inventing and inventions had driven them.

After a second, Cavanaugh went on, "And, sadly, the repercussions do not end there."

Felicia looked at him, puzzled as to what else might be at stake, but his gaze seemed to have turned inward.

"While this project is not my first as the head of a syndicate, it is the most prominent of my investment projects to date. It's the project my coterie of investors are most interested in seeing succeed. If we" — he refocused on William John, then included Felicia with his gaze — "do not deliver on the promise of that investment, do not live up to the assurances of success I gave, then my carefully nurtured reputation as an investment syndicate leader will be . . . severely compromised."

Only now that he'd considered the possibility — if not likelihood — of the Throgmorton steam engine failing had Rand realized just how much he'd staked on its success. "Of course, on top of that, my own funds will take a sizeable hit." But that was the least of his worries.

Silence fell — a moment of staring into the abyss as they all dwelled on the consequences of failure.

Perhaps unsurprisingly, it was William John who first stirred and said, "Well, we'll just have to make sure the engine works as advertised."

Rand took in the young inventor's unwavering determination and had to wonder . . .

Regardless, there seemed no other way forward, yet long acquaintance with the species had taught Rand that where time was a factor, even when deadlines loomed, inventors could not be trusted to keep their focus.

He felt as if the circumstances were forming up around him and all-but-physically herding him into taking on a role he never had before. Into taking a large step beyond the comfort of the arenas in which he was knowledgeable and embarking down a path of unknown risks and unforeseeable challenges.

Nevertheless . . .

He glanced again at Miss Throgmorton, then looked at William John. "I agree. At this point, I can't see any alternative way forward — not for any of us — other than to persevere, get the engine working, and present it successfully at the exhibition."

William John nodded, his expression resolved and sure.

Rand glanced at Miss Throgmorton. If they were to have any hope of succeeding in time, they would need her support as well.

Felicia met and returned Cavanaugh's gaze. Only when he faintly arched his brows did she realize he was waiting for — asking for — her agreement. She blinked, then cleared her throat and said, "I agree. There seems no other viable way to proceed." Until the last moments, she hadn't realized just how dire — how absolute and inevitable — the consequences of failure would be.

Only now did she fully comprehend what was hanging over their heads.

Yet another revelation she would need time to fully assimilate.

Cavanaugh nodded. "So we three are re-solved."

Rand shifted his gaze to William John. "Given how much is riding on the outcome, I'll remain and assist you as required, at least until you get the engine going. I can't work on the mechanics as you do, but I am very good at managing time and resources, and we'll need everything running smoothly if we're to succeed in attaining our mutual goal."

Far from being put out by the thought of having someone looking over his shoulder, William John's face lit with eagerness. "I'll be delighted to explain the engine to you." He paused, his mind clearly going to the invention, then he grimaced and refocused on Rand. "The boiler will be too hot for us to dismantle it today, but I can show you the workshop and explain what does what and where our current problems lie — if

46

you'd like that?"

Rand nodded and pushed out of the armchair. "That sounds an excellent place to start."

He glanced at Miss Throgmorton. A faint frown on her face, she was sitting with her hands clasped in her lap, staring at the low table. As if feeling his gaze, she looked up, and he caught her green eyes. He inclined his head. "Until later, Miss Throgmorton."

She dipped her head in reply. "Lord Cavanaugh. I'll have a room prepared for you." To her brother, she added, "I'll see you both at dinner."

William John waved vaguely and headed for the door.

Rand followed and wondered just what he'd let himself in for.

TWO

Rand followed William John into the front hall. The younger man led the way to the wooden door Rand had earlier noted.

Someone had shut the door, no doubt against the still-definite smell, but apparently oblivious, William John lifted the latch and started down the stairs. "Our laboratory-workshop takes up most of the lower level of the house. My father set it up when he was a young man, and it's been in use ever since."

Descending the spiral stairs on William John's heels, Rand asked, "How do you get heavy machinery into the workshop?" The stairway was too narrow to get even a smallish engine down.

"Ah. As I said, it's a lower level of the house — not a cellar. The land behind the house is lower than in the front, so we have a pair of double doors that open to a paved courtyard at the rear of the house — we just roll the engines in and out."

They rounded another curve, and William John halted. "Damn!"

Rand stopped two steps up and looked over William John's head at the drifting murk blanketing the enclosed space below them. A noxious stench, sulfurous and metallic, rose from the cloud. The miasma wafted, veiling benches and the large bulk of an engine, plus any number of other contraptions dotted about the wide, stone-walled chamber.

"I forgot the door was shut." William John clapped a hand over his nose and mouth and plunged into the fug. He rushed across the room to a pair of large wooden doors, fumbled with the latch, then pushed the doors wide.

The cloud of heavy gases shifted, then settled again. William John stood on the flagstones outside and frantically waved his arms, attempting to encourage fresh air to flow in, but his efforts were largely ineffectual.

He dragged in a breath, then rushed back through the haze to the stairs. Climbing to where Rand had waited, William John sighed. He looked down and across the room. "Perhaps we'd better leave any inspection until tomorrow."

Rand grunted in agreement. "I doubt inhaling tainted steam will do either of us any good." He turned and led the way back up the stairs.

William John followed; even his footfalls sounded disappointed. "My man, Corby — well, he used to be Papa's, so he's accustomed to dealing with explosions. He'll see to getting the place tidied up first thing tomorrow."

Rand merely nodded. He emerged into the front hall to find the butler hovering.

At the sight of Rand, the butler — middleaged, tallish, of average build, with thinning brown hair and a stately manner — came to attention and bowed. "Lord Cavanaugh. Welcome to Throgmorton Hall." The butler straightened. "I regret we were somewhat distracted when you arrived. My name is Johnson. Should you require anything during your stay, please ring and we will endeavor to meet your needs. Miss Throgmorton asked for a room to be prepared. If it's convenient, I can show you to your room now."

Rand realized he felt as if, in driving up the Throgmorton Hall drive, he'd stepped into some strange and unpredictable world; a butler who, despite appearing strictly conventional, referred to dealing with an in-house explosion as being "somewhat distracted" seemed all of a piece. "Thank you." Taking a few moments to reassess the situation appealed to his naturally cautious self. "I would appreciate shedding the dust of my journey."

Johnson bowed again. "Indeed, my lord. I'll have a maid bring up some water. If you'll follow me?"

Rand turned to William John; the younger man was standing, frowning at the floor. "I expect we'll meet at dinner."

"What?" William John blinked owlishly, refocused on Rand, then his face cleared. "Oh yes. I'll look forward to it."

Rand resisted the urge to shake his head, nodded instead, and followed Johnson up the stairs. One thing he'd already ascertained: William John was as vague and as given to fits of absentmindedness as his father had been.

The room the butler led Rand to was a pleasant bedchamber located in the northwest corner of the first floor. Comfortably furnished, with upholstery, curtains, and bedspread in a striped fabric that was neither masculine nor feminine, the room felt airy and was blessedly uncluttered. The bed was a half tester, wide and well supplied with pillows. Two side tables flanking the bed, an armoire, a tallboy, a desk with a straight-backed chair set beneath one window, plus a small dressing table tucked into a corner with a stool before it, rounded out the furniture.

Two windows looked out over the grounds, one facing north, the other west. Late-afternoon light streamed into the room through the west-facing window. Noting that his bags had already been unpacked and his brushes and shaving implements laid ready on the dresser, Rand dismissed the hovering Johnson, then crossed to look out of the west window. As he'd expected, that window afforded an excellent view of the drive leading to the forecourt, plus the woodland beyond, and, farther to the north, the shrubbery.

After surveying the scene, he moved to the other window. From there, he could see the eastern edge of the shrubbery and the stable and stable yard more or less directly ahead. Farther to the east lay a structured garden. From the profusion of blooms and their sizes and colors, Rand suspected it was a rose garden.

As he watched, a lady walked purposefully from the rear of the house toward the arched entrance of the garden, a basket swinging from her hand. Despite the distance, Rand recognized Miss Throgmorton.

He'd been acquainted with William Throgmorton for over four years. Rand had known William had a son, of whom he was quite proud.

The old inventor had never mentioned a daughter.

Rand watched as Miss Throgmorton halted in the middle of the garden, dropped her basket, then set about attacking the tall bushes with what, from her rather vicious movements, he assumed was a pair of shears.

He focused on her, his senses drawing in to the point he didn't really see anything around her. Just her, her lithe figure topped by her flaming red-gold hair, lit to a fiery radiance by the warm rays of the westering sun. Regardless of the distance, he sensed the vitality that animated her; for some reason, she all but shone in his sight, a beacon for his senses.

A magnetic, compelling, distracting beacon.

How long he stood and stared he couldn't have said; footsteps approaching along the corridor had him shaking off the compulsion and turning to face the door.

After the briefest of taps, the door opened, and Shields — Rand's groom, who, in a pinch, also served as his gentleman's gentleman — came in.

"Ah — there you are." Bearing an ewer, Shields nudged the door closed, then advanced to set the ewer on the dresser. "I've unpacked, and I brushed that blue coat of yours for the evening. If that'll suit?"

Rand nodded. "Yes, that's fine."

"Are we staying for a while?" Shields asked.

Rand frowned. "A few days at least."

Shields grunted. "Just as well we were on our way to Raventhorne, then. At least we've both got clothes enough for a stay."

Putting his back to the view, Rand leant back against the windowsill. "What are your thoughts on the household here?"

"Despite what we saw when we drove up, it's a well-run house. Calm and well-ordered, even if a mite eccentric. The staff are longtimers, all of them — and if they're not that old, then their parents were here before them. Very settled, they are, and . . . I suppose you'd say they're content."

"The explosions don't trouble them?"

"Seems they're used to them — and apparently, there's never been anyone hurt. Just lots of noise and nasty smoke."

Rand nodded. A well-run household and contented staff were excellent indicators of

54

the qualities of a house's master. Or mistress, as the case might be.

He straightened from the sill and turned to look out of the window again.

"Country hours here, so dinner's at six." Shields retreated toward the door. "Do you need me for anything else?"

Rand shook his head. "Not today." His gaze flicked to the stable. "How are the horses?" He'd purchased the pair only two months ago; they were young and still distinctly flighty.

"They didn't approve of the bang and the smell, but the stable's well away from the house, and they settled happily enough."

"Good." Rand paused, then said, "I doubt I'll need the horses for the next few days at least. Other than keeping an eye on them, I won't need you for much, but let me know if you see or hear anything that strikes you as odd."

"Aye. I'll do that. I'm off for my tea, then."

Rand heard the door open and shut. His gaze had already found and refocused on Miss Throgmorton.

She was still attacking the roses.

Rand wavered, prodded by an impulse to go down and speak with her. About what, he wasn't all that clear. Judging by the energy with which she was clipping, she was still distinctly exercised over what his arrival had revealed.

She'd had no inkling of Rand's or the syndicate's existence. More, Rand sensed her antipathy toward inventing — an attitude that had reached him perfectly clearly during their meeting in the drawing room — had a deeper source than mere female disapproval of such endeavors.

Yet her support would be vital in keeping her brother's nose to the grindstone, and they all needed William John to finish the invention within the next three weeks.

Rand wasn't sure how much he could actively help William John — that remained to be seen — but at the very least, he could ride rein on the younger man and ensure he remained focused on solving the issues bedeviling his father's machine. William John had already shown strong signs of the absentminded mental meandering Rand had observed in many other inventors.

In his experience, time was the one dimension to which inventors rarely paid heed.

Yet in this case, time was very definitely of critical importance.

Rand refocused on Miss Throgmorton.

He drew out his fob watch and checked the face, then tucked the watch into his pocket and headed for the door.

He had time for a stroll before dinner.

In the rose garden, Felicia deadheaded roses with a vengeance. With her left hand, she gripped the next rose hip; with her right hand, she wielded the shears. *Snip!* She dropped the clipped hip into her basket and reached for the next.

She'd hoped the activity would allow her to release some of the emotions pent up inside her. And, in truth, simply being out of the house and breathing fresher air had eased the volcanic anger, fueled by hurt, that had welled within her on learning of her father's and brother's subterfuge.

Snip.

Her father was dead; she couldn't berate him. As for her brother . . . while she *could* berate him, she and the household — not to mention the too-handsome-for-his-own-good Lord Cavanaugh and his syndicated investors — needed William John to keep his mind on his work. Berating him wouldn't help.

Snip.

Besides, she knew her brother well enough to know he would feel no real remorse; encouraging her to believe that the funds she'd been drawing on to keep the household running had been royalties from previous inventions would have seemed to her father and William John to be the easiest path.

They wouldn't have wanted her to worry over using money received from others for an invention they hadn't yet got to work.

Their sleight of mind still hurt.

And she was now quite worried enough, and in that, she wasn't alone. Even William John was uncertain. Unsure.

He'd been growing steadily more nervous over recent weeks — more nervous than she'd ever known him. She'd wondered why. Now, she knew.

This time, her father and brother had embarked on a gamble that might not pay off.

She nudged the basket along with her foot and reached for the next dead rose.

Unlike previous projects, where she'd insisted they worked only with capital they already possessed and also left untouched a cushion of funds on which the household could fall back on should the project fail, this time, there was no cushion. No funds to fall back on.

No way to keep going.

Snip.

This time, if the invention failed, they would have to sell the Hall and let the staff go. There'd been Throgmortons at the Hall for generations; everyone would be devastated. The loss of their home would hurt William John even more; without his laboratory-workshop, he would be rudderless. As for her . . . she had no idea what such a future would hold for her, other than that it would be bleak. She'd had her Season in London and hadn't taken — and she hadn't taken to life in the capital, either; it had been far too superficial for her taste. Now, at the age of twenty-four, the best she could hope for was a life as a paid companion or as an unpaid poor relative in one of her distant cousins' households.

If she'd been a different sort of female, she might have given way to despair, but she didn't have time for any such indulgence. As far as she could tell, there was one and only one way to avoid the abyss that had opened up before them — William John had to get the dratted modified steam engine to work.

Snip.

If she wanted to save the household, the Hall, William John, and herself, she needed to do all she could to keep her brother's mind focused on that task and ensure that all possible burdens were lifted from his shoulders.

William John was a year older than she was, but it had long been she who managed everything around him.

A distant step on the gravel path circling the house had her raising her gaze. Lord Cavanaugh — he who, from her year's experience of London society, she had instantly recognized as belonging to the too-handsome-for-his-own-good brigade — was crossing the lawn. He wasn't out strolling; there was nothing idle about his stride. He'd seen her and, apparently, was intent on speaking with her.

While ostensibly clipping another dead rose, she watched him approach. Over six feet tall, with wide shoulders, a well-muscled chest, narrow hips, and long, strong legs, he cut a powerful figure, well-proportioned and rangy. Also distinctly mature; she judged him to be in his early thirties. He was still wearing the clothes he'd arrived in — a fashionably cut coat over a fine linen shirt, a neatly tied ivory cravat, tightly fitting buff breeches, and top boots. The subdued style, exquisite cut, and expensive fabrics marked him as a gentleman of the ton's upper echelons, yet it was his features that had prompted her to give him the label she had; his dark, walnut-brown hair, the thick locks fashionably trimmed, framed a face of cool calculation tinged with the autocratic arrogance often found in those of the higher nobility.

He was a marquess's son, after all.

The long planes of his face were spare, even austere, with sharp cheekbones on either side of a patrician nose, and firm, chiseled lips above a squarish chin. Straight dark-brown eyebrows and surprisingly thick dark lashes set off those eyes of molten caramel that she'd already discovered were unwarrantedly distracting.

Those eyes were currently trained on her. Trapped under his gaze, to her irritation, she felt her lungs contract until breathlessness threatened. And the closer he came, the worse the effect grew.

Her father's cousin, Flora, who lived at the Hall and was nominally Felicia's chaperon, had already been won over by Cavanaugh when, in the immediate aftermath of the recent explosion, he'd attentively assisted her to the bench by the front steps.

Flora had heard his name when he'd introduced himself; as soon as she'd caught her breath, rather than join Felicia, Cavanaugh, and William John in the drawing room, Flora had rushed upstairs and combed through her correspondence.

Flora's correspondents numbered in the

multiple dozens, all ladies like herself for whom keeping abreast of everything to do with the haut ton was a lifelong occupation.

Courtesy of Flora, Felicia now knew that Lord Randolph Cavanaugh was the second son of the late Marquess of Raventhorne and was wealthy and eligible in every way — no real surprise there — but to the consternation of the grandes dames, Lord Randolph tended to avoid the ballrooms and, consequently, was as yet unmarried. That, she had to admit, was surprising and had raised a question — purely a curious one — in her mind. What would it take in a lady to interest Lord Randolph Cavanaugh?

The object of her purely idle curiosity reached the entrance to the rose garden. From the corner of her eye, she watched as, his gaze fixed on her, he ducked beneath the archway and slowed to a prowl. He pretended to glance at the roses, then, as he halted a yard away, returned his gaze to her.

She really did not like the way her nerves were tightening in response to his focused look. Before he could speak, she briefly glanced his way. "We keep country hours. Dinner will be served at six o'clock."

One of his dark brows faintly arched. "So I've been informed."

His voice was deep, a purring rumble.

Lips and chin firming, she reached for another rose hip. Anything to force herself to look away from him — to give herself a reason for doing so. Admittedly, in the drawing room, he'd almost flabbergasted her by asking her opinion — asking for her agreement in forging on as they were — yet she wasn't at all sure that had she disagreed, he wouldn't simply have ignored her stance.

Gentlemen like him might well possess ingrained manners and act on them without thinking. That didn't mean he'd actually cared about how she felt, and she would be a fool to further encourage him.

Snip.

"I saw you out here and thought I'd get some air — and kill two birds with one stone."

Inside, she stiffened. Air she understood, but what else was he thinking to slay?

When he didn't immediately offer up a clue, her wits — unaccountably skittering in myriad directions though they were — came up with the answer. She debated for only a second; better she keep the reins of any conversation in her hands, and she stood to learn as much about him from his questions as he stood to learn from any answers she deigned to give. Pausing in her pruning, she slanted him a glance. "What do you wish to know?"

A faint smile edged his lips — and her eyes and her senses found another point of distraction. Luckily, he'd relaxed somewhat and, thrusting his hands into his pockets, he glanced down as if marshaling his words.

Rand had looked down to hide his satisfied smile. Her response to his vague allusion confirmed his initial assessment that Miss Throgmorton was a lady of uncommon intelligence. That was hardly surprising given she was William Throgmorton's daughter, but it was one of the points he'd wanted to verify. Her being intelligent would make working alongside her in managing William John and the completion of the steam engine a great deal easier.

Regardless, he took a second or two to consider his next words. She was . . . prickly. Somewhat unaccountably, and the reason for that was a part of what he needed to learn. He drew breath and, without looking up, said, "Forgive me if I misread, but during our meeting in the drawing room earlier, I got the impression that you were . . . shall we say, opposed to inventions? Whether specifically your father's and brother's or in a more general sense, I couldn't tell." He looked up and met her green eyes — sum-

64

mer green, the soft green of summer grass. "However, given the present circumstances, I'm curious as to your attitude, and why you seem to have taken against inventions."

And if, therefore, you're going to get in my way. Mine, my investors', and William John's.

He didn't say the words, but as her eyes narrowed on his, he felt confident she understood.

She stood with her shears held laxly in one gloved hand and stared into his eyes. Then her lips firmed, and she turned back to the rose bushes. "I am not against inventions." She reached for a dead rose. "It's inventors I have little sympathy or time for."

She paused, the fingers of one hand cradling the withered bloom; her shears remained raised, but didn't sweep in. He could almost hear her debating whether or not to explain her stance to him. He knew when she accepted that, given the circumstances, he had reason to ask and, possibly, a right to know.

"There's a truth I learned long ago." Her tone had hardened; her diction was clipped. "When it comes to anything that impacts on their inventing, inventors like my father and my brother are inherently, innately selfish. They live and breathe their work and are deaf and blind to all else about them —

to house, estate, staff, friends, family. Everything. Were the house to literally crumble about them, they wouldn't notice — would pay it no heed whatever — not unless and until it directly interfered with their work. Only then would an issue other than the invention itself become important — important enough for them to afford it an iota of their attention."

Now that Felicia had finally faced the question no one before had ever thought to ask her, and had started to answer and, in doing so, had opened the box into which for so many years she'd stuffed all her resentments, she discovered that continuing was easier than curbing her tongue. "I saw what my father's unswerving devotion to his inventions meant for my mother. She was a Walpole, higher born than Papa, but theirs was a love match — and of that I am sure, that there was love on both sides to the very end. Yet my father's inventions always came first. Throughout all my mother's life, Papa's inventions kept eating up all their funds, leaving Mama cut off from society — even the small circle of local society. She couldn't entertain, sometimes not for years. People were kind, but she wouldn't attend dinners on her own, and Papa would never make the time to accompany her. For years,

66

we lived under the most straitened circumstances, with Mama's constant role being to pinch and scrape and eke out the funds left after Papa's depredations, just to keep up appearances and make sure there was food on the table. Not that Papa or William John ever noticed what they were eating. Our staff, bless them, have stuck with us through thick and thin, but through most of my parents' marriage, times were far more thin than thick."

Cavanaugh shifted. "Your father is considered a very successful inventor. I know he had many successes."

She made a scoffing sound. "He did, indeed, but, monetarily speaking, virtually all his successes were minor. All brought in some funds, but it was never enough to cover my father's — and more recently, William John's — hunger for the latest valve or piston or cylinder or gear. There's always something they simply must have. The drain on our funds was — and still is — never ending."

She sensed rather than saw him lift his head and glance around — at the well-maintained house, the grounds, the gardens.

"Yet you seem to have managed well enough."

She laughed cynically. "Up to now." She

paused, then in a quieter tone went on, "I saw what inventions made of my mother's life. I learned that the obsession with inventions isn't something even love can triumph against. When she fell ill, at her request I took up the reins of managing the household. Unlike Mama, I have a good head for numbers — and I was more than up to the task of arguing and nagging my father until he agreed to set aside funds for keeping up the house. Mama died eight years ago. Papa's successes mostly occurred after that, and I managed to cling to sufficient funds to keep the good ship Throgmorton on an even keel." She paused, then snipped another dead rose. "At least, so I thought."

After a moment, she turned, dropped the dead rose into her basket, then raised her gaze and met Cavanaugh's eyes. "I might as well confess that I hold a deep and abiding antipathy toward inventing — the process. Had I known how matters stood, if it had been up to me, after Papa died, I would have drawn a line under the steam engine project and returned the unused funds to you and your syndicate." She paused, then inclined her head and swung back and shifted to face the next rose bush. "That said, I know William John wouldn't have agreed, and quite aside from being male, he's also older than me." She cut another dead rose and more evenly said, "In addition to the reasons he gave — of wanting to establish himself — I suspect he feels a certain filial obligation to get the engine working as my father envisaged as a form of tribute to Papa — a final triumph."

His gaze fixed on her profile, Rand murmured, "I can understand that."

"It might be understandable, but is it sensible?" She snipped another rose, resurgent tension investing the movement.

Before Rand could formulate any answer, she shot a sharp glance — one a very small step away from a glare — his way. "After Papa's death, the only reason I gave way and acquiesced to William John continuing to work on the steam engine project was because there was money still coming in — as I thought, from royalties from earlier inventions."

She turned back to the bush; he could only see her profile, but even that looked flinty. The next dead rose fell to a savage slice of her shears.

"Both Papa and William John lied to me about the source of those funds. They didn't just encourage me to believe something that wasn't true — they lied. Directly. Several times each. They intentionally deceived me"

— Rand almost winced as she took off another dead rose — "so that I would think there was enough money — sufficient money, at least — to be made from inventions after all. They bought my support with lies."

Rand suddenly found himself skewered with a green gaze that was all daggers.

"You can imagine how I feel about that."

He could.

"And" — she turned back to the rose bushes — "how I therefore feel about everything to do with inventors and inventing."

He'd wanted to know, and now, he did. Rand looked down, studying the edge of the flagstone path while he absorbed all he'd heard, all he'd sensed behind her words, and readjusted his strategy.

He knew too many inventors to doubt anything she'd said. The emotional and physical neglect she'd described wasn't uncommon but an all-too-frequent outcome of inventors' single-minded focus on their works.

As for her hurt on learning she'd been lied to . . . He knew all about betrayal by one's nearest and dearest, those a man — or a woman — should have been able to trust.

The realization left him feeling a closer

kinship with her than he'd foreseen.

Unfortunately, he could do nothing about what lay in her past, any more than he could do anything about what lay in his.

Experience had taught him that forward was the only practical way to go.

He raised his head, studied her for an instant, then quietly said, "Just for the record, although I might fund inventions and intend to work alongside your brother in bringing his current project to fruition, I would definitely notice if the house started to crumble in even a minor way."

She glanced at him sidelong and briefly met his eyes. "You're an investor, not an inventor."

He smiled tightly. "Indeed." He didn't want her tarring him with that brush.

She gave a small humph and turned back to snip another dead rose.

Rand studied her face, the flawless complexion — milk and honey with a golden tinge courtesy of the summer sun — framed by a wealth of tumbling red-gold locks that made his fingers itch.

And I would definitely notice if you were unhappy or distressed or under pressure of any sort, especially if it was due to something I'd done.

The words remained a quiet statement in

71

his mind; he was too wise to utter them.

He straightened and caught the swift glance she threw his way. "Thank you for confiding in me." He held her gaze. "I can't promise that this will pan out as we all hope, but rest assured I will do everything I can to ensure the weight of your father's last invention is lifted from you, your family, and the household as soon as possible."

Openly, she searched his eyes. "Do you think it's possible? That at this late stage, William John can sort out the mechanisms that to date have eluded him?"

He didn't look away. "I can't say. However, I can guarantee that our only option is to forge ahead and do everything possible to assist William John in that endeavor."

She looked toward the house. For a moment, he thought she would merely nod in dismissal, but, instead, she raised her chin and said, "Thank you for the assurance of your support." She paused, then went on, "While I might not be overjoyed about the project continuing, I understand the situation and accept that it must. That, as matters stand, we all need this invention to be a success." Finally, her eyes touched his again, and she gracefully inclined her head. "Rest assured that I'll do nothing to make the road to success more difficult."

Rand tipped his head in response. "Thank you." That was the assurance he'd come to the rose garden hoping to get. He stepped back. "I'll see you at dinner."

She murmured an agreement and returned to trimming the roses.

Rand turned and walked out of the rose garden, then he slid his hands into his pockets and strode across the lawn. On his way to the rose garden, he'd passed the still-open doors of the workshop; a breeze had sprung up, and the sulfurous fog had almost cleared. He turned his steps west. Circling the house would afford him time to sort through his thoughts as well as giving him the lie of the land.

Speaking of which, he should learn Miss Throgmorton's given name. Not that he expected to get all that much closer to her, fascinating creature though she was. She was intelligent, prickly, and capable — more than clever enough to manipulate any man.

Precisely the sort of clever lady he'd long ago barricaded his heart against.

And if his heart wasn't involved . . . given the circumstances, pursuing any sort of relationship with her was entirely out of bounds.

Yes, he was aware of the visceral tug he felt in her presence, but that didn't mean he had to do anything about it.

Aside from all else, he was there, walking the lawns of Throgmorton Hall, for one burningly urgent reason. He had to ensure the Throgmorton Steam-Powered Horseless Carriage made its debut in appropriate style at the upcoming exhibition.

If he failed . . .

Unlike the Throgmortons, he wouldn't be ruined, but the setback would be severe.

Clearly, he and William John would get no active help from Miss Throgmorton, not that he could imagine how she might actively assist. But she'd agreed to manage the household around them, around the completion of the invention, and that was really all he could hope for from her.

He walked on, boots crunching on the gravel of the forecourt as he approached the front door, through which he'd left the house.

As he started up the porch steps, he inwardly admitted he would have preferred Miss Throgmorton to be more engaged with the project — to be an invested supporter, rather than a highly reluctant one.

But he'd gained a clear statement of commitment, and having heard the reasons behind her attitude to inventing, that was realistically all he could hope for.

It's enough to go on with. The words rang in his mind as he opened the door and walked into the front hall.

THREE

Felicia swept through the door of the breakfast parlor at her customary hour of eight o'clock. Dinner the previous evening had been an entirely uneventful and rather stiff affair; she'd still been grappling with the ramifications of the revelations Cavanaugh's arrival had brought, William John had been frowning and muttering over what had caused the explosion, and Cavanaugh had seemed disinclined to push further regarding the invention, perhaps wanting to wait until he'd seen it. He'd spent more time chatting with Flora than with anyone else.

As usual, Felicia found William John already at the table, frowning direfully at several diagrams while he sipped his coffee, but she nearly jumped when Cavanaugh rose from his chair farther around the circular table.

Her eyes wider than she would have liked, she managed to smile with reasonable composure and wave him back to his chair. "Good morning, my lord." *I didn't expect to see you before noon.* "I trust you slept well?" She headed for the sideboard.

"I did, thank you." He resumed his seat. "The bed was comfortable, and after the constant noise of the capital, the silence of the country at night is a welcome relief."

She glanced briefly his way. "You live in Mayfair?" Why had she asked that? She didn't need to know. She gave him her back and concentrated on helping herself to a portion of kedgeree — and tried to drag her wits away from their sudden obsession with whether her bodice was straight and her hair properly pinned.

"I have lodgings in Jermyn Street."

Of course he did. The street inhabited by all the most fashionable bachelors.

"That said, I spend most of my time in my office in the City."

Turning, she approached the place opposite him. Johnson arrived with a teapot and a fresh rack of toast; he quickly set them down and pulled out and held her chair for her. She thanked him with a smile, sat, then glanced again at Cavanaugh. "I suppose you have to meet and discuss projects with your investors."

He lowered his gaze to his plate of ham

and eggs. "That, and meet with my contacts so that I hear of any new inventions looking for funding." He raised his gaze and, across the table, met her eyes. "That takes more hours than I like, but it's essential to keep on top of the field. Inventions arise more or less unheralded — one has to keep one's ear to the ground."

She nodded and, fixing her gaze on her plate, sampled the kedgeree, then settled to consume it. To her irritation, she was keenly aware of her every movement. Was there a bit of herring on her lip? She must be careful not to overload her fork.

Such thoughts — such awareness of her appearance and how a gentleman might be seeing her — were so alien, they jarred.

What was the matter with her?

Whatever it was — whatever affliction Cavanaugh had inflicted on her — she needed to ignore it.

Feeling his gaze on her, she very nearly squirmed.

"You know," William John said, "I think you're correct." He leaned across to show Cavanaugh a diagram. "If I move the inlet valve to here, then the gauge should be more sensitive to the changes in pressure." William John frowned. "Theoretically, anyway."

Cavanaugh shrugged. "At times, one simply has to try things and see if they work."

Slowly, still frowning, William John nodded. "Once we have the workshop cleared and the boiler replaced, we'll try it. That, however, won't be the only change we'll need to make."

Accustomed to her brother's ramblings, Felicia, nevertheless, pricked up her ears at his use of "we." Ever since their father's death, with respect to the steam engine, William John had always spoken in the singular.

She continued to eat her kedgeree and sip her tea, and surreptitiously watched as Cavanaugh made another suggestion, and William John readily discussed the pros and cons . . . freely, without the slightest reservation.

In less than twenty-four hours, Cavanaugh had won her brother's confidence, something she knew was not easy to do.

Clearly, she would be wise not to make assumptions about Lord Randolph Cavanaugh. It wasn't yet nine o'clock, and already, he'd surprised her twice.

She was surprised again when Cavanaugh turned to her and asked if William John's proposal to commandeer the footmen and gardener for cleanup duties in the workshop would inconvenience her.

She was tempted to say it would, but she'd promised to assist as she and the household could. She shook her head. "There's nothing on their plates this morning that they can't do later, once they've finished in the workshop."

Cavanaugh turned back to William John and continued — artfully, gently, almost imperceptibly — to steer her brother, again and again drawing his peripatetic mind back to the issue at hand and keeping him firmly on the shortest path to completing the necessary modifications to the engine.

Felicia had to be grateful for that; if left to himself, William John had a tendency to follow whatever vague notion popped into his brain. From comments he'd let fall, she'd long ago formed the opinion that her brother's brain was literally awhirl with thoughts, even more so than their father's had been.

Now Cavanaugh had won William John's trust, Cavanaugh was in a position to harness William John's undoubtedly able mind and keep it focused on fixing the engine.

Watching the pair, for the first time since learning of the true nature of what faced them all, she felt a smidgen of hope.

With Cavanaugh at the helm, they might just win through.

Finally, William John slapped his palm on his pile of diagrams. "Right, then!" He looked at Felicia for the first time since she'd entered the room and grinned. "It's time we got working."

The enthusiasm in his eyes . . . she hadn't seen that for quite some time. She found herself smiling back, then she set down her empty teacup, pushed back her chair, and rose as both men came to their feet.

She turned and made for the door; she had her usual morning meeting with Mrs. Reilly, the housekeeper, to attend, then she needed to take stock of the kitchen garden with Cook and decide if they should try for another crop of peas.

Cavanaugh and William John followed her into the front hall. William John made straight for the door to the workshop stairs, but Cavanaugh hesitated. When, heading for her sitting room on the other side of the hall, she glanced his way, he caught her eye. "Don't you want to see how things are in the workshop?"

She slowed, her gaze steady on his. "No. I don't go down there. I haven't been down since I was twelve years old."

His eyes narrowed, as if he sensed there was some tale behind that.

She summoned an entirely meaningless

smile, turned, and walked on.

Rand watched the fascinating — and now enigmatic — Miss Throgmorton walk to the door of the room opposite the drawing room, open the door, and disappear inside, shutting the door firmly behind her.

He shook aside the feeling of . . . he didn't know what. Ridiculous to feel that, now, he needed to find out what had happened when she was twelve years old that had kept her out of her father's workshop ever since.

With a shake of his head, he strode after William John and started down the stairs.

He had to admit that William John's performance in the breakfast room had certainly borne out his sister's view; William John had been utterly oblivious to her presence. He hadn't even looked her way when Rand had asked her about the footmen.

Rand was well aware that inventors — most of them — behaved in exactly that fashion, that their minds were so blinkered they were aware of nothing beyond their invention. Yet since he'd spoken with Miss Throgmorton, his eyes had been opened to the harm that trait could cause.

There was, sadly, nothing he could do to alter or even ameliorate that.

He reached the bottom of the stairs, raised

his head, and surveyed the challenge before him.

William John and the Throgmorton steam engine.

That was a challenge he could do something about.

Although the workshop doors had been closed during the night, they'd been propped open again at daybreak, and the air inside the laboratory-workshop was now fresh and clear.

Rand paused on the last stair and scanned the chamber. With no wafting cloud to obscure his view, he took in the racks and shelves that filled every available foot of wall. Every inch of storage space was crammed with cogs, tubes, pistons, valves, pipes of every conceivable sort, and a cornucopia of engine parts. Two large, moveable racks were hung with a plethora of tools. The paraphernalia for welding was piled on a large trolley.

There were no windows; given the likely frequency of explosions, that was probably a good thing. Instead, a gantry with multiple beams hung from the ceiling; it was rigged with gaslights that, once lit, would shed strong, even light over much of the room.

A large, rectangular frame, roughly five feet long, three feet wide, and reaching to chest height, held pride of place, positioned squarely in the center of the space between the stairs and the double doors. Suspended within the frame was the steam engine designed to power the Throgmorton version of John Russell's modification of Trevithick's horseless carriage.

Although presently smudged with soot and grease and liberally sprinkled with coal dust, the engine was a gleaming mass of copper and steel pipes and cylinders, of connections and joints and screws. The body was smaller than Rand had expected, between three and four feet long and possibly the same in width, and about two feet in height. Regardless, the combination of solidity and complexity made it an impressive sight.

There was no carriage, only the engine; the frame supported the engine's body at bench level so William John could easily poke and prod and tinker, as he was presently doing, crouched on the other side of the frame.

Unfortunately, it was obvious that the engine wouldn't be working anytime soon. The gleaming boiler that was essentially the heart of the contraption was ruptured, its sides peeled back like a banana skin.

Frowning slightly, Rand stepped down to

the workshop floor. The flagstones were littered with bits and pieces of metal. One of the tool racks had been tipped back over the welding equipment, and tools lay scattered amid the debris.

Something metallic crunched under Rand's boot, and he halted.

William John straightened and, across the wreck of the boiler, smiled at Rand. "It's not as bad as it looks."

Rand couldn't stop his brows from rising. "I'll have to take your word for that." He glanced around, peering deeper into the far reaches of the chamber that extended beneath the house. "Where's the carriage part of it?" He glanced at William John. "It is built, isn't it?"

"Oh yes." His gaze almost lovingly cataloguing what remained of the engine, William John went on, "We keep it in the stable, tucked safely away. We won't bother putting the engine into the carriage until we have the engine working perfectly."

Rand hid his relief and nodded at the blown boiler. "That certainly appears wise." He hesitated, then said, "Your sister mentioned you'd blown several boilers over the past weeks."

William John frowned at the engine. "We — Papa and I — redesigned the feed of heat off the burner to the boiler. We increased the efficiency and therefore the steam generated, but that's led to difficulties with the mechanisms downstream, especially the controls. We can achieve smooth and significant acceleration, but deceleration . . ." His frown deepened. "Papa died before we'd fixed the problem, and up to now, everything I've tried . . . Well, I've improved the system to the point we can accelerate and decelerate once, but further acceleration seems to be cumulative, and then . . ." William John gestured at the ruptured boiler. "I still haven't got it right."

Footsteps coming down the stairs had both William John and Rand glancing that way. "Ah," William John said, "this will be Corby, plus Joe and Martin, the footmen."

A dapper-looking man of fifty or so appeared. He halted, and the two footmen Rand had previously seen halted on the stairs behind.

The older man bowed to Rand. "My lord." Then he looked at William John. "Are you ready for us to tidy the place, sir?"

"Yes, please, Corby." William John's wave encompassed the entire workshop. "Sweep, tidy, and clean. All of you know where most things go. As usual, if you find any bit of metal or tool that you don't recognize, just leave it on the bench" — William John pointed to a workbench set to one side — "and I'll sort it out later."

Rand watched the footmen walk deeper into the chamber and return with brooms and brushes. Corby pulled out a bag of rags tucked behind some piping. While the footmen started sweeping, Corby commenced lovingly wiping the pipes and cylinders of the engine, removing the grime that coated them.

Rand looked at William John. The younger man was frowning vaguely at the engine and muttering under his breath. Rand circled the engine and halted beside William John. "Explain to me how the engine works. Start at the point where you turn it on."

All vagueness dropping from him, William John eagerly and enthusiastically complied.

Rand put his mind to ensuring he understood. When William John went too rapidly, he stopped him and hauled him back.

William John traced the path of the steam from the ignition of coal in the box beneath the boiler, through the various modifications he and his father had made to the way the steam was generated within the boiler before it moved through the complicated series of pipes, cylinders, and valves to the piston chambers — also modified — that would ultimately drive the twin shafts to turn the horseless carriage's wheels.

The explanation took time. They walked from one side of the engine to the other as William John pointed to this and that.

Relatively early in the exercise, Shields came down the stairs and offered his services to Corby, who readily accepted and set Rand's man to wiping off the grime deposited on the various racks of equipment.

While William John declaimed and Rand questioned, Rand noticed their four helpers paid closer and closer attention. He had to admit the mechanism of the engine — that such a thing could work — was enthralling.

"And finally" — William John indicated a set of levers mounted on a panel attached to the frame — "these are the controls that allow us to manage the output."

"And that," Rand said, "is where things are going wrong."

"Yes, but not with the levers themselves. They're fairly simple and should work perfectly, at least in what they do. It's the result of what happens that's out of . . . well, control." William John frowned. "Once we have a new boiler in place, I'll be able to show you what I mean." He pointed at a row of gauges that were mounted on the engine, facing where Rand assumed the driver would sit. "I've a suspicion it's something to do with these gauges and the valves they're connected to that's causing the buildup of steam in the boiler, but until we have the new boiler in, I won't be able to investigate."

Rand bit back a comment to the effect that they didn't have time to investigate anything. Fix, yes. Explore and investigate, no.

William John turned to survey the state of the workshop. Rand followed his gaze, noting that the floors were once more clear of debris, the tool racks and welding equipment had been straightened and wiped clean, and the engine was now gleaming and free of all smuts.

William John smiled. "Thank you, gentlemen — if you've finished with your tidying, let's make a start on removing this." With one hand, he thumped the side of the ruptured boiler.

Both footmen and Shields, plainly curious, put away their implements and readily drew near. Corby tucked his rags away and joined the group.

Rand stepped back and watched as William John, wielding a wrench and directing the others on what he needed them to do, set about releasing the gaskets that locked the ruptured copper boiler in place amid the plethora of tubes and pipes.

When it came to doing anything to his invention, Rand had to admit that William John remained unrelentingly focused. No hint of vagueness intruded as he loosened this nut, then that, all the while telling Shields, Joe, and Martin just where to put their hands as they supported the boiler as well as the various loosened pipes, tubes, gauges, and valves. Corby hovered, handing tools to his master as and when required.

Leaving them to their task, Rand drifted to the open double doors. Pausing on the threshold, he looked out and around. The paved area before the doors was level with the floor of the workshop, with only a narrow drain set between two rows of flagstones to allow rain to drain away rather than spread under the doors and into the workshop. Straight ahead, a walled kitchen garden lay on the other side of the paved area. Beyond it, a swath of lawn was bordered by the surrounding woodland. To the right, lawns stretched away, eventually joining the south lawn, while to the left, a gravel path, more than wide enough for a carriage, ran along the side of the house and around the northeast corner.

Rand raised his gaze and, beyond a short stretch of lawn, saw the end of the stable block; presumably, the path was an extension of the section of the drive that linked the forecourt and the stable. He could appreciate the foresight; once the engine was working, the path would make it easy to bring the carriage-body to the workshop.

On turning back into the workshop, he spied a series of pulleys and thick chains piled with a conglomeration of heavy beams and iron struts in a corner near the doors. Presumably a part of the mechanism by which the engine would be lifted out of its supporting frame and lowered into the carriage.

Rand surveyed the workshop — the racks and shelves, the purpose-built frame and benches. It was clear the Throgmorton males had spent considerable time and thought — and expense — on their favored domain. Despite Miss Throgmorton's plaint that the rest of the house was invisible to her father and brother — something Rand suspected was true — he doubted the men's devotion to their workspace had contributed to keeping Miss Throgmorton out of it.

That she hadn't been down there for over a decade . . . he had to wonder why.

With a rattle and a clang, Shields and

Martin hauled on cables connected to a smaller set of pulleys attached to the ceiling above the engine. William John and Joe held back tubes and pipes, and, with a screech of metal on metal, the ruptured boiler rose out of the body of the engine.

"Excellent." William John released the parts he'd been holding, seized the freed boiler, and guided it away from the rest of the engine, toward the open space before the doors. "Let's set it down here. Gently, now."

Shields and Martin let the cables out slowly, and the boiler lowered to the floor.

"Right." William John signaled, then released the webbing that had cradled the boiler. Straightening, he looked down at the twisted metal.

Rand joined him. "It looks like the seams gave way."

William John humphed. "Indeed." He crouched and ran his hands over the sides of the boiler. "I wonder if we can beat it out and resolder . . ."

Rand stared at the crumpled, folded-back metal. "No. We can't." He'd learned enough from other inventors about the risks one ran in resoldering such things — namely an increased risk of re-rupturing. "The second soldered seam will be weaker than the first."

William John looked up, and Rand caught the younger man's eyes. "We don't have time to take that risk. If it explodes again, we'll have lost days and got no further. We need a new boiler."

William John stared at him for a moment, then grimaced. "Yes. You're right. I keep forgetting . . ."

About the exhibition and their deadline. From their earlier discussions, Rand had already realized that. He turned his mind to the logistics required. "I assume you have a cart we can use to ferry the boiler to the nearest blacksmith's. He can reuse the metal, which will get us a better price on the replacement."

His gaze on the destroyed boiler, William John waved toward the stables. "Struthers — our stableman — knows which cart to use."

"Shields?" Rand glanced at his man.

Shields nodded and made for the double doors. "I'll fetch it."

Rand looked at William John. "Where is the nearest blacksmith?"

With a sigh, William John straightened. "In the village. The forge is at the far end of the village street." He frowned. "Mind you, I'm not sure Ferguson will agree to do the job. He wasn't best pleased last time, when he made this one — I only just talked him around." William John glanced sidelong at Rand. "We might have to beat out and re-solder this one after all."

Rand didn't bother wasting breath restating his refusal to hear of any such thing. It was increasingly apparent that there was an ongoing need for someone to steer William John — to unrelentingly herd him along the surest path to success. Rand turned to the doors as the distant rattle of a cart's wheels reached them. "We'll see," he replied. And was determined that they would.

After they'd loaded the ruptured boiler into the back of the cart, Rand took the reins and, with William John beside him, drove out along the drive and into the lane leading to Hampstead Norreys.

Throughout the short journey, William John remained sunk in his inventor's thoughts, occasionally muttering about pressures and gauges.

When they reached the intersection with the village street, Rand turned the plodding horse and set it walking northward, through the center of the village. Although Hampstead Norreys was by any measure a small village, in addition to the inn, it possessed a Norman church in a well-kept yard and several shops. Rand noted a large and prosperous-looking general store and post office, a bakery, a butcher's shop, a shop that, from the goods displayed in the window, he took to be a haberdashery, and a gentleman's outfitters.

The blacksmith's forge lay at the far end of the village, separated by a row of old trees from the shops along the west side of the street.

Rand drew the cart to a halt in the yard in front of the smithy.

William John blinked and returned to the here and now. He shook himself and climbed down from the cart.

Rand set the brake, tied off the reins, and joined him.

A large man with heavily muscled arms came slowly out from the shadows of the smithy. Behind him, in the depths of his workshop, a furnace glowed and spat the occasional spark. Wiping his hands on a rag, the man nodded to Rand, then, with significantly less enthusiasm, nodded to William John. "Mr. Throgmorton. What is it today?"

"Ah yes. Good morning, Ferguson." William John waved to the boiler in the back of the cart. "I'm afraid we've had another accident."

The blacksmith seemed to sigh. He lumbered up to the side of the cart and looked down at the lump of crumpled metal. He shook his head. "You will keep putting them under too much pressure. There's ought I can do to help you, and no point at all trying to repair that."

"Yes, well." William John shifted. "We want you to make a new one."

"A new one." Ferguson frowned. "I don't rightly know whether there's any point in that, either. With what you're doing to them, the seams just won't hold."

A thought occurred to Rand. While William John applied himself to securing Ferguson's assistance, Rand turned his sudden notion around in his mind . . . and decided it was worth pursuing. Or at least, asking if it was possible.

Ferguson was still shaking his head, a craftsman patently fed up with having his creations mangled.

When William John paused for breath, Rand spoke up. "Mr. Ferguson. I'm Lord Randolph Cavanaugh. I'm the lead investor in a syndicate backing Mr. Throgmorton's invention. I appreciate your point about the seams being necessarily a weak point in the construction of the boiler, especially as Mr. Throgmorton is putting the system under pressure. However" — Rand threw a glance at William John, including him in Rand's question — "I wonder if it's possible to construct a boiler that's balloon-like — with no seams but only an inlet and outlet."

Rand saw blankness overtake William John's expression as his mind turned inward to evaluate the notion. Rand looked at the blacksmith. He was frowning, too, but more in the way of working out how to do what Rand had suggested.

William John blinked several times, then his face came alight. "By golly, I think that would work." Eagerly, he looked at Ferguson. "Can you create such a thing, Ferguson?"

The big man was looking distinctly more interested. "If I was to work from a sheet and bend it . . ." He stared unseeing between Rand and William John for several more seconds, then he refocused on Rand and nodded. "Aye, I think I can do it — and you're right. It'll get around a lot of the problems Mr. Throgmorton here has been having."

Rand smiled. "Well, then, the only question remaining is how fast you can have the new boiler ready."

William John leapt in to describe the outlets he would need added to the top of the boiler, and, in turn, Ferguson questioned William John as to the connection between the heating system and the boiler.

Once they'd thrashed out the details to their mutual satisfaction, Ferguson looked at Rand. "As it happens, my lord, I've not got much on today. I can start this new boiler straightaway, but it'll need to cool overnight before I can do the final additions — so tomorrow afternoon would be the soonest."

Rand nodded. "I'll add a ten-percent bonus to your bill if you can get the new boiler to the Hall by noon tomorrow."

For the first time since they'd arrived, Ferguson grinned. He dipped his head to Rand and touched a finger to his forehead. "I'll take you up on that, my lord." He looked toward William John. "Tomorrow by noon, I'll have it to you."

"Excellent!" William John clapped his hands together and beamed.

"I'll relieve you of this lump." Ferguson turned and roared to his apprentices. Two hulking lads appeared, and he directed them to lift the twisted wreck of his previous creation from the bed of the cart and carry it inside.

Satisfied — and faintly chuffed at having been able to make a real contribution to the invention, however small — Rand climbed back to the cart's box seat and untied the reins. William John, happy as a grig, climbed up and sat, and Rand turned the horse out of the smith's yard and set it trotting back down the village street.

A wagon laden with produce of various types had drawn up outside the general store, and the driver and a lad were carting boxes and crates inside. As a gig had halted outside the butcher's shop on the other side of the street, Rand had to halt the cart, yet with the issue of the boiler resolved and no reason to rush back, he was content to sit on the box and wait.

William John, of course, was miles distant, no doubt mentally back in his laboratory-workshop.

Rather than get too close to the wagon being unloaded, Rand had halted a short distance up the street. He was idly scanning the various denizens of Hampstead Norreys, mostly the female half of the population busy about their morning shopping, when the door to the general store opened, and Miss Throgmorton stepped out onto the pavement.

A gentleman had held the door for her; he followed close behind, and Miss Throgmorton turned to speak with him, plainly continuing a conversation struck up inside the store.

Rand frowned. "What's your sister's Christian name?"

"Hmm? What? Oh." Absentmindedly, William John volunteered "Felicia," then returned to his ruminating.

Presentiment tickled Rand's nape as he watched Felicia Throgmorton chat animatedly to the gentleman as, side by side, they walked down the street, then crossed to the opposite pavement. The pair paused outside the bakery, exchanged several more words, then Miss Throgmorton farewelled the gentleman and went into the shop.

For a moment, the gentleman remained standing outside; Rand wished he could see the man's expression. Then, with a decidedly jaunty air, the gentleman turned and continued down the street.

The wagon wasn't yet ready to move. Rand elbowed William John.

"Huh?"

Rand nodded down the street. "Who's that man?"

William John sat up and peered over the now-depleted wagon. "The one walking toward the inn?"

"Yes. Him."

William John studied the man, then shook his head. "Never seen him before."

"He's not a local?"

"No. I can't tell you who he is, but I'm quite sure of that."

At that moment, the wagon driver came out of the store, tipped his hat, and called his thanks to Rand, then the wagoner climbed up and set his horse plodding slowly down the street.

Rand shook the reins and set the cart rolling in the wagon's wake. Ahead, the unknown gentleman strode along, then turned under the archway of the inn.

By the time the cart had drawn level with the inn yard, the man had disappeared.

Rand faced forward. He waited until the wagon had turned left, back along the lane to Ashampstead. Then he turned the cart right, into the lane, and set the horse trotting back to Throgmorton Hall.

A personable gentleman, apparently unknown in those parts.

Rand reminded himself that it was none of his business to whom Miss Felicia Throgmorton chose to speak. However, a personable gentleman unknown in those parts who happened to strike up a conversation with the daughter of William Throgmorton might be set on gaining rather more than just Miss Throgmorton's smiles.

And that, most definitely, legitimately fell within Rand's purview.

FOUR

On their return to the Hall, given Miss Throgmorton was still in the village, Rand put aside the issue of the unknown gentleman and what business he'd had with her and followed William John into the workshop.

William John had explained that, despite not having the boiler and therefore no steam to harness, there were various tests and trials he could run, all part of his search to rectify the problem of the uncontrollable rise in pressure resulting from the improvements he and his father had made to the engine.

"You make one thing work better, and some other part fails." William John shook his head. "It's always the way, but you can never predict exactly where the new problem will be — not until you run the damned thing."

Rand perched on a stool and, for the next

hour, watched as William John changed this and adjusted that.

Finally, they heard the luncheon gong rung rather forcefully, and Rand realized he'd heard the gong earlier, but rung less stridently.

He fished out his watch, checked it, and, somewhat surprised, reported, "It's after one o'clock."

William John stepped back from the engine and sighed. "We worked so hard to increase the efficiency — it's what we absolutely needed to do. But now we've done it, that's upended the balance that gives us control of the power." He frowned at the pipes and gauges. "I'm sure that's what the problem is, but be damned if I can figure out how to correct it."

Rand rose from his stool. "It'll come to you." He fervently hoped so; if not, they were sunk. "Meanwhile, we'd better appear at the luncheon table or your staff are going to complain."

William John grinned. "They do, you know. Complain that I don't turn up in time and dishes get cold." He frowned in puzzlement. "I don't know why they get upset — I still eat everything."

Rand inwardly shook his head. He waved

William John to the stairs and followed him up.

Luckily, as it was high summer, there was a cold collation laid out on the dining table, so as yet no noses had been put out of joint by their tardiness. William John led the way into the dining room. He greeted his sister with a wave and made straight for the table.

It appeared that Miss Throgmorton had already finished her meal and was making for the door.

Rather than follow William John through the doorway, Rand stepped back and waited for Miss Throgmorton to step into the corridor.

When she did and halted, he inclined his head to her, but didn't move aside to let her pass.

Briskly, she nodded. "Good afternoon, Lord Randolph."

Rand caught her gaze. "All of my friends and most of my acquaintances call me Rand. Given we are working together in common cause, perhaps you might use that name, too." He summoned a deliberately charming smile. "I do get tired of being my lorded."

Her lips curved, and she inclined her head. "Very well."

Trapped by the warmth of his caramel

eyes, a warmth that had only grown more definite with his smile, Felicia hesitated for only an instant before suggesting, "And given our connection" — she shot a glance through the doorway to the dining table, where William John was already seated — "I daresay it would be appropriate for you to use my name. It's Felicia."

Cavanaugh — Rand — gracefully inclined his head. "So we're agreed." He hesitated, as if debating the wisdom of his next words, then said, "I was in the village with William John, visiting the blacksmith about replacing the boiler."

"I see. How did that go? I know Ferguson was losing patience over the continuing destruction of his work."

"Indeed, but we might have made a minor breakthrough with the boiler's construction — no doubt we'll know once the new boiler is delivered. Ferguson promised it by noon tomorrow."

She allowed her brows to rise. "That's . . . excellent." She very much doubted that it had been William John who had reinvigorated the blacksmith's interest.

But rather than claim credit, Cavanaugh — Rand — continued, "While in the village, we happened to notice you speaking with a gentleman — one William John couldn't place. I thought the man looked vaguely familiar, but I didn't see his face well enough to be sure." Those molten caramel eyes held hers trapped. "Did he mention why he was in the area?"

She didn't appreciate having been watched, much less being quizzed. Yet there was no reason she shouldn't answer, especially given the arrangements she'd made with the gentleman in question. "He's an artist from London. He does sketches for the *London News,* and during the summer, he's traveling through the villages of the Home Counties, sending in sketches of country vistas and views."

Rand nodded. "I've seen those sketches — they're quite good."

"Indeed. And the reason the gentleman approached me was that the villagers had told him about the Hall, how it sits surrounded by woodland, and he was keen to take a look at the house with a view to doing a sketch of it for the paper." Still returning Rand's gaze, she calmly stated, "I've invited him for afternoon tea. I suggested he arrive about half past two, and I'll take him for a stroll about the grounds before tea. On fine days such as this, we — Cousin Flora and I — take tea on the terrace outside the drawing room, if you would care to join us."

Cavanaugh — Rand — hesitated, then slowly said, "Thank you, but no." He glanced into the dining room. "I'd better remain with William John."

She couldn't help but smile. "Keeping his nose to the grindstone?" When Rand lightly shrugged, she let her smile widen. "I assure you, he needs no encouragement. It's usually a battle to get him to lift his nose *off* said grindstone."

Rand's lips curved. "So I've discovered." He brought his gaze back to her face. "Nevertheless, he seems given to . . . distraction. And we no longer have time for him to pursue every idea that comes to him."

She nodded. "Very true."

When Rand continued to look at her and made no move to step aside, she tipped her head and asked, "So, do you know Mr. Mayhew — the artist?"

Rand blinked. "Is that his name?"

"Mr. Clive Mayhew." She studied Rand's face. "Does that ring any bells?"

"No." Rand couldn't keep his frown from his eyes. "If he's an artist, it's possible I've met him in London. I know several artists, and I'm connected to others, so our paths might have crossed at some function." That said, his claim to have recognized the man had been false — a ruse.

He studied Miss Throgmorton — Felicia — and wondered whether he should share his misgivings . . . not that he could be certain, even in his own mind, exactly what was making his nerves twitch. Was it seeing the personable Mayhew with her . . . or knowing an unknown gentleman had suddenly arrived in the vicinity of such a critical invention?

She held his gaze steadily — as if aware there was more to his interest in Mayhew than he'd yet owned to.

Rand drew in a breath, glanced briefly at William John, busily eating and utterly oblivious to Rand and Felicia's conversation, then he looked at Felicia and quietly said, "I've been working with investors and inventors for more than five years. I've learned first-hand that when an exciting invention is nearing completion, other inventors or other investors sometimes take steps to . . . ensure that exciting invention doesn't come to fruition."

Her eyes widened. "You think Mayhew has been sent to . . . sabotage our engine?"

Our engine. He was making headway on that front at least. "You have to admit that Mayhew suddenly appearing out of the blue . . ."

Her lips set; her chin firmed. "Papa was always careful. From childhood, he taught us never to speak of what he was doing or even where the workshop was — not to people we didn't know well, well enough to trust."

"Sound advice." Then Rand wrinkled his nose. "But Mayhew's an artist. I have to admit it sounds like paranoia speaking, yet . . ." After several seconds, he focused on Felicia's green eyes. "Can I suggest it might be wise to avoid all mention of our current project and to steer Mayhew well away from the workshop?"

Her eyes on his, she slowly nodded. "I certainly won't mention the engine or even inventions in general — what possible interest could that have for an artist? And if he asks, we'll know that, regardless of being an artist, he's here for some nefarious purpose. I can also make sure he doesn't see the workshop, but it would help if you could ensure that all the doors are kept shut during the afternoon."

He nodded. "I'll make sure they're shut and stay that way." He still wasn't happy at the thought of her strolling the lawns with Mayhew, but he really had no justification for suggesting she put the man off.

She'd been frowning, unseeing, past him; now, she looked up and met his eyes. Determination and a sort of female confidence gleamed in hers. "I could put Mayhew off, but frankly, if he is a saboteur trying to get access to the engine, given we — you and I, at least — are alert to that possibility, I would rather we give him the chance to show his true colors."

He didn't like it, but something about the resolution in her eyes warned him arguing would not be in his best interests. Not on any front.

He forced himself to incline his head. "I'll keep watch while he's here."

"Hoi, Rand! Do you want any of this roast beef?"

They both turned to see William John peering at a dish on the table.

Shaking his head, Rand looked back at Felicia.

Just as she put out a hand and touched his sleeve. "You'd better go, or there'll be no roast beef left."

He had to fight the urge to close his hand over hers, to hold it against his arm. His smile a trifle stiff, he inclined his head and stepped into the dining room, allowing her too-tempting hand to fall away. "One thing." He halted and locked his gaze with hers.

"While you're with Mayhew . . . take care."

She widened her eyes at him. "Of course." Then her lips curved lightly, and she turned and walked on, into the front hall.

Rand watched her go, then turned and made for the roast beef.

Felicia used to think her father's admonitions regarding his inventions and the workshop to be, as Rand had put it, paranoia speaking. Now, however, with so much riding on the success of the steam engine, she was more than willing to err on the side of caution.

She was waiting in the drawing room when Johnson announced that Mr. Mayhew had called. Leaving Flora, who she'd warned of the artist's visit, to organize for afternoon tea to be served on the terrace, Felicia walked out to greet Mayhew.

He was glancing around, apparently taking in the lines of the front hall. He turned at the sound of her footsteps, and a charming smile wreathed his face. "Miss Throgmorton."

He accepted the hand she offered and, very correctly, bowed over it.

"I'm delighted to welcome you to Throgmorton Hall, sir." She was more than capable of behaving in as charming a manner as he; her year in London had taught her how to be pleasantly civil while keeping gentlemen at a safe distance. Smoothly retrieving her hand, she waved toward the front door. "As I mentioned earlier, I suggest we stroll around the house before taking tea with my aunt. The light about the house is at its best at the moment. Even though it's summer, the trees in the woodland are so tall, they cast long shadows over the lawns from afternoon onward."

"Yes, indeed." Mayhew clasped his hands behind his back and kept pace beside her as she walked to the front door, propped wide to let the sunshine stream in.

Felicia noted that the door giving onto the workshop stairs was firmly shut. Rand's doing, without a doubt; William John rarely remembered.

She walked onto the porch and halted, then glanced at Mayhew. "As you can see, the shadows are already encroaching on the lawn." She looked to left and right. "Keeping to the lawns, we can stroll all the way around the house. Which way would you prefer to go?"

Mayhew favored her with another charming smile; he seemed to have a ready supply that stopped just short of ingratiating. "I'm happy to be led by your experience, Miss

Throgmorton."

"In that case" — she waved toward the shrubbery — "let's circle to the right."

She picked up her skirts and descended the steps. Mayhew kept pace; she watched as he looked around — exactly as one might imagine an artist would.

He was as tall as Rand, but had narrower shoulders and was one of those men with a tendency to stoop, as if trying to disguise his height.

He scanned the woodland and the shrubbery as they approached. When they reached the arched entrance to the shrubbery, he paused to look back at the house. After several moments of studying it, he shook his head. He turned to follow her onward, saw her watching, and smiled wryly. "My apologies. I'm always looking for the right view. Sadly, that isn't it."

She smiled spontaneously. "No need to apologize. That is why you're here, after all."

He inclined his head. "You're more understanding than many a young lady. Most imagine that they are the most . . . well, fascinating aspect of any view. And while that's so in a way, I'm generally focused on landscapes and buildings. People are . . . more difficult to accurately capture."

Felicia looked at him with burgeoning

interest. "That's an insightful comment."

He was looking down as he walked. He snorted softly. "It's simply the direction in which my talent runs."

They circled through the shrubbery, then walked past the stables and into the rose garden. Again, he halted within the rose garden and looked back at the house.

"Now, this is a very pretty composition, but, sadly, I would have to capture it soon after dawn." He glanced at her and gave a rueful grimace. "I am definitely not at my best before noon."

She laughed. She was finding it increasingly difficult to imagine Clive Mayhew as a saboteur. But as they strolled on, between the beds of roses, it occurred to her that while he might be a saboteur, he might also genuinely be an artist; the one did not preclude the other. "Did you bring some of your sketches? You said you would this morning."

"Indeed." He patted his pocket, and a faint rustling reached her ears. "I thought perhaps I could show you — and is it your aunt? — over afternoon tea."

"Mrs. Flora Makepeace is my father's widowed cousin. She'll be joining us for tea, and I'm sure she'll be as delighted as I to view your work."

"Now you're just being kind, but I hope my poor efforts will be at least of passing interest."

Felicia smiled. "I'm sure they will be. You cannot be too modest when your sketches are published by the *London News.*"

Was his story of being a sketch artist for the popular pictorial news sheet an invention? She glanced at his face, but his expression remained untroubled — innocent of guile.

They reached the end of the rose garden, and she led the way on, along the swath of lawn that ran behind the kitchen garden. For just a few yards — before the walls of the kitchen garden intervened — the doors to the workshop were visible to their right. She was on Mayhew's left; she needed to keep his gaze on her. Airily, she asked, "Have you had a chance to exhibit your work in the capital?"

He flicked a glance her way and sighed. "Sadly, no — although I must confess that's one of my most cherished ambitions." His lips twisted cynically. "Along with every artist in the land, of course."

"It must be quite . . . cutthroat." She caught his eye. "Having to find a patron."

His gaze on her face, he nodded, and they passed the point beyond which the garden walls hid the workshop doors.

Felicia led Mayhew onto and down the south lawn, then they followed the tree line and circled past the old fountain, now no longer in use.

Just past the fountain, Mayhew, who had been constantly glancing toward the house, halted. He stared at the front of the house, from that perspective seen at an angle. "This is the spot." He made the pronouncement with absolute certainty. After a moment, he looked at Felicia. "Miss Throgmorton, I would very much like yours and your family's permission to sketch your home from this angle for inclusion in a series I'm doing for the *News*, featuring England's country homes in the Home Counties."

Not once had Mayhew even obliquely referred to inventions or workshops; he hadn't even asked about the house itself, seemingly only interested in its visible exterior — precisely as an artist with his declared interest would be. Felicia smiled and inclined her head. "There's only my brother I need to consult, and I know he'll see no reason to deny you."

"Excellent." Mayhew looked at the house. His expression eager, he went on, "That's the west face, so I'll need the afternoon light, as now." He glanced at Felicia. "Perhaps I could come and sketch tomorrow afternoon — from about two o'clock, if that would be convenient?"

"I know of no reason it wouldn't be. We lead a quiet life, and Cousin Flora hasn't mentioned any visits, so I believe that arrangement will suit." With a wave, she indicated the raised terrace that ran along the house's south face, overlooking the long lawn. "But let's join Flora and ask, just to make sure."

They walked back to the house and up the steps to the terrace. Flora was waiting, seated at the round wrought-iron table, which had already been set with plates, cups, and saucers, with a multitiered cake stand in the table's center. Felicia made the introductions. Flora gave Mayhew her hand and smiled in her usual soft and comfortable way, then she waved them both to sit.

Mayhew held Felicia's chair. Once she'd settled, he claimed the third chair at the table.

Despite Flora's overtly gentle and feminine appearance, Felicia knew her chaperon was shrewd and observant. Flora poured tea and chatted in amiable vein, professing her delight at the thought of Mayhew sketching the Hall. She confirmed Felicia's expectation that there was no reason Mayhew couldn't ply his pencil the following afternoon and approved of his choice of view.

Flora waited until Mayhew had sampled one of Cook's lemon cakes and sipped his tea before leaning forward and declaring, "I have to confess, Mr. Mayhew, that I am quite impatient to see the sketches Felicia said you would bring to dazzle us."

A faint flush stained Mayhew's long cheeks. He shot Felicia a self-deprecating glance. "I wouldn't describe my work as 'dazzling,' ma'am." He set down his cup and reached into his pocket. "However, I have brought several of my sketches — of Ashampstead and of the river nearby. I hope you'll recognize the view and approve of my poor talent."

He withdrew a roll of paper about nine inches long that was wound about a thin wooden rod. Seeing Felicia look curiously at the roll, Mayhew explained, "I carry my sketches in this way so they don't crease."

"Ah. Of course." Felicia watched while Mayhew unrolled several sheets of fine artist's paper from the spool. When he handed the curling sheets to her, she eagerly took them. Flora quickly cleared a space on the table between her and Felicia, and Felicia laid the sketches down.

She and Flora stared, mesmerized by the pencil-and-ink sketches that had captured views with which they were both familiar with such accuracy and felicity that the scenes were not just instantly recognizable but the sketches somehow conveyed a sense of the atmosphere pertaining to each place. The sketch of Ashampstead village street on a market day was abustle with life, while the delicate sketch of the pool on the river Pang to the east of Hampstead Norreys invoked a sense of bucolic peace.

Once she'd looked her fill, Felicia glanced up and, across the table, met Mayhew's eyes. "These are exquisite. You are, indeed, very talented."

Somewhat to her surprise, Mayhew didn't smile but lightly raised one shoulder, as if he remained unsure of his skill or was, for some reason, uncomfortable acknowledging it.

Looking again at the sketches, Felicia felt vindicated in having agreed to allow him to sketch the Hall; such an opportunity, dropped into her lap by Fate, shouldn't be lightly passed up, and if it helped Mayhew continue and gain more confidence in his work, well and good.

"I admit," she said, raising her gaze once

119

more to Mayhew's face, "to being intrigued to see what you make of the Hall, sir. It was a lucky chance that sent you our way."

Flora added her compliments, too.

Mayhew blushed anew and, yet again, disclaimed — although with the evidence of his talent lying before Felicia and Flora, he might as well have saved his breath. Then, with all three of them transparently pleased with the outcome of Mayhew's visit, they settled to finish their tea.

From the shadows of the woodland bordering the south lawn, Rand watched the trio on the terrace as they laughed, smiled, and chatted.

It wasn't difficult to assess how Felicia — and Flora, who Rand considered a sensible and supportive lady — viewed Mayhew. They'd both relaxed and were smiling with genuine delight upon the supposed artist.

Although Rand had retreated to the workshop with William John after luncheon, he'd set Shields on guard by the stable. Shields had hurried around to the workshop to warn Rand that Mayhew had arrived, riding a rather poor-quality nag — Shields being the sort to notice such things.

Leaving William John muttering at his engine, Rand had climbed the stairs and confirmed that the door at the top was firmly shut. He'd waited behind the panel and had heard Mayhew arrive and speak with Johnson, then Felicia had come and taken Mayhew outside.

Rand had descended to the workshop and, assisted by Shields, had closed the large double doors. William John had noticed the light dimming. He'd blinked, then crossed to the wall and fiddled with a knob, setting the gaslights in the gantry above his workbench blazing. Then he'd returned to his invention, ignoring Rand and Shields and all else about him.

Rand had dismissed Shields, who had clattered back up the stairs and out via the front hall. Rand had counseled himself to patience, but hadn't been able to squash the impulse to ease one of the big workshop doors open a fraction — just enough to peer out.

He'd glimpsed Felicia and the artist walking through the roses, then had watched Felicia lead the man down the lawn, until the pair had passed out of sight behind the kitchen garden.

That had given Rand an idea. He'd confirmed that William John had no intention of emerging from the workshop before the gong rang for dinner. With Felicia and Mayhew still screened by the walls of the kitchen garden, Rand had slipped out through the double doors. He'd shut them behind him, then swiftly circled the kitchen garden to the corner where he could see Felicia and Mayhew walking down the south lawn, their backs to him.

He'd walked quickly across the lawn and into the woodland that so helpfully surrounded the house.

From the cover of the trees, he'd watched Felicia and the artist stroll the lawns, eventually fetching up at a spot almost directly across from where Rand had been standing. After some discussion, apparently pleasing to both, they'd repaired to the terrace, where Flora was waiting with the teacups.

Mayhew had shown them some papers — presumably some of his sketches. Rand hadn't been able to get a clear view of Felicia's face, but from the expression on Flora's, Mayhew's sketches were very definitely worthy of admiration.

As the trio consumed their tea and cakes and conversed in pleasant vein, Rand shifted in the shadows and wondered if he was being overly paranoid. Or overly something else.

Could Mayhew simply be what he purported to be? A sketch artist whose works were published in the *London News* and who was eager to find new vistas to draw?

Certainly, Mayhew had shown no interest in the workshop doors, although given their location, they could easily be taken to be doors to a cellar for storing produce from the kitchen garden. Yet Rand wasn't even sure Mayhew had noticed the doors; he'd seemed more interested in Felicia and, later, in the long views of the house.

As Rand watched, Mayhew made some comment, then collected his sketches. Felicia rose and went indoors; a moment later, she returned and resumed her seat. Presumably, Mayhew was leaving, and Felicia had gone to ask for his horse to be brought around.

Rand shifted, uncertain and faintly irritated. He tried to get a better sense of — a clearer insight into — the instincts that were so firmly insisting that Mayhew was a threat. Which instincts? And a threat to what?

Given his focus on the invention, he'd assumed the prickling tension had to do with that, warning him he should see Mayhew as a threat to the Throgmorton engine.

But what if it wasn't that? What if his instincts were bristling because they saw

Mayhew as a threat in another sense?

As a threat to Rand because of his fascination with Felicia Throgmorton.

Cloaked in the trees' shadows, he wrestled with the realization that — almost without him being aware of it — that second option had become a possibility.

Just because he'd decided he wouldn't think of finding a wife until after he'd established his position in the investing world didn't mean Fate would fall in with his plans.

Concealed in the wood's gloom, he watched as Mayhew rose, and Felicia got to her feet. With smiles and bows, Mayhew took his leave of the ladies, then walked back along the terrace and around the corner of the house to where his horse would be waiting in the forecourt.

Rand studied Felicia as she remained by the table, watching Mayhew depart; he couldn't see her face.

Rand's lips twisted, then he shook his head, made his way out of the trees, and strode for the workshop doors.

He could pretend all he liked, but the truth was that, regardless of whether Mayhew had any interest in the Throgmorton steam engine, Rand and his prickling instincts would still see the artist as a threat.

A different type of threat, yet a threat nonetheless.

As for which type of threat Mayhew actually represented . . . at that point, Rand didn't know. He couldn't even make an educated guess.

FIVE

As dusk turned to darkness outside the windows and the clocks throughout the house chimed for ten o'clock, Rand sat at the desk in his bedchamber and penned a letter to his half brother, Ryder, and Ryder's wife, Mary.

The couple had known Rand had been on his way to visit them; not appearing and not sending word wasn't an option.

Even if Ryder wasn't inclined to worry unduly, Mary would fret, and then Ryder would act — most likely by asking questions in London — which wouldn't be helpful. Aside from avoiding such an outcome, Rand wanted to make his excuses to his nephews and niece and assure the whole family that he would join them at Raventhorne Abbey as soon as the problems with the Throgmorton Steam-Powered Horseless Carriage were resolved.

As his nib softly scratched across the

paper, Rand felt increasingly sure that he wouldn't be free to visit the Abbey until after the twenty-second of the month — after the exhibition at which the invention was to be unveiled. Until then . . . he expected to be living on tenterhooks.

They had to meet that deadline and meet it successfully. Any alternative would harm him, his investors, the Throgmortons, and their household — it was as simple as that.

Not that he communicated any of his anxieties to Ryder and Mary. Forging his own path meant doing things himself, and while Ryder, as the Marquess of Raventhorne, possessed significant power, and Mary, as a Cynster, had her own brand of power, too, in the arena Rand had chosen as his own, that sort of power was, if not entirely impotent, then as near as made no odds.

Increasingly, these days, men like Rand were being judged by their achievements. One's birth helped, but the achievements mattered more.

He reached the end of his missive, signed his name, then blotted the page. He folded the sheet, inscribed Ryder's direction, and used the stick of wax supplied to seal the flap, pressing his signet ring to a melted blob, then waving the letter to cool the seal.

That done, letter in hand, he turned down the lamp, rose — and froze, staring out of the window into the country dark.

Had he just glimpsed a figure drifting through the near-black shadows edging the lawn?

He stared, but could no longer see anything to suggest someone was out there. The figure — if figure there had been — had been moving southward. If there was someone there, they would now be out of his sight.

Rand frowned. Slowly tapping the letter against his fingertips, he stood looking through the window while he reviewed the reasons his mind might be playing tricks on him by imagining a figure flitting through the woods.

Despite his and, indeed, Felicia's initial suspicions of Mayhew, they all — meaning Felicia, Flora, Johnson, Shields, and, reluctantly, Rand — had agreed that the man had shown no sign whatever of being anything other than what he purported to be — an artist keen on sketching the Hall.

They'd discussed the matter over the dinner table, then called in Johnson and Shields for their views of Mayhew. Johnson had served the Throgmortons for decades and was well aware of the threat to the family a seemingly innocent man might pose, and Shields, as a Londoner, had been born suspicious, yet neither man saw Mayhew as harboring any sinister intent.

Grudgingly, Rand had accepted that his heightened instincts were, in this case, heightened for another reason entirely — one that had nothing to do with any threat to the Throgmorton engine.

In accepting that . . .

He snorted softly and turned from the window. He opened the door and walked along the corridor into the gallery, then descended the stairs. A salver for letters for the post was sitting where he'd assumed one would be — on the side table in the front hall. He left his letter on the salver, on top of one written by either Felicia or Flora, judging by the delicate writing.

As he was about to turn away, his gaze fell on the door to the workshop. It was closed, and he'd checked the bar across the double doors on the lower level himself before he'd followed William John upstairs for dinner.

The workshop was secure. The invention was safe.

There was no danger to anyone — at least, not tonight.

Yet his nerves — his instincts — were still twitching.

His lips setting, Rand turned and went up the stairs.

Five minutes later, he settled in the bed, closed his eyes, and — somewhat to his surprise — fell instantly asleep.

A clanging commotion jerked Rand awake. The noise didn't stop. Whatever it was continued to clatter and bang.

He leapt from the bed. As he grabbed his trousers, he glanced at the window — and, in the faint silvery light shed by a crescent moon, saw a man fleeing across the lawn to dive into the wood.

Cursing, Rand thrust his legs into his trousers and shoved his feet into his shoes. He shrugged on a shirt and headed for the door.

The clanging was slowing, but hadn't ceased.

Still buttoning his shirt, he strode down the corridor — and saw Felicia, swathed in a silk wrapper and carrying a candlestick, in the gallery ahead of him.

He caught up with her as she started down the stairs. Going down three and four at a time, he waved at her. "Stay back!"

On reaching the hall tiles, he glanced over his shoulder — only to see her hurrying down.

She pinned him with a furious glare. "Don't be ridiculous."

Cursing anew, this time under his breath, he turned and strode on. He hauled open the door to the workshop — the clanging had come from there, but had almost stopped, fading in a rather curious way.

All below him lay in inky darkness.

Tight-lipped, he swung around, seized one of the candles left on the hall table, lit the wick from the candle Felicia — her expression stoic, but concern leaping in her eyes — held steady. Then he turned once more to the workshop stairs.

"Wait!"

Rand looked around to see William John, the skirts of his dressing gown flying about him, a lighted candelabra in his hand, come hurrying down the stairs.

Johnson appeared behind his master, and Shields, Corby, and the two footmen came thundering down in their wake.

"It's all right," William John assured them all. "If they'd got through, the sound would have changed."

"What was that racket?" Felicia asked.

William John grinned. "It's an alarm Papa and I rigged up. It goes off if anyone tries to force the workshop doors." He pushed past Rand and started down the workshop stairs.

"Come on. I'll show you."

Everyone clattered down the stairs, even Mrs. Makepeace, Cook, Mrs. Reilly, Mr. Reilly, and their four daughters — the maids of the house.

In the workshop, William John threw the switch that, with a buzzing hum, set the gaslights blazing. He stood back and surveyed the doors, then laughed. "It worked perfectly." He pointed to a structure mounted on the wall high above the double doors. "See there? That's our alarm."

Rand had noticed the contraption earlier, but had assumed that, it being connected to the bars that secured the doors, it was merely some mechanism to lift them that was no longer in use. He came to stand beside William John and studied the mechanism of gears and levers, and what appeared to be several saucepans with their handles cut off. He debated asking how it worked, but feared William John would immediately demonstrate. If the noise had been so loud it had hauled the entire household from their beds, then in the stone-walled workshop, the cacophony would be horrendous. Nevertheless . . . he glanced at William John. "Very effective." He had to give credit where it was due.

"It was, wasn't it?" William John beamed.

"I've been wanting to test it for an age, but there's nothing like a true test of an invention to give one confidence."

Rand shared a glance with Felicia, who had halted on the last stair, then dryly murmured, "Indeed."

Felicia turned to the others, arrayed on the stairs behind her. "All's well. Someone must have tried to force the doors, but no one got through."

"Should we check outside?" Shields looked at Rand, as did both footmen.

Remembering the figure he'd seen fleeing into the night, Rand shook his head. "Whoever they were, they'll be long gone." And with so much woodland all around, their chances of catching anyone were slight. "But I believe we must treat this as the sign it unquestionably is. Someone knows of the Throgmorton engine and has, tonight, targeted it."

Rand glanced at Felicia.

She nodded slightly, in support.

He looked at the others and went on, "We'll need to mount a guard — despite the alarm mechanism, several men, acting together, might think to push past it and damage the engine before fleeing." He focused on Shields, Corby, and the footmen. "We'll need two men here at all times during the night."

Corby exchanged a glance with Shields, then volunteered, "I'll draw up a roster. We've Struthers and his lads from the stable, too, so it shouldn't be too much for anyone."

Rand nodded. "After the recent excitement, I'm sure we'll be safe for the rest of the night. Whoever it was who tried to break in will need to regroup."

Everyone nodded in agreement. All except William John, who was still admiring his successful alarm mechanism.

Rand tipped his head in dismissal and turned to William John. While Felicia urged everyone to return to their beds, Rand, with William John, checked that the doors were, indeed, still shut tight. William John assured Rand that as long as the bars were set in their place — as they were — the alarm system could be relied on to give notice should anyone attempt the doors again.

Stepping back, looking up, and smiling at the alarm mechanism, William John sighed happily. "Papa would have been so pleased."

Again, Rand met Felicia's eyes, then, at her direction, William John turned off the gaslights, and he and Rand followed her up the stairs.

Felicia paused in the hall. The rest of the

household had already reached the gallery and were dispersing to their rooms. She turned to William John — and Rand, who was closing the workshop door, something William John hardly ever remembered to do.

One glance at William John's face informed her that her brother was overwhelmingly delighted at the perfect performance of one of his inventions and remained untouched by any apprehension over what had caused the alarm to go off.

Rand, on the other hand, looked as concerned as she felt. It was more to him than William John that she said, "After the alarm went off, I saw a man run away from the house and plunge into the woods."

William John blinked.

Rand regarded her levelly. "Heading past the rose garden?"

She nodded. "Yes."

His jaw set. "I saw him, too." He grimaced. "There's so little moonlight, I didn't get a decent look at him."

"Nor did I." She saw the question forming in Rand's eyes and stated, "And no, he didn't look familiar in any way, but it was so quick and the light so poor, I couldn't swear it wasn't Mayhew, either."

William John frowned. "I thought we'd

decided the artist was no threat."

"That's what we'd concluded," Rand agreed, "but that doesn't mean our assessment was correct. It seems a trifle too coincidental that Mayhew appears in the area, inveigles an invitation to the Hall, visits, and hours later, in the dead of night, someone tries to break into your workshop." He looked at Felicia. "Cast your mind back. Did Mayhew do or say anything at all that might suggest he'd noticed the workshop?"

"No." She frowned, thinking back yet again. "As I said earlier, I'm not even sure he saw the doors. If he did glimpse them, he certainly paid them no attention at all." She paused, then shook herself and fixed her gaze on Rand. "Regardless, Mayhew is supposed to return tomorrow — no, today." A quick glance at the longcase clock against the hall wall confirmed it was nearly two o'clock. "He said he would come in the early afternoon to do his sketch. If it was he who tried the workshop doors, perhaps he won't turn up. But if he does . . ."

Rand grunted and waved her and William John toward the stairs. "If he does, either he's the innocent artist we all think him, or he possesses enough nerve to be a real threat to the invention."

"We still won't know, though, will we?"

William John climbed the stairs on her other side.

"We'll simply have to remain vigilant," Rand replied.

He and Felicia parted from William John at the head of the stairs. Side by side, they walked around the gallery and down the corridor that led to their rooms. Rand reached his door. He paused with his hand on the knob, then inclined his head and, through the dimness, wished her a good-night.

She returned the salutation and continued to her room. Once inside with the door firmly shut, she exhaled.

Despite all the excitement and distractions, keeping her gaze from Rand's chest, the solid muscles and impressive width imperfectly concealed behind the screen of his fine linen shirt, had required far more effort than she'd liked. Yet she'd clung to her composure and had managed well enough; she doubted he or anyone else had noticed her difficulties.

She crossed to the uncurtained window through which she'd seen the fleeing man. Crossing her arms over her silk wrapper, she stared down at the night-shrouded scene and thought of what was to come.

Prior to tonight, she and Rand had already

started to form a . . . partnership of sorts. Until he'd arrived and she'd learned the truth of how matters stood, she hadn't comprehended the significance of her brother's current invention with respect to her own life. Given she now understood that reality, Rand was quickly coming to feature as . . . a collaborator. Someone whose aims coincided with her own. Someone she could rely on, at least as far as protecting the invention and steering it to a successful unveiling went.

That some man had attempted to break into the workshop proved beyond doubt that *someone* — be it Mayhew or some other man — wanted to sabotage the project.

She and Rand would have to work together to guard against that happening. His alarm mechanism notwithstanding, William John couldn't be relied on to recognize, much less react appropriately to, a threat posed to his invention, not until an attack materialized and was actively under way. *Then,* he would defend his engine to the death. Meanwhile, however, he would be absorbed with correcting the issues preventing the engine from running for more than a handful of minutes without exploding.

For all their sakes, William John needed to

devote his time and his brain to that. No one else could fix the engine.

And she and Rand would be thrown together even more in organizing its defense.

She had to admit that a large part of her found the prospect . . . enticing. It promised a sort of excitement that had rarely come her way.

More, however, as she stood staring unseeing into the darkness, she realized that, for the very first time in her life, she felt . . . protective toward an invention.

Before Rand had arrived on their doorstep, she hadn't thought of the engine much at all, and when she had, it had featured as a nuisance.

After she'd learned the truth, she'd accepted that the engine meant something to her — to her future.

And after this direct attack . . .

She searched through her feelings for the emotions underlying them — and felt her brows rise as she considered what she sensed.

She would defend the invention as if it were . . . hers, in a way. Hers to protect — like a mechanical child. A mechanical nephew — the fruit of her brother's brain.

Given her until-recent attitude to inventions, that struck her as odd, yet she couldn't deny or dismiss the protectiveness that had surged inside her when she'd heard the alarm and seen the man fleeing across the lawn.

She'd known the invention had been attacked, and her response had been instant and instinctive.

She'd been — and still was — prepared to fight to ensure the engine, her father's last project, succeeded.

Not from any especial devotion to her father or even her brother. Not purely because her future might well hang on the engine's success. But primarily because someone had dared to attack the engine — and through that, attack them. Her, William John, their household — and Rand Cavanaugh.

Her features eased; she considered that conclusion, then allowed a smile to bloom.

Now, she understood her reaction.

Her people — those she considered her responsibility — had been threatened. Of course she would fight to defend them.

Reassured and feeling more settled, she lowered her arms and turned from the window.

She climbed beneath the covers, lay down, and settled her head on her pillow.

No matter how unthreatening and innocent Clive Mayhew appeared to be, she would continue to be on her guard against him. If he truly was innocent, it wouldn't matter. If he wasn't . . .

She closed her eyes and relaxed into the softness of her feather mattress. She thought of Mayhew's visit later that day as sleep drifted closer.

On the cusp of dreams came the reflection that she was exceedingly glad that Rand had thought to come to the Hall, that he'd opened her eyes to the reality of what was going on, and she was beyond words relieved that, over dinner, he'd said he would stay, not just until the engine was fixed and running smoothly but until they'd successfully unveiled it at the exhibition.

He would be there, by her side, throughout this unforeseen adventure.

She slid into sleep thoroughly pleased about that.

SIX

On his way to the breakfast parlor that morning, Rand paused in the front hall as Johnson emerged from the direction of the kitchen. "Johnson, has that letter I left last night gone out?"

"Indeed, my lord." With a covered dish in his hands, Johnson half bowed. "I sent both letters off with the stable lad first thing this morning. The post is collected from the village promptly at nine o'clock."

Rand smiled. "Thank you." So his letter to Ryder was on its way. Perhaps it was just as well he hadn't known of the attack to mention it, not if he wanted to avoid a visit from his sometimes-overpowering big brother.

He followed Johnson into the breakfast parlor. Felicia and William John were already at the table. After exchanging a "Good morning" with Felicia, Rand helped himself from the sideboard, then circled the table to claim the chair he'd sat in the previous day — the one facing Felicia. The light streaming in through the windows at his back illuminated her expressive face. He could, he felt, stare at it for hours.

He wasn't entirely surprised when, once he'd settled and essayed his first mouthful, she shot him a look and stated, "Regarding Mayhew's visit this afternoon, I've decided it would be best to continue to be on guard. We can't be certain he wasn't the man who attempted to break into the workshop last night."

For once, William John was listening. He frowned, his expression suggesting he wasn't convinced of Mayhew's involvement.

"I agree." Rand reached for the mug Johnson had filled with coffee. "But regardless of whether the perpetrator was Mayhew or not, the attack last night is proof incontrovertible that someone — someone in the vicinity — is set on gaining access to the Throgmorton engine. Given how close we are to the exhibition, we have to assume that person's intent is to sabotage the invention and prevent it from being successfully presented at the exhibition."

William John grimaced. Pushing away his empty plate, he sank his hands into his trouser pockets and stared at the tablecloth in front of him. "I know Papa had an invention sabotaged years ago, while he was transporting it to the factory that had commissioned it, but he managed to fix it." William John looked up and met Rand's gaze. "In that case, the blackguard was a competing inventor. Are there other inventors in direct competition with us over the steam engine? I haven't heard of any, but since Papa's death, I haven't been corresponding with any others in the field."

Rand took a full minute to evaluate what he knew and how best to explain it. Eventually, after glancing at Felicia and noting that she, too, was waiting for his reply, he said, "I don't know of any directly competing inventors. As far as I know, the Throgmorton Steam-Powered Horseless Carriage is the only such invention being unveiled at this year's exhibition. In the eyes of most inventors and investors, the concept of a steam-powered horseless carriage has proved unviable — precisely because of the problems you and your father have worked to address. I haven't heard of any other inventor who is still pursuing that dream — at least, not in England. And I doubt the Throgmorton engine will have come to the attention of inventors on the Continent — not yet."

He paused, considering, then concluded, "Overall, I think it unlikely that some other inventor is behind last night's attack." He drew breath and went on, "That isn't to say there aren't others who have a vested interest in eradicating any suggestion that steam-powered horseless carriages might yet be a viable proposition."

Felicia frowned. "If not other inventors, then who?"

"Other investors — and that's just one group." Rand felt his face harden. "With steam-powered vehicles, you would also have to consider the owners and operators of the railways — and they are an exceedingly powerful lot. Then there's the toll-road operators, who have taken a hard stance against steam-powered vehicles — they would infinitely prefer the notion vanished without trace." He paused, then met Felicia's eyes. "And as for the politics . . . who knows who has interests that such an invention — a successful one — might threaten?"

Felicia studied his face, his eyes, then she tipped her head, and her lips and chin firmed. "It sounds as if it's pointless to speculate on who might ultimately be behind the attack and what their motives might be. To me, that means we need to maintain our vigilance against any and all further attack — who might be behind such attacks doesn't change what we need to do."

Rand nodded. "Well said. I agree." Shields had already reported on the rotation Corby and he had devised. Rand outlined their plan. "So as well as William John, there will always be at least one extra man in the workshop throughout the day. And at night, two men will be on duty at all times."

Felicia was listening intently. Rand glanced at William John. Their inventor appeared to have drifted back to mentally wrestling with tubes and valves. Rand returned his gaze to Felicia's green eyes. "That should ensure the invention remains safe — unsabotaged."

She nodded, then, holding his gaze, pushed back her chair. "Meanwhile, I'll keep a close eye on Mr. Mayhew while he completes his sketch." She swiveled on the chair, about to rise, then paused and said, "Regarding Mr. Mayhew . . . just in case he is involved, presumably working as an agent for someone else, I thought I might use the hours while he's here to tease more information from him as to his background, his connections — the usual sorts of things a lady might bring up in conversation."

Rand hadn't wanted to ask, but was quick to nod encouragingly. "You never know what he might let fall, especially if he's distracted with his sketching."

She cut a swift glance at her brother. "My thoughts exactly." She rose, and Rand came to his feet.

William John grunted as if their movement had disturbed his train of thought. He pushed back his chair and stood as well.

As Rand rounded the table, Felicia turned to the door. "Of course, once Mayhew completes his sketch, there'll be no reason for him to return."

"True." Rand followed her into the front hall. "But even if he doesn't openly return here, we won't know if he remains in the area. There are too many villages and hamlets within easy reach to check."

"Indeed." She nodded. "I'll see what I can learn this afternoon."

With that, she sailed off to what Rand had learned was her sitting room — on the other side of the hall from the drawing room. Mrs. Reilly was already waiting by the door, a sheaf of papers in her hands. The housekeeper followed Felicia inside and shut the door.

William John, his hands sunk in his pockets, his head down — deep in thought — had already ambled past, heading for the workshop stairs.

Rand studied the closed sitting room door. Even more than previously, he didn't like the idea of Felicia Throgmorton interacting with Mayhew, especially alone upon the lawn at some distance from the house. Then again, Rand wouldn't be far away, and he most certainly would be watching like a hawk. The thick woods that circled the house were proving to be a blessing.

He wished he could think of some alternative, but in the circumstances, it was undoubtedly wise to learn what they could about Mayhew, and in accomplishing that, Felicia stood a far better chance of success than he.

If learning that William Throgmorton was dead and the invention Rand had so much riding on was not yet complete had been a rude shock, learning that someone was intent on sabotaging said invention was an even more unwelcome complication.

Inwardly shaking his head, with nothing more he could usefully do at that point, Rand walked to the workshop stairs and followed William John down.

When Clive Mayhew arrived, Felicia was seated with Flora in the drawing room, waiting to welcome him.

Johnson announced the artist, and Felicia,

with Flora at her back, walked into the front hall to find Mayhew piling an easel, a folding stool, and a rather battered artist's satchel into Joe's arms.

Felicia smiled and gave Mayhew her hand. After bowing over it, then greeting Flora, Mayhew bestowed a charming smile on Felicia and stated, "If you don't mind, I would like to commence sketching straightaway. The light's particularly fine this afternoon, and I don't want to risk losing it."

"Of course." With a wave, she gestured toward the still-open front door. "I'll come with you and see you settled." She glanced at Flora. "If you'll excuse us, cousin?"

Flora smiled. "It's such a lovely day. I believe I'll take my embroidery onto the terrace. Enjoy your sketching, Mr. Mayhew." With a gracious nod to Mayhew, Flora retreated to the drawing room.

Felicia walked toward the door. Mayhew fell in by her side.

"That spot not far from the old fountain was simply perfect," Mayhew said. "I need look no farther for the perfect view."

"Excellent." With a tip of her head, Felicia signaled to Joe to follow them with Mayhew's equipment.

With Mayhew looking about, an open, apparently relaxed expression on his face, they crunched across the forecourt and tramped over the thick grass toward the spot Mayhew had selected the previous day.

He turned and walked backward as they neared it, his eyes narrowed as he considered the vista. His feet slowed, then he halted. "Yes. This is it."

The position he'd chosen lay just beyond the shadow cast by an old oak that grew at the edge of the woods. Joe came up and set down his burdens. With a quick "Thank you," Mayhew picked up his easel and, with efficient, practiced movements, set it up, then he lifted his satchel, unbuckled the flap, reached inside, and carefully drew out a sheet of fine-grained paper.

Felicia watched as Mayhew attached the paper to the board of the easel with pins, then he searched in the satchel again and drew out three pencils. He set the pencils on the tray of the easel and bent to prop the satchel against the easel's rear leg.

Then he unfolded his stool and set it before the easel.

Puzzled, Felicia said, "I thought you used ink as well as pencil."

Mayhew flashed her a smile. "I do. But I add the ink later, at a desk. I can get all the detail I need down with pencil, then later, I pick out the strongest lines with ink to complete the sketch." His expression turned faintly awkward. "Do excuse me if I sit."

Felicia waved him to his stool. "Of course." She watched him settle, then asked, "Do you mind if I watch?"

He was already assessing his subject, but in reply, he threw her a vague smile. "By all means." He looked back at the house. "Some of my brethren dislike anyone near when they work, but as I often sketch in busy streets, I long ago lost all such sensitivity."

"Ah — of course." Felicia surveyed the thick grass; courtesy of the warm day, it was dry. She'd draped an old shawl over her elbows in the hope she could remain. She shook out the shawl, spread it on the sward to the side and a little back from Mayhew's stool, then sat. From her position, she could see his sketch as it came into being. She also had a clear view of his profile.

She bided her time as with swift, sure strokes he laid in the initial lines of his creation. It was pleasant in the shade, with the distant sounds of Reilly snipping canes in the kitchen garden and the occasional clop of hooves and jingle of harness from the stable overlaid by the twittering calls of birds flitting in the woods at her back.

After a time, Mayhew sat back, his gaze

rising, then dipping as he compared his rendering with the reality before him, then he set down the pencil he'd used to that point and picked up another.

"Can you talk while you work?" she murmured.

"Hmm? Oh — yes. To a point. If I get caught by a difficult section, I might forget to listen, but in general" — he shot her a swift glance, one that invited her to laugh with him at himself — "I can manage well enough. So if you have questions, by all means, ask away. It's not often I get to sketch with a delightful lady looking on."

She suspected he meant questions about his sketching. Her expression relaxed, faintly smiling, she asked, "Did you train to be an artist, or is this a natural talent?"

"Very much a natural talent. My family would have had a fit if I'd set out to be an artist."

"So what did you set out to be?"

"An idle gentleman, like the majority of my peers."

"And what changed that?"

"You might say my art called to me. Being idle, I was ripe for distraction, and this — sketching — became my chosen vice."

"Do you live in London, then?"

"I have lodgings there — nothing salubrious, being a younger son and all."

"What of your family? Are they in London, too?"

He paused for a moment, but Felicia judged that to be more because he was paying a great deal of attention to the perspective between the house and the stable. Sure enough, a moment later, he straightened on his stool, and his pencil moved on to the shrubbery, and he murmured, "What was that? Ah yes. My parents. They now spend their days at home in Sussex. My brother and sisters are scattered about London. They spend more time in tonnish circles than I do." Smiling, he glanced her way. "Us bachelors tend to lurk on the fringes, but I've been known to be hauled to a ball or two by my sisters or sister-in-law."

Felicia smiled and continued her questioning, apparently lighthearted and inconsequential, yet his answers were painting a picture of him that she recognized from her year in London. The Clive Mayhews of the ton, the idle, drifting younger sons, were personable, charming, with unexceptionable manners — the sort of gentlemen chaperons approved of as escorts to the theatre and the opera and to the occasional ball, but unless love struck, they were never going to be regarded as eligible *parti*. They

153

were innocuous stand-ins, safe arms on which a young lady could lean.

Other idle younger sons might be a great deal more dangerous, but those like Mayhew constituted no threat.

Felicia realized *that* was what lay behind her continuing vacillation over casting Mayhew as their current villain. While, logically, she accepted she had to suspect him and continue to be on her guard, when she was with him, his character and personality were such strong reminders of the sort of man he was, she found it difficult to view him as any sort of threat.

Indeed, at no time had she sensed that he posed any danger to her. Her antennae had been well honed during her year in London; she knew beyond question that no matter how attentive and charming Mayhew might be, he had absolutely no designs on her.

As his sketch took shape and the answers to her questions took longer to come, and sometimes didn't come at all, it became crystal clear that the one thing Clive Mayhew was extremely serious about was his art.

Wryly smiling to herself, Felicia couldn't help thinking that, when it came to interacting with them, an artist was no different from an inventor.

By the time the first sketch was done — or, as Mayhew explained, done to the point of being ready for the application of ink — it was time for afternoon tea.

Apparently having decided that the cool shade beneath the oak was too tempting, Flora came drifting over the lawn, with Joe and Martin lugging the wrought-iron table behind her.

Johnson followed with a chair. In short order, the footmen returned with two more chairs, and Johnson carried out the tea tray.

Once they were settled about the table and Flora had poured cups of tea, Mayhew showed Flora his sketch. "It's the first — I'll essay another after tea. The second attempt is usually better."

"Dear me!" Flora studied the sketch, then swiveled on her chair to stare at the house. "You've quite captured it. It's a remarkable likeness."

"Thank you." Mayhew sipped his tea and watched while Felicia took the sketch from Flora and studied it.

As with the other sketches of his she'd seen, he'd not just depicted the house and, with simple lines, somehow conveyed the gardens and grounds, he'd also managed to capture a feeling of the place — its inherent atmosphere. She raised her gaze, met Mayhew's eyes, and handed the sketch back to him. "I feel quite honored to have been able to watch as you created it. Thank you for permitting that."

Mayhew took the sketch and inclined his head gracefully. "Thank you for permitting me to sketch here. It truly is my pleasure."

"Is there any chance of us getting a copy of your best sketch once it's published?" she asked.

Mayhew arched his brows. "I should be able to get you one of the first-run prints. The final sketch itself is the property of the paper, but they allow me a few prints for my own collection."

"If we could have a copy to hang here, dear Mr. Mayhew, that would be lovely." Flora looked thoroughly pleased; Felicia could imagine Flora sharing that news with her far-flung correspondents.

"I'll see what I can do," Mayhew returned with a smile.

While he drew out his spool-like contraption and carefully added the sketch to the sheets already on the roll, Felicia reflected that there really wasn't any reason — any fact, any tiny incident, or even a word said

— to suggest that Mayhew was in any way linked to the attack on the engine.

That morning, Rand's man, Shields, and Struthers had gone into the village and discreetly inquired about any strangers seen in the area. Struthers knew who to ask. But other than Mayhew, there'd been no one sighted even riding through.

Of course, as Rand had pointed out, there were many small villages and hamlets within a few miles — lots of places a stranger might be lurking. Impossible to search them all.

Yet no matter how she tried, she couldn't imagine Mayhew as the man she'd seen fleeing into the woods last night.

Telling herself that continuing to suspect him was futile, she relaxed, smiled, and chatted.

They finished their tea. Mayhew rose and prettily thanked both Felicia and Flora for their hospitality — a subtle hint that he wished to return to his sketching.

When, laughing, Flora tasked him with that, Mayhew looked sheepish. "The light will only last for so long, and" — he turned to view the house — "you must admit the lines are particularly sharp at the moment."

Now that he'd pointed it out, Felicia could see what he meant. The westering sun lit the front façade and left every line of the house sharp and stark. She could appreciate why Mayhew had chosen this position from which to sketch . . . which itself suggested that the sketch was his reason for visiting the Hall. If he'd wanted to sketch the house from the rear, from where he could see the workshop doors . . . Instead, he'd shown absolutely no interest in them.

The table had been placed to the side of where Mayhew had elected to site his easel; they could leave the table and chairs as they were without interfering with his view. Smiling, increasingly at ease with Mayhew — the artist who patently was just an artist — Felicia rose as Flora pushed to her feet.

"In that case," Flora said, "we'll leave you to your sketching, Mr. Mayhew. Do drop by if you find yourself in the neighborhood again."

"Thank you." Mayhew hesitated, then said, "Actually, I've been so greatly taken with the scenery hereabouts — it's particularly well-suited to my style — that I've been thinking of taking a short holiday and remaining in the district to work on more sketches, entirely for myself."

Felicia blinked as alarms jangled in her brain.

"How lovely!" Flora replied. "It really is a very pleasant region of the country."

"Indeed." Mayhew glanced at Felicia, meeting her gaze. "I was wondering, Miss Throgmorton, given that I will be remaining in the area, if you would be agreeable to me calling on you sometime — purely a social call?"

What? Her gaze on Mayhew's perfectly serious face, for the first time in years, Felicia felt flustered. A faint blush rose to her cheeks, yet no matter how she stared, she couldn't see — couldn't sense at any level — that Mayhew was attracted to her.

So why was he asking leave to call?

Her own words from that morning echoed in her head. *Of course, once Mayhew completes his sketch, there'll be no reason for him to return.*

Assuming he was innocent of having designs on the engine had been her rationale.

Her suspicions of Mayhew came roaring back.

Before she'd gathered her wits enough to form any reply, Flora, smiling benevolently, declared, "Of course we'd be delighted to see you, sir, whenever you are free to call."

Mayhew shot a questioning look at Felicia.

She'd rallied by then and managed a creditably gracious smile. "You'll be very

159

welcome, sir." What else could she say?

Mayhew bowed elegantly. "Thank you, ladies. For now, I wish you a pleasant afternoon and evening."

With Flora, Felicia took her leave of Mayhew.

Flora linked her arm with Felicia's as they strolled slowly across the lawn toward the open front door. Knowing full well that Flora didn't need the support, once they were out of Mayhew's hearing, Felicia arched a brow at her chaperon.

Flora smiled. "Petunia told me about your suspicions of Mayhew." Petunia was the lady's maid Felicia and Flora shared. "I've been living here since your mother died, and I've learned enough of the way things are regarding inventions to comprehend the situation. Given Mayhew asked to call again . . . well, my dear, let's just say that I believe in that old adage about keeping one's friends close and one's enemies closer."

Such words coming from the soft and matronly Flora made Felicia want to laugh; if the situation hadn't been so serious, she would have. Instead, as they neared the forecourt, she patted Flora's arm. "I believe I agree with you on that."

■ ■ ■ ■

Rand stood with his back against the bole of an ancient beech and watched Felicia and Flora retreat into the house.

He'd been in position for the past several hours; Johnson had tipped him off after Mayhew and Felicia had walked onto the lawn. Rand had left the workshop via the rear doors, stridden around to the stable, and slipped into the woods beyond, then he'd worked his way around under the cover of the trees until he'd found this spot; situated just inside the edge of the woods directly behind Mayhew's back as he sat before his easel, the tall beech had branches that draped nearly to the ground. Being in full summer leaf, the dipping branches effectively screened Rand while allowing him to study Mayhew.

Unfortunately, he wasn't close enough to have eavesdropped on the conversations between Mayhew and Felicia, and, later, Flora. He'd had to try to guess what was being said from expressions and gestures, and through most of it, Felicia had had her back to him.

Rand debated showing himself — debated what benefits or problems might accrue.

He wasn't close enough to see the details of Mayhew's work, but after the ladies had left him, Mayhew had fixed a fresh sheet of paper to his easel and was swiftly and efficiently sketching, to all appearances deeply immersed in his work.

Rand had to admit that even now, when he couldn't know he was under observation, Mayhew still looked and behaved as an artist would.

That tipped the scales toward the possibility that Mayhew was, in fact, simply an artist. If so, then there was some other man lurking with intent to destroy the engine.

Rand frowned, possibilities, conjecture, and speculation whirling in his brain.

Minutes ticked by. Mayhew's hand worked at speed, rapidly covering the paper with what, from Rand's position, appeared to be scribbles in shades of gray. Comparing what was taking shape with the earlier sketch, Rand suspected Mayhew would finish soon.

Making up his mind, Rand pushed away from the tree and quit the safety of its draping canopy. Silently, he worked his way to the right — Mayhew's blind side as he looked from the house to his sketch. Eventually emerging onto the lawn, Rand settled his coat, then, as if he'd been taking a constitutional on the south lawn, strolled toward Mayhew.

Mayhew was so engrossed, he didn't see or sense Rand until he halted a mere yard away.

Mayhew looked up with a start. "Ah." He blinked, then inclined his head. "Good afternoon." Mayhew gestured with his pencil. "I've permission to sketch the house."

Rand nodded. "Felicia — Miss Throgmorton — mentioned you would be by. Mayhew, isn't it?" Rand offered his hand. "I'm Lord Randolph."

It was useful to have a first name that could be taken for a surname.

Mayhew rose, transferred his pencil to his other hand, and gripped Rand's. As their hands parted and Mayhew subsided onto his stool, he asked, "You're a neighbor?"

Rand shifted to study Mayhew's sketch. "I'm a friend of the family. I'm visiting for a few days before I head home."

"I see." Mayhew waited, but when Rand said nothing more, Mayhew raised his pencil and continued sketching.

Sliding his hands into his pockets, Rand considered the sketch and inwardly frowned. He did, in fact, know several artists. One of Mary's connections was the famous portraitist Gerrard Debbington.

163

Through attending several exhibitions of Debbington's works, Rand had met other artists; it was becoming fashionable, once again, to be the patron of a talented artist.

Mayhew was talented. Rand had learned enough of art to appreciate that. There was something in the way he laid down lines that was insightful, that drew the observer into the picture.

Mayhew's sketch was just lines on paper, yet it conveyed much more.

Rand's inner conviction that Mayhew was behind the attack on the workshop wavered.

His hands sunk in his pockets, Rand shifted, then said, "You're exceptionally good."

Mayhew glanced briefly his way. A smile touched his lips. "Thank you." After a second in which he added two fine lines, he murmured, "Grudgingly given praise is often the most satisfying."

Rand laughed — he couldn't help it. "That's . . . very true." He chuckled and inclined his head. "Touché, Mr. Mayhew."

Oh, this was not good. Rand sternly told himself he didn't want to like Mayhew. He still thought the artist turning up at just that time, his glimpse of a man lurking, and the attempted break-in was too much co-incidence to swallow.

Returning to his purpose, he took advantage of Mayhew's breaking the ice to further his knowledge of the man via the usual information men such as they might exchange during just such an impromptu meeting. They spoke of London, of clubs and hells, of the theatre and the latest generally known scandals. Mayhew knew his way about London and was also well acquainted with Fleet Street and the newspaper offices, as well as with the City — although whether his knowledge of the Bank of England and other such buildings was because of his use of their facilities or because he'd sketched them, Rand wasn't sure.

Somewhat to Rand's consternation, Mayhew responded to all his queries — the subtle probes as well as the outright questions — with easy candor and with answers that painted him as precisely who he purported to be, namely, the younger son of an established family who had taken to sketching to supplement his income and make his mark.

There was absolutely nothing Mayhew let fall that supported the thesis that he was an agent of some inventor or investor intent on sabotaging the Throgmorton steam engine.

Of course, as Rand well knew, the ton had no shortage of accomplished liars.

Finally, Mayhew rose from his stool, pushed it aside, and stepped back from his easel. After a moment of comparing the sketch with the house, he nodded. "That's it." Gathering his pencils in one hand, Mayhew reached around the easel for his satchel. He glanced up at Rand. Seeing the slight frown on Rand's face, he said, "This is the second sketch I've done. The light's going, but I've got all I need to be able to complete the inking at the inn. They have a room under the eaves that has lovely light — perfect for the work."

Rand nodded his understanding. He watched as Mayhew folded his easel, collapsed the stool, then shouldered his satchel and lifted easel and stool.

Rand waved toward the forecourt. "I'll walk with you."

Mayhew's lips quirked, but with an inclination of his head, he accepted Rand's escort.

They were halfway across the lawn when Mayhew, his gaze fixed on the stable, said, "I mentioned to Miss Throgmorton that I was thinking of taking a short holiday in the area and might call in at some time. However, I've recalled that my arrangement with the *News* requires several more sketches of other villages before I can call my time my own. Consequently, I'll be out of the area for a few weeks." Mayhew glanced at Rand. "Could I ask you to convey that to Miss Throgmorton and Mrs. Makepeace, and to assure them that I'll drop by with the sketch I promised them when I return?"

Maintaining a genial but uninformative mien, Rand inclined his head. "I'll pass the message on."

They reached the stable yard. This time, Mayhew had arrived in a gig. While he strapped his easel and folding stool to the back of the seat, Rand noted the stamp on the gig's side that proclaimed it the property of the Green Man Inn in Basildon. The horse between the shafts bore the same inn's brand.

With his equipment stored, Mayhew slung his satchel onto the seat and climbed up. He nodded at Rand. "I'll bid you a good day, Lord Randolph."

"Good sketching," Rand dryly replied.

Mayhew grinned, snapped off a salute, then shook the reins.

Rand stood back and watched the gig rattle down the drive. Even when the trees hid Mayhew from sight, Rand remained staring after the artist.

Wondering.

Especially over what Mayhew's last message might mean.

Was the artist simply an artist and temporarily moving out of the area purely in order to satisfy his employer?

Or had Mayhew merely claimed to be leaving in order to paint himself as no threat?

Had he decided on a few weeks in response to Rand's presence at the Hall, assuming that, as Rand had intimated, in a few days, Rand would be gone?

There were fifteen more days until the exhibition. Artist or no, that left Mayhew plenty of time to return and sabotage the engine.

Frowning, Rand turned and headed toward the house.

He still didn't know what he thought of Mayhew, but as for the artist taking himself off . . .

As he mounted the porch steps, Rand couldn't bring himself to place any reliance on that.

Seven

The following day, after having had Johnson strike the gong to summon William John and Rand to the luncheon table three times, all to no avail, Felicia gathered her skirts and started down the workshop stairs.

"Ridiculous men!" She muttered more pointed imprecations as she carefully made her way down the spiral staircase. If she gave up on them and ordered the table to be cleared, then, as sure as eggs were eggs, a minute later, they would be wandering into the dining room looking for sustenance.

Truth to tell, as it was now well past one o'clock, she was surprised their stomachs hadn't accomplished what the gong and their ears had not.

She slowed as she rounded the stair's last curve and looked down into the workshop.

Although she'd made no effort to conceal her approach, her slippers hadn't made that much noise. Neither man had realized she was there.

They were staring at the engine, each, in their own way, radiating frustration. William John was scowling; his hair stood up in clumps — he'd clearly clutched at it several times. As for Rand, he'd rested his forearm on the bench and was leaning on it, his expression one of focused exasperation.

She shifted her gaze to the object of their ire. It was the first time she'd given the engine at the center of their now-joint mission more than a cursory glance. The contraption was a fantastical construction of pipes and tubes, cylinders and pistons, all wrapped around a gleaming copper boiler. Pipes curved and bent, creating a knotted skein of sleek metal that glowed softly under the harsh lights.

Unexpectedly mesmerized, she stared. She was conscious of a tug, as if prompted by some inner compulsion to unravel and understand the complex construction.

She tried to draw back, to pull away; she managed to keep her frown from her face when she didn't succeed.

She stepped down to the workshop floor. It might have been years since she'd walked upon it, yet everything seemed the same — still familiar.

Instead of berating both men for not

responding to the gong, she heard herself ask, "What's wrong?"

Ferguson, the blacksmith, had delivered the new boiler the morning before; she'd seen it being carried in, an oval balloon in shining copper, quite unlike any boiler she'd previously seen. It now sat in the center of the welter of pipes.

Although Rand looked up at her question, William John didn't. Instead, he clutched his hair with both hands and wailed, "I don't know!"

Before she had a chance to react, he pointed dramatically at the boiler. "That's the new boiler." She drew closer, and he hurriedly added, "Don't touch it. It's hot." He frowned. "In fact, it's too hot, which I think is part of the problem."

She told herself she shouldn't ask, yet the words "What is the problem?" popped out of her mouth.

"It's the throttling back that just isn't working." William John whirled to face the large board on which he'd pinned his diagrams.

Felicia walked around the engine so she could see more clearly.

"This is the boiler." William John pointed to the diagram. "Although it doesn't look like that anymore, for our purposes, it's the same. It sits on top of the burner, and that's all working as we'd hoped. We've drastically improved the efficiency of the generation of steam from a given amount of coal, which was one of our primary aims to improve Russell's modifications to Trevithick's design. So we've got that right, and all the rest" — he waved to the pipes, valves, and pistons that connected in a tangle of pieces between the boiler and the representation of what Felicia vaguely understood was a drive mechanism — "works faultlessly. Exactly as required. But it seems we can only drive the carriage at an ever-increasing pace. We can ease back a little, but the slowing is quickly overcome by the pressure building in the boiler. The valves that used to work to allow us to slow still work, but they don't reduce the pressure sufficiently, and it just keeps mounting."

Felicia frowned at the diagrams, her eyes tracing pathways through pipes and pistons.

"At present," Rand said, "the power escalates at an ever-increasing rate. If we allow it to run for even ten minutes, it'll blow up."

Felicia grimaced. "That's the last thing we need — another explosion." After several moments, she glanced at William John. He looked more dejected and defeated than she'd ever seen him.

She didn't look at Rand, but she'd heard the same low ebb in his voice.

That odd compulsion prodded at her, nagging, all but whispering: *What could it hurt?*

To her, the problem appeared reasonably straightforward. She must have retained more from her earlier years than she'd realized; the diagrams were as readily interpretable as Mayhew's sketches.

The suggestion circling her brain might well be ludicrous, yet given the men's dejection, what would it hurt to voice it? There was nothing more at stake than her pride.

She focused on the diagram of the boiler and its immediate connections, mentally working through her argument again, then she drew in a breath, lifted one hand, and tapped on the paper. "When you throttle back, this valve releases, doesn't it?"

William John had gone back to staring at the engine. He returned to the board of diagrams, halted by her side, and looked at where she pointed. He nodded. "Yes. That's the one."

"If you've drastically increased the efficiency of generating steam," she said, "shouldn't there be more than one?"

William John blinked. He opened his mouth, then shut it. Then his face came alive. "We reengineered the pistons, but we left everything else as Russell had it."

Behind Felicia, Rand straightened. "But she's right, isn't she? You've allowed for the extra power in the forward drive, but you haven't adjusted the release."

William John was nodding feverishly. "Yes. That's it!" He stepped closer to the board and jabbed a finger at the offending valve. "We need to double the size of that, and I think we should run two in parallel. Yes, that's right — in series won't do it. Parallel, it should be." His voice was rising, excitement building. He started to mutter, all but babbling as he rethought his approach.

Emboldened, Felicia raised her voice and said, "And is there any reason you can't attach a valve to the boiler itself? One with a high enough limit so it will only release if the pressure rises beyond safe levels?"

William John pulled up short. He thought, then peered at the diagram of the boiler. "You mean directly on the boiler? We'd need it to be recast."

"We haven't got time for that, so what about here?" She pointed to one of the two connectors at the top of the boiler. "Can't you change that and insert a valve with a gauge there?"

Rand came to stand beside her. "Can that

be done?" From his tone, William John's excitement had infected him, too. "I assume if so, we would be able to test the rest of the engine without constantly having to turn it off whenever the pressure in the boiler gets too high."

William John's eyes were alight. "Yes — *yes!* We can do that. We must have the right bits here somewhere — we can figure it out, and then . . . Yes! That's it!" He turned to Felicia; his expression ecstatic, he waved his arms in the air. *"Eureka!"*

She had to laugh — then she felt strong hands fasten about her waist, and Rand, laughing, too, spun her about, picked her up, and, stepping away from the engine and board, whirled her around.

Their excitement sank into her and bubbled through her veins. As the workshop whirled about her, she smothered a squeal. Her hands fell to Rand's shoulders and gripped; as he slowed, she looked down into his face, wreathed in relieved delight. He grinned boyishly up at her, and something nebulous and elusive tugged at her heart. His eyes met hers, and his expression grew a touch more serious; he held her gaze for several seconds, then, slowly, he lowered her to the floor.

As he released her, he said, "You have no

idea how close we were to admitting ultimate defeat."

She arched a brow at him, then shot a
glance at William John. "Am I allowed to
say I find that hard to believe?"

William John humphed, but he was still
grinning and didn't seem able to stop.

Before he could start assembling the bits
and pieces to create his new valve assembly,
she firmly stated, "Now I've helped solve
your problem, you can solve one for me.
There's a cold collation waiting upstairs,
and thus far, only Flora and I have turned
up to eat it."

It was difficult, but she did her best to
mock-glare at them both.

"Great heavens! Is it lunchtime?" Rand
consulted his watch.

"Good!" William John said. "Now we
know what we're doing, I'm as hungry as a
horse."

She shook her head at him, then turned
and led the way to the stairs.

Rand followed her up, with William John
happily clattering behind.

Relief was still pouring through Rand, so
intense he almost felt giddy. He'd spoken
truly. He and William John had been at their
wits' end. He'd greatly feared they'd been
staring failure in the face.

Felicia's insight testified to the benefit of having a fresh pair of eyes look over a problem. He and William John had been studying the diagrams for so long, they hadn't been able to see the valves for the pipes.

Yet as he followed Felicia into the dining room, he had to own to being impressed by the ease with which she'd taken in the problem, then unerringly put her finger on the source. He'd worked alongside inventors long enough to appreciate that seeing through all the layers of obfuscation created by complicated mechanical systems to the heart of a problem required a certain clarity of mind.

In his experience, it took a special type of brain and mind to be able to "see" at that level.

Felicia said nothing about her success as she resumed her seat beside Flora, who had already finished her meal.

Rand smiled and made his and William John's excuses, then claimed the chair opposite Felicia.

As usual, William John sat at the head of the table, opposite Flora. Transparently released from all worries, glib and gay, he rattled on to Flora, heaping accolades on his sister's head for her invaluable assistance.

Felicia, Rand noticed, looked pleased, but also faintly disturbed.

To fascinating and occasionally enigmatic, he could now add intriguing.

From where he sat, there was definitely more to Felicia Throgmorton than he'd had any reason to suppose.

The next day was Sunday. Rand and William John went down to the workshop immediately on returning from church.

The previous afternoon and evening, they'd worked together — Rand acting as William John's assistant — to make the modifications Felicia had suggested. They'd had to leave the connections to harden overnight before testing the new valves.

They could barely wait to fire up the boiler.

Then they watched the gauges. Watched and waited as the pressure built.

The valve released precisely as it should. "Yes!" William John raised his fists to the ceiling.

Rand grinned, but kept watching. Only when the new valve continued to release, maintaining the pressure in the boiler at the maximum safe level, did he finally relax.

Unfortunately, that wasn't the end of their

difficulties. William John reattached the drive shaft — he'd dismantled it while they'd concentrated on working on the boiler — only to discover that now, although the issue with the pressure was resolved, even with a steady pressure applied, he couldn't get the pistons to remain in strict tandem. After five minutes of running, they were sufficiently out of rhythm to have the drive shaft groaning.

After an hour of poking at the pistons and their connections, clearing all the tubing, and then studying the diagrams, William John had once again resorted to tugging his hair. "I don't understand it," he wailed. "We've increased the pressure, but it's now under control and steady. The timing shouldn't have changed."

It occurred to Rand that, as with the earlier problem, this one was almost certainly more about design than the actual mechanism. "Why don't we carry on with those changes you wanted to make to the drive shaft itself and wait until your sister comes to pry us away for lunch, then see if she can suggest a way forward?"

William John had looked ready to throw a spanner at the board. Rand's words gave him pause, then he shrugged. "Yes — why not? We're getting nowhere here — let's move on to something we can do."

When, after Johnson had struck the gong twice with no result, Felicia again made her way down the curving stairs to the workshop, it was to find William John and Rand waiting for her with welcoming smiles on their faces.

Frowning, she paused on the last stair. "What is it?"

William John leapt to tell her — in detail.

And, once again, she found herself, however reluctantly, inexorably drawn into considering, studying, and evaluating the problem.

When William John finally fell silent, and both men waited, patently expecting her to offer them a solution, she frowned at them. "Yesterday . . . that was very likely just luck. A fluke. A moment that won't be repeated."

William John looked at her beseechingly. "Please." He gestured to the diagrams.

"We're stuck." Rand's tone was less cajoling and more definite. "You're here, you understand the problem — just look and see if anything strikes you."

She humphed, but consented to fix her attention once more on the diagrams. The more she traced the connections, the more she felt as if her mind was sinking into the structure of the engine, making sense of the complexity in a way that was almost beyond her conscious grasp. As if some deeply buried part of her recognized the challenge and rose to meet it.

This difficulty was . . . trickier. There were more possibilities, more points at which things might be going awry.

She lost all sense of time as, with her eyes, she traced, tracked, and backtracked.

As if from a distance, she heard slow, ponderous footsteps on the stairs, heard Flora's voice raised in a question that cut off when Rand said something.

She almost smiled as she realized what she was doing — that she was just like her father and brother in being able to cut herself, her mind, off from everything around her . . .

She used to consider that a flaw. Now . . .

She blinked, looked more intently, then she stepped closer to the board, swiftly ran through her thoughts once again, then with a fingertip, she tapped each of the four feed lines to the pistons. "These are the source of your problem — you haven't equalized the lines. The pressure going into each is equal, but because the lines are different lengths, the pressure delivered to the pistons is fractionally different. It didn't matter, at least not so much, when you were running with much less power. Now you've increased the power, the pistons will be noticeably out of time after even a relatively short run."

She turned to William John and saw his eyes widening, widening, then a huge grin split his face.

He beamed at her. "You've done it again!"

She found herself grinning back. She glanced at Rand and saw him grinning, too, transparently relieved and delighted. An undeniable spurt of triumph rose and washed through her.

William John was muttering, then Flora harrumphed and said, "I'm very glad you've worked out your problem, but luncheon is still waiting. At least it's a cold collation and won't be spoiling."

Along with a still-smiling Rand and a muttering William John, Felicia — reluctantly — turned away from the diagrams and started up the stairs in Flora's wake.

Three steps up, Felicia glanced back — at the board, the gleaming bulk of the engine, the clutter of the workshop. Facing forward again, she finally understood something of what had driven her father and still drove her brother. That moment of triumph when one solved a critical issue and got things right . . . however fleeting, that feeling of euphoria was addictive.

They trailed into the dining room and sat about the table, helping themselves to the various dishes and, in short order, settling to eat.

An atmosphere of pleased satisfaction reigned, and for a while, they all savored it in silence.

Rand ate and thought — and couldn't shake, much less sate, his burgeoning curiosity. Eventually deciding there was no reason he couldn't ask, he looked across the table and caught Felicia's gaze. "I own to being curious about your talent. Were you much involved in your father's work?"

She blinked at him. "No. I wasn't involved at all." She glanced at William John, then added, "I was never . . . asked. As I mentioned earlier, I haven't set foot in the workshop for years. Yesterday was the first time in . . . a very long time."

William John's expression was entirely serious when he said, "Obviously, it's been far too long since you were there. Thank God you ventured down yesterday."

"Indeed." Rand looked from William John to Felicia, then back again. He hesitated, but the point was too important not to be addressed. "I've worked with a lot of inventors over recent years. Many work in teams, often of just two members, sometimes three.

Rarely more. Your father was one of the exceptions — he worked alone for most of his life. But you two . . . If I was assessing your inventive strengths, I would say that while William John has clearly inherited your father's aptitude for engineering and assembling mechanical devices, you" — he nodded at Felicia — "have inherited your father's brilliance in conceptualization and design." He looked at William John. "Those are distinctly different sets of skills, and both sets are essential for successful invention."

William John leaned forward, his gaze going to Felicia. "Rand's right. I couldn't see what the problems were until you pointed them out. I can fix them once I know what's amiss, but I couldn't identify them — and you could. And you did that not just once, but twice." William John sat back and grinned broadly at Felicia. "You, dear sister, are an inventor, too."

Felicia felt she should scoff — at least humph and dismiss the notion as nonsensical — yet the warmth of that moment of triumph still lingered in her veins, seductive and alluring, and as she glanced from William John to Rand and read the sincerity in their expressions and open gazes, seduction on a different level bloomed.

They — both of them — saw her and her abilities, her instinctive skills that she'd neglected and ignored for so long, as valuable. As worthy of nurturing, worthy of inclusion. Worthy of encouragement and support.

She knew how she'd gained those skills — she'd absorbed them during her earlier years when she'd run free in her father's workshop, side by side with William John. Even after she'd been effectively excluded and had stopped going downstairs, she'd been forced to listen to her father discuss his inventions ad nauseam — of course she'd taken a lot in.

If, now, Rand and William John thought she could contribute to the invention in a real and meaningful way . . .

It seemed that an entirely unexpected and novel path was opening up before her.

Do you want to take it?

Something in her leapt at the thought.

She blinked and looked down at her plate. Apparently, she truly was her father's daughter — the notion of working alongside William John in the workshop was powerfully attractive.

Both Rand and William John — and to a lesser extent, Flora — were waiting for her reaction to William John's assertion. When she didn't deny it, Rand evenly said, "We've less than two weeks before the exhibition. I suggest that from now on, we consider you, Felicia, as a contributing partner in our efforts to get your father's last invention working well enough to present it to the world."

She looked up, and Rand was waiting to capture her gaze.

"Would it be possible," he asked, "for you to make time to assist in the workshop?"

William John leaned forward as she glanced his way. "In case we stumble over another obstacle and need your insight." He looked like an eager puppy begging her to come and play with him.

She felt her lips twist in a reluctant smile. She drew in a breath and inwardly acknowledged the instinctive compulsion to agree that had leapt to life inside her. But she wasn't yet ready to fling restraint to the winds and unreservedly embrace this unexpected twist of fate — this new role that Fate seemed to be offering her.

Yet . . . she held William John's gaze, recognizing his sincerity, then she looked at Rand. "We all need the Throgmorton steam engine working perfectly as soon as may be. If you require my help, I'm sure I can manage an hour or so to assist in whatever way I can in that endeavor."

His expression satisfied, Rand inclined his head.

Flora looked bemused.

William John beamed and slapped his palms to the table. "Well, then. That's settled." He pushed to his feet and looked at Rand. "We'd better get on."

Clive Mayhew returned to London that evening. Burdened with his easel, folding stool, and satchel as well as his bag, he alighted from the train at Paddington Station and managed to find a hackney to ferry him to his lodgings in Mortimer Street.

Juggling his bags and equipment, he unlocked the front door, then struggled up the narrow stairs to his rooms on the first floor.

With a sigh and a wince, he set down the easel and stool in a corner of the shabbily furnished living room, then laid the satchel on the small table beside the single armchair angled before the hearth. He paused to light the sconce on the wall, then carried his bag through a secondary door into the bedroom beyond.

After depositing his bag on the bare floor by the narrow bed, he returned to the living room. The rooms had been closed up; the atmosphere was musty and close. He crossed to the single window, unlocked the sash, and pushed it up. A bare breath of breeze wafted in.

A scarred tantalus stood against the wall below the window. Mayhew checked the bottles, found one with several inches of brandy remaining, and poured one of those inches into a glass.

Finally, glass in hand, he sank into the armchair. After downing a gulp of the poor-quality brandy and grimacing at the taste, he reached for his satchel, flipped open the flap, and drew out the sketches he'd made over the previous days.

They weren't bad. Not bad at all. Cruick-shank at the *News* would pay well for them.

Unfortunately, not well enough.

The last sketches in the pile were the pair from Throgmorton Hall. He'd risen early that morning to finish them, sitting at the small desk beneath the window in his room at the Norreys Arms.

He'd propped the window open and the faint rustle of the trees in the woods had, at first, been the only sound, that and the faint trickling of the nearby stream. He'd inked in the sketches, soothed by the country peace flowing all around him.

The views of the Hall were exquisite — even if it was he who said so. As both were from the same viewpoint, they were similar, yet the changing of the afternoon light had resulted in subtle differences.

His thoughts shifted back to the household at the Hall — to Miss Throgmorton and Mrs. Makepeace.

They'd welcomed him warmly and had been genuinely interested in and impressed by his sketching.

They'd been . . . nice. Honest, straightforward, comfortable people who assumed those they met were equally honest and straightforward.

What would they think of him if they ever learned his true purpose in wrangling an invitation to the Hall?

For long moments, he toyed with the notion of stepping back from his uncle's scheme. It was crazy and risky — what did he know of inventions and engines? He'd agreed because it had seemed so distant and in an arena he cared nothing about.

But meeting Miss Throgmorton and Mrs. Makepeace had brought living people into the picture. *Nice* people.

Clive raised his glass and, his gaze unseeing, took a long sip.

He could honestly say that until agreeing to act for his uncle, he'd never knowingly and deliberately done another harm — at least, not as an adult. He knew right from wrong and had never intentionally crossed that line.

Of course, he still hadn't managed to blot his copybook, but he had tried.

Uncertainty — fueled by welling discomfort over his covert role — rose beneath his skin, an increasingly persistent itch. He shifted in the chair and refocused on his sketches — those on his lap and the two he still held in one hand.

Surely — *surely* — he could find some other way to assemble the necessary to get Quire off his back?

He stared at the sketches of Throgmorton Hall, and the conviction that he couldn't do as his uncle wanted grew. His wits skittered this way and that, like a mouse desperately seeking a way out of a maze.

The sound of the street door opening jerked him from his thoughts. As heavy footsteps climbed the stairs, on a spurt of panic, he remembered he hadn't relocked the front door.

He gathered his sketches and set them on top of his satchel. He had only seconds to steel himself before the door to the living room opened, and two heavy, beefy mountains of men marched through.

The latter closed the door and stood, feet

apart, before it — as if Clive might rush past the other and attempt to escape.

The first man steadily advanced, his small eyes locked on Clive. The bruiser halted by the chair. His expression impassive, he studied Clive for an unnerving few seconds, taking in the nearly empty glass, then his gaze shifted to the sketches and the satchel on the side table.

Clive tensed — which brought the mountain's gaze back to his face.

Finally, the man spoke, his voice surprisingly light. "The guv'nor wants his money."

Gripping his glass, Clive slowly nodded. "I said I'd have it for him in a few weeks — on the twenty-fifth. He agreed to wait."

The mountain nodded back. "That he did, and the guv'nor is a man of his word. He just sent us around to remind you of that."

And to remind Clive of the detailed and quite hideously violent promises their "guv'nor," Quire, had assured Clive would come to pass should Clive fail to meet his latest deadline.

"I haven't forgotten."

The mountain studied him for another few seconds, then glanced at the sketches. "Seems like you've been out playing."

Fighting down the urge to reach for the

sketches, Clive straightened in the chair. "I'll get paid for those."

"P'raps." The mountain returned his unnerving gaze to Clive. "But not nearly enough."

Clive inclined his head. "True. But I have other . . . irons in the fire, so to speak."

The mountain chuffed out a laugh. "Irons in the fire, heh?" The behemoth exchanged a grinning glance with his friend. "I must remember to share that with the guv'nor. He'll enjoy a good laugh."

Clive's blood chilled at the reminder of one of the more gruesome threats their master had made.

The behemoth's gaze returned to Clive's face, and now cruelty was etched in the man's expression. "The guv'nor said to remind you that if you fail to turn up with the entire sum, interest and all, the very first thing he'll have us break is those lily-white hands of yours. Every single bone. He's given you a last chance — don't disappoint him."

Having delivered that chilling ultimatum, the brute turned on his heel and marched toward the door. His mate opened it and stepped back.

The first man went out and started down the stairs. The second man, until then silent, pinned Clive with eyes that held less expression than a dead fish's. "I'd listen to him if I were you."

The man turned and went out of the door and quietly shut it behind him.

Clive stared at the panel. Only when he heard the street door shut did he manage to haul in a breath.

Slowly, he exhaled.

After several seconds, he raised his glass and tossed back the last of the sour-tasting brandy. Then he shuddered. He glanced at the sketches lying on his satchel. After setting the empty glass on the floor, he picked up the sketches, stowed them in the satchel, then rose, the satchel held between his hands.

He stared at the satchel.

He had only one talent to his name — only one way of earning a living.

Those at Throgmorton Hall enjoyed a pleasant home in a lovely, peaceful setting. They plainly had the wherewithal to keep the place up even while throwing money at inventions.

Having one invention fail wouldn't be the end of the world for them.

Not succeeding in making that invention fail would be the end for him.

■ ■ ■ ■

That evening, as dusk deepened, edging toward night, Rand stepped out onto the terrace. He breathed deeply, then walked down the steps onto the lawn, slid his hands into the pockets of his trousers, and started pacing.

He had no destination in mind; he let his feet wander where they would. His room had been warmed by the afternoon sun, and he'd felt a need for fresher air to clear his mind and settle his somewhat peripatetic thoughts.

His feet took him eastward, toward the darkness of the woods. Before he reached the trees, he turned north, slowly pacing the stretch of sward that sloped gently upward from the south lawn, skirted the rear wall of the kitchen garden, then leveled off not far from the roses.

As he walked, he glanced to the side, into the wood. The trees grew thickly in that area, directly behind the house, and the undergrowth clogged the spaces between. Although it seemed the closest concealed approach to the workshop doors, the area was near impassable; the man he'd seen fleeing after the attempted break-in had raced away to the northeast and plunged into the woods that presently lay ahead on Rand's right.

He'd gone searching on the morning after the scare. He'd found the path the man must have taken, but with the ground summer hard, there'd been no sign to mark the man's passing. That path twisted through the woods to eventually join the lane a little way from where the village street ran off it. Anyone from the village, including a guest of the Norreys Arms, would have had an easy run home.

Admittedly, the would-be burglar could just as easily have come from farther afield; at that hour, a gig or horse left in the lane wouldn't have been seen by anyone.

And in the small hours of the morning, no one would have seen the man returning to his lair.

Given that, Rand had jettisoned any notion of pursuing their man by tracking him.

His gaze on the grass before his feet, he passed the kitchen garden and continued up the slope toward the rose garden. The combined scents from the blooms wafted past on a faint breeze, teasing his senses — reminding them of the fascinating, enigmatic, and intriguing lady who tended the bushes.

195

He knew himself well enough to acknowledge that he was — to his mind, surprisingly — attracted to her. Not just physically, but intellectually, emotionally, and even by dint of his business. To him, she was a lure of many facets.

After his experience of and his consequent antipathy toward ladies clever enough to manipulate him, he'd assumed that the last lady he would feel drawn to would be one who, in his estimation, possessed a mind capable of running rings around his.

Felicia Throgmorton definitely possessed such a brain. She might hide it, disregard it, yet he, at least, couldn't overlook it, not after her recent and undeniably critical contributions to the Throgmorton project.

What surprised him was that knowing she possessed such a mind in no way dampened her allure. If anything, that she could and clearly did understand inventing at a fundamental level had only increased his interest in her.

Increased the sense that she — and she alone of all the ladies he'd ever met — somehow fitted.

Fitted him, his life, and the aspirations and private goals he hadn't — until the last days — thought much about.

His attraction to her — recognition of

what sort of attraction it was, its depth and escalating strength, and what, at some point, it would push him to do — had prodded him to focus on those until-now nebulous goals.

He wanted to marry. He wanted a family. He definitely wanted a hearth and a home and a wife to share both with.

In short, he wanted everything Ryder had found with his Mary.

The family at Raventhorne figured in Rand's mind as the shining epitome of his ultimate desire.

That was what he wanted his life to contain.

Up to now, he'd kept his attention firmly fixed on accomplishing his business goals, telling himself that even defining his more private goals could wait. He was only thirty years old, after all.

Yet the instant he'd seen Felicia Throgmorton on the Hall's front steps — his virago with rose-gold hair — his senses had focused on her in a way they never had with any other lady and taken his emotions and a good part of his wits with them.

Everything that had happened since — his reactions to Mayhew and the incident of the break-in to the growing ease and understated understanding between Felicia and himself — had only further entrenched his feelings, until, now, they shone as an inner certainty.

The only consideration stopping him from pursuing her openly was the Throgmorton steam engine.

If she didn't view him in a complementary way, then pressing his suit before the project was successfully completed would make working together on the engine awkward. More, he didn't know how she might react to a declaration from him; she might even back away from helping William John altogether, and that, he simply could not risk. There were too many people relying on them delivering the project on time.

With her help, he was confident they would succeed. Without her help, he was no longer so sure. All he'd seen to that point seemed to prove that William John's strengths alone wouldn't be enough.

So he would wait until they had the engine working and presented it at the exhibition. Then he would ask for her hand.

He nodded to himself, pleased to have thought his way to that clear and unequivocal stance.

Of course, waiting didn't mean he couldn't use the time to learn more of her. Indeed, for any number of reasons, it would be wise to gain some understanding of her complicated and convoluted relationship with inventors and inventing.

They'd managed — entirely by chance — to get her into the workshop long enough for her to respond to their need and demonstrate her understanding.

They'd opened a door they hadn't known existed, and today, they'd managed to wedge that door open.

That didn't mean she couldn't slam it shut.

Today's advance was no guarantee that he or William John wouldn't, in some way, unintentionally step on her toes and prompt her to step back.

She'd agreed to help them and clearly understood both why she needed to and what was at stake. But ladies could always change their minds.

When it came to her and inventing, he felt like he was blundering in the dark — a feeling he didn't appreciate.

He'd started plotting a campaign to tease more insights from her when the soft swish of silk reached his ears.

Surprised, he looked up — and realized that his wandering feet had set him on course for the entrance to the rose garden.

Even as, blinking, he focused on the heavily shadowed arched entrance, now a mere yard away, Felicia, her eyes on the ground, walked purposefully out, under the arch.

She walked directly into him.

"Oh!"

He'd had a second to halt and brace himself.

She all but bounced off him.

Before she could stagger back, he grasped her upper arms and steadied her.

She sucked in a breath, and tension streaked through her.

Ignoring the rush of physical awareness that raced over him, he ducked his head and looked into her face. "It's all right. It's only me — Rand."

She blinked at him, her eyes luminous in the semi-dark; the unexpected collision had affected her, too — in her wide eyes, he saw the same awareness that was prickling under his skin.

Then she let out the breath she'd held in a soft exhalation; the line of her shoulders eased, and she raised a slim hand to her throat. She looked into his eyes with transparent relief. "My apologies. I wasn't looking."

"No need to apologize. I didn't see you coming, either." Yet he'd realized in time that, had he wished to, he could have avoided the collision, but that was something he saw no reason to mention.

"Well, then. Thank you." She sounded faintly breathless.

She stepped back, and, reluctantly, he released her and lowered his arms.

She stared at him for a second; he cursed the shadows that fell over her face and prevented him from reading her expression.

Then she tensed a touch and shifted as if intending to step past him.

Before she could bid him goodnight and leave, he reached out, looped her arm with his, and smoothly turned her around, effectively anchoring her beside him as he stepped toward the rose garden. "Please — walk with me." Pausing under the arch, he gestured down the flagstone walk. "It's a beautiful night, and your roses are in bloom."

Short of wrestling free — something he felt fairly certain she wouldn't do — she had little option but to fall in by his side. She humphed and dryly replied, "So I've noticed."

But her feet obligingly followed his.

"Have you been strolling long?" he asked.

"No. My room was stuffy, so I came out to get some air."

Greatly daring, he loosened the guard on

his tongue. "Am I allowed to say I'm glad?"

She looked down, then, in a plainly curious tone, asked, "Why?"

His face shrouded by the deepening shadows, he grinned and gave her half the answer. "Because I'm curious. After our previous discussion in this garden, having learned of your antipathy to inventing and inventors and your very sound reasons for that, I was . . . shall we say, taken aback? . . . to realize that, regardless of your stance, you are very definitely an inventor, too." He paused, his senses confirming she was listening, and that although she'd stiffened slightly at his reference to her talent, she hadn't tried to halt or pull away. His voice even, his tone intrigued but not demanding, he went on, "If you'll consent to sharing your thoughts with me, what I would particularly like to know is why you have, apparently doggedly, kept yourself out of the workshop and away from all inventing until now."

That afternoon, while they'd been working on the modifications to the pistons' feed lines, William John had confirmed that he hadn't known of his sister's abilities, and that as far as he could remember, she'd never been a collaborator in any of his or his father's inventions in even the smallest way — indeed, that she'd never previously shown the slightest interest in any invention whatsoever.

Felicia narrowed her eyes, but as she kept her head bent and her gaze directed at the path before their feet, the gesture had no effect on the gentleman who had so adroitly claimed her company. Her senses, thrown into disarray by their collision, hadn't yet completely settled. Her nerves were still flickering, all too aware of his powerful, very male presence so close beside her.

She shouldn't have acquiesced, but her silly feet had followed his lead . . . just as her thoughts were now following his.

Given that, invention-wise, he seemed intent on involving her as a collaborator, his question — his curiosity — was, perhaps, understandable. And while his wasn't a question she'd ever posed to herself, she did know the answer.

Raising her head, she looked down the path along which they were slowly strolling. She half expected him to press, but he remained attentively silent. Encouraging, but content to allow her to marshal her thoughts.

More than anything else, that silent yet focused attention prompted her to speech. "When I was a young girl, I spent a great deal of my time in the workshop, along with William John. I expect my . . . talent, as you call it, stems from those days. From all the hours I spent listening to Papa talk through his work. Probably because, until recently, he'd always worked alone, he was one of those inventors who, when he was working, spoke his thoughts aloud." She paused, remembering those days. "Instead of dolls, I had wrenches and spanners. And I still can't embroider to save my soul. In place of the usual lessons a young girl learns, I was playing at building things with gears and levers. Mama loved Papa too much to try to curtail my time with him, and I adored — simply adored — the different world that existed downstairs."

She stared unseeing into the deepening darkness that cloaked the end of the garden. "But that time passed. William John and I grew older, and as we did, Papa focused on William John, of course. I was a girl, and increasingly, Papa paid less and less attention to me — and feeling cut out, I went down to the workshop less often. That meant I spent more time upstairs with Mama, and that made me aware of the . . . counter side of Papa's obsession with inventions. As the months and years went on, I saw and increasingly understood the pressure Papa's obsession placed on everyone else, but on my mother most of all. Papa left her to manage everything. He cared for nothing but what went on in his workshop. By then, I'd stopped going down there. I simply couldn't — not while knowing what him working down there was costing Mama."

She drew breath and raised her head. "I grew increasingly angry — and what you've termed my antipathy grew and grew, until ultimately, I turned my back on everything to do with inventing." She paused, then went on, "If it wasn't for William John — if it had been left to me — I would have closed the workshop after Papa's death."

The long-fermented rancor elicited by her father's behavior still pulsed in her veins.

She tipped her head toward Rand and felt her curls brush his shoulder. "Given all that, it's hardly surprising that I simply didn't realize I . . . had any real ability in that sphere. Even after Papa died, the very last thing I would have thought of doing was going down to the workshop and offering my help." She thought of it, then softly snorted and looked down. "Had Papa been alive . . . what happened two days ago would simply never have occurred. He never — ever — thought of me as a potential colleague. He had William John, and I was just a girl."

They'd reached the end of the path. The seconds they took to swing around to pace back toward the house were time enough for her to realize and acknowledge another truth. As they strolled freely again, she murmured, "In hindsight, me distancing myself from inventing was a mistake on both my and Papa's parts. Had I participated in his work, even if only occasionally, I would have understood what drove him." She drew breath and admitted, "It wouldn't have changed how I felt about inventing, but . . . I would have understood him."

She frowned and looked down, suddenly aware that she now had regrets she hadn't previously harbored. Nevertheless . . . raising her head, she stated, "I still firmly believe that people — especially those close to us, the people we love, our family — are in all situations and at all times more important than any invention could ever be."

His voice, deep and faintly gruff, rumbled across her senses. "Even as engrossed in inventions as I am, I entirely agree."

She glanced at his face, but the shadows were now those of full night, and she couldn't make out his expression.

Rand continued, "Inventions should help,

not harm — not in any way, not even in their developmental stages. There is no other purpose behind inventing, so to cause harm while inventing . . . to me, that runs counter to any inventor's purpose."

Her explanations and revelations had pushed him to consider his own views, to review his own feelings. How far would he go in pursuit of an invention if someone dear to him stood to be harmed, even if only emotionally? The answer was very clear in his mind. He couldn't imagine allowing such a situation to proceed.

"Thank you for trusting me enough to explain." He glanced at her face and, through the dimness, met her shadowed eyes. "It helps to understand how you feel about things."

Despite the darkness, he saw her lips curve. "In that case, I claim turn and turn about." She tipped her head, her eyes still on his. "What led to your interest in inventions? From what did such an esoteric interest spring?"

When he didn't immediately answer, she murmured, "It would help to understand how you feel about things."

That surprised a short laugh from him. "Very well." He faced forward and wondered where to start. Then he knew. "I had no interest in inventions until six years ago."

When he didn't go on, she prompted, "What happened six years ago?"

She'd been open and honest — and brave — in telling him all she had. He couldn't be less, do less. "Six years ago, my mother died. She fell to her death from an upstairs window while trying to escape being taken up for the attempted murder of my half brother, who was and still is the Marquess of Raventhorne. She tried to kill him so that I would inherit — a scheme I and my other brothers and sister had no notion of. She . . . was a master manipulator and had pulled the wool over all our eyes. Everyone knew she didn't like Ryder, but that she would do such a thing . . ." He shook his head. "It was incomprehensible."

"You're close to your half brother — the marquess?"

"Nothing so mild as merely close. That was why our mother's treachery . . . hurt so much. Ryder's six years older than I am, and I'm the eldest of the four children my mother bore our father. To the four of us, Ryder was our hero. He was the magnificent big brother who always took care of us. Even now, he's our family's rock — the one all of us would turn to for help, knowing he'll always — *always* — gladly give it." He felt his lips twitch upward. "Ryder's our shield, and I suspect he'll think of himself as that to his dying day."

She paced beside him, then softly said, "It must have been — must still be — quite something to have a brother like that."

He glanced at her, reminded that her older brother had never supported her; in truth, it was she who supported William John. Rand closed his hand over hers where it rested on his sleeve. "As I said, we're more than close." His thoughts rolled on, and he drew in a deep breath. "It was the aftermath of my mother's death that set me on the path to becoming an investor who specializes in inventions. I was twenty-four when she died, and I'd . . . done nothing worthwhile with my life to that point."

He paused, letting an echo of those long-ago feelings, the strongest ones that had pushed him down his present path, ripple through him again. "I had never wanted to nor expected to inherit the marquessate. Managing a noble estate had never been of interest. But the shock of my mother's death opened my eyes and made me ask what I stood for. What the name of Randolph Cavanaugh would mean to others — and I realized that, at that time, me and my name meant nothing at all."

He glanced briefly at her and saw she was watching him. "I came to that realization a few weeks after we buried my mother. I decided on that day that I would carve a place for myself in the world, so that the name of Randolph Cavanaugh would some-day mean something."

"So that you would leave a positive mark on the world."

He inclined his head. "In whatever way — it didn't truly matter how. So I started investigating what arena I might have a more-than-passing interest in and discovered the answer was investing. For several years, I stuck as close as I could to another nobleman — a connection of my sister-in-law, Ryder's wife, Mary — who has long been an acknowledged force in investment circles. He was kind enough to teach me everything I needed to know. Through him, I stumbled into investing in inventions, and it was there I found my place."

He met her eyes. "Inventions — evaluating and assessing them, then working out what the most useful require to bring them to fruition — called to me. Captured me." He held her gaze. "Possibly in the same way that you were drawn back into inventing when the chance — the need — was placed before you. Investing in inventions drew me

210

in and held me as nothing else ever had."

They'd returned to the archway, and he led her beneath and out onto the lawns, now silvered by the light of the rising moon. "I like — no, I thrive — on the challenge of finding a worthwhile invention, then supporting the inventor logistically and financially to transform that invention into an established success."

Her gaze lingered on his face, on his profile, then she looked toward the house. "You bring passion and drive to an invention's development. Trust me, for any inventor, that's a boon in itself."

The dry words had him inclining his head.

After a moment, she glanced his way. "It seems we share the experience of having been influenced by the actions of one of our parents to the point that our reactions propelled us down our respective paths."

He thought about that, then murmured, "Perhaps. But we differ in that, while my reaction to my mother's scheming pushed me into investing in inventions — an occupation that fulfills me, and with which I'm increasingly content — your reaction to your father's shortcomings has kept you out of inventing and inventions, an arena in which you plainly are able to make real and meaningful contributions."

He didn't say more. Didn't elaborate on the contrast, but instead, left her to think it through and see that truth for herself.

After several moments of considering his words, Felicia murmured an agreement. He was right. Inventing and inventions and the contributions she might make . . . The prospect elicited a response from deep inside that was nine parts eager excitement and one part pure desire.

She wasn't sure what she felt about that. Turning assumptions about herself on their head left her mentally dizzy — uncertain of her footing.

They'd walked down the lawn and around to the terrace. As she raised her skirts and, still leaning on his arm, climbed the steps, she was aware of a certain expectation in the air — of this being a moment in time when her life was poised on the cusp of a new direction.

Exactly what that direction might be, where it might lead, and what it might hold . . . that, she had yet to learn.

Rand halted outside the drawing room door. She drew her arm from his and faced him.

Through the enfolding shadows, he looked into her eyes.

And she looked into his.

Finally, he said, his voice deep and low, "It seems that both of us have, indeed, been working our way out of the emotional coils generated by one of our parents — working to define ourselves, to define our paths into the future."

"From all you've said, you've advanced further than I have. I'm . . ." She hesitated, but they'd passed the point of being cautious. "After the revelations of recent days, I feel I'm only just starting my journey."

It was a catharsis of sorts, to speak so openly to another who understood.

Rand quietly asked, "Did you enjoy it — helping William John see his way to solving his problems?"

She blinked, then nodded. "Yes, I did. It was . . . invigorating. As if I was stretching a muscle I hadn't used in years."

"Did you feel the lure — the one I know all true inventors feel? Did it feel right — that it was right and proper? Did it feel as if you have a place in inventing?"

"Yes." Her reply came so quickly, he knew he'd touched on something she truly had experienced. She went on, "At least to your first question. As for the others . . ." She frowned. Even though he couldn't see her eyes, he knew she was looking inward.

Then she shook her head and met his

gaze. "I can't yet say. I'll have to take them under advisement."

They were alone in the night, standing close.

He felt the tug of attraction, of building desire, a tangible sensation that pushed him to shift closer still — to draw her to him.

They'd both spoken openly of things they had — he felt quite sure — never revealed to any other. They'd started, deliberately, down the path of understanding each other better than anyone else in the world.

The temptation to take the next step — to draw her into his arms and set his lips to hers — thudded in his blood.

He teetered on that indefinable edge, but held his breath and braced against it — achingly aware of the compulsion, but not yet willing to take the plunge and risk . . . any sort of awkwardness that might drive her from the workshop she'd only so recently reentered or strain the cooperation he now knew to his soul he needed from her if the Throgmorton engine was ever to see success.

Was it wrong to put that in the scales? To weigh his responsibility to all the others against what he felt for her?

Regardless, his voice lower still, a touch of gravel in his tone, he said, "Promise me you'll tell me when you learn the answers."

Felicia held his gaze and felt his words resonate deep inside. Tension had risen between them — but this wasn't a tension she'd felt before. This tension excited. Tempted and lured.

But he made no move, and she told herself she was grateful for that. They'd met only five days before. Surely that was too short a time to have developed a meaningful connection. And yet . . . there they were.

In the dark of the night with secrets already spoken and shared.

Still holding his gaze, she inclined her head and stepped back from the lure. "Goodnight." Her voice had lowered to a sultry tone.

Her nerves leapt and prickled as she turned, opened the French doors, and slipped into the drawing room.

As she crossed the shadowed space, absentmindedly avoiding the furniture, she told herself she was deeply glad he'd refrained from reaching for her; if he had, God alone knew what she might have done.

She passed through the open drawing room door and walked slowly into the front hall. She'd been kissed before, been waltzed and wooed, yet nothing had prepared her for Randolph Cavanaugh and his effect on her senses, her wits — on her will.

Nothing had prepared her for her own desire — no other man had ever evoked it. She'd never before had to deal with this sparkling compulsion.

Yet another novel and unexpected twist in her new direction — courtesy of Lord Randolph Cavanaugh.

Rand stood on the night-shrouded terrace and let Felicia walk away from him.

He waited — not thinking, not allowing his mind to speculate — until he felt enough time had elapsed for her to have gained her room.

Only then did he haul in a deeper breath, shove his hands into his pockets, and turn to look out over the south lawn.

The silvered expanse remained empty.

Lips setting, he opened the door through which Felicia had gone, stepped inside, then snibbed the lock. He checked the second pair of French doors and found them already locked. Satisfied that he could trust Johnson to have seen to the rest of the house — the butler must have glimpsed Rand and Felicia outside and left the French doors, the pair most often used by his mistress to go outside, unlocked — Rand followed Felicia's trail across the darkened room and up the stairs.

Her room lay opposite his, her door a few paces farther down the corridor. He hesitated, vacillating in the darkness between his door and hers; on hearing no sounds from her room, he turned and entered his.

He hadn't bothered to leave a light burning. After shutting the door, he crossed to the uncurtained window and stood looking, unseeing, at the dark shapes of the trees in the woods.

In retrospect, he'd been a coward to allow that moment on the terrace to pass. He should have seized the chance when it offered and trusted to Fate to see him right.

At least it was only a step forward he hadn't taken; he hadn't lost any ground. He would continue onward — and hope his moment of strategic caution wouldn't be one he would come to regret.

EIGHT

Two mornings later, Felicia entered the breakfast parlor at eight o'clock to find William John and Rand already at the table.

Both were frowning.

They raised their heads and nodded a reply to her cheery "Good morning." In William John's case, his gaze remained unfocused and his nod absentminded, but Rand's attention locked on her. His gaze, intent, swept her, then rose, and he met her eyes. He smiled fleetingly and inclined his head, then he glanced at William John and his frown returned.

She helped herself from the sideboard, then joined them at the table, sliding into her usual chair opposite Rand, with William John to her right.

As she poured herself a cup of tea, William John muttered something, then more volubly grumbled, "I just don't understand it. It *should* work perfectly, but it's *not*."

She told herself it wasn't any of her business — except, of course, now it was. She'd agreed to help, even if she remained uncertain of the wisdom of doing so. If she grew to enjoy the pastime and fell victim to its lure, what then? She was a lady, a female, and nothing could change that. She took a bite of the slice of toast she'd liberally slathered with raspberry jam, then glanced at Rand.

He was waiting to catch her eye. "As you can hear, William John's stumped."

Her brother turned to her and eagerly explained, "It's something to do with the drive mechanism. Now everything else is working perfectly, it's somehow getting out of kilter. I think we need an adjustment to the gears, but I can't see where. And there's some other wrinkle in the pressure in the lines. Not major, but I suspect if we don't get it perfectly correct, the engine will work for only a relatively short time before . . ." He raised his hands in a "who knows?" gesture. "It'll probably blow a gasket or something and come to a shuddering halt."

Rand's gaze hadn't left her face. "We were wondering if you would take a look at the problems. You might see something William John has missed."

She glanced at William John, only to have

her brother fix her with a pleading look and reach across and grasp her hand. "Please, Felicia." He squeezed her fingers. "I know it's not something you expected to have to do, but any insights you have — any hints you can give me — would be greatly appreciated." He held her gaze, then quietly stated, "I need your mind to work my way through this."

She heard the sincerity of his plea and saw it in his eyes. Inside, a stone wall of resistance, built through years of enforced disinterest and bolstered by self-protective caution, wavered, then crumbled and fell. She felt herself nod. "All right." She glanced at her plate. "Just let me finish my toast and let Mrs. Reilly know I'll meet with her later, and I'll come down and see . . . what I can see."

They hovered, both of them, as if despite having gained her agreement to assist, they thought she might change her mind or be distracted by the household. She had to smother a cynical snort.

Less than fifteen minutes later, the pair all but shepherded her down the stone stairs, William John leading the way, with Rand following behind her. On reaching the workshop floor, William John went straight to the engine, suspended within its special frame.

To her eyes, the engine seemed to have grown.

William John saw her taking note of all the extra pipes and tubes. "I've added the connections to the levers the driver manipulates." He pointed to a board clipped to one side of the frame. "That slots into the front wall of the carriage in front of the driver's seat."

"Ah. I see." She promptly ignored the extra pipes and tubes and focused on the engine beneath.

William John pointed, directing her attention to a complex set of gears that lay between the pistons and the twin drive shafts. "When I start it up, all runs smoothly. I can increase the power and therefore the speed and all is well. With the throttle fully open, everything powers along. The instant I start to throttle back, the gears start to grind. I'm sure if I let the machine continue to run, they would eventually jam, which would be disastrous."

"Hmm." After a moment of frowning at the interlocking cogs, Felicia turned to the board on which the diagrams were displayed. She went to stand and stare at the drawings. After a minute in which both men

remained utterly silent and watched her —
she could feel their gazes on her back —
she reached out and, with one finger, circled
the set of cogs, levers, and rods that made
up the gears. "The issue lies here, and,
again, it's because you've increased power
to such an extent, everything downstream
has to be readjusted."

She glanced at William John. "You're not
going to do anything to further increase the
power output, are you?"

He moved to join her before the board.
"No. We've more than doubled the output
of Trevithick's engine. We don't need more
power — at least, not at this point."

"Good." She eyed the board, almost
surprised at the way her mind was already
juggling options. It hadn't required conscious thought — a conscious instruction to
her mind to solve the problem — but rather
a deliberate direction to her higher mind to
get out of the way of an ability that was
instinctive and intuitive.

After another minute, she pointed to the
largest of the cogs. "Can you make this bigger? Or is there some other way to . . .
expand the capacity? That's what we need
to do — you've increased the power, so now
you need to compensate and expand the
control to handle the extra power."

William John stared at the cog in question, then pulled a face. "I'm not sure we can make it any bigger, but what if —"

Rand slid onto a high stool on the other side of the heavy frame and watched brother and sister discuss and debate their options. And gave thanks to whatever deity was watching over him and this project. If they hadn't stumbled on Felicia's unexpected talent, they would have already run aground. Instead . . . as he watched Felicia and William John standing shoulder to shoulder before the board, their attentions fixed unwaveringly on the diagrams, both entirely sunk into the workings of the Throgmorton engine, Rand felt quiet confidence well and solidify.

In common with many of the more productive inventors, William John didn't care where ideas for improvement came from. That the ideas he was, even now, eagerly seizing on and working to find ways to implement were coming from his younger sister didn't even impinge on his ever-grasping mind.

As for Felicia, the more Rand heard of her and William John's increasingly quick-fire exchanges, the more he realized she had an instinctive feel for where her skills ended and William John's began. Again and again, she seemed to mentally walk to some definable edge and then turn to her brother.

And unfailingly, without so much as a pause, William John would pick up the inventive baton and carry it on.

It took the pair the better part of an hour for William John to reach the point where he was smiling again and, fired by confidence, declared that he would soon have the problem with the gears resolved.

Another hour passed as the pair investigated the problem with the control levers. They ultimately came to an agreement on the best way to rework the settings — "It's the sensitivity of the movement that's at fault," Felicia had said — but agreed to leave that adjustment until after all else was working correctly.

Accepting that verdict, William John set about dismantling the control panel from the engine.

Felicia watched him work for a moment, then glanced at Rand and stepped away from the engine and the board of diagrams. "Mrs. Reilly will be waiting. I should go up."

Engrossed in his task, William John merely grunted.

Rand watched as Felicia plainly battled an impulse to remain and, perhaps, even tinker herself, but then she straightened her spine and took another step toward the stairs. She caught his eye. He smiled and inclined his head. "Both William John and I are more grateful than we can say for your assistance."

"Yes, well . . ." Her eyes were drawn to the engine. Then she murmured, "I suppose, now, that it's partly my responsibility, too."

After another second, she drew breath, determinedly turned away from the engine, and, with a brief nod his way, headed for the stairs.

Felicia climbed the stairs to the front hall — and, with every step, felt as if she was having to physically pull herself away.

As she'd suspected, the ineluctable thrill of solving William John's puzzles — of meeting the challenges — was well-nigh addictive.

On reaching the front hall, she paused and drew in a deep — very deep — breath.

As she exhaled, Mrs. Reilly looked around the green-baize-covered door at the rear of the hall.

On sighting Felicia, the housekeeper's face lit. "There you are, Miss Felicia. Are you ready to go over the menus, miss?"

"Yes, indeed. You've timed it well." She needed to get her mind back into its usual rut — no, it wasn't a rut. Dealing with the household was her normal and rightful occupation. Poking at inventions in the workshop was merely a temporary, if necessary, distraction and would never amount to anything more. "Come to the sitting room." She gestured to the door across the hall and led the way.

She and Mrs. Reilly settled in the sitting room and spent a comfortable half hour discussing menus and recipes. Somewhat to her surprise, Felicia found her mind drifting . . . Disconcerted, she hauled it back and focused firmly on the task before her.

Subsequently, determined to keep her mind on matters domestic, she went down to the kitchen to check with Cook regarding the bounty currently issuing from the kitchen garden and was taken by that worthy on an inspection of the beds burgeoning with summer vegetables.

They returned to the house with just half an hour to spare before luncheon. Felicia spent the minutes with Flora in the drawing room, idly sharing views on the information Flora's wide-ranging correspondents had recently reported, while inwardly, Felicia wondered how matters were progressing below stairs.

Somewhat to everyone's surprise, Rand and William John responded to the first striking of the luncheon gong. They ambled in, smiles on their faces — and Felicia found herself smiling back.

William John dropped into his chair and beamed at her. "Putting in those extra cogs has done the trick!" He included Rand with his gaze. "We're nearly there!"

"Don't get too excited yet," Rand advised, but he continued to smile. As he took his seat, he said to Felicia, "As you suggested, William John has concentrated on making the gears work properly first, before he endeavors to adjust the controls."

"Mind you," William John said, helping himself to the platter of pickled vegetables Felicia had handed him, "I'm increasingly certain we'll have yet more to do to get the controls to precisely how we want them — we'll see once I put the modifications we discussed in place. However" — his beaming smile returned — "I still say we're almost there." He met Felicia's eyes, then looked at Rand. "We will get everything done in time."

Her expression mild, Flora glanced from one to the other. "How many days remain before this exhibition you and the invention have to be at?"

Rand replied, "We have ten days until the day of the exhibition. However, we'll lose two of those traveling to Birmingham." He paused, then, his gaze meeting Felicia's, said, "We have until the morning of next Thursday to have the Throgmorton Steam-Powered Horseless Carriage assembled and running perfectly. That reminds me." He looked at William John. "What about the carriage itself?"

William John swallowed and waved toward the stable. "It's deep in the stable and properly covered. We can wheel it out when we're ready."

Rand paused.

Imagining what he was thinking, Felicia inquired, "How long is it since you've cleaned the carriage?"

William John frowned. "A few months . . ." After a moment, he grimaced. "Six months at least."

"Hmm. I believe we should have the covers off, and I can send the Reilly girls" — to Rand, she explained — "our maids, to clean and polish it." She refocused on William John. "Are there any moving parts they need to be wary of?"

He shook his head. "No, just the wheels, and the brake will be on. They can wipe and polish to their hearts' content. Once they have the covers off, I'll come and take a look, just to be certain there's nothing amiss." He glanced at Rand. "You'll want to see it, too."

Rand nodded. "If there's anything that needs fixing or adjusting to get the carriage ready for the exhibition, we should get that done."

William John grinned. "All the better to have everything ready to go the instant we have the engine fully adjusted and working perfectly." He smiled at them all. "I can feel it in my bones — we're nearly done!"

To her surprise, Felicia felt herself react to her brother's rousing words — felt her heart surge with anticipation and pride.

Inventing was proving even more addictive than she'd thought it would be.

With the others, she pushed back from the table and rose. *At last, Papa, I understand.*

The following days passed in a blur of activity. Felicia moved her meetings with Mrs. Reilly to later in the morning to accommodate William John and Rand's continuing requests for her assistance in the workshop — their urgings for her to bring her mind downstairs and apply it to the latest glitch in the engine's systems.

To her abiding amazement, she continued to find interacting with her brother, following his lines of thought and catching where he went wrong, challenging in an intriguing and satisfying way. Even though it might take her a few hours, invariably, her mind supplied a way around whatever obstacle William John had encountered.

Rand sat and watched and quietly encouraged — if the pair of them faltered, he would pose a question, starting them off again. To her, he was a necessary catalyst — one who lent the spark that fired her resolve, and that, in turn, drove her to find the way over or around the next hurdle.

During those hours in the workshop, the three of them merged into a highly effective team.

And when William John made an adjustment she'd suggested and it worked . . . the thrill of pleasure that coursed through her was worth every iota of effort; the effect only grew stronger and more intense as the days rolled on.

She'd told Rand truly; if her father had encouraged her to become involved, even if only tangentially, in his inventions, she would have understood his and William John's obsession and would have viewed their behavior in more tolerant and supportive vein.

Nevertheless, contributing or not, she

would have remained the practical one — the one who ensured the household ran smoothly around the laboratory-workshop. But her view of the workshop would have — and, indeed, had — changed; she now saw that space and what went on in it as an integral part of life at the Hall and not as an offshoot to be endured and otherwise deplored.

She was well aware that for her change of heart, for her rekindled interest in inventions, and for her greater understanding of her father and her brother, she had Randolph Cavanaugh to thank.

She'd spent the past two afternoons with the Reilly girls — Petunia, Primrose, Poppy, and Pansy; as she'd explained to Rand, the girls' father was the gardener and loved his flowers. As a group, they'd set about cleaning and polishing the carriage the engine would eventually power along the roads.

William John and Rand had examined it carefully, going over every panel and checking the wheels and struts, and pronounced it whole and in perfect repair. Once they'd left, armed with cloths and all manner of polishes, Felicia and the maids had fallen on the carriage and set to with a vengeance.

In midafternoon, Felicia returned to the house to join Mrs. Reilly in the sitting room to check over the weekly orders for the grocer and the butcher. On entering the sitting room, Felicia smiled at the housekeeper, who was waiting by the empty fireplace. "By tomorrow, your girls will have the carriage spotless — spick, span, and gleaming."

A fond mama, Mrs. Reilly beamed. "They're good girls, and they've been excited to do their bit for one of the master's inventions. And it started with your father and all — like a bit of a memorial for him, isn't it?"

"It is, indeed." Felicia sank into her favorite armchair and waved Mrs. Reilly to the one facing it. "I have to admit that I've never before felt so excited myself. Lord Cavanaugh, William John, and I went over the engine in fine detail this morning — we believe that after the last adjustments William John is making, the engine will be ready for its final tests. And then we'll be able to lift it into its place in the carriage, hook everything up — and the carriage will go." She couldn't help sharing a smile with the older woman, who had seen the household through the ups and downs of so many inventions over the years. "We're trying to contain ourselves, but we all believe the engine will perform splendidly!"

"That's good to hear, miss. A happy outcome all around."

"Indeed." Salvation beckoned on so many fronts — for her and William John, for their household, and for Rand and his investors as well. Felicia drew in a breath, then focused on the lists Mrs. Reilly held on her lap. "So — is there anything particular we need to get in?"

After she and Mrs. Reilly had made their decisions on the purchases for the next week and the housekeeper retired to write out her orders, Felicia crossed to the escritoire that stood against the wall between the windows. She owed her aunt-by-marriage a letter, and her cousins, too.

She was sitting at the escritoire, filling a page with the usual local news, when a firm tap fell on the door.

Puzzled, she called, "Come."

She grew even more puzzled as, her expression unusually grim, Petunia — who, when she wasn't busily cleaning the horseless carriage, acted as lady's maid for Felicia and Flora both — propelled her youngest sister, Pansy, into the room. "No help for it, Panse." A force not to be denied, Petunia pushed a clearly reluctant Pansy to the middle of the room, then stood back, folded her arms, and fixed a stern look on the young housemaid. "Now, my girl, you tell Miss Felicia what Diccon asked."

Pansy looked from Petunia to Felicia. Straightening, she scrunched her now-dusty white apron between her hands and bent a wary gaze on Felicia.

Although nearly ten years older than Pansy, Felicia had known the girl from birth. She had no idea what this was about — why Petunia had brought Pansy to her and not to the girls' redoubtable mother — but endeavored to smile encouragingly. "What did Diccon ask, Pansy?"

Pansy screwed up her face, but after a second during which she seemed to order her thoughts, she replied readily enough, "Diccon — he's the lad as helps at the butcher's, miss — we got to talking yesterday, when I was in the village with Poppy and Primrose, while I was waiting for them to come out of the general store. They got stuck in the queue behind Miss Limebeck, so I sat outside to wait, and Diccon came up, and he and me got talking." Pansy paused, her blue eyes wide and her expression serious. "Then out of the blue, Diccon asked if I could get ahold of the plans that Mr. William John works from."

Shocked, Felicia sat back.

Pansy saw her reaction and nodded. "Aye

— I was shocked and all, too. I said no and asked Diccon who wanted them — the plans. Obviously, it wouldn't've been him. He said as how one of the ostlers at the Arms said a gent from London, who called in for a drink in the tap, had said to him after, as the gent was leaving, that if he — the ostler, that is — could get ahold of the plans, he'd see gold for his trouble."

When Pansy fell silent, her blue eyes huge, her hands still wrapped in her apron, Felicia — horrified — looked at Petunia.

Arms still crossed, the older maid nodded soberly. "That's not the end of the tale. Panse here came home and — eventually — had the sense to tell Pa after lunch today. Pa went off then and there to the village. He found Diccon, who told Pa it was Harry at the Norreys Arms who'd asked him. Pa went to see Harry. Of course, Harry — being the silly knockhead he is — tried to say he didn't know anything about it. But Pa and Joe-the-barkeep wore Harry down. In the end, Harry said it was like Diccon had said. The gentleman called at the tap night before last — that's when he spoke to Harry. Yesterday morning, Harry — knowing Diccon often speaks with Pansy — got Diccon alone and asked him to ask Pansy, just like Diccon did. Harry thought that if the plans were just lying around the place, no one would miss them."

Petunia, Pansy, and Felicia shared a look. The notion of William John not noticing, within the hour if not sooner, that one of his precious diagrams had been moved, let alone stolen, was simply too fanciful to contemplate.

"Like I said," Petunia went on, "Harry's a knockhead, and Diccon's too good-natured and trusting. Pa asked Harry when the gent said he'd be back, but seemed he'd already called in again early this afternoon, and Harry'd told him he couldn't get the plans. Apparently, the man looked angry and swore, then he shrugged and got back on his horse and rode off."

"Did Harry have any idea who the man was?" Felicia asked. "Could he describe him?"

Petunia shook her head. "He said he reckoned the man was from London from his accent, but as the man was a gent — both Harry and Joe-the-barkeep agree on that — his accent doesn't necessarily mean he lives in London, does it?"

"No," Felicia agreed. "It just means he's from a good family and went to a good school."

Petunia nodded and went on, "Harry

swore he'd never seen the man before. Both he and Joe said the man had a hat pulled low and a muffler wound round his face. Harry couldn't see anything but the gleam of the gent's eyes." Petunia paused, then added, "The only thing Harry could say was that the horse was from the Crown at Pangbourne, and the man rode away in that direction — he assumed heading back to London."

Felicia stared unseeing at the maids while she digested the unwelcome and troubling news.

Petunia lowered her arms and straightened; Felicia glanced at her. "Pa just got back with the news. He said he had to get on with lifting the potatoes if we was to have any for the table tonight, and that Pansy and I should come in and tell you the whole."

Felicia summoned a weak smile for the girls. "Thank you both for coming and telling me — and please thank your father as well."

Petunia and Pansy curtsied, then Petunia followed her youngest sister out of the room.

Felicia stared at the door for several moments. Then, frowning, she rose and headed for the workshop.

Rand was standing by the engine, cleaning one of the several levers William John had removed from the control panel, when he heard Felicia's light footsteps coming down the stairs. He turned and was waiting, when she reached the last step and her gaze swept the room, to meet her eyes.

She held his gaze for a moment, then stepped down and walked closer.

Taking in her sober expression and the frown in her eyes, he arched his brows. "You don't normally grace us with your presence at this hour."

She looked at William John, who hadn't raised his head from his intent examination of the pins connecting the control panel to the engine, then returned her gaze to Rand's face. "There's been a development of which, I believe, you both need to be informed."

Alerted by her tone, William John looked up, then straightened, a wrench in his hand. "What's happened?"

Briefly, she told them what she'd just learned, concluding with "So although we know that some gentleman tried to get our staff to steal the plans, there's little more to be gleaned."

Her tale had sent a slight chill through Rand, but . . . . "This really shouldn't come as a surprise. As we've already discussed, there are various parties who would prefer the Throgmorton Steam-Powered Horseless Carriage to never see the light of day." He focused on Felicia. "However, as the man involved has already quit the area, there's no sense wasting our time — time we don't really have — in trying to trace him or those who sent him."

"He'd hidden his face, too," William John pointed out. "Without any way to identify him, it's difficult to point to any particular gentleman as our villain."

Rand inclined his head, wondering if there was more to the man having so assiduously concealed his features.

Felicia put his speculation into words. "Given we can't identify the man, then he could have been Mayhew, but I understood he was planning to be out of the area for longer than a few days."

"If it was him, he would have wanted to conceal his face," William John said, "but equally, as I understand it, we have no reason to think he's in any way involved with these attempts to sabotage the engine or that he even has an interest in inventions."

He looked at Rand and Felicia both.

Reluctantly, Rand nodded. "You're right. We have no evidence that Mayhew is a threat. On the other hand, this, on top of the attempted break-in, is irrefutable evidence that someone — some decently bred gentleman most likely hired by as-yet-unknown others — is intent on sabotaging this project."

William John grimaced and nodded.

Felicia looked grave. "What should we do?"

"When it comes down to it, there really isn't much more we can do, other than ensure that the guards we already have on duty understand that the threat is real and keep alert throughout their watch." Rand met Felicia's eyes, then William John's. "Despite our successes, we still have a lot to do to prove the engine and then get it inserted into the carriage and check that over, too — all before we set out for Birmingham."

"Six full days before we need to leave." William John nodded decisively. "We'll make it."

"What about the journey?" Felicia met Rand's gaze. "Surely that would be the perfect opportunity to . . . well, thrust a spoke in the carriage's wheels."

He nodded. "But against that, during the journey, we'll have extra guards to keep the steam carriage safe. Whoever our ill-wishers are, they will expect that and would presumably conclude that, in reality, it will be easier for them to strike at the invention here, while it's still at the Hall."

Felicia frowned, then refocused on Rand's face. "Is there any way to guess who is behind these attacks?"

Rand thought, then shook his head. "There are too many possibilities, none of which we can discount — too many groups that might have hired a gentleman like the one who recently visited the Norreys Arms. Sadly, 'gentlemen' like him are easy to come by in the capital."

He paused, then, when both Felicia and William John seemed to wish it, he listed their possible opponents. "Other syndicates working on similar projects — I don't know of any openly working on a steam-powered carriage at this time, but if they kept the work secret, they might now view us as a real threat. Then there are the usual suspects who hold strong views on allowing any steam-powered carriage to succeed. They managed to discount Trevithick's original, managed to ignore Russell's improvements and the works of others who'd attempted similar modifications. Yet none of those inventions held the promise of the Throgmorton engine. If they understand the potential, then they would be very keen to see our project fail. And we mustn't forget the railway companies, the toll-road owners, and all their shareholders. And last but not least, any inventor who feels envious or threatened, or feels he's been in any way damaged by your father's past successes — this is, after all, William Throgmorton's last great invention."

Felicia and William John pulled almost identically dejected faces.

After a moment, Felicia said, "So at this stage, there's no chance of identifying who was responsible and therefore no sense in wasting our time attempting to gain sufficient evidence to point a finger." She nodded more definitely. "This evening, we should warn the men mounting the night watches of the increased chance of another attack." She met Rand's eyes, then inclined her head and turned toward the stairs. "I'll speak to the rest of the household now. They, too, will need to remain alert."

Rand watched her go, then turned back to William John, who, apparently, had consigned all responsibility for increased security into Rand's and Felicia's hands and had dived back into the engine.

A certain tension pervaded the house. Watchful and on guard even during the day, alert for the slightest movement or noise out of place, the household went about their business, eyes peeled, ears strained.

But there was suppressed excitement running beneath the tension — a sense that no one would be taking aim at the steam engine if it wasn't a worthy target, implying that William Throgmorton's last great invention was, indeed, slated to be a spectacular success.

Two nights after the discovery of the attempt to steal the plans, after Flora had retired, Felicia remained in her sitting room, determined to complete her letters to her cousins. She lost track of the time, then Johnson tapped and looked in.

The butler smiled when he saw her. "You're late, Miss Felicia."

She glanced at the clock and saw it was nearly eleven o'clock. "Good gracious." She looked at the letter she was writing. "I'll just finish this page, then go up."

Johnson smiled benignly, then circled the room, checking that the windows had been locked.

Felicia laid down her pen with a sigh and looked up. "A last and final check?" Johnson usually did his final check soon after he wheeled the tea tray away.

"Indeed, miss. Given the circumstances,

one cannot be too careful, and I have to admit I sleep a lot easier if I check the locks late."

She nodded. "No blame to you. As whoever wishes to break in and steal the plans or sabotage the invention has presumably learned that the workshop doors cannot be forced, then it must surely be on the cards that they might attempt to gain access through a door or window on this level and make their way down to the workshop."

Johnson somewhat diffidently remarked, "Lord Cavanaugh did canvass that possibility with me. It seems you and he think alike, miss."

She smiled. "That's not really surprising. We're both committed to ensuring this invention remains safe all the way to the exhibition, and as you know, William John is somewhat . . ."

"Absentminded?" Johnson smiled. "Indeed, miss. But a very clever gentleman, nonetheless."

Felicia allowed her smile to grow and inclined her head. "As you say, Johnson." Seeing he had completed his circuit of the room's windows, she said, "I'll be going up momentarily. You can turn down the lights elsewhere."

"Yes, miss." Johnson bowed. "I'll see you

in the morning."

Felicia remained in the chair by the escritoire and let her mind wander — first to assessing the steps they'd taken to secure the Hall, searching for any weakness and finding none, then to the revelations of recent days and the changes those revelations had wrought.

Eventually, with the house settling to nighttime quiet about her, she rose, turned off the twin sconces she'd had burning, and made for the door. She opened it and stepped into the front hall, shutting the panel quietly behind her. As per her instructions, Johnson had turned the two small sconces in the hall and the one on the stair landing to their lowest setting; they cast the faintest of pale glows, just enough for someone like her, familiar with the house, to be sure of their way. She started toward the stairs.

She was halfway to them — exposed in the very center of the open expanse of tiled floor — when she heard a boot scrape on stone.

On the stone of the stairs leading up from the workshop.

Before her mind registered the oddity of any intruder coming up the workshop stairs, her heart started to race.

Her breath caught in her throat, and she swung toward the door to the stairs in time to see it slowly open.

A figure appeared in the doorway. Male, tall, powerfully built.

Even in the poor light, she recognized those shoulders. At some level beyond that of normal senses, she recognized him.

Her heart leapt and raced again — this time, for a very different reason.

She exhaled in relief and smiled. "Rand. Checking the guards?"

He tipped his head as he walked toward her. "That, and checking your brother's masterpiece of an alarm system. It's quite ingenious."

He drew level with her, and she turned. Side by side, they continued toward the stairs, with him shortening his stride to accommodate hers.

"And you? This is later than usual for you, I think?"

She waved toward the sitting room. "I was writing letters and forgot the time." Ruefully, she glanced at him. "Thank you for checking the alarm. Sadly, William John doesn't possess a practical bone in his body — he would never think to do it."

Rand shrugged, those wonderfully wide shoulders shifting fluidly beneath his well-cut coat. Amusement ran beneath his words as he said, "I've worked with quite a few inventors in recent years. None are what you could term 'practically minded.' "

She smiled. "I suppose it's an upshot of single-minded focus."

"Indeed. So it seems."

Wreathed in shadows, they started up the stairs, and she felt his gaze on her face, not intent so much as assessing.

"I have to say," he murmured, "that the three of us complement each other in a rather unique way. William John is unquestionably a whizz at mechanical construction — he truly is your father's heir in that way. You, meanwhile, provide the essential insights into design — without your input, for all his brilliance, William John wouldn't have been able to solve the problems the improvements to the power of the engine caused."

When he didn't go on, smiling, she prompted, "And you?"

"I," he stated, "arrange the finance, but in this case, I've also been pressed into a role I've never had the chance to fill before, that of managing the project — doing whatever's needed to facilitate William John's efforts and also ensuring the project remains secure."

She glanced at his face; his features were calm, his expression at ease and assured. "Have you enjoyed the managing?"

Slowly, he nodded. "Far more than I would have imagined." He glanced at her and, in the faint light, met her eyes. He smiled. "I've come to see William John's subterfuge, which was what got me involved and us all to this point, as a boon."

She chuckled. "In that, we're something of a pair. As I told you several nights ago, being brought into the project as I have been has . . . widened my horizons in a way I had no idea was even possible."

Rand felt satisfaction well within him — fueled by his delight in his new role and even more by her pleasure in hers. They reached the landing and turned to continue up the next flight, and he asked, "What about William John?"

Her reply came instantly. "I have never, ever, seen my brother so . . . simply happy. He loves what he does, but I suspect he's never felt so free to simply be himself, with others he trusts to manage everything around him."

Rand grinned. "You to manage the house and assist him as required, me to manage the project, and William John free to simply build machines."

"Exactly."

Emboldened by the ease he sensed between them, he ventured, "And what about you?" He glanced at her and through the dimness met her eyes. "Are you happier, too?"

Her lips curved, and she looked ahead. "Indubitably. I feel more settled than I've felt . . . possibly ever. I had no idea I'd retained enough of what I must have absorbed in my early years to contribute to any invention as I am, much less that I would find that activity so rewarding."

His satisfaction welled and overflowed. Knowing she was content set the seal on his own contentment.

After several seconds, she said, "Amazing though it seems looking back on the confusion from which we started, it's all coming together, isn't it?"

If he'd been at all superstitious, he wouldn't have replied, but given their recent advances, he felt they were entitled to hold to hope. "Yes. It's been something of a scramble, but it is, indeed, coming together nicely. There are only the final tests to run, then we can install the engine into the carriage and be on our way to the exhibition."

They reached the head of the stairs, and she made a soft scoffing sound. "It'll never be that easy."

He inclined his head. "True. But we can hope."

She chuckled. Deeper shadows engulfed them as they walked around the gallery and on into the corridor that led to their rooms.

Peace and a sense of companionship quite unlike anything Rand had ever known lapped about his consciousness, soothing, supporting, indescribably comforting. Him and her walking through the quiet of a slumbering house . . . simply felt right. The conviction that she was the perfect lady for him had taken root in his soul. Practical, down to earth, solidly supportive, with an innate understanding of inventions and inventors that no other young lady could possibly have, she was a foil perfectly fashioned to complement him.

He would be a fool not to seize her.

They reached their doors — one on either side — and halted.

This time, he didn't hesitate, didn't let the moment when she turned to bid him goodnight elude him. His eyes seeking hers through the enveloping shadows, he caught her hand; with his eyes locked on hers, he raised her fingers to his lips and pressed a kiss to her knuckles. He waited a heartbeat to see her eyes flare, then smoothly drew her closer, nearer — to him — and as his other hand slid around her waist, urging her closer yet, he bent his head and covered her lips with his.

He'd intended it to be a gentle caress — a statement, an assurance, and a glimpse of what might be.

But he'd misjudged.

His inner self leapt at the chance to taste her, to steep himself in the pleasures of her mouth, of her lips and tongue . . .

Felicia's head spun. She'd been kissed before, but never like this — with such direct and compelling mastery that she and all her senses had surged in response. Her lips parted beneath the temptation of his; she quelled a delicious shiver as his tongue teased the slick softness, then slid between and settled to explore.

To engage and expand her senses.

Her wits had gone wandering; to where, she didn't care. Instinctively, she came up on her toes the better to participate in the enthralling exchange; she leaned into him, her hands coming to rest, palms flat, on his chest.

Even through the fabric of his coat and shirt, she felt the alluring heat of him. Beneath her hands, she sensed the reality of a flesh-and-blood man.

Desire bloomed. She'd never felt it before, yet she knew it for what it was and embraced it.

Angling her head, she surrendered to a temptation she hadn't even thought to resist and kissed him back.

Minutes of heated communion had passed before Rand's wits punctured the fog of his senses enough for him to realize how definitely she was returning his caresses. Not shyly or tentatively but absolutely determinedly. With deliberation.

Desire leapt and passion ignited.

He tightened his hold on her, dipped his head, and steered the kiss into even deeper waters.

She made a wordless sound in her throat, clutched his lapels, and followed his lead with her own brand of ardor.

Need — sudden and shocking — flared and surged.

The unprecedented force — fierce and demanding — was enough to rock him. To free his wits from the engrossing fog of desire so he could assess . . .

Too far, too fast.

He knew that, yet . . .

It was an effort to draw back from the kiss. To — eventually — lift his head and allow their lips to part.

He looked down as her lids rose and her wide eyes slowly focused. As he watched, a faint frown invested her expression.

He was holding her against him, within one arm; his other hand was still wrapped about the fingers he'd kissed.

Then he saw her eyes search his, search his expression. He cleared his throat and murmured, "That was intended as a thank-you."

She blinked. "What for?"

He felt his lips curve — saw her eyes track the gesture. "For being you."

Shackling his impulses wasn't easy, but he managed to force himself to release her. His arm falling from her, he stepped back. At the last, he opened his hand and freed her fingers. Felt them only slowly slide away.

He had to clamp down on a flaring impulse to seize them again.

She continued to stare at him through the dimness, studying him, yet in no way rejecting his advance.

That knowledge shook his resolution — the assumption that he would allow her to sleep alone that night. He drew in a tight breath, inclined his head by way of a good-night, then turned and stepped to his door.

Not yet, not yet. He kept his feet moving. Their connection had evolved so very quickly; she would need time to absorb and accept. Until she did . . . he had to give her time.

It couldn't be yet.

Felicia watched Rand open his door and, without a backward glance, go into the room and shut the panel.

Still, she stood staring, her heart thudding. Slowly, she raised a hand and touched her fingertips to her throbbing lips.

This, then, was how it felt to be swept off one's feet.

To be caught up in a maelstrom formed of desire, to fall prey to the need and hunger that flowed in desire's wake — passions she'd never until now experienced.

Minutes ticked by as she stood outside her door and considered and weighed and experienced again the feelings he and that revealing kiss had evoked.

She felt the rippling echoes sink deep, to her soul.

Eventually, the tumult of her senses faded. Slowly, she turned, opened the door, and walked into her room.

NINE

The following morning, Felicia remained, if not precisely trapped in dreams of where extending such a kiss as she'd been a party to last night might lead, then at the very least, powerfully distracted.

Rand and William John had already departed the breakfast table before she reached it, for which she was thankful. William John wouldn't notice her abstraction, but the source of it certainly would, and the last thing she wished was for the fact that Rand had started to inhabit her dreams to somehow become evident.

With her blushes spared, she sat and consumed her tea and toast, then girded her loins and, with wholly spurious calm, made her way down the spiral stairs to the workshop. Halting on the second last step, she looked out at the sight of both William John and Rand engrossed in some adjustment that had both of them all but diving

255

headfirst into the bowels of the engine.

Then, as if sensing her presence, Rand looked up.

Their gazes locked, then the line of his lips eased into a smile — one that started a warm glow spreading beneath her skin.

Clasping her hands before her, she managed to haul in a tight breath and drag her gaze to her brother's downbent head. "Do you need me for anything this morning?"

William John looked up, saw her, and grinned. "No. Fingers crossed, but after those last changes to accommodate the increased power, the whole seems to be reconciled. I've got a few more checks and a handful of possible adjustments to do, and then we should be ready to run the final tests."

Keeping her eyes on her brother's face, she nodded. "Very well. I'll get back to my usual day, then." She turned to leave — and let her gaze briefly touch Rand's. "Send for me if you need me."

With that, she retreated to the sitting room. After working her way through her usual meeting with Mrs. Reilly and having learned that the household had run out of ink, she decided to walk into the village and rectify the shortage.

A basket on her arm, she set off through

the woods, following the path the man she'd seen fleeing the house after the attempted break-in had taken. Above her head, birds flitted in the branches, and the sun shone warmly from the summer-blue sky. The air was fresh and clear; with her basket swinging, she walked along, smiling delightedly for no reason beyond her happiness with her life as it was — as it now was, post the changes consequent on Lord Randolph Cavanaugh arriving at her home.

The path was the shortest route to the village; soon, she was in the general store. After chatting with the owner, she purchased two bottles of ink. On quitting the store, she paused on the pavement to settle the ink bottles in the bottom of the basket. Satisfied with their arrangement, she raised her head and stepped — directly into a gentleman who had to have crossed the road to materialize so suddenly before her.

Gripping the basket with both hands, she fell back.

The gentleman stepped back, too. "My apologies, Miss Throgmorton." Mr. Mayhew smiled at her. "Well met, dear lady." His gaze fell to her basket, and he held out a hand. "Let me help you with that."

"Er . . . good morning, Mr. Mayhew — it's not at all heavy." Nevertheless, Felicia found herself surrendering the basket — then wished she hadn't; she'd have to get it back from him before she left him. She hid a frown. "I confess I hadn't expected to see you back quite so soon, sir."

Mayhew's charming smile lit his face. "I arrived last night. The weather's been unusually benign, so my sketching for the *News* went faster than I'd anticipated. I've been able to take that short holiday I mentioned earlier than planned."

"I see." With the engine so near completion and the exhibition only a week away, Mayhew's reappearance — as he'd admitted, earlier than he'd flagged — opened a deep vein of suspicion inside her. Endeavoring to keep all sign of wariness from her face and voice, she waved down the street. "I was about to head home."

"Ah." Mayhew glanced in that direction, then met her eyes. "I wonder if you would take tea with me, Miss Throgmorton. In the inn." He tipped his head toward the inn on the opposite side of the street. "I would like to show you my most recent sketches — I would value your opinion."

She searched his eyes, but they and his expression remained open, and nothing more than honest earnestness shone through. She remained unsure if he was genuine or not, but she knew all the staff at the inn, and taking tea in a public place posed no risk. Besides, she told herself, as she smiled and inclined her head in acceptance, learning more about Mayhew wouldn't hurt. "Thank you, Mr. Mayhew. I would be delighted to take tea with you and view your recent sketches."

He beamed at her and offered his arm.

She laid her hand on his sleeve, and they crossed the street and entered the inn.

At that time of day, even the tap was quiet, and the ladies' parlor alongside was empty of occupants other than them. She led the way to the table beneath the window, where the light streaming in offered steady illumination.

As previously, Mayhew had his ever-present satchel slung over one shoulder. After setting her basket on the floor by her chair, he opened the satchel, extracted a sheaf of sketches, then hung the satchel on the back of the chair opposite her, sat, and placed the sketches on the table before her.

Despite all wariness, she reached for the pile with unfeigned eagerness. If these were as good as those he'd earlier shown her and Flora, they would be worth looking at.

Sure enough, as, slowly, she turned page after page, she was treated to a cornucopia of gentle country scenes, each with some small detail that delighted. Every view was exquisitely and evocatively rendered, displaying a fine eye as well as a fine hand at work. That Mayhew was an exceptional artist was undeniable.

The serving girl appeared and, deep in his sketches, Felicia vaguely heard him order tea. The tray arrived, and she roused herself enough to pour, then, sipping, continued her perusal of Mayhew's recent work. Given that there were more than twenty sketches in the pile, she could understand that he might feel a short holiday was in order.

She finished studying the final sketch and laid it with its fellows. Then she raised her gaze. "These are very impressive, sir."

He smiled self-deprecatingly. "I'm glad you think so, Miss Throgmorton."

"It was a pleasure to have the opportunity to view them." She inclined her head. "Thank you."

Mayhew's smile faded. "Actually" — he leaned forward, his forearms on the table and his cup cradled between his long-fingered artist's hands — "I was especially glad to meet with you again." When she glanced up, he caught her gaze. "I wanted to ask if you and your family would permit me to sketch the Hall again, this time from different angles."

Without waiting for any answer, he rolled on, "The setting is rather unusual, as I'm sure you're aware — the woods all around lend the house a subtle, almost-fairy-tale quality, and the lines of the building are classic, of course, which only adds to the unexpectedness of seeing it in what otherwise appears to be wild and untamed surrounds." He focused on her eyes. "Please say you'll consider allowing me to do at least a few more sketches. The house has fired my imagination, so to speak."

He was clever enough to stop talking at that point and simply sit staring at her in obvious and expectant hope.

Felicia set down her empty cup and returned his steady regard while her mind raced. He might be an agent acting for some other inventor with the intent to sabotage the engine. Against that notion, he wasn't asking to sketch inside the house. Seeking to confirm that, she said, "Different views of the house from different spots outside?"

He nodded. "Yes. Exactly."

How could he possibly threaten the engine? He'd be a hundred or more yards from the house at all times.

She still wasn't sure — and wasn't sure why that was so. At no time had Mayhew, by word or deed, given her cause to suspect him.

The timing — the coincidences surrounding his initial appearance in the village — had sparked both her and Rand's suspicions, and his reappearance at such a critical juncture would only further feed their wariness. And although there was nothing more substantial than coincidence to support their suspicions, at least in her case, despite Mayhew's charm and all the evidence of his undeniable talent, her suspicions showed no signs of abating.

Yet if he was a sneaky gentleman intent on harming the invention, she would really rather keep him in view — stuck behind his easel on the lawn.

She stirred. "Perhaps if you come to tea this afternoon and discuss your request with Mrs. Makepeace and me, we might see our way to granting it." She smiled to soften her refusal to immediately agree; she wanted a few hours to think — and to consult Rand.

She pushed back from the table, and Mayhew hurriedly got to his feet and assisted her to hers. She smiled easily in thanks. "If you will call at three o'clock?"

"I'll be there." His charming smile was very much in evidence as he picked up her basket and insisted on escorting her back to the street.

On the corner, she claimed her basket and was firm in declining his escort along the lane and down the woodland path. "It's not far, and I know these woods like the back of my hand."

With a last nod from her and a half bow from him, they parted — both still smiling.

As she walked down the lane to where the path from the house joined it, Felicia had to wonder if Mayhew's smile was as much a façade as hers.

Rand had been loitering in the doorway of the forge, waiting for Ferguson to refine the curve on a brace that would anchor the engine into the carriage and, meanwhile, idly scanning the village street, when he saw Felicia exit the inn on the artist's arm.

"Damn it — he's back." Eyes narrowing, Rand had pushed away from the archway against which he'd been leaning. His hands gripping his hips, he'd watched as, at the far end of the street, Felicia had firmly dismissed Mayhew and, parting from him, had continued on alone, walking with her usual free stride along the lane in the direction of the Hall.

She hadn't seemed distressed in any way. As for Mayhew, he seemed pleased. Rubbing his hands together, the artist was smiling as he turned toward the inn.

Rand watched Mayhew walk back to the inn and disappear inside.

A litany of possible actions — reactions — scrolled through Rand's mind. In the end, the considerations that stopped him from marching down the street, into the inn, and making it indisputably clear to Mayhew that Felicia Throgmorton was spoken for were twofold.

The first — and most telling with respect to protecting the invention — was that as Rand had led Mayhew to believe he was a family friend passing through, Mayhew would not be expecting Rand to still be at Throgmorton Hall. Mayhew, Rand judged, came from a circle only slightly below his own; he knew how Mayhew would have interpreted his words — he would have assumed that, seven days on, Rand would be gone by now.

That raised the interesting question of whether Mayhew had retreated for a week, waiting until he assumed Rand would have left in order to ensure a clear run at the Hall. Simply by asking around in the village, Mayhew could have learned that, other than the absentminded brother who toiled away in the workshop every day, occasionally blowing things up, there was no true male protector residing at the house.

The more Rand thought of it, the more he felt that it would be wise to allow Mayhew to remain unaware of Rand's continuing presence. Unless Mayhew thought to ask Ferguson, he was unlikely to learn that Rand was still about.

The second consideration that held him back from confronting Mayhew was more personal. Felicia herself might not — yet — understand where she stood vis-à-vis Rand. They hadn't yet progressed to the point of a declaration.

To his mind, the kiss they'd shared last night had certainly raised the prospect, but he hadn't spoken.

Once again, he debated that decision, but waiting until after the exhibition, when there would be no urgent business-related pressure hanging over their heads — no possible consideration that might impinge on her decision to accept him, or that she might imagine had influenced his decision to ask for her hand — still seemed the best way forward.

Waiting to speak remained the better option.

The niggling understanding that he was uncertain enough of her — of his appeal to her — to want more time to convince her to be his, he pushed to the back of his mind.

"M'lord."

Rand lowered his arms and turned as Ferguson came walking out from the depths of the forge, waving the reformed brace.

"This is ready now. Good and strong — should do the job."

Rand accepted the curved length of solid iron. "Put it on the Throgmorton tab."

Ferguson nodded genially. "Aye. I'll do that." Rand had already assured the man he would stand guarantor for William John.

Rand had tied the horse he'd ridden from the Hall to the ring beside the forge door. He moved around the bay and stowed the brace in the saddlebag. Then, over the horse's back, he looked at Ferguson, who had remained in the doorway. "I want to give this fellow a run. Is there a way I can circle around" — he tipped his head — "to the west, preferably, that will eventually take me back to the Hall?"

"Oh aye. There's a good run down the edge of Farmer Highgate's fields. If you go that way" — Ferguson pointed away from the village — "then turn left and left again, you'll come to it — a bridle path, it is. You won't miss it."

Rand thanked the blacksmith, then swung

up to the bay's broad back. He rode out of the yard, turned north, then, as directed, west. True to Ferguson's word, Rand found the bridle path easily enough and took the circuitous route back to the Hall, giving the inn a very wide berth.

By the time he'd reached the Hall's stables, Rand had started to question just why Felicia had, to all appearances, encouraged Mayhew. She'd gone into the inn with him; however innocent their meeting, Rand had to wonder why she'd agreed to it.

After leaving the bay in Shields's capable hands along with orders to deliver the brace to the workshop, Rand strode across the lawn to the house with uncertainty itching just beneath his skin. He didn't know Felicia that well; he'd never seen her in society. Perhaps the artist, charming to his toes, was more to her taste than a gentleman who thought investments were exciting . . .

Abruptly, he halted, drew in a deep breath, then exhaled and, struggling not to clench his jaw, walked on.

There was that kiss in the dark last night. He shouldn't — couldn't — forget that. She'd responded. She'd been as intrigued as he with the prospects — with the promise.

He shouldn't doubt her.

Not without evidence to the contrary.

Just because he didn't trust women, especially not those clever enough to be manipulative, that didn't mean he couldn't trust her.

He reached the house, opened the side door, and stalked inside. Even as his long strides ate the carpet, at the back of his mind was the realization of what his present state — his churning thoughts — portended.

He knew how irrationally Ryder acted over Mary, and his big brother was the epitome of calm reason. This morass of uncertainty was, apparently, an unavoidable outcome of allowing oneself to fix on a particular lady, to place her above all others.

He'd already reached the point where Felicia was that for him — the lady he'd placed on his pedestal, the one lady he wanted for his own.

Johnson was crossing the front hall as Rand walked onto the tiles.

"Ah — Johnson. Do you happen to know where Miss Felicia is?"

"Indeed, my lord. She's in the garden hall." Johnson pointed past the breakfast parlor. "It's toward the end of the corridor, my lord."

"Thank you." Rand drew in a breath, reminded himself to be calm — that he'd as yet said nothing to Felicia about her being his — then strode in search of her.

She was arranging peonies in a bowl when he walked into the narrow garden hall.

She looked up at him and smiled. "Has William John and his incessant muttering driven you upstairs?"

"No." He leaned back against the bench alongside where she was working and crossed his arms. "I went into the village to have a brace reforged. I was waiting outside the blacksmith's and saw you with that artist."

Her gaze on her hands as she cupped and shifted blooms in the bowl, she nodded. "Yes. Mayhew is back. He met me as I was coming out of the general store. He invited me to tea so he could impress me with the sketches he's done over the last days." She paused, then glanced at Rand, briefly meeting his eyes. "He must have been hard at work to have produced so many in just seven days. They were as good as his sketches of the Hall. I recognized some scenes from a hamlet near Basildon, so he must have traveled up there."

He frowned. "So his story of having to do

more sketches for the *London News* rings true?"

"So it seems."

To his ears, she sounded equivocal, possibly unconvinced, but at the very least unimpressed.

"The reason he wanted to make a point of the quality of his work was to pave the way for him to request permission to return here and do more sketches of the house."

He stiffened, muscles throughout his body hardening.

Before he could say anything, she straightened and, dusting her hands, faced him and met his eyes. "I suggested he come for afternoon tea and speak with me and Flora about it. I know there's no chance of winkling William John from the workshop — and we need him to finish the last adjustments as soon as possible, so better he isn't distracted — but would you care to join us?" She tipped her head, her eyes still on his. "We could see what you make of Mayhew and his return."

Her last comment, especially her use of "we," shifted Rand's perspective. He studied her expression, but wasn't sure what he sensed. "You don't believe him?"

She humphed and turned to lean back against the bench beside him. "I believe him

270

about his ability to sketch — that's beyond doubt. But as for the rest . . . I have to admit I'm not inclined to trust any charming gentleman who comes waltzing up our drive."

Rand turned his head and stared at her.

Eventually feeling his gaze, she glanced at him, then her lips twitched and she faced forward again. "I trust you, but that's for a lot of other reasons, and you've never tried to charm me, which in my book is a very large point in your favor."

Faintly, he arched his brows. "Duly noted," he murmured.

Belatedly, Felicia realized that this was the first time he and she had been alone since that amazingly distracting kiss in the night, yet rather than suffering from any feeling of awkwardness, she felt comfortable, at ease, and, yes, relieved. Relieved he was there to share her concern over Mayhew and what his reappearance might mean.

"Is having Mayhew back, even for afternoon tea, a wise idea?"

She glanced at Rand. "I can't see any way of being sure. And while I could easily have put him off, at least until after the exhibition, it occurred to me that if he is the agent of some other inventor — or some other person who wants our engine to fail — then keeping him in plain sight might be a better option than refusing his request. Consider" — she gestured toward the French door that gave access to the lawn at the rear of the house — "the very thing about this house that makes it so attractive for him to sketch, or so he claims, also makes it terribly easy for him to approach quite close without us knowing. He could hide in the wood and watch us fit the engine to the carriage and so on."

Facing forward, she paused, then went on, "There's also the fact that if Mayhew is an agent working against our interests, then I, for one, would like to know who he's working for." She glanced sidelong at Rand and caught his eyes. "Wouldn't you?"

He stared at her for a full minute, then grimaced. He faced forward and blew out a breath. "What — exactly — did he say?"

She told him. "He didn't ask to be shown around inside or to sketch inside the house."

After a moment, he demanded, "Has he ever asked about the workshop or about what your brother does?"

"No." She hesitated, then admitted, "The only things he's shown any interest in are those that affect his sketching."

"Hmm." After another significantly more brooding silence, Rand said, "I assume you hope to give him enough rope to hang himself, so to speak."

She nodded. "For him to at least show his true colors."

"How, exactly, do you see his next visit and his next round of sketching leading to that end?"

She grimaced. "I don't know. But he has returned, and he wants to come here and sketch. Presumably, he has a reason for that. Given we're on guard against him — and with him back in the neighborhood, I assume we'll be maintaining our night and day watches with even greater stringency —"

"I'll be rearranging the watches so that during the night, there'll be three men awake and alert at all times."

"— then I propose we give Mayhew the opportunity to ask questions about the workshop, or about William John's occupation, or even to attempt to see the workshop or speak with William John." She frowned. "If we're right in thinking that he's not just an artist but also a would-be saboteur, then with only a week to go before the exhibition, he'll be wanting to make some definite move to achieve his ends very soon."

A sudden thought occurred, and she turned to Rand. "You said we'd have to leave here on Thursday morning to get to Birmingham in time. If Mayhew fails in his task while here, but gives us no reason to have him arrested, then surely damaging the invention while it's on the road to the exhibition will be his next cast. We'll need to organize more guards."

"That won't be hard — you can leave that to me."

To his discomfort, Felicia's proposed interaction with Mayhew left Rand prey to contradictory impulses.

His protective, possessive self didn't want her anywhere near Mayhew — a charming gentleman-artist who Rand had yet to inform of his interest in the delectable Miss Throgmorton. Against that . . . he could appreciate her reasoning, and if it hadn't been her but some other lady involved, he would probably have readily agreed with her suggested way forward. More, the sense of camaraderie that in the last twenty minutes had deepened between them was . . . seductive. He liked the feeling of working closely together, even when their goal was to expose Mayhew and whoever he worked for.

Apparently taking his silence for acquiescence, she asked, "So will you take tea with us this afternoon?"

"No." He met her eyes. "When I spoke with Mayhew last time he was here, I told him I was a friend of the family visiting for a few days. I suspect he'll imagine I've left by now, and if he's a villain, it'll be to our advantage for me to play least in sight." He paused for a heartbeat, then went on, "However, that doesn't mean I can't watch, and while you're serving him tea, I'll hover close enough to hear all that's said."

She frowned. "Perhaps that was why he was away for barely a week — because he knew you were here and thought it wiser to wait until you were gone."

"Very possibly. If you recall, he intimated to me that he would be away for longer — a few weeks — yet in barely a week, he's back."

"Hmm. Despite his charm and innocuous appearance, it's little things like that that keep me wondering about him." Felicia paused. She was quite pleased with the way the discussion had unfolded; for a minute, when Rand had first come striding in and she'd told him about meeting Mayhew and inviting him to tea, she'd feared that Rand was going to convert to some overbearing, arrogant, and pompous male, but he'd throttled any such impulse, and the discussion had proceeded on a sensible, rational plane. She straightened away from the bench. "For now, let's see what direction he takes when he comes for tea at three o'clock. Flora will be with me, of course."

Rand caught her gaze and held it for a second, then he, too, pushed away from the bench and straightened to his full height. She raised her gaze to his face, and he looked down at hers. Then he nodded. "All right."

He half turned to leave, but then swung back — and she found herself swept into his arms.

She looked up in surprise as he bent his head, then his lips found hers, and her lids fell, and with a fleeting inner smile, she gave herself over to returning the caress.

His lips were firm, masterful; at their command, she parted hers and almost shivered with delight as his tongue slipped past the slick curves to claim her mouth, to stroke and tempt.

She leaned into him, pressed her hands to his chest, and stretched up, the better to meet him. Through the kiss, through the pressure of his lips, she sensed his approval.

His encouragement.

She seized the opportunity and pressed her own kiss on him, and he let her. Let her explore the communion of their mouths, the simple, unalloyed pleasure of such caresses.

He'd splayed his hands on her back; now, they moved in long, slow strokes, up, then down, urging her closer, molding her slighter frame to his much larger one. Her breasts swelled, the peaks tightening almost to the point of discomfort. That he knew what he was doing — how each touch, each increment of pressure, affected her — was never in any doubt, but that he allowed her to play, too, thrilled her. Drove her to push her hands up, over his shoulders. She sank her fingertips into the broad muscles of his upper back, testing their resilience, then gripping and claiming them as, in response, he angled his head, and the kiss heated by several degrees . . .

Her head spun. Her wits, she realized, had flown.

Not that she cared — not at that moment as warmth and a hunger she had never before felt yet instantly recognized flowered and unfurled within her.

This time, Rand held tight to their reins. This time, he'd braced for the potent lure of her response; he was determined to indulge both her and himself, yet still retain control.

He'd managed, more or less — passably

at least — yet as the exchange spun out, kiss for kiss, and the lure of her lips, her mouth, her tongue, of the svelte, feminine body so vibrant and tempting in his arms only grew, and he sensed the rising tide of desire silently surging, he knew that with every second that passed, the inevitable drawing back would only be harder. More difficult — more of a wrench.

He had to end this, even though it went against the clamoring of his inner self. There was more than pleasure in this embrace; with no other woman had he found the sense of center — of being centered, of being whole and perfectly balanced — that he found in her arms.

She pressed against him, and his heart leapt, and his body hardened. He wanted her with a rapidly escalating passion — a passion that, until now, he'd endeavored to keep leashed.

If he didn't end this . . .

His chest swelled as he drew in a steadying, fortifying breath. Clinging tight to his purpose, to what remained of his eroding will, he eased back from the kiss.

Inch by inch, lightening the pressure — releasing their senses to return to the world.

Felicia recognized his direction. In the same way she'd blithely followed his lead into the encounter, she accepted the necessity to follow him out of it.

Step by step, gently — accomplishing the inevitable drawing back without a hint of rejection on either part.

Without the slightest hint of anything other than wholehearted togetherness.

Even when their lips, at last, parted, they stood with their faces close, breathing the other's breath, at close quarters, their gazes briefly touching from under lowered lids.

Finally, as if in orchestrated concert, they both drew deeper breaths, raised their heads, and, lowering their arms, drawing their hands from each other, stepped back.

The separation impinged, much as if she'd lost something she valued, then her wits cleared, and she focused on his face.

She took in the faintly smug smile that slowly curved his lips.

Not quite frowning, she moistened her lips and saw his eyes track the movement of her tongue. "What was that for?" She was suddenly very sure there had been some purpose that had prompted his sudden, unplanned action.

He raised his eyes to hers, then his smile softened. "That was to remind you that there's more to working with me than cogs and gears and chasing saboteurs."

"Indeed?" She arched her brows.

His smile deepened. Still holding her gaze, he raised one hand and lightly ran the back of one finger down her cheek . . .

She couldn't quell a delicious shiver of reaction.

For a second, they both froze.

The moment held, fraught, the air between them charged, as if they stood on a precipice but couldn't yet move.

His eyes on hers, he knew and sensed it, too. "Later." He drew breath and lowered his hand. "After the project is completed and we're free to think of only ourselves."

With that, he inclined his head, then stepped back, turned, and walked away, leaving the room and heading toward the front hall.

Presumably back to the workshop.

Discovering she could, she drew in a long, deep breath and turned back to the peonies.

Very little thought was needed to conclude that he was correct. What with the engine, the exhibition, and would-be saboteurs, they had too much on their collective plate at the moment to think of other things.

Personal things.

Not that, all in all, they hadn't just taken a step closer to what they both, quite clearly, desired in that sphere.

She humphed. "Men!" She picked up the vase, destined for the table in the front hall, and determinedly carried it forth.

"Thank you, Mr. Mayhew." Felicia handed Mayhew a full cup and saucer for Flora, and he carried it to the older lady, comfortably ensconced on the sofa in the drawing room.

When Mayhew returned, Felicia handed him his cup, then sat back with her own and watched as Mayhew elegantly arranged his long limbs in the armchair opposite hers. She and Flora had been waiting in the drawing room when Mayhew arrived; the instant he had, she'd rung for the tea tray. That had also been the signal for one of the footmen to inform Rand, who had retreated to the workshop with William John after luncheon, that their visitor had arrived.

Felicia didn't doubt that, by now, Rand was near, lurking out of sight — either in the front hall or more likely on the terrace given she'd left the doors propped wide. She sipped and waited for Flora to open the discussion.

Smiling in her customary, sweet fashion, Flora lowered her cup and said, "Dear Felicia tells me that you wish to draw more sketches of the Hall, Mr. Mayhew."

"Yes, indeed." His charm to the fore, Mayhew launched into an explanation of how the Hall in its rather unusual setting called to him.

Although Mayhew's gaze flicked her way several times, Felicia kept silent and observed. Closely.

Eventually, Mayhew ran down, and Flora responded with a smiling "I can see you're extremely devoted to your art, sir."

Felicia seized the moment. "Is there any particular aspect you had in mind to sketch on this occasion?" She half expected him to own to a wish to sketch the house from the rose garden, or from some other angle that would give him a view of the workshop.

Mayhew smiled and waved toward the terrace. "The perspective from that side is by far the best. I would like to make several sketches from that direction." He turned and glanced out of the open doors. "From farther down the lawn — toward the woods."

"I see." Flora smiled benignly. "I'm sure we can have no objection to that." She cast a faintly questioning look at Felicia.

Caught in the act of raising her cup, Felicia inclined her head, sipped, then lowered her cup. "Indeed."

"Actually, my dear Mr. Mayhew," Flora

said, "I was wondering if you're acquainted with the Mayhews of Tonbridge. Gerrard and his wife, Kitty."

Hiding an inner smile, Felicia listened as Flora embarked on just the sort of inquisition a widowed lady of her years might be expected to have an interest in; in truth, Flora rarely had the chance to air her interrogatory skills, but given they wished to know more of Mayhew, inquiring as to his family connections was potentially pertinent.

However, Flora uncovered no inherently suspicious connections, and, rather more telling, Mayhew suffered her questions with easy grace. His charm and ready-to-please air never faltered.

Felicia — straining her ears for any hint of an out-of-place intonation and, with her eyes sharply focused, searching for any sign of a mask — had reached the point of acquitting Mayhew of being anything other than the charming and easygoing artist he seemed, when a sudden *pop!* sounded.

The distinct and rather odd noise apparently came from outside, reaching them through the open doors. They all glanced that way, and Felicia realized William John must have the workshop doors open, or at least ajar. The noise had come from there, from around the side of the house.

She glanced back in time to see an expression she couldn't read flash across Mayhew's face. It was there and gone so quickly, she had no idea what it might have meant.

The instant Mayhew saw her looking his way, his smile returned, combined with an inquiring look.

She waved dismissively. "Just a pipe clanking. They sometimes do when the sun heats them."

It hadn't been any pipe, but a valve blowing. She recognized the sound. What the devil was William John doing? He was supposed to be finishing off and getting ready for the final tests, not blowing valves.

Felicia drained her cup. She saw Mayhew had done the same. "Perhaps," she said, setting down her saucer and reaching for his, "you and I should go outside, and you can show me the view you'd like to sketch."

"Excellent." Mayhew rose and, with ready courtesy and his never-failing charm, took his leave of Flora, shaking her hand and promising to mention her to a distant relative who they'd agreed she might have met.

When Mayhew straightened and looked her way, Felicia waved him to the open doors and the terrace beyond, then led the way.

As she stepped onto the terrace flags, she swiftly glanced to her left, but if Rand had been there, he'd beaten a retreat. With Mayhew by her side, she descended the central steps to the lawn and started strolling down its length.

Mayhew, with his long legs, easily kept pace. After several moments, he glanced at her face. "I do hope you don't think I'm" — he gestured vaguely — "taking advantage, as it were."

Puzzled, she glanced at him. "No. You're quite welcome to sketch the house." *You're not welcome to interfere with our invention.*

"Oh, right, then." Mayhew's smile returned, and he looked ahead, then pointed to the large oak at the bottom of the lawn. "I think the best spot will be somewhere around there."

Felicia had been wondering where Rand was. She'd glanced at the woods bordering the lawn several times, but hadn't seen him. Then from the corner of her eye, she fleetingly glimpsed a shadowy figure keeping pace along one of the deer trails.

He was too far away to hear their words, but close enough to watch and observe.

They reached the oak, and Mayhew halted. He turned and surveyed the house, then he embarked on a voluble examination of angles and light and shadow.

She listened and observed, yet not once did she glimpse anything incongruent in his actions or words, not even in his tone or his expression.

Mayhew was an artist intent on sketching the house. There wasn't anything else — any hint of ulterior motive or mission — to be seen.

Was that because their imputed ulterior motive didn't exist, or was it there, but he was glib enough not to let it show?

Could Mayhew be this superbly duplicitous?

Felicia eyed him and simply didn't know.

Eventually, he fell silent. After several moments of staring at the house, now frowning slightly, he turned to her. "I don't like to ask it of you, but to make this sketch the best it can be, I need something — some object — in the foreground to anchor the perspective and make sense of the view." He caught her gaze. "You'll have seen how I do that in some of those sketches I showed you earlier. The object in the foreground. Like the pump in the inn yard, or the signpost in one of the landscapes."

She did remember and nodded. After a second's hesitation, she asked, "What sort of object do you need for this view?" She tipped her head toward the house.

He drew breath and, with one of his most appealing smiles, said, "I would really like you." He swung to gesture with both arms. "Sitting in one of those chairs from the terrace — the cane armchairs. Just there." He waved at the spot, then looked toward the house, eyes narrowing as if examining the effect he wanted to create. His voice soft and low, he murmured, "If you have a flowy gown, something in a pale and lightweight fabric, and a parasol . . . that will do wonders for contrasting with the sharp lines of the house, throwing them into greater visual relief."

Felicia consulted her instincts. Mayhew was standing only feet away, yet her instincts still did not see him as a threat; they never had. It was her mind that harbored suspicions of him.

And if she was sitting out here with him . . . he wouldn't have any chance to wander closer to the house, to perhaps attempt to get into the workshop. Meanwhile, she would have an opportunity to further interrogate him in a setting and at a time when he might let down his guard.

She'd already observed that, when they were working, artists and inventors were much alike; they became absorbed and forgot about the wider world and, indeed, most else.

She looked at Mayhew and met his eager, almost childishly pleading gaze. "All right." She nodded. "I'll sit for you."

She wouldn't be alone with him; she felt absolutely certain Rand would be only as far away as the nearest cover.

After weathering Mayhew's abundant gratitude and making arrangements for him to return at two o'clock the next day, Felicia walked him back to the forecourt and waved him on his way.

He was now driving a gig, hired from some inn during his travels, she assumed; she hadn't recognized the brand on the rear panel.

Once Mayhew had rattled out of sight around the curve in the drive, she looked around, expecting to see Rand emerge from the woods. When he didn't, she walked around to the south side of the house and climbed the steps at the end of the terrace.

Stepping onto the flags, she saw Rand waiting, leaning against the balustrade outside the drawing room.

Unhurriedly, she walked toward him, very aware of the way he watched her as she approached. His gaze appeared dark and intent, ruthlessly focused, and something powerful lurked behind the molten caramel of his eyes.

The touch of that gaze felt delicious and left her faintly breathless.

Nevertheless, she summoned a slight smile and, with it curving her lips, she halted beside him. He straightened from the balustrade. She placed her hands on the stone coping and looked down the lawn.

He settled beside her, idly glancing in the same direction before he brought his gaze to her face. "Anything?"

"He reacted to the valve blowing." A sudden thought occurred, and she slanted a glance at his face. "Did you arrange that, by any chance?"

He shrugged. "We wanted to test Mayhew — I asked William John to fake something minor."

She humphed. "Well, Mayhew reacted, but as I wasn't warned, I only caught the tail end of his response." She frowned as she replayed the moment in her mind. "There was something in his eyes . . . but I can't say what it was. It might have been nothing more than surprise, yet it seemed rather more calculating." She shook her head. "Other than that, there was absolutely nothing in his behavior to point to — no hint of awareness of the invention and not a single sign he has any designs on gaining entrance to the house."

She looked up and briefly met Rand's eyes. "It's intensely frustrating. On the one hand, I feel ready to declare him nothing more than the artist he purports to be — and I really don't think there can be any doubt that he truly is that. But whether he also intends to tamper with the invention . . . as to that, I'm still in two minds."

She fell silent, frowning out at the lawn.

Rand looked down the green expanse to the oak tree and strengthened his hold on his temper's reins. "I heard you agree to sit for him tomorrow. What the devil possessed you?"

Somewhat to his own surprise, his tone suggested that, while her agreeing to sit for Mayhew very definitely didn't meet with his approval, he was prepared to hear that she had some logical and rational reason for doing so.

The glance she threw him, the light in her green eyes, suggested she'd heard and interpreted his words in just that way. A faint smile curved her lips as she proved him right. "If I'm sitting for Mayhew, then he, in turn, will be sitting before me, under my eye the entire time. He will have no opportunity to sneak away anywhere." She paused, then, meeting his eyes, admitted, "I'm leaning toward accepting that Mayhew is simply an artist, and his appearance here at this time is, indeed, nothing more than coincidence. However, it would be best for us to settle our suspicions of him once and for all, so if he reaches the point of finishing his sketch without doing or saying anything to suggest an interest in the invention, I plan on mentioning the workshop and, possibly, the engine, and seeing if he rises to more specific bait."

He narrowed his eyes on hers. "What if he professes an interest and asks to see it — workshop or invention?"

She held his gaze and lightly shrugged. "I'll play it by ear." Her chin firmed. "Regardless, it's time we knew for certain whether or not Mayhew poses a danger to us. William John will be running the final tests tomorrow, and the exhibition is only days away — if Mayhew is intent on sabotage, we need to flush him out."

He didn't disagree and couldn't argue. He held her gaze steadily. "I'll be in the woods, as close as I can be. I'll be watching Mayhew's every move."

Her smile bloomed, warm enough to banish all his fears. "Yes, of course. I was counting on that."

TEN

At three o'clock the following afternoon, Felicia was seated at the far end of the south lawn in one of the cane armchairs from the terrace; her back was to the house, and her parasol was raised, artfully shading her face.

Before her, Clive Mayhew sat behind his easel, his entire focus on the sketch he was creating with swift, sure strokes.

Felicia wasn't even sure he saw her as an animate entity.

It had taken a good few minutes for him to direct her into the correct pose. She'd been sitting with her shoes flat on the grass, her head raised a fraction and tilted to her left, with the parasol riding over her left shoulder for the last thirty minutes.

About them, the summer afternoon stretched, somnolent and lazy. The air was weighted with the smell of freshly cut hay, the sweet scent wafting under the hand of an oh-so-gentle breeze. Insects — bees in the kitchen garden, perhaps — droned in the distance, while nearer to hand, the occasional bird chirped in the thick undergrowth beneath the wood's trees.

Felicia stifled a sigh. She was already well and truly bored. Before she'd struck her pose, she'd glimpsed Rand in the dappled shadows of the wood — not behind Mayhew but to her left. The last glimpse she'd had of him, he'd been leaning with one shoulder propped against a bole, arms crossed, his gaze undeviatingly fixed on her and Mayhew.

For his part, Mayhew had been so focused on the view he'd intended to sketch, he'd spared not a glance for the woods; she would wager her mother's pearls he was utterly oblivious to their watcher beneath the trees.

Even if Mayhew did look searchingly around, she doubted he would spot Rand; that helpful bole would largely screen him from Mayhew's sight.

Without shifting position, she studied Mayhew. He was seated on his folding stool, his attention wholly on his sketch. He was using several pencils, one, then another, gripping those not in use in his left hand while his right hand moved swiftly across the paper. He didn't seem to even look to decide which pencil was which; his fingers seemed to know them by feel.

Again, the proof that Mayhew truly was an artist was displayed for anyone to see.

Felicia inwardly sighed and started composing a suitable incidental comment with which to allude to inventions and inventors.

She'd almost crafted a workable sentence when a massive *bang!* exploded from the house — from the workshop.

She managed not to react — to turn and stare — but Mayhew had blinked and was now staring at the house.

"It's just another pipe." It wasn't — this time it was something even more troublesome than a valve. Mayhew glanced at her, and she waved dismissively. "The staff will take care of it."

Mayhew hesitated, then settled to his sketching again, although Felicia noted he glanced toward the house — toward its rear — more frequently than before.

She could only pray that the workshop door hadn't blown open and that clouds of steam weren't gushing forth.

That morning, she'd worked with William John to solve what they had hoped was the last little glitch that had kept the engine from running perfectly; they'd been so pleased and heartened — buoyed by a sense of impending success. Now . . .

Damn it! We haven't all that many days left.

Mayhew looked at her sharply. Briefly, she smiled, erasing her frown, and schooled her features back into her pose of bucolic serenity.

Rand was steadily and stealthily making his way back toward the house. Mayhew was all artist, at least at that moment, and given how near to completion the engine was and how close the exhibition, Rand felt compelled to see what had gone wrong — what had blown now.

This time, it hadn't been anything he and William John had arranged.

As Rand retreated, he glanced back frequently, but Mayhew and Felicia remained seated as they had been, at the far end of the lawn. From all Rand had seen, he suspected Felicia would, indeed, need to tempt Mayhew to test the man's interest in the engine. Rand had to admit he was increasingly feeling his and her suspicions regarding Mayhew owed more to paranoia than reality.

He was still some way from the house, following a deer trail through the wood, when, after checking on Mayhew and Felicia yet again, he noticed Flora, who in her role as chaperon had been seated prominently on the terrace, had quit her post and, presumably, gone into the house.

That suggested the explosion was serious.

His heart sinking, Rand increased his pace.

He plotted his course. He would make for the part of the wood nearest the kitchen garden, then risk crossing the lawn to the wall; the wall was taller than he was and would allow him to reach the workshop with little chance of Mayhew spotting him.

Again, he glanced back. Mayhew was still sketching, and Felicia was still posing; neither had altered their position.

Rand faced forward, lengthened his stride, and headed for the workshop.

Felicia remained all but boneless in the chair. Her mind, however, was elsewhere, focused on the engine in the workshop. Trying to imagine what had caused the noise, she turned her thoughts to the diagrams on the board. What had she missed? Where among the pipes, pistons, and tubes could an excess of pressure have built up?

She was engrossed in reviewing the design of the engine when Mayhew looked at her, then rose from his stool.

Felicia blinked. Was it the shifting shadows

of the oak beneath which he sat, or had his features hardened?

But then he smiled. "This is truly excellent. It'll be one of my best works to date. I just need you to hold that pose for a few minutes more." He stepped around the easel and, with one hand, indicated his satchel, which he'd left leaning against the rear corner of the armchair. "I need a different pencil for the final strokes."

Felicia faintly smiled and obediently held her pose, her chin at the required angle and her gaze on the trees at the end of the lawn to her left.

Mayhew approached and crouched down beside the chair. She heard him open the satchel, heard the rustle of paper as he searched inside.

After a moment, she sensed him straighten.

Still in the wood, Rand drew level with the wall enclosing the kitchen garden. He pushed through the undergrowth to the edge of the lawn. Pausing just inside the wood, before walking into the open and across to the screening wall, he looked down the lawn, intending to time his emergence to a moment when Mayhew looked down at his sketch —

The artist was no longer behind his easel.

Felicia wasn't in the chair.

Her parasol lay to one side, discarded.

Rand swore. He burst from the undergrowth and raced onto the lawn. He ran full tilt down the slope and on, toward where Felicia had been.

His thoughts churned like a raging river, then abruptly cleared.

He and Felicia had been right — Mayhew was their villain.

Mayhew hadn't seen any way of getting to the invention to sabotage it, so had taken Felicia instead.

Mayhew intended to use her as a hostage to ensure the Throgmorton engine never made it to the exhibition.

Rand swore between his teeth and ran faster.

For a host of desperate reasons — of which the invention was the least — he had to catch them.

He had to reach Felicia and seize her back.

Deep in the wood beyond the end of the south lawn, Felicia struggled and fought, but Mayhew's hold seemed unbreakable.

Instead of fetching any pencil, he'd come up behind her, and before she'd had a chance to react — to turn her head and look at him — he'd clapped a hand over her mouth, seized her arm with his other hand, and hauled her out of the chair.

Then he'd propelled her straight into the wood — onto this path that led more or less directly away from the Hall.

He held her with her back to his chest, one hand still wrapped across her face, immobilizing her head and holding it hard against his shoulder. His other arm was cinched tightly across her waist, allowing him to force her to walk ahead of him, step after step.

She knew all the paths through these woods. This one eventually led to a track along which it was possible to drive a gig.

She'd been in the drawing room when Mayhew had arrived, but — now she thought of it — she hadn't heard the sound of wheels on gravel; she would wager a considerable sum that his gig would be waiting on the track at the end of the path.

Frantically, she struggled against his hold, but he was far stronger than she and continued to force her along the path.

She'd agreed to sit for him to learn whether he was a saboteur or not, to prick him into revealing himself as either innocent artist or dangerous threat, but at no point had she imagined this. The damned villain was kidnapping her!

She locked her knees and tried to keep her feet from moving, to make every step a battle, yet no matter how she stumbled and staggered, he still succeeded in pushing her on.

"You blackguard!" Her imprecation was all but smothered behind his hand.

Being unable to scream only made her feel more helpless.

In mounting fury, she wrestled, tipping side to side, trying to overbalance him, but he only cursed and tightened his grip about her waist until she could barely breathe.

She desisted, hauled in as deep a breath as she could, and fought to focus her wits. She couldn't win free of Mayhew by main force. She had to use her brains.

Rand would be coming . . . if that unplanned explosion hadn't drawn him back to the house. Nothing had been happening with Mayhew, after all.

She knew Rand would follow as soon as he realized they'd gone, but until he saw they'd vanished . . .

Her lungs expanded as she drew in a huge breath. If she wanted to escape Mayhew, she would need to save herself.

Think!

She couldn't believe this was happening

301

— not to her.

A spurt of pure fury seared through her, and, lips and chin setting, she threw herself violently against Mayhew's hold.

He swore again, this time more ferociously, and halted. In grim silence, he gripped hard, then harder, waiting for her to give up.

Eventually, she did, momentarily slumping.

Ruthlessly, he thrust her onward.

As she staggered before him — still resisting every step of the way — he lowered his head and spoke by her ear. "Stop struggling, you little fool." His words were clipped, his tone beyond tense. "I don't want to hurt you. I just need you for leverage to ensure your damned brother doesn't finish his steam engine and get it to Birmingham. I'm sure once he realizes you're missing and gets the note I'll have delivered, he'll see the sense in doing as he's told. Once the day of the exhibition rolls around and the Throgmorton engine fails to make an appearance, I'll let you go."

She was accustomed to people with one-track minds. "And until then?" She managed to make the words intelligible despite speaking around his palm.

"I've rented a cottage — you and I will be

safe enough there."

Safe? All he was worried about was physical safety?

What about my reputation?

She didn't bother wasting breath wailing the words. He was an artist, right enough. She'd already noted how like inventors the species was, and this only proved it. Their world revolved about themselves, and they never even thought to consider the welfare of anyone else.

Anyone else affected by their plans, by their actions.

A thought struck. She shoved her head back into his shoulder and managed to mumble, "Mrs. Makepeace and the staff — they know who you are."

Mayhew softly snorted. "They won't raise any hue and cry — not with your reputation at stake. And they won't make any fuss later, either. Once you return home, everyone — you included — will consider the incident best buried and never mentioned."

So he'd thought of her reputation in that regard — as a threat to ensure his subsequent safety.

He didn't know about Rand. About her and Rand.

If she was locked away with Mayhew for days, when he released her, her reputation would be effectively nonexistent among those who knew. That included Rand. And while she might hope that he would still wish to pursue his "later" with her — she was fairly certain he would trust her word regarding her virginity and, after all, she could prove it — he was a man who had reason to distrust women; this wouldn't help. And then there was Rand's brother, the marquess, let alone his sister-in-law! Rand hailed from the upper nobility. If his family ever found out about her sojourn in a cottage with an artist — and she had no faith the incident would remain buried for all time — she would be ostracized.

Even if Rand married her, she would still be looked down on and sneered at, and any children they had . . .

She couldn't let that happen — not to her or to him.

She felt her resolve harden, like steel infusing her spine.

There'd been no sound of pursuit. It was up to her to get herself out of this.

Her first step had to be breaking from Mayhew's hold.

Drawing every bit of determination she possessed to her, she focused her mind on the path. She traced it in her memory.

Thus far, the path had been more or less

level, but not far ahead, there was a left turn where the lie of the land was deceptive. Beyond the turn, the path sloped steeply downward. And at the lower end of the incline, where the path swung right, a huge beech, standing above the path to the left, had spread a tangle of roots over and across the path. The roots were usually at least half buried by leaf mold, but the hard, contorted lumps were there, just below the loose surface.

If she could manage to unbalance Mayhew just there . . .

She held herself back, conserving her strength, yet she didn't cease her ineffectual resistance. Didn't make his task any easier. If she had, he might have started to suspect she was planning something, so she still pushed back against him, forcing him to exert his strength to keep her staggering and stumbling on before him.

The crucial bend in the path drew nearer. She strained her ears, but could still detect no hint of pursuit.

They reached the turn. She drew breath and dug in her heels, balking for all she was worth — Mayhew hissed through his teeth and shoved her on, following close on her heels.

As she'd hoped, the incline caught him by

surprise.

Instinctively, his feet moved faster as he tried to catch his balance. She added to their momentum by forging ahead herself, pulling him further off balance, until they were rushing toward the end of the incline and the looming beech.

In a skidding swoosh of dead leaves, they reached the crucial spot beside the beech.

The instant she felt the hardness of a root beneath the leaves, she wrenched to the side, flinging all her remaining strength into twisting from Mayhew's hold.

He didn't let go. He clutched her tighter.

His boot soles skidded on the buried roots, and he fell.

Felicia fell on top of him. One of her elbows drove deep into his midsection, her knee came down between his legs, and he gasped and hawed.

Then his hands were desperately pushing her up and off him.

She grabbed up her skirts, scrambled to her feet, and fled.

Back up the incline, back onto the flat, then she was racing along the path toward the Hall.

Behind, she heard a furious, if gasping, bellow, and then, far too soon, Mayhew was pounding after her.

Desperately clutching her skirts high, she raced across a clearing and on along the path. Her lead over Mayhew wasn't enough. After struggling with him for so long, her strength was gone; she was already flagging. He would catch her before she could break free of the woods.

Was there anywhere she could hide?

She frantically searched her memories, but couldn't think of any place safe enough.

A stitch in her side jabbed painfully. Panting, she flung herself across another clearing and raced blindly into the next bend — and ran headlong into Rand.

He staggered under the impact, but his hands clapped about her shoulders, and he caught her. Held her.

"Thank God! Are you all right?" Relief nearly drove Rand to his knees. Inanely, he blurted out, "I thought I'd lost you."

Felicia was gasping, swaying between his hands. She shook her head. One hand at her breast, she managed to gasp, "Mayhew." She swung and pointed. "He's coming."

Their collision had pushed her back around the bend. Rand looked in the direction she pointed — across the clearing she'd just traversed — as Mayhew skidded to a halt on the far side.

For a second, Mayhew stared at them —

at Rand. Mayhew's expression blanked. Then he turned and fled.

Rand tensed to give chase, but he glanced at Felicia, and his feet didn't move.

He thought he'd lost her, but she'd found him — she'd fought and striven to run back to him — and he had her beside him again.

He wasn't going to — couldn't make himself — quit her side.

Not again.

Not so soon.

She stared at him, then, as if understanding his dilemma, she slipped one hand into his.

He gripped her fingers tightly — and she gripped back — then she turned and tugged. "Come on. Let's at least see where he goes."

She ran as best she could, gamely pushing on, and he held himself back to keep pace with her.

She warned him about the tricky incline. At the bottom of the descent, she pointed to where the carpet of leaves was scuffed. "That's where I managed to make him fall and broke free."

They continued on as the path narrowed, and the trees closed in.

Then from some way ahead of them, they heard the muted rattle of wheels and the quick clop of a horse's hooves.

Felicia slowed, then halted. She sighed. "He's got away."

Rand halted beside her. He looked at her, felt her fingers warm and real beneath his. Then he tightened his grip and pulled her into his arms.

Crushing her close, he bent his head and kissed her.

Hard, sure, with every iota of passion in his possessively protective soul.

And she seized him in return; sinking her fingers into his hair, she held him to her.

To their kiss as it raged, fueled by emotions neither could control. That neither had yet even had a chance to own.

Need and want combined to give birth to a ravenous hunger.

Desire swelled, and passion surged.

But they were too exposed — too much at risk — there in the depths of the wood.

Rand broke from the kiss and, with his gaze, raked their surroundings. Nothing disturbed the stillness around them.

He looked back at Felicia as she drew in a steadying breath. Their eyes met, and their gazes held.

So much lay between them — so much needed to be said — yet now was not the time.

Patently, not the time.

After a moment, somewhat gruffly, he offered, "I doubt we'll see Mayhew again."

Slowly, he lowered his arms, releasing her from their cage. When she stepped back, he reached out and closed his hand about one of hers. "We'd better get back to the house."

She nodded, and they set off, walking slowly but steadily along the path.

"He was intending to kidnap me and hold me in a cottage to force William John not to present the engine at the exhibition. He said he would let me go once the exhibition was over."

He managed to grind out, "Did he hurt or harm you in any way?"

She shook her head. Then on a spurt of shaky laughter, she said, "I suspect I hurt him significantly more when I tripped him and fell on him."

"Good." He would prefer to tear Mayhew limb from limb, but that could wait.

As they tramped beneath the trees, through the soothing woodland quiet, his wits started to settle and function again. "Mayhew has to be working for someone. I've no idea whom." He glanced at Felicia and briefly met her eyes. "I'm going to send to Raventhorne Abbey. It's not far, and my brother can and will provide the men we need to ensure we get the engine and carriage to Birmingham safely — on time and in one piece."

Her gaze on the path, she nodded.

They reached the edge of the woods and walked onto the lawn.

Felicia waved at the jumble of items strewn on the grass. "He even left his things — his satchel, easel, and stool."

Rand halted and considered the sight. "Those are his tools of trade. He must have wanted very badly to stop the invention succeeding."

"I'll send one of the footmen to gather them up. Who knows? If we ever catch up with Mayhew, they might prove useful in some way."

He saw no reason to argue. In his experience, artists were protective of their equipment. If they did catch up with Mayhew, his well-used easel, stool, and satchel might help to pry loose the name of whoever had hired him.

They started up the long slope of the south lawn. Looking ahead, Felicia heaved a resigned sigh. "I suppose we'd better go and see what William John blew up this time."

Rand nodded because she expected him to. In reality, the Throgmorton engine and William John's endeavors had sunk low in the scale of what was important to him; they now rode well below the lady whose hand he held firmly in his grasp.

The lady his inner self had already decided he should never, ever, let go.

ELEVEN

The moon was riding high in a black and cloudless sky as Rand slowly paced the terrace. Night had fallen hours before, but the emotions roiling inside him, along with the inevitable conjectures — the what-ifs that rose to plague him — hadn't yet settled enough to allow him to relax, much less sleep.

His hands clasped behind his back, his gaze fixed unseeing on the flagstones before his feet, he slowly walked the balustraded expanse; at least he'd stopped pausing to stare through the darkness at the far end of the lawn.

Beyond a bruise or two, Felicia had suffered no hurt — or so she'd assured him and Flora. They'd shared what had happened with the older lady, as well as with Shields, Johnson, and the rest of the staff; by mutual agreement, they'd decided not to distract William John with news of the attack on his sister. Although, on several occasions, he'd been present when Felicia, Rand, and Flora had discussed the artist, they seriously doubted he'd paid attention enough to remember, and the explosion that had distracted Rand and Flora and given Mayhew the chance to seize Felicia had ruptured several pipes and a gasket. William John needed to keep his mind on the engine; all final testing would have to be successfully completed by Tuesday evening — forty-eight hours from now. They were running out of time.

Unsurprisingly, Mayhew had vanished. On returning to the house, Rand had dispatched Shields and Struthers to the Norreys Arms in the vain hope Mayhew had returned there. Instead, they'd learned that the artist hadn't been putting up at the inn. Presumably, since returning to the area, he'd been staying at the cottage he'd hired to hold Felicia. That suggested the cottage would not be easy to find.

Given the circumstances — given the timing — there was no sense in attempting to pursue Mayhew. Not at this time. Later, Rand vowed, there would be a reckoning, but for now, he had to let the artist go.

By the time Shields and Struthers had returned with their report, Rand had had a letter for Ryder waiting. He'd sent Shields to Raventhorne to deliver the missive. By horse, the Abbey was only about three hours away.

To Rand's surprise, the knowledge that Ryder would have received Rand's request by now, and the safety of both Felicia and the invention on the way to and at the exhibition was thus assured, hadn't calmed him as much as he'd expected.

Hadn't eased the tension gripping him to any noticeable degree.

He knew what had caused that tension to rise, accepted it as inevitable — an unavoidable consequence of the connection that had come to be — yet acceptance didn't make the inner turmoil, the primitive and potent passions roiling in his gut, any easier to subdue.

He paced on. With those primal emotions still churning within him, he felt like he imagined a caged tiger would — poised on the edge of dangerous violence.

The faint scrape of a sole on stone had him whirling — to see Felicia step out of the drawing room into the moonlit night.

Like him, she was still dressed as she had been at dinner; the pale green of her silk gown, its lines clinging to her slender figure, converted to a more silvery hue in the moon's argent light.

He'd halted. Her gaze had been on him from the first. Slowly, she glided to meet him.

To his eyes, she was his goddess — the one he worshipped. His senses locked on her, and her nearness reached for him like a physical caress and set his nerves flickering.

Waiting.

Strung out and aching.

Through the long windows, Felicia had seen Rand pacing implacably, the long planes of his face hard, chiseled, his expression almost forbidding. Something inside her had responded to the sight; as she neared, she sensed that the restless, turbulent compulsion that had driven her downstairs, that had intensified in the instant she'd seen him, pressing her to go to him, to soothe him and seek her own solace with him, was of a piece with the powerful feelings transparently gripping him.

She didn't stop until she stood before him, close enough that, even through the shadows, she could read his eyes, his face.

Deliberately, in a gesture akin to a gentle challenge, she steadily held his gaze and let her lips lightly curve. "I couldn't sleep, either." She'd pitched her voice low, her tone suggesting she viewed her state — and his, too — as inevitable, a truth she'd only just realized.

She turned her head and looked down the lawn — to where Mayhew had seized her and dragged her into the woods. For a moment, she remained silent, marshaling her thoughts and her words, then she drew in a deep breath and said, "I know you don't want to hear this, but I want to — indeed, I need to — thank you. Properly."

Since returning to the house, she'd attempted to thank him several times, but every time, he'd managed to adroitly sidestep and divert the conversation.

In the cool of the night, she wasn't about to be gainsaid. Evenly, she continued, "If you hadn't been watching — hadn't cared enough to spend your afternoon loitering in the woods being supremely bored — if you hadn't been there to see and come racing after me, I wouldn't have escaped Mayhew. He would have caught up with me and seized me again. Then he would have carted me off and done as he'd said, and the Throgmorton engine would have remained at the Hall and not been presented at the exhibition."

She drew in a deeper breath and faced him, her gaze steady on his face. "The invention would have failed. You and your investors would have lost your funds. Your reputation would have been severely damaged. William John would have been ruined and any hope he has of becoming an established inventor would have vanished. The household would have been ruined, too — we would have had to sell up. The workshop would be lost, my family as it has been would cease to be, and I . . ." She focused relentlessly on his shadowed caramel eyes. "I would have been damaged goods. There would have been no future for me, and if William John and I managed to avoid ending destitute, it would only be by the charity of others."

His jaw tightened as if he was holding back words — a dismissal he knew she wouldn't accept. Her own expression firming, determined to say all she felt she must, she went on, "So hear me, Rand Cavanaugh, and know that, from the bottom of my heart, I thank you for being there when I needed you to be."

Even as the words fell from her lips, she realized that was, for her, the critical and most fundamental point. He was the first and only man in her life to have shown her such simple yet steadfast loyalty. No matter they'd known each other for mere weeks, she knew beyond question that he would always be there if she needed him, that she could rely on him as she had never been able to rely on any other.

The insight left her feeling both vulnerable and invincible.

Rand looked down at her, into pretty green eyes, silverpale in the moonlight, his self, his senses, locked on her while he fought to keep back the words he felt he could not yet — did not yet have the right to — say. She and William John and the household at the Hall would never be destitute; he wouldn't allow it.

Yet while he battled to suppress those words, others — fueled by a source even more powerful — rose to his tongue. "I don't want your thanks. I don't want your gratitude." Even to his ears, the words sounded gravelly and dark. Belatedly, he tried to rein himself — his true inner self — back, but it was too late. Far too late. He held her gaze and succinctly stated, "I just want you."

Her eyes widened. Then she blinked and tipped her head, regarding him with a frown slowly investing her eyes and her expression.

He suddenly realized she might misconstrue; the possibility horrified, and he hurried to clarify . . . For a moment, he was lost, then, as if a dam broke, words rushed to his tongue. "That kiss in the woods today — and the one before. In neither case did I kiss you because I intended to seduce you . . . or rather, I do hope to seduce you, but not in any way to your detriment." The more rational part of him wondered where the hell he was going with this, yet her expression said she was listening, and the words kept flowing. "I said we should leave dealing with whatever was between us until later — until this business with the engine was over and done with, and we would be free to think of ourselves." His eyes locked with hers, he shook his head. "This afternoon, when I thought I'd lost you, my world came crashing down. I had thought other things" — his wave encompassed the world beyond the lawn — "were more important — or, at least, equally important — but in that, I was wrong. This afternoon taught me exactly how wrong."

All of him — all he was, every last particle of his being — was focused on her. Blindly, he reached for her hands, gathered her fingers in his, and gently squeezed. "Regardless of the brevity of our acquaintance, something in me knew you for what you were in the first instant I saw you. *You* are the most critical thing — far and away the most important thing — to me. To my life, to my future — to the future I want to have."

His eyes on hers, he raised one of her hands to his lips and brushed a soft kiss to the backs of her fingers. "I want you. I want you to be mine — to be my wife. I want you to share your life with me and become the lynchpin of mine." He lowered her hand, but continued to hold her gaze as he softly said, "After this afternoon, that's what I want. You."

Felicia had stopped breathing; as the last word sank into her soul and resonated there, she dragged in a shallow, shaky breath and tightened her grip on his fingers. Holding fast to that anchor, holding hard to his gaze, she gathered her courage. Sincerity and honesty were the strengths behind his words; standing before him in the moonlight, she wanted to — felt compelled to — give him the same. "No simple phrase can carry enough meaning to respond to that." Her heart thudded in her chest, its cadence a compulsion all its own. "You arriving at the Hall, you being the man you are, was the catalyst that opened my eyes on so many levels. Because of you, I found my talent for helping with inventions and, finally, gained some understanding of my father and William John. Because of you, I've lifted my head and seen that my life's horizons are much broader than I'd known. But most importantly, you and your regard have brought me to see the possibility of a different type of partnership."

She paused, her eyes steady on his as, in her mind, she looked back over the last days. "I didn't know how you felt — that you felt this way about me — but you had already said enough to make me consider, to make me think about how I felt about you. And yes, this afternoon brought a revelation for me as well. When I realized what Mayhew intended and how his plans would inevitably affect me and the future I wanted . . . in that moment, just how desperately I wanted that future struck home."

Again, she paused, needing to ensure that her next words carried the full weight of her own sincerity, her own honesty. "The events of the afternoon rendered in stark clarity what I need to make me whole — to give me the chance to live my life, to live a full and rounded life, to the very best of my abilities."

He shifted fractionally closer; his fingers gripped hers more tightly. The intensity of his focus on her never wavered. "And what is that thing you need to make you whole?"

She let her lips curve, let her eyes light with the emotion behind her answer. "You."

His smile bloomed, then she was in his arms. She moved into his embrace as his arms closed about her. She tipped up her head as he lowered his, and his lips found hers.

Anticipation and promise — both were equally vibrant in that kiss. Equally heady.

His lips moved on hers, tantalizing and tempting. She kissed him back, following his lead, wanting, needing, hungry for more.

The kiss drew out, sensations stretching and spinning — an unspoken vow in the silvery night.

She broke for just a second to murmur against his lips, "I want you. I need you." She gripped his lapels for emphasis.

He feathered kisses over her jaw and cheeks. "Not half as much as I need and want you."

Their lips met again, fused again. This time, it was he who drew back, just a fraction, to say, "You called this a different partnership. That's what I want, too. I want a marriage of minds as well as bodies."

She looked up at him and wouldn't have been surprised if he saw stars in her eyes. "Sharing inventions as well as a family?"

"Precisely." He held her gaze for several

seconds — as if committing to that and reading her corresponding acceptance — then he bent his head and their lips met again, and this time, metaphorically, he took her hand and drew her into the dance.

Into the swirling whirl of their desires, into the heat of their rising passions.

His lips turned demanding, commanding, and, eager to learn what more lay in store, she parted her lips, and he plunged into her mouth and explored.

He kissed her deeply, in patent relief and with a passion their words had freed from all restraint.

Gladly, exuberantly, she followed him into the burgeoning flames, returning each caress with equal fervor. For long moments, they communed in the dark, exploring and learning, clinging to each other as their senses waltzed and their wits fell away.

With deliberate focus, she set her senses free — let them soar.

Opening herself to the moment, sinking herself into the kiss, she set herself to savor every moment, every nuance.

Every thudding beat of her heart, the steadily escalating heat of the kiss, the increasing hardness of the muscled arms that surrounded her and held her to him. The potent thrust of his tongue that she welcomed with her own, prelude to a more intimate joining.

She wanted to — needed to — get closer. She pressed herself to him and gloried in the hard ridge that impressed itself against the softness of her belly. She might be an innocent, but she was no prude; the raw evidence of his desire for her set her pulse racing.

Sliding her hands up, over the contours of his heavily muscled chest — drinking in its splendor yet again — she raised her palms to his cheeks and framed them, the better to meet his heated forays as he devoured her with single-minded passion.

Her senses, her wits, had drawn in; she no longer had any interest beyond the merging of their mouths — beyond following the path that had opened between them and merging their bodies and, ultimately, their lives.

Between them, the heat and an increasingly explicit hunger grew and swelled. Welled, until it became a pounding beat in her blood, a driving force too powerful to deny.

On a gasp, she pulled back, although their lips parted by less than an inch. They were both breathing raggedly. Giddy, her lips all but brushing his, she whispered, "Is it wrong to want to give in to this — this hunger, this need? To fling all restraint to the wind and follow this path to its ultimate end?"

She raised her lids enough to see him do the same. Their gazes met and held.

He looked into her eyes and, with simple candor, replied, "We're going to marry. I'll be your husband, and you'll be my wife. Between us, indulging our desires — yours for me, and mine for you — will now and forever be our right."

She let a heartbeat pass, savoring the prophesy of his words, then she slid her hand to his nape and drew his lips to hers. "Good," she declared and kissed him.

In open invitation and none-too-subtle demand.

Rand responded, feeling a rightness and an eagerness he'd never before felt, but they were on the open terrace. Gently, he drew back, raising his head to look down at her face — at her swollen lips and shining eyes. At the glow in her cheeks and her desire-etched expression. "Your room or mine?"

She weighed up those options. "Mine. Petunia — my maid — won't come up in the morning until I ring."

He nodded, forced his arms to release her, then he caught her hand and, without another word, led her back into the house. He paused to lock the French doors behind them, then she took his hand and drew him into the front hall and up the stairs.

She led him down the corridor to her room at the end. She opened the door, and he followed her inside.

He shut the door, then swiftly glanced around the room as, smoothly, he drew her into his arms. A wide tester bed stood against the far wall. She hadn't drawn the curtains over the wide windows; the moon was at its zenith, sending more than enough silvery light pouring in for their purpose.

There was something about making love in the moonlight — in a light that rendered white curves pearlescent.

As their lips met again, as she came up on her toes to meet and match him, he once again found himself battered by contradictory impulses — to seize and rush ahead, or to linger and savor.

In the end, he deferred to her. Although he kept his hands on their reins, he let her lead, let her script their play, drawing her back only when her open and unbounded enthusiasm had her racing ahead too fast. Then he caught her hands, captured her lips in a kiss designed to corral her wits, and refocused her on the sensation she'd missed, that in her eagerness she'd failed to properly savor. Once she had — once she'd tasted and gloried — he released her to resume her exploration.

They divested each other of their clothes, piece by piece stripping the garments away, revealing themselves to each other inch by inch.

Felicia marveled anew, thrilled to her core at being able to sate her senses with the resilient splendor of his bare chest. With the fascinating display of rock-hard muscles sheathing heavy bones.

To her surprise, she felt little modesty in allowing him access to her naked curves. She was too absorbed drinking in the wonder of his body, his inherent strength, and the sense of control, of reined power that, unclothed, he emanated.

To an untried lady, that should have spelt danger; instead, to her, he personified wonder.

They'd turned and shifted as they'd disrobed; now, finally naked, they stood beside her bed. She moved into his arms, and their bodies met skin to skin for the first time, and a sharp shiver of awakened awareness, potent and sweet, raced through her.

She lifted her arms and draped them over

his shoulders; with her greedy hands splaying over thick muscle and heated skin, she stretched up against him, her nerves sparking at the sliding contact.

He closed his arms around her, bent his head, and recaptured her lips.

As, eager and wanting, she returned the caress, his hands spread on her back, and he urged her closer yet.

She pressed her body to his — and felt her senses leap, then shudder. Felt her heart thud — felt his thud against her breast. Felt his erection, a hot, heated rod, against her belly.

Then he bent his knees and, with one arm banding her upper thighs, hoisted her against him. She broke from the kiss to look down at his face, and he tumbled them onto the bed.

She gasped, then lost what little breath she'd gained as he stretched alongside her, and his hand closed over her breast.

From that moment, her education began, as with caresses and knowing touches, strokes and hot kisses, he opened her eyes to the breadth of her own senses, to the elemental strength of her own passions and desires.

She'd known him for barely two weeks, yet he seemed to have known her forever;

he knew just where to touch to make her gasp and tremble, over just what spot to languidly trail his fingertips to make her burn.

Soon, her senses were in tumult, and her nerves had tightened. Wings of heat beat steadily beneath her skin, the flames flaring hotter wherever he touched. Wherever she touched him.

Body to body, they rolled amid the sheets, the soft silkiness of her skin abraded by the hair-dusted roughness of his. The peaks of her breasts cinched tight as the crinkly hair adorning his chest rubbed across them.

His hands sculpted her body, making her arch, making her breath catch as sensation peaked, then fell — only to rise with the next stroke, the next brush of his lips across her skin. The heaviness of his limbs, the promise of his weight, had her sensuously sliding her body against his, tangling her legs with his, exploring and learning, seeking every last source of pleasure, for herself and for him.

Sensation built. And built. Pleasure escalated, wave upon wave, the next always greater than the last.

Suddenly, she needed his lips on hers, needed his kiss to anchor her as her senses and her perceptions whirled.

Her world had shrunk to them — him and her in the billows of her bed.

Delight had never been so sharp and sweet, and the pleasure his increasingly possessive, increasingly explicit caresses sent rolling through her continued to burgeon and build.

She felt his hand between her thighs, and she gasped and clung.

His fingers stroked, his touch sure and artful, and her mind locked on the sensations each knowing caress sent lancing through her.

Desire swelled, a never-before-tasted elixir; she found it well-nigh addictive, compelling her, driving her on.

Into passion.

The flames flared, brighter, near incandescent in intensity as they consumed her from the inside out.

Then with a blunt fingertip, he circled the nub of nerves hidden between her folds, and she lost her breath and arched against him as sharp pleasure streaked through her.

He slid one long finger into her sheath, and she caught her breath on a half sob. Her mind seemed to overload, struggling to assimilate the pressure of the intrusion, the alienness of it, along with the sudden wanting that filled her. He murmured something, his voice dark and mysterious, then he stroked. Her body responded, rising and riding each gentle thrust, and she discovered she ached for more.

Discovered a need welling inside her, one she'd never felt before — a need that grew and swelled until it thundered in her blood.

Urgency blindsided her, and gasping, she clutched at him, needing him closer.

Abruptly, their play seemed a great deal more serious, more desperate — her heightened need sharpened to an acute ache.

She wasn't an innocent — she knew what this was. She needed him now.

Now.

Rand understood her wordless call — her demand, the command carried in her grip as she sank her fingertips into his upper arms and tried to drag him over her.

More than ready, he complied. Passion was a drumbeat in his blood, more forceful than ever before. He lifted over her, bracing his arms and taking his weight on them as he spread her legs with his and settled his hips between her thighs.

They were both burning. Desire had flushed her skin a delicate rose, visible even in the moonlight. Her breathing was ragged, her breasts rising and falling, her hands urgent on his skin.

The soft flesh at the apex of her thighs had flowered for him; the scalding slickness of her welcome bathed the head of his erection as he nudged the swollen lips at her entrance, then eased slowly in.

She caught her breath and stilled. From beneath lids weighted by passion, her eyes glinted, and she caught her lower lip between her teeth — waiting, wanting, and yet unsure . . .

Unable to resist, he lowered his head and kissed her. Caught her lip and drew it from her hold, then sank deep into her mouth and, with unrestrained ardor, claimed.

Her attention shifted as he'd known it would. He seized her senses, trapped them in the kiss.

Then he flexed his spine and drove slowly, powerfully, home.

Home.

Her maidenhead ruptured, and her sheath closed around him in glorious welcome; her small cry was smothered between their lips, and she arched wildly beneath him.

And it was his turn to catch his breath, to break the kiss and clench his jaw and, with his head hanging close beside hers, battle his instincts as he fought to give her a moment to accustom herself . . .

Although tension still held her, he sensed

that she paused, then he heard a soft "Oh," the syllable, barely breathed, laden with wonder.

If he could have smiled, he would have. Instead, he eased the reins he'd so desperately clung to, and slowly, with care, moved upon her, inside her.

Immediately, instinctively, she rose to his beat, to the challenge and the promise, reaching for it, stretching and grasping, and then racing with him as he drove them on.

What followed was a lesson in what could be. She might have been a novice, but he learned, too.

Learned of the difference a true connection of the heart made to what had previously been a merely physical pleasure.

This was hunger.

This was desire.

Everything before paled in comparison.

Her perfume — an elusive blend of honeysuckle and rose — wreathed about him, and he breathed deeply, drawing the scent into his body, into his mind, an indefinable part of her, now, an ineradicable part of him.

They were both desperate, their skins slick with passion, their breaths ragged as together they pushed on. And on . . .

Abruptly, passion's peak reared before them.

Undaunted, they flung themselves up — straight to the pinnacle. Together, they raced — and leapt.

Her senses fractured a second before his. The invisible rack tightened one more time, and she, her body, the strong muscles of her sheath, clutched him violently for one last instant, then she broke, and release took her.

He had only a heartbeat to look down at her and glory before his own release roared through him. He dropped his head to the curve of her throat and groaned long and deep as ecstasy wracked him and he emptied himself into her welcoming heat.

A minute later, his arms quivered and gave way, and, exhausted and spent, he collapsed upon her.

Felicia wrapped her arms as far around him as she could reach. She didn't know why, but she welcomed his weight, the blanket of his body warm and solid over hers.

She lay beneath him; every last muscle in her body felt wrung out and limp. As for her mind, she hadn't known her faculties could be so overwhelmed — so suborned by sensations, feelings, and emotions that nothing else could intrude. Her body — every nerve, every muscle, every square inch of her skin — felt steeped in glory. In pleasure that, until now, had been unimaginable.

As for that moment in which their passions had peaked and the dam had broken . . . she was quite sure she'd seen stars. Even now, with her body weightless, apparently floating on a sea of satiation, pleasure still thrummed beneath her skin.

Beyond that moment on the terrace, she hadn't paused at any point along their path, the one they had followed that had led them from then to now. At no point had that path felt anything but right — the right and proper path for her.

Also, she'd sensed, for him.

Their commitment had been mutual; their need had been, too.

Certainty was there, among all the other emotions swirling through her. As her body relaxed even more, sinking deeper into the mattress under his weight, she felt him stir.

He raised up and, through the waning moonlight, searched her face. His expression was lax; she was sure hers was, too.

He shifted, raised a hand, and brushed her tangled hair back from her forehead. "Are you all right?"

His concern reached her clearly. Softly, she smiled, lifted her hand, gripped his fingers, and weakly squeezed. Her eyes holding his, she murmured, " 'All right' doesn't do justice to how I feel — I'm not sure words can."

Relief showed in his face. "Good." Then he disengaged and lifted from her.

He reached for the rumpled covers, shook them free, then drew them over their cooling bodies. He settled beside her and slid an arm around her; yielding to his gentle urging and her own impulse, she turned to him, settled her head on his chest, in the hollow beneath his shoulder, and felt his arm close protectively about her.

Holding her to him even as they slept.

She smiled and lightly touched her lips to his chest.

He smoothed a hand over her hair, then she sensed him settle, his heavy body relaxing just that touch more as sleep crept up on him.

She closed her eyes and felt slumber ease its clouds over her, too.

This was the first time in her life that she'd slept with anyone else. It should have felt odd. Instead, it felt perfect.

She'd found her place — the place that was right for her, a place into which she fitted perfectly.

On the cusp of sleep, revelation shone in

her mind.

This was the place she'd spent her life waiting to find — lying in the arms of a good, kind, caring, passionate, protective, and purposeful man.

TWELVE

When Rand opened his eyes, the sun was well up, and soft sunshine streamed across the foot of the bed. During the night, he'd turned onto his stomach, and Felicia — his wife bar the ceremony — lay facing him, her head on the pillow beside his.

From beneath still-heavy lids, he drank in the sight of her and felt his heart swell. She was, quite simply, the woman for him.

As his mind drifted over the events of the night — the feelings, the sensations, the glory — awareness tugged at his mind.

Something had woken him. What?

Then he saw Felicia's fine brows draw down, a slight frown forming, then her lashes rose.

She looked into his eyes. For several heartbeats, they stared at each other — the simple fact of them sharing a bed underscoring just how much between them had changed since the previous day.

339

Her gaze softened, and her lips curved. But then the frown, which had lightened, returned.

She blinked and, still frowning, lifted her head from the pillow. "What's that noise?"

Rand turned to his side and came up on one elbow, looking down the bed toward the source of a distant rumbling. That was what had woken him — an unexpected cough, followed by that purring murmur.

It was coming from outside . . .

He looked at Felicia as she turned to look at him.

Dawning realization lit both their faces.

"It's the engine," she breathed.

They both looked toward the window. The noise had to be escaping through the open workshop doors.

Rand flicked a glance at the carriage clock on Felicia's dressing table. "It's barely six o'clock." He looked back at the window. "William John must have thought of something."

Her brother had spent the previous afternoon and evening working feverishly to repair the damage from and rectify the cause of the latest setback.

Felicia was listening intently to the steady purr; in the quiet of the morning, it was just loud enough to reach them. The thrum of sound remained steady, but the tone changed — increasing in pitch, then decreasing, then, after several minutes, increasing smoothly again.

On tenterhooks, she waited, but no sudden bang or even a hiccup disturbed the steady, rumbling purr.

Then, from below, they heard William John bellow to the morning, *"It works!"*

Felicia looked at Rand, wonder in her face. "He's fixed it!"

Rand met her eyes, then together, they thrust back the covers and lunged for their clothes.

Minutes later, Rand stuffed his cravat into his coat pocket and opened the bedroom door for Felicia. She'd thrown on a day gown, but hadn't bothered with petticoats; the material of her skirt clung to her hips and legs as she hurried along the gallery and down the stairs ahead of him.

It was so early, none of the staff were yet about. Other than the steady purring of the engine, no other sound disturbed the morning quiet.

They hit the tiles of the front hall, and Rand strode to the door to the stairs leading down. He flung open the door and led the way.

He and Felicia all but leapt down to the

workshop floor, where William John, his expression ecstatic, was literally dancing around the engine, which continued to thrum smoothly, the gears rotating, the drive shafts smoothly engaging and thrusting.

William John saw them. "Watch this!" Gleefully, he paused by his temporary control board and shifted the handle that controlled a lever. The engine smoothly accelerated, gears and shafts moving faster and faster, then he held the handle steady, halfway to full speed, and the sound leveled and all movement continued at the increased pace. "Keep watching!" He lowered the handle, returning it to its original position, and the engine slowed, but didn't stop.

"That's it!" William John spread his arms, encompassing the entire machine. "The riddles are all solved, and it works exactly as Papa intended."

Felicia seemed unable to drag her eyes from the purring engine. Rand could understand; after all their efforts, the disappointments and frustrations, to see it working, apparently so effortlessly, was breathtaking.

Beaming in delight, William John bounded to Felicia, caught her hands in his, and swung her into his mad dance. "Balance!" he declared. "It was all about balance —

just like you said."

"You fixed it!" Felicia's eyes were bright, her expression radiant. "You did it!"

"*We* did it. I wouldn't have thought about balancing things without you." Grinning, William John dipped his head toward Rand and met his eyes. "And we'd never have had the funds to persevere if it wasn't for Cavanaugh."

Grinning back, Rand saluted the pair of them. Then his gaze fell to the engine. "What brought you down so early?"

"I woke to an epiphany." William John whirled Felicia to a halt beside Rand, then stepped closer to the engine and pointed to several long tubes that now formed a web along each side. "I realized we needed to equalize all pressure directly, from the boiler on, and not just rely on our single pipe to deliver to both pistons. That also meant running equalizer tubes back from both drive shafts and both pistons to get the controls working correctly."

Felicia had drawn closer to study the new tubes. She stepped back with an expression of relief. "Of course."

William John grinned at her. "As I said, balance in all things."

Rand smiled at William John's exuberance, then he returned his gaze to the engine. After a moment, he sobered. "Have you completed the tests yet?"

William John regarded the engine with obvious fondness. "Not yet. I'll do that today."

Rand exchanged a sidelong glance with Felicia. "For the sake of our peace of mind, what's say you run the tests twice?"

Transparently content, William John shrugged. "If you like." His grin resurfaced. He drew out his watch and consulted the face, then, with evident satisfaction, tucked the watch back. "But it's been chugging along sweetly for over half an hour, and it's still perfectly in tune, perfectly aligned. Nothing's going to blow now."

"Nevertheless," Felicia said. "Just to be sure, run the tests twice. How long will that take?"

"I need to let the boiler cool between tests, so I'll get the first set run today, then we can perform the second round tomorrow, while we make the final preparations for seating the engine into the carriage." Over Felicia's head, William John met Rand's eyes. "It'll take us all of the next day — the day after tomorrow — to fix the engine into the carriage, then put the completed machine through its paces."

Rand nodded. "We're going to meet our

deadline, but with no days to spare. We'll need to leave on Thursday morning to get the carriage onto the exhibition floor by late Friday afternoon."

"That's when it has to be there?" Felicia asked.

Rand nodded again. "But as it appears Fate has finally decided to smile upon us, I'm increasingly certain we'll make it." He met William John's, then Felicia's eyes. "I believe we can look forward to seeing what Birmingham, Prince Albert, and the inventing world make of the Throgmorton Steam-Powered Horseless Carriage."

The following days passed in a state of organized chaos.

Shields returned from Raventhorne Abbey while they were still at the breakfast table, with the entire household in alt over the news that the engine's problems had been solved and it was finally working as it should. After confirming that the Marquess of Raventhorne would arrive with a goodly number of guards on Wednesday afternoon — Rand had asked Ryder to come on that day — Shields, along with Joe and Martin, followed William John down to the workshop for a demonstration of the magnificent machine.

Subsequently, throughout Monday, William John dutifully ran the first round of final tests. Felicia elected to serve as his assistant, pointing out that two pairs of eyes and ears were preferable to one, especially when they all had so much riding on the outcome.

Meanwhile, Rand took over the sitting room. He spread maps of the area on a low table, and, with Shields and Struthers, plotted the route they would take to the exhibition and planned where they would halt along the way, every decision made with an eye to being best able to protect the invention — and Felicia and William John, too. "In Birmingham, we'll put up at the Old Crown. It's on our road in, and it's the most suitable place to accommodate us all."

Rand scanned the list of roads and inns they would halt at — for lunch as well as for the night of Thursday. Then he held out the list to Shields. "Ride to Banbury and arrange for rooms there, then go on to the Old Crown and do the same. As Ryder will be with us, use his title — it never hurts."

He exchanged a grin with Shields, who took the list and rose.

"I'll take note of the roads as I go," Shields said, "and look for places that might hide an ambush. If I leave now, I'll be back by

Wednesday morning, in time to help lift the engine into the carriage."

"Yes — look for anywhere that might conceal an attack." Rand got to his feet, along with Struthers. "Meanwhile" — he looked at Struthers — "let's see if there's anything we can do to help prepare the body of the carriage."

He and Struthers spent the afternoon oiling and rechecking every moving part of the now-gleaming carriage.

Rand spent the evening with Felicia, Flora, and William John, all of them buoyed by the rising tide of excitement that had infected the whole household.

That excitement lent spice to his and Felicia's later encounter, one that settled them both, in some indefinable way, drawing them even closer. As if with each passing day, they aligned just a little more perfectly with each other.

Tuesday saw the engine clear the final round of tests with flying colors, and the carriage readied in every way possible for the moment when the engine would be lifted and lowered into the cavity in front of the carriage's forward driving board. That was one of William Throgmorton's original modifications, placing the engine in front of the passengers, rather than behind.

That evening, Flora and the household staff organized a celebration. As Johnson, who proposed the toast, stated, the staff had lived with the invention through thick and thin, over all the months since their late master had commenced working on the project, and as they wouldn't be at the exhibition to observe its moment of glory, it was only fitting that they drank to the success of the engine and its inventors here and now.

After a nudge from Felicia, William John rose to the occasion and thanked everyone for their forbearance, truthfully adding that success wouldn't have been achieved without the help of everyone there, before concluding with the observation that those at the Hall today were the first to see history in the making, and that tomorrow, the future would be here.

By general consensus, the household retired for an early night. Rand followed Felicia to her room, and, after clinging to each other through the throes of a distinctly exploratory bout of lovemaking, they slept slumped in each other's arms as the moon sailed across the sky.

Then the sun dawned, and Wednesday was upon them.

Shields returned to report that their route

to Birmingham held few places where at-
tackers might lie in wait and that the required rooms for their party, including the
barn for the steam-powered carriage that
Rand had insisted they needed for their
overnight stay in Banbury, had been secured.

Immediately after breakfast, it was all
hands on deck in the workshop. With the
outer doors propped wide, William John and
Rand released the heavy locking bolts that
had anchored the iron wheels of the frame
supporting the engine to the workshop
floor, then all the men put their shoulders
to the massive frame, heaved, and started it
rolling, slowly and ponderously, out of the
workshop in which it had sat for nearly two
full years.

Foot by foot, the frame emerged through
the doors and rolled onto the flagstones of
the courtyard between the house and the
kitchen garden, exposing the engine to the
lazy, hazy summer sunshine.

There were murmurs of approval and
wonder from the women of the household
— from Flora, Mrs. Reilly, her four daughters, and Cook — all of whom had lined up
along the front of the kitchen garden to
watch.

Finally, the engine in its frame was halted

in the middle of the courtyard, parallel to the house, and chocks were pushed beneath the frame's wheels to stop it from shifting.

"Now" — William John straightened and dusted his hands — "we have to assemble the gantry and pulleys."

He, Joe, and Martin returned to the workshop, reappearing moments later, lugging armfuls of heavy struts and braces, which they laid on the flagstones. While William John sorted the pieces, Joe and Martin fetched two large steel beams, then under William John's direction, the men started constructing the gantry to either side in front of and across the frame containing the engine.

When Felicia asked how long assembling the structure would take and William John airily suggested two hours, the women lost interest and drifted back to their work.

All except Felicia; this was, in that moment, her most important task. Arms crossed, she watched critically as the gantry took shape. Once the major struts had been locked into position, she inquired of William John, then conscripted Rand, Struthers, and Shields to assist her in rolling the carriage part of the invention out of the stable and around to the courtyard.

The carriage stood waiting in the stable,

with every surface polished and gleaming. The seat was of golden oak, and the side panels, metal guards, and forward and rear plates had been painted a deep green, the better to display the solid brass of the levers and fittings.

At Rand's suggestion, Felicia climbed to the seat, sat, and used the wheel to steer the carriage, propelled by the three men, out of the stable yard, onto the drive, and around onto the wide path that ran along the rear of the house to end at the courtyard. She had to concentrate at first, but by the time they reached the courtyard and she applied the brake, halting the carriage with the nose of its empty forward compartment mere inches from the engine's frame, she had a wide grin on her face, and excitement once again fizzed in her veins.

William John and Joe were up on ladders set on either side of the frame, fixing heavy-duty pulleys with their dangling chains to the gantry's massive upper beams. Once that was done, the pair climbed down, and everyone stood back and considered their next move — raising the engine out of the frame, sliding the frame away, rolling the carriage into place under the suspended engine, then lowering the engine into position in the carriage's body. "After that," William John said, "I'll slide beneath the carriage and secure the engine in place, then attach the shafts to the axles."

Everyone glanced at each other, then Rand suggested they fortify themselves with luncheon before embarking on the most crucial stage of the assembly process, and all agreed. Johnson, Shields, and Struthers elected to have their meal brought out to them so they could remain with the engine — on guard against anyone who might think to slip out of the woods and tamper with it. After all the watches the men had stood protecting the invention over the past weeks, they were not of a mind to allow anyone to sabotage it at this late stage.

Relieved on that score, Felicia, Rand, and William John retreated into the house.

Rising excitement ensured they didn't dally over the dining table. As soon as they'd sated their appetites, they returned to the courtyard to find the entire staff once again in attendance.

The moment was another milestone in the long journey to get their father's last invention to the exhibition. Felicia stood back and watched as, with William John on one side of the frame and Rand on the other, all the male staff set their hands to the thick chains of the twin pulleys and hauled back, hand over hand, and the engine slowly rose from its support inside the frame.

William John and Rand steadied the massive beast, both calling to the men so they maintained an even lift on both pulleys, keeping the engine level with the ground.

There was a tense moment when one of the chains caught, then jerked free, but everyone clung to calm, and, once the engine stopped its sudden swaying, the men slowly raised it the last foot, until, finally, it hung suspended, clear of the frame.

The men on the chains were stationed at the rear of the frame — opposite the end where the carriage sat, with its empty compartment ready to be wheeled under the engine.

With the engine free of the frame, William John pulled on his side of the frame, and Rand set his hands to the other side and pushed, and the heavy iron frame, now without the weight of the engine, rolled slowly toward the kitchen garden, leaving the space beneath the engine clear.

The instant the frame was out of the way, William John hurried to the carriage, waving Felicia to climb to the seat. "We'll push — you steer."

She clambered up and, after glancing back and seeing Rand and William John poised at the rear of the carriage, she faced forward and released the brake.

Slowly, the carriage rolled forward.

"Keep it straight," William John called.

Felicia gripped the wheel with both hands and held it rigidly straight. The engine neared, level with her head. "When should I stop?"

Forward movement ceased, and Rand and William John strode past Felicia, one on either side. Both halted beside the engine cavity and looked up at the engine, then down at the locking blocks onto which the engine had to be lowered.

A flurry of rushing steps had Felicia, Rand, and William John looking toward the rear of the carriage. All four Reilly daughters as well as Cook and Mrs. Reilly had come to brace their hands on the rear board of the carriage. Mrs. Reilly looked at William John. "We'll push — you two let us know how far."

Smiling, Felicia faced forward. She shared a look with Rand, who grinned. Then he looked across the engine compartment at William John and nodded. "Your call."

With literally everyone bar Flora actively assisting, it took another ten minutes to get the engine compartment positioned to perfection beneath the engine, and then the men, who had been grunting and shifting as they continued to support the weight of the engine, lowered the beast slowly — and then even more slowly as William John and Rand shifted it fractionally so that its foot plates with their bolt holes were perfectly aligned with the supports inside the carriage — until finally, the engine touched the supports. William John and Rand did a last frantic check, reported that the positioning couldn't be bettered, and at last, the engine was set fully down, the chains went lax, and the Throgmorton Steam-Powered Horseless Carriage was almost complete.

Relief rippled through everyone, then excitement soared, even more heightened — more expectant — than before.

Then Mrs. Reilly gathered the female staff, and in a group, they headed back around the house to resume their normal duties. After waving to Felicia, Flora followed.

Rand came to help Felicia to descend from the carriage's seat. William John had already turned to instruct the men in moving the gantry away from the carriage. With grunts and much muttering, with all the men lending a hand, they half lifted, half pushed the massive gantry by degrees until it was clear of the carriage.

William John directed Shields, Struthers, and Johnson to, between them, roll the now-empty frame around the carriage and back into the workshop. While they took care of that, William John, assisted by the other men, fell to dismantling the gantry.

Taking the structure apart required much less time than it had taken to put it together. Leaving the men to carry the individual beams, struts, and bracing into the workshop, William John came to stand beside Felicia and Rand and study the engine sitting snugly in its compartment. "Now to hook everything together."

He swung about and disappeared into the workshop, only to reappear seconds later pushing one of his racks of tools. He angled it beside the carriage, then extracted a board with wheels on one face, set the contraption on the flagstones, then he picked up a wrench, lay flat on the board, and grinned up at Felicia and Rand. "Wish us luck." William John kissed the wrench, then with his feet propelled himself under the engine.

Fascinated, Rand and Felicia bent to look and saw William John screwing in the large bolts that would hold the engine in place.

After a moment, Felicia asked, "How long will it take to connect everything so we can test the carriage as a whole?"

William John paused in his tightening, then replied, "An hour at least. More likely two."

She straightened and looked down at his feet. "In that case, I'll leave you to it."

"No sense in hanging about," William John blithely confirmed. "If I want anything, I'll call one of the men, but most of what needs to be done in hooking everything up is down to me."

Rand grinned and, with Felicia, moved away from the carriage. "He sounds happy as a grig."

"Indeed." Felicia couldn't stop smiling herself. She looked back at the carriage as they strolled toward the terrace. "I can barely believe we're nearly there."

She and Rand shared an expectant glance — then the sound of many horses clopping up the gravel drive reached their ears.

Rand's face lit. "That, I believe, will be the party from Raventhorne."

"Oh." Felicia halted and looked down at her green cambric gown. She shook out the skirts and hoped they weren't too crushed; at least she'd managed to avoid any grease. Raising her gaze, she met Rand's eyes. "Is my hair still neat?"

He smiled reassuringly, drew her nearer, and linked his arm with hers. "Don't worry.

I seriously doubt Ryder will notice."

"But he's a marquess."

"Yes, he is, but he's not at all high in the instep, not unless someone annoys him — and trust me, you won't."

They diverted into the workshop and, dodging around the men stowing the pieces of the gantry away, made for the stairs to the front hall. As they climbed, she shot Rand a glance, but his expression stated he was looking forward to seeing his brother, so she bit back her uncertainties and hurried on.

They stepped into the hall just as Johnson swung the front door wide.

She approached the doorway, with Rand immediately behind her.

The sight that met her eyes had them widening.

A large body of horsemen was milling in the forecourt.

She knew Rand had asked his brother to send a troop of reinforcements to help guard the carriage, so the number of men didn't come as a shock. Similarly, the tall, tawny-haired, exceedingly well-set-up gentleman standing beside a huge dappled gray was no great surprise; Rand had expected his brother to accompany his men.

What did make Felicia blink and slow,

then halt — balk — on the threshold was the raven-haired beauty in an exquisitely cut riding dress that the marquess — it had to be he — was in the process of lifting down from the back of a superb black Arab.

Viewing the scene from behind her, affection and amused resignation in his tone, Rand murmured, "I might have guessed — Mary's come as well."

"The marchioness?" Felicia's voice had risen to a squeak.

She felt Rand's gaze touch her face, then his hand settled in the small of her back and gently propelled her forward. "Don't worry. Mary will take great delight in befriending you. She's very much one for family."

Fractionally heartened, Felicia walked forward and composed herself, waiting with Rand at the top of the porch steps with her hands clasped before her and a welcoming smile on her face.

She hadn't thought of the point until Rand had mentioned the likelihood of his half brother joining them, but there was no denying she would not be considered a good catch — not for Lord Randolph Cavanaugh. She had no real dowry and no particular prospects of wealth or high social connections to recommend her.

That said, she'd been prepared to accept Rand's assurances that his half brother would welcome her with open arms, but she'd hoped to have time to find her way with the marquess before she had to face his wife.

Felicia felt passingly sure that Lady Mary would take a much dimmer view of a penniless inventor's daughter as Rand's choice of wife.

The marchioness was smiling down at her husband, sharing some joke as she leaned her hands on his broad shoulders and he lifted her effortlessly down to the gravel. For a second, as he steadied her, his hands locked about her tiny waist, and she gazed, still smiling laughingly, up into his face as he looked down at hers, the connection between the pair shone so brilliantly, Felicia felt a pang of yearning. And of hope. The marquess and marchioness had, apparently, been married for some years, yet they still looked at each other like that.

Would she and Rand share that sort of connection? Time, she supposed, would tell.

On releasing his wife, the marquess turned to address his men, instructing them to take their horses and follow Struthers, who had appeared to take the gray's and the Arab's reins.

Meanwhile, patently eager, the marchioness looked about. She hadn't spotted Rand and Felicia before; as her gaze landed on them, waiting on the porch, her face lit with a smile of transparently genuine delight. Tossing the train of her habit over one arm, still beaming, she walked quickly toward them.

Deciding that Lady Mary's delight was most likely occasioned by seeing Rand, girding her loins and stiffening her spine, Felicia, with Rand keeping pace by her side, descended the steps to meet her hopefully soon-to-be sister-in-law.

Lady Mary halted before them. Without even a glance at Rand, her ladyship's vivid cornflower-blue eyes, large and quite striking, fixed on Felicia's face. "Good afternoon, Miss Throgmorton. I'm Mary, Ryder's wife." If anything, the marchioness's delighted smile only grew brighter. "I cannot tell you how positively thrilled I am to meet you." Lady Mary held out her hand; she'd already removed her gloves.

All but blinded by the marchioness's unrestrained friendliness, Felicia lightly grasped Lady Mary's fingers — only to have Mary grip more tightly and draw her into a scented embrace. "I truly am *so very glad,*" Mary whispered in Felicia's ear, then Mary released her and stepped back, her smile now holding a degree of reassurance.

Felicia couldn't hold back; she smiled sincerely and more brightly in return, then she recalled herself and bobbed a curtsy. "Welcome to Throgmorton Hall, my lady."

Mary's eyes promptly narrowed, although they still gleamed with happiness. "No ceremony among family — and please, no 'my ladys.' Just Mary will do." With a swift grin that banished her mock-sternness, she swung to Rand and stretched up to kiss his cheek. "Rand. So at last, you've found your lady." Dropping back to her heels, Mary looked expectantly from one to the other. "Please tell me I can wish you happy."

Rand looked at Felicia. Briefly, she met his gaze, then she looked at Mary and admitted, "We do plan to marry, but we haven't told anyone yet."

"Excellent!" Mary swooped on Felicia again, kissed her cheek, then linked her arm in Felicia's and turned her toward the house. "That is such *wonderful* news!"

Bemused — amused, as she had a shrewd suspicion her would-be sister-in-law intended — Felicia allowed herself to be towed up the steps. Given Mary was shorter than she, once they reached the porch, it was easy enough to keep pace with her, yet as they passed into the front hall, and Felicia indicated the drawing room door, and they continued in that direction, it became clear that Mary favored a much more energetic stride than the languid glide normally favored by high-born ladies.

Flora was waiting in the drawing room to greet their guests. Mary bubbled with effervescent charm. After being introduced to Flora, she turned to Felicia. "I realize you would not have been expecting me. Please don't go to the trouble of making up a separate room — I'm more than happy to share the room you've set aside for Ryder." Her eyes twinkling, she confided, "I would, regardless."

Being of an older generation, Flora was faintly shocked, but Felicia found herself smothering a laugh. Mary was nothing like the censorious, hoity lady she had envisioned.

Then Ryder and Rand walked in, and there were more introductions.

Felicia found her hand held in Ryder's warm clasp as with a lazy smile and transparent sincerity, he welcomed her into the Cavanaugh family. Although his gaze appeared as lazy as his smile, she had a shrewd suspicion his hazel-green eyes saw everything there was to see — and then a bit more.

No matter that Ryder moved slowly and was elegantly dressed, there was no hiding the power in his body — and Felicia received the distinct impression the mind that controlled that power was equally formidable.

Mary and Ryder were a handsome and intrinsically powerful couple, yet they were also assured, confident, and clearly accepted the prospect of Felicia filling the place at Rand's side. Both made no bones about their approval of her, and she realized the only criterion they had for Rand's choice of wife was that Rand had freely chosen her.

Her inner uncertainty faded and, under the consistent, persistent warmth emanating from both Ryder and Mary, eventually dissipated entirely, and she relaxed.

While Mary chatted with Flora, the pair comparing their acquaintances to determine if they had any in common, with Ryder, amused, looking on, Rand seized the moment and bent his head to murmur in Felicia's ear, "Mary is correctly termed a 'force of nature.' Unless she wants to do something you don't want her to, it's easiest to just let her run."

Chuckling, Felicia met his eyes. "So it seems."

Shortly afterward, they were waiting for the tea trolley to be ferried in and Mary was telling Rand, Felicia, and Flora of the latest exploits of her and Ryder's three children, when a soft cough heralded a purring hum — one Rand and Felicia instantly recognized.

Her eyes widening, she met Rand's gaze. "William John's started the engine."

They leapt to their feet — with Ryder and Mary a mere second behind. "Which way?" Mary asked.

"We can go via the terrace." Rand turned in that direction, but even as he took the first step, the purring started to fade.

Fade, not stop.

Felicia seized his sleeve and tugged. "He's driving the carriage around the house."

The four of them rushed into the front hall, with Flora following more slowly. As, her hand in Rand's, Felicia followed him out of the front door, she glanced back and realized the entire household was hot on their heels and making for the porch.

She, Rand, Mary, and Ryder halted at the top of the steps. The rest of the household crowded behind them. As they all looked toward the corner of the house, some of

Ryder's men, along with Struthers and Shields, came running along the edge of the drive, waving and cheering.

Then the carriage came into view, smoothly rolling on its steel-banded wheels around the corner of the house.

Perched behind the steering wheel, William John was smiling fit to burst. He steered the carriage into the forecourt, slowing as he approached the steps.

Then he turned off the engine, and the carriage halted, and he pulled on the brake.

He beamed up at his audience, then spread his arms wide. "I give you the Throgmorton Steam-Powered Horseless Carriage!"

Everyone — literally everyone — whooped and cheered.

Simple happiness and satisfaction permeated the house. All the staff went about with a smile on their faces, while Flora, Felicia, Rand, and William John couldn't stop beaming with a combination of relief and exuberant triumph. Mary and Ryder were pleased for them and added to the joy with an indulgent air.

And as the hours passed and the carriage was further tested and trialed, then driven back into the workshop and locked away, with guards stationed both inside and outside both entrances, a sense of sharp-edged excitement intensified and gripped all those who would travel to the exhibition.

After dinner — served as usual at six o'clock, as they planned an early start the next morning and Mary and Ryder had denied any need to hold back to a more fashionable hour — the company gathered in the drawing room. Mary sat with Flora on the sofa, with Felicia in the armchair at one end. Mary asked Felicia what the exhibition would be like. Felicia had to confess she didn't know, never having attended one before. Between them, they speculated, with Flora adding her assumptions to theirs, but as none of them had the slightest experience of such events, it was all truly guesswork.

Then they noticed that the three men — Rand, Ryder, and William John — were standing before the windows and plainly making plans.

Mary swiveled to view the three, then, in a commanding tone, called, "Gentlemen." When all three swung to look at her, she waved them to the armchairs facing the sofa. "Obviously, it's impossible to make any firm plans without Felicia's and my input, so might I suggest you join us and we make a start?" Her cornflower-blue eyes wide, in all apparent innocence, she continued, "Don't forget you'll need to let Shields and the other men know of our decisions so they'll be ready when required tomorrow and will also know which way to go."

Felicia saw Rand glance at Ryder, but the marquess only smiled amiably and ambled to take the chair opposite his wife. "Indeed, my dear."

Rand followed his brother's lead, with William John, frowning faintly, trailing behind.

Once the men had claimed their seats, the five of them — with Flora adding a comment here and there — worked through the details of their trip. In the main, the discussion was led and directed by Mary — with the acquiescence of her husband and Rand. While they progressed through the stages of the journey, first to Banbury and thence to Birmingham — with William John contributing his estimations of the carriage's likely speed, and all three men spending some time discussing the mounted guards and the possible reaction of the horses to the engine — Felicia took due note.

She couldn't help but smile.

Rand had claimed the armchair alongside Felicia's. After he reported on the accommodation he'd arranged for their party along the way — to general approval — under cover of Mary asking William John what their day at the exhibition might be like, Rand reached across and grasped Felicia's hand where it rested on the chair's arm. He'd noticed the small smile playing over her face. When she glanced his way, he arched his brows. "What is it?"

She studied him for a second, then looked at Mary. "I was thinking that, having seen Mary in action, I now understand how it's done."

He suspected he knew, yet still he asked, "How what's done?"

Felicia's smile deepened, and she met his eyes. "I believe your sister-in-law is teaching me how to manage a husband."

Rand uttered a soft groan. "I should have kept you two far apart."

"Nonsense — she's an excellent teacher."

Rand shook his head in mock-seriousness. "Mary is a highly corrupting influence, at least in the matter of managing." He paused, then slanted Felicia a look from beneath his lashes. "Besides" — he lowered his voice — "when it comes to managing me, you need no instruction. As I recall, you 'managed' exceedingly well last night."

She fought not to laugh, even as a delicate blush tinged her cheeks. "Hush." She threw him a warning look, but he could tell she was quietly pleased.

Rand sat back. He continued to hold her hand, feeling her fingers relaxed and accepting under his. As he listened to his brother, his very dear sister-in-law, and his soon-to-be brother-in-law discussing their expectations of the exhibition, he felt peace with a definite undercurrent of contentment roll through him.

At that moment, his world was perfect — even more perfect than he'd imagined it might be. The Throgmorton steam engine had proved to be an even more impressive invention than anyone could have foreseen, and the lady sitting quietly beside him embodied the promise of a future beyond anything he had dreamed.

Fate — or whatever power it was that ruled the universe — had moved its various cogs and gears into alignment to raise the prospect of the ultimate result.

All they needed to do to claim the ultimate prize, with its many ribbons, was get the Throgmorton Steam-Powered Horseless Carriage to the exhibition on time.

THIRTEEN

The next morning dawned bright and clear, a brilliant summer day in the heart of England's green and leafy land. After an early breakfast, the party traveling to the exhibition gathered in the forecourt, packed and ready to depart.

Although Mary had ridden the relatively short distance from Raventhorne the previous day, Ryder had ordered their traveling coach to follow, and it had arrived later that afternoon. Now, with its team of four horses between the shafts, the coach stood ready on the gravel. The footmen piled Mary's, Ryder's, Rand's, Felicia's, and William John's bags into the boot or lashed them onto the roof behind the coachman.

Then the guards, all mounted and wearing livery — tabards displaying the Raventhorne coat of arms — came clopping down the path from the stable. The Hall household, gathered about Flora on the front porch, chattered and watched. The rising tide of excitement was palpable, investing swift smiles and the rush of action as everyone hurried to take their place.

As per their deliberations the previous evening, their company formed up in a small cavalcade. It had been decided four riders — three of Ryder's men plus Shields — would lead the way, followed, at what they hoped would be a safe enough distance of one to two hundred yards, by the steam-powered horseless carriage, with William John at the wheel.

Rand would sit beside William John, at least for the first leg of the journey, but Ryder, Felicia, and Mary had all stated their wish to ride with William John at some point. All were eager to experience the thrill of bowling along with no horse before them.

Behind the horseless carriage, separated again by a few hundred yards, would come four more mounted guards, closely followed by the traveling coach, with a pair of outriders bringing up the rear.

Ryder handed Mary, then Felicia, up into the coach, then shut the door; he'd elected to ride and, if need be, act as a messenger back and forth along their line.

Mary and Felicia promptly hung out of

the windows, just in time to see Rand stride up.

Rand met Felicia's eyes, then he looked at Ryder. "Ready?"

"Quite." Ryder smiled his lazy smile. "We're an impressive sight."

Rand turned to look along the line, then nodded. "Indeed, and now" — he swung to grin at Mary and Felicia — "it's time we got under way." His expression sobered and turned determined. "Keep your eyes peeled." With that and a brief salute, he strode back up the line.

Ryder, too, saluted Mary and Felicia, then gathered the reins of his huge gray hunter and swung up to the saddle.

Distantly, they heard the clatter of horses moving off, then came the soft cough followed by a purring hum they now recognized as the steam-powered engine starting up.

Mary and Felicia exchanged a look, then both shifted to the other side of the carriage and hung out of the windows to peer ahead and witness the moment. Courtesy of the curve of the drive, they could see the steam-powered carriage, with William John behind the wheel; as the first group of riders had disappeared between the avenue's trees, the steam carriage was now at the head of the line.

Rand climbed up to the seat and sat beside William John. The steam carriage purred for another minute — no doubt to let the advance guards get far enough ahead for the horses not to be spooked by the engine — then William John adjusted a lever and the sound of the engine changed; he released the brake, and with a small lurch and the crunch of gravel under its wheels, the steam carriage rattled off.

The company assembled on the porch gave vent to a resounding cheer.

William John and Rand responded with triumphant grins and waves.

Smiling more broadly than she ever had, Felicia watched the steam carriage roll out of sight down the drive, then she sat back, settling against the luxurious leather seat. She saw her own excitement reflected in Mary's bright-eyed smile and admitted, "This feels like a dream that I hadn't dared to dream actually coming true. Until Rand arrived, and even in the weeks after that while we struggled to get the invention working as it should, I could never quite imagine that we would ever reach this point — setting off for the exhibition with a working engine leading the way."

Mary continued to smile, but faintly — almost wryly — arched her brows. Her gaze drifted to the window beyond which Ryder sat his horse, waiting for the guards ahead of the traveling coach to move off. "One thing you can say about the Cavanaughs," she confided, "is that they are dogged and never give up."

Felicia considered that, then inclined her head. "Those certainly seem to be family traits."

Then Ryder called an order, and the coach lurched into motion. Mary shifted to the window alongside which her husband was riding, and Felicia quit the rear-facing seat to sit beside Mary.

Felicia straightened her skirts, then sat back. Her gaze passed over the trees lining the drive.

Keep your eyes peeled.

There — among the shadows.

She blinked, then stared. As the carriage rolled on, she turned to look back, trying to spot what she thought she'd seen.

"What is it?" Mary asked.

Felicia frowned. "I thought I saw someone lurking in the wood, but . . ." With a sigh, she sat back and faced forward. "When I looked again, there was no one there. I must have imagined it."

"Shall I tell Ryder?" Mary asked. "He'll stop, and he and the guards can search."

Felicia thought for a moment, then shook her head. "It might have been a curious farmworker or some such person, and it doesn't matter now — we're on our way." She glanced at Mary and smiled. "Besides, we should keep as close as possible behind the steam carriage — we don't want anyone slipping in between."

"True." Mary settled against the seat. "If anyone wants to sabotage the engine, they'll have to catch us first and then go through the guards." Her smile turned edged. "They'll never manage that, so, I believe, we can relax on that score."

After seeing the men Ryder had brought as guards, Felicia had to admit that was a reasonable assessment and conclusion.

As they rolled out of the drive and turned onto the lane leading away from the village, then almost immediately turned right onto the lane heading north toward Oxford and Banbury beyond, she imagined how their cavalcade would appear to all those they passed.

Imagined how the Throgmorton Steam-Powered Horseless Carriage would look to others — like a fantastical machine from the future.

As she swayed with the motion of the carriage, she inwardly sighed, touched by a combination of happiness and sadness as she thought of her father.

It was an abiding pity he hadn't lived to see this moment — to see William John complete the invention and drive it off to the exhibition. How proud her father would have been of William John.

And, perhaps, of her.

Standing cloaked in shadows, Clive Mayhew watched the Throgmorton machine rumble down the drive. One small part of him cursed, but a larger part of his mind was fascinated.

Enthralled.

As for the rest of his mind, that had taken a firm stand, lecturing and hectoring him on his fall from grace.

He now deeply distrusted his uncle's stance. And despite the black cloud of despair and desperation that hung over his own head, he was nevertheless increasingly sure that for his own sake, he needed to pull back and step away from the action he'd agreed to undertake. To turn aside from that particular path to monetary salvation.

His attempt to seize Miss Throgmorton had been calculated to bring about his uncle's desired end without physical harm to any person or, indeed, to the machine, even though he hadn't, at that time, set eyes on it.

The thwarting of that attempt — the manner in which it had been thwarted — had shaken him. He'd seen the looks on both Cavanaugh's and Miss Throgmorton's faces, signaling their contempt and his loss of all gentlemanly status in their eyes.

Their expressions had haunted him. Had started the voice in his head niggling, asking questions such as *What sort of man are you?* And some deeply buried part of him had surfaced and warned that there was no point erasing his debts if, in the process, he lost all standing in his world — and, most especially, with himself.

He hadn't thought of himself as overburdened with morals, yet in that moment when Cavanaugh and Miss Throgmorton had looked at him, his inner self had flinched. Had cringed. And he'd turned and run away.

Now, as he listened to what he realized was a quite fascinating advance in steam-powered carriages hum its way toward the exhibition in Birmingham, he felt that deeply buried part of him strengthen and take firmer hold.

He set his jaw, then softly reiterated, "I'm not going to do it."

He waited to see how clinging to that resolution of yesterday felt — whether it still fitted him, the man he truly was. And it did; it resonated and felt right.

He drew in a breath, slowly exhaled, and felt immeasurably better — lighter — than he had.

He was, thank heaven, a complete failure when it came to illicit and underhanded sabotage. In reality, he felt more comforted than bothered by that conclusion. How he would pay his debts, he didn't know, but he would find some way — some legitimate way. Some way that wouldn't make him ashamed to be Clive Mayhew.

Perhaps he could grow serious about his sketching. His family had never encouraged him to think his sketches worth anything, but Cavanaugh and the Throgmorton ladies had thought them better than merely good. The *London News* used his sketches here and there, but they didn't want art so much as recognizable depictions of this or that, and they didn't pay much. Perhaps he should gird his loins and offer his private portfolio to some art dealer and see what might come of it?

One way or another, he would find a way.

The mounted guards and the traveling coach had followed the steam carriage and were now long gone. The Hall's household had returned indoors, and the stable-man had retreated to the stable. Clive turned and quietly made his way out of the wood, eventually emerging onto the lane.

Now what?

He stood in the lane and debated. Given his new direction, his first move should be to free himself from all ties to his uncle's scheme. "I'd better tell the old codger that I won't be doing his dirty work."

He grimaced at the thought of going back to London. He rather fancied remaining in the country until he had added substantially to his portfolio, so he would have some hope of securing cash quickly on his return to town, the better to keep Quire at bay, at least long enough to test the waters with some art dealers.

He'd been gazing, unseeing, along the lane the steam carriage, the horsemen, and the traveling coach had taken; as, frowning, he refocused, he realized he didn't have to go to London — his uncle would be at the exhibition in Birmingham in two days' time.

His resolution firmed. "I'll go to the exhibition, find him, and tell him — then I'll see if I can get a closer look at the

Throgmorton engine and whatever other machines are on show."

He'd recognized the tug he'd felt as the steam-powered engine, gleaming in the well of the carriage, had puttered past. It was the same tug he felt when he saw certain buildings in certain landscapes. For some odd reason, his artist self was attracted to the new machines.

"Who knows?" Turning, he continued down the lane toward the track along which he'd left the gig he'd hired. "Sketching mechanical inventions might be the next big thing."

Later that night, Felicia lay in the bed in her room in the Reinedeer Inn in Banbury and listened to the creaks as the timbers of the old inn settled. The footsteps that, earlier, had tramped past her door had faded, and silence had descended on the upper floors. If she strained her ears, she could dimly hear the distant sounds of revelry issuing from the taproom.

Relaxing between the crisply laundered sheets, she let her mind wander. In retrospect, the day had passed in a curious mix of excitement and enforced patience.

She, Mary, and Ryder had not only taken turns riding beside William John in the horseless carriage, but also, at her brother's insistence — after he'd taught Rand how to drive the engine to the point that Rand had tooled the steam-powered carriage along the winding lanes with increasing confidence — they had each been taught to steer and manage the engine. To their considerable surprise, it hadn't proved that difficult, and each of them had thoroughly enjoyed their moments behind the steering wheel.

Passing through villages had also been a thrill; people had dropped what they were doing and rushed to watch the horseless carriage putter past. More often than not, the steam carriage had been cheered on, certainly by the children, who had thought it a great lark to run alongside and shout questions. Only a few ancients had scowled and raised their fists. Most other adults had contented themselves with staring in wonder, then, once the steam carriage had passed, shaking their heads and returning to their interrupted tasks.

In contrast to the thrills and excitement, riding in the closed coach for hours on end had been enervating. It had also left her with plenty of time to imagine possible attempts to sabotage the engine while they were resting overnight at the inn.

But when the traveling coach had rocked

to a halt in the inn's yard and she and Mary had been helped down to the cobbles by Rand, she'd seen the steam carriage being pushed into a barn and heard Ryder issuing orders to his men, setting a rotation of groups of four men at a time to watch the carriage. On top of that, William John had looked around the barn, seen the hay bales stacked along one side, and announced his intention of sleeping there, within sight and sound of the precious invention.

Rand had exchanged a look with her, and neither they nor Ryder and Mary had argued.

Although there'd been plenty of light still remaining in the day, none of them had felt any desire to wander the town. Instead, they'd eaten an early dinner in the splendor of the inn's Globe Room, which dated from Elizabethan times — as did a great deal of the half-timbered inn — then they'd spent an hour going over their plans for the next day and their arrival in Birmingham.

She was dwelling on their decision to take the road through Stratford-on-Avon, rather than swing farther north to the larger highway through Warwick, when a soft knock sounded on her door. She hesitated for only a second, then thrust back the covers and, the wooden floor cold beneath her bare feet, pattered across to the panel. "Yes?" she softly inquired.

"It's me — Rand."

She unbolted the door and held it open while he slipped inside, then she closed the panel and slid the bolt home again. She turned to him as his hands closed about her waist, hard palms burning through the fine linen of her nightgown.

He looked into her eyes and arched a brow. "Do you mind if I stay?"

She smiled and raised her arms to drape them over his shoulders. "Of course not." As she stepped into him and stretched up on her toes, her lips hungry for his, she murmured, "I hoped you would come."

As she pressed her lips to his, she felt his curve, then they firmed, and the kiss deepened, and he waltzed her and her greedy senses into the flames of what was becoming a familiar and welcome fire.

He'd shared her bed for the past four nights, and she'd already grown accustomed to having him there.

As he steered her back until her legs met the mattress, she gave thanks that Flora had deemed the presence of Mary, Felicia's soon-to-be sister-in-law, as well as that of Rand, her all-but-announced fiancé, sufficient chaperonage in the circumstances and had elected to remain and hold the fort at the Hall.

Mentally blessing Flora for her sense, Felicia set her fingers to Rand's neckerchief. "You're wearing far too many clothes."

He didn't bother replying, instead devoting himself to rectifying that situation.

Then he drew her into his arms, kissed her with undiluted passion, closed his fists in the folds of her nightgown, then he broke from the kiss, stepped back, and drew the garment off over her head.

Hot as a flame, his gaze streaked over her. Before the nightgown even hit the floor, flicked loose from his fingers before he reached for her, she was in his arms, crushed to him, skin to naked skin, and they were burning.

With that delicious flame she'd come to crave.

He took her down to the bed, and they rolled across the sheets, seizing and savoring, seeking and claiming.

Neither felt any need to rein in their rampant desires; both gave the moments their all — their undivided attention and their unstinting commitment. Him to her, and her to him.

Through gasps and smothered cries, through moans and achingly guttural groans, giving and taking and sharing.

At the end, when, exhausted, wrung out, and deeply sated, they lay side by side on their backs in the bed, they each turned their head and met the other's gaze — sank into the emotions dwelling there — then softly smiled.

She rolled onto her side, into him. He raised one arm and draped it about her, drawing her closer, and she settled her head on his chest, her hand splayed over his still-thudding heart.

A minute passed, then he reached down and drew the coverlet over their cooling limbs.

She settled her head, then murmured, "We're nearly there. I'm still not sure this isn't a dream."

He pressed a kiss to her hair. "No dream. We — William John, you, and I — have worked for this. One more day, then we'll see what success we can wring from our endeavors."

Her thoughts returned to her earlier consideration of the next day's route. After a moment, she ventured, "Do you think, as we approach Birmingham, that the danger to the steam carriage — the potential for attack — might increase?"

Rand didn't immediately dismiss the idea.

However, after considering the likely scenarios, he murmured, "I can't say for certain, but I think there are several points that will work in our favor and make it unlikely that any attempt at sabotage will be essayed at this late stage — at least, not on the road. Just as we are, all the other inventors with exhibits will be coming into Birmingham tomorrow. As the exhibition hall doesn't open until noon, I doubt any inventors will have brought their inventions into town early — fearing tampering before they get their invention safely into the hall. But all exhibitors must have their inventions in place by six o'clock, so all the other inventors will be converging on the exhibition hall, as focused on getting their inventions onto the hall floor at much the same time as we will be — I can't imagine any will have time to spare to think about causing problems for us."

She shifted on his chest. "That's the other inventors. What about people they or others might have hired — like Mayhew?"

"That's the second point working in our favor. The horses have grown used to the steam engine. You might not have noticed, but from after lunch, as we traveled, Ryder gradually brought his men and their mounts closer and closer to the steam carriage. By the time we traveled up Horsefair to this place, the horses were treating the steam carriage as if it was any other carriage." She looked up, and he met her gaze. "Tomorrow, the guards will travel much closer, especially as we come into Birmingham. That will make it all but impossible to approach the engine closely enough to do it any damage."

He smiled. "And as we'll make straight for the exhibition hall, there'll be no later chance for anyone to tamper with it. The organizers of the exhibition are well aware of the potential threats — they know their reputation depends on them keeping all the inventions safe overnight and through the exhibition. They'll have guards everywhere."

"So once we place the steam carriage on the exhibition floor — essentially, placing it into the organizers' hands — we can be assured it will remain safe?"

He pulled an equivocal face. "Theoretically, yes. But the exhibition itself is liable to be crowded, so we'll have our own guards in place as well, to ensure the engine remains safe throughout, but until the exhibition ends and we take the steam carriage out of the hall, its safety remains the responsibility of the organizers. Once it leaves the hall, it becomes our responsibility again, but as the presentation of the invention will have been accomplished, I can't see anyone bothering to make an attempt at sabotage then. There would be no point."

"Ah. I see." She smothered a yawn.

He settled her more comfortably against him. Within seconds, he felt her limbs relaxing, growing that telltale touch heavier. He brushed his lips across her temple. "Did you enjoy your driving lesson?"

He felt her lips curve.

"Yes. It was . . . exhilarating. I can understand why William John is so in alt."

Rand smiled to himself as her words trailed away and her limbs grew heavier yet. Seconds later, she was asleep.

Still smiling, he closed his eyes and sensed a satisfaction that glowed bone deep, deep enough to wreathe about his soul.

He, too, was in alt, but his contentment owed nothing to any invention.

He owed his state to the woman in his arms and to the emotion that had prompted him to set aside his prejudice against clever ladies and understand all she was, and all she meant and would mean to him.

Feeling her weight soft and safe and secure in his arms, still inwardly smiling, he surrendered to sleep.

Although, the following day, their party set out with every member infected by heightened alertness, as Rand had predicted, the journey from Banbury to Birmingham passed without incident. They maintained their vigilant cavalcade into the bustle of the busy town, passing along Digbeth and around the famous Bull Ring marketplace, around St. Martin's Circus, then puttering and clattering all the way up New Street to Victoria Square and the Town Hall, in which the exhibition was to be held.

The Town Hall was a memorable building. They pulled up outside, and Rand alighted from the steam carriage. After one glance at the organizers waiting with their lists before the steps, he went to the traveling coach, reaching it in time to hand Felicia down. He noted her survey of the building and murmured, "It was designed by the inventor of the Hansom Cab — Joseph Hansom. He modeled it on the Temple of Castor and Pollux in Rome."

Standing beside Ryder and Mary, who had joined her on the pavement, Felicia studied the colonnaded façade with a critical eye, while Rand went with William John to speak with the organizers. A ramp had been erected over one side of the steps leading into the building. After registering their arrival and receiving instructions, Rand and William John returned, and with the help of all the men, pushed the Throgmorton Steam-Powered Horseless Carriage up the ramp and into the foyer of the exhibition hall. More organizers were waiting there to take charge of each invention. They had a small army of porters, some of whom were directed to take the steam carriage away. A small man, swathed in a gray dustcoat and with round spectacles perched on his button nose, directed six porters. "Down the aisle to the space reserved for it — number twenty-four."

The porters nodded and took charge, carefully pushing the steam carriage on through the foyer and into the exhibition hall.

Although the hall's double doors stood open, from where the Throgmorton party had been halted behind a cordon, they couldn't see into the space.

William John stared after the disappearing steam carriage, a pained expression on his face.

Felicia put a hand on his sleeve. "All the

porters are wearing gloves — did you notice?"

"They are?" William John blinked, looked around to confirm that, then reluctantly conceded, "I suppose they have to take the best of care."

"Indeed." Felicia linked her arm with his and drew him inexorably away.

They returned to the horses and traveling coach. Rand and William John joined Felicia and Mary inside the coach, and their now-much-less-impressive party headed back into the town, retracing their route to the Old Crown Inn.

The inn was crowded; it was fortunate that Rand had sent Shields days before to reserve rooms for them. As Shields had used Ryder's title, the rooms they were shown to were among the best the inn had to offer, well-appointed and comfortable.

Their party gathered for dinner in a private dining room. Ryder had ensured that all the men had been summoned to join them.

At Rand's suggestion, they applied themselves to the tasty meal served by their hosts; only when the plates had been emptied and jugs of ale had done the rounds of the long table did he and Ryder turn to the task of organizing the watches on the steam carriage during the exhibition and on leaving the hall at the end of the event.

Seated beside Mary, the pair of them flanked by Rand and Ryder, Felicia listened as Rand, Ryder, and William John discussed the potential weaknesses in the organizers' arrangements.

"The official guards will be there until the end of the day, but there are only so many of them, and exhibitions such as this are always crowded," Rand said. "There'll be streams of people — not just inventors and investors, but all sorts of interested members of the public, even children — passing up and down the room and milling around the inventions."

William John, seated opposite Felicia, frowned. "Not in the morning, though." He screwed up his face in concentration. "I can't remember." He looked at Rand. "Is that right?"

Rand nodded. His expression serious, he glanced around the table at all the men. "Although it's the organizers' responsibility to keep the hall and all the inventions in it secure until the end of the exhibition, once the doors open to the public at one o'clock, I strongly suspect the organizers' guards will be overwhelmed. However, I believe we can place our faith in the organizers and their guards until one o'clock. In addition, the exhibitors — in our case, William John and me — must report to the hall at ten o'clock. Between ten and twelve, the organizers and their team of assessors examine the inventions, and William John and I need to be present throughout that time."

"But you don't need extra guards through those hours." Ryder looked at Rand for confirmation.

"No, we don't. We'll both be there, beside the steam carriage, waiting to show the assessors around it and demonstrate how it operates, and while some of the other inventors might leave their exhibits and mill around, there won't be so many that, between us, we won't be able to keep an eye on them all." Rand glanced at William John. "Between twelve and one o'clock, William John and I will remain with the steam carriage, just to be sure."

Sober and serious, William John nodded.

Rand turned to survey Ryder's men. "After that, however, immediately the doors open to the public at one o'clock, we will need you — about five or even six at a time — to stand guard around the steam carriage."

Shields glanced at the other guards. "Right, then." He looked at Rand. "We've enough of us to stand six at a time. We'll rotate so that we each get a chance to take a gander at the other machines on show, if that'll suit?"

Rand inclined his head. "Indeed."

"So," Shields went on, "we're to keep all the punters away from the steam engine?"

"They can look," William John said, "but you'll need to keep them sufficiently far back that they can't touch."

"Either William John or I will be there throughout the exhibition," Rand said, "standing before the steam carriage to answer any questions." He paused, then went on, "Even though, prior to the public viewing, the steam carriage will have been examined by the assessors and demonstrated to them, establishing that it works, the most critical point at which our invention must shine is when we have our chance to present it to Prince Albert — so tampering or sabotage remains a real threat until the steam carriage is successfully presented to the Prince." Rand glanced around at the men. "Albert is scheduled to arrive at half past two. After the usual welcome speeches, he'll start examining the exhibits, commencing from the first exhibit on the left and progressing down that side of the hall to the end, before returning along the other side."

Rand looked at William John. "We're number twenty-four, and I believe there are fifty exhibits in all." Looking at the men, he said, "I managed to get a glimpse of the plan of the exhibits. The hall is a long rectangle, and the exhibits are arranged against the two long sides, leaving a wide central aisle. The steam engine's spot is almost at the end of the hall on the left side."

The men all frowned, envisaging the hall in their minds' eyes.

Ryder asked, "Are there any side halls or annexes opening from the main hall?"

"None that were marked on the organizers' plan." Rand frowned faintly, then offered, "I've been in the hall before, and as far as I recall, it's just one large rectangular hall. There may be doors here and there, but no other spaces open from it."

Ryder sat back. "If the exhibits are arranged more or less against the walls, that makes protecting them from any interference from the passing crowd easier." Touching a finger to the condensation on his ale glass, he drew a line on the wooden tabletop. "Here's the wall, and here" — he drew a rectangle beside it — "is the steam carriage. If we place a cordon of men in a shallow arc extending to either side, virtually to each of the neighboring exhibits, then we'll block anyone approaching the steam carriage from either side. No one will be able to slip behind it, even if the two of you are distracted by others asking questions."

Rand, William John, Ryder, and the other men fell to discussing the precise placement of the guards. Watching them, Felicia felt a seductive sense of relief — surely, with so many focused on protecting the steam carriage, nothing would go wrong.

The knowledge that, in the matter of failing, they were approaching the last hurdle hovered at the back of her mind.

Beside Felicia, Mary murmured, "Ryder and I are acquainted with Albert. It would likely be some sort of royal solecism were we not to present ourselves to him at some point in the proceedings." She glanced at Felicia and met her eyes. "The question is, what would be the most useful point at which to step forward and make our presence known?"

Much struck, Felicia arched her brows. "What would you suggest?"

At that moment, the placements of the guards was resolved to all the men's satisfaction. Mary leaned forward and asked Rand, "What happens after the Prince arrives? You said there would be the usual speeches, then he'll speak with the exhibitors — there must be some sort of protocol in place."

Rand shrugged. "From what I've seen in the past, Albert speaks with each inventor, and they explain their invention to him. He'll move down the line, but he will linger if some invention catches his eye. Then he'll spend longer, asking questions and examining the machine."

"The public will be milling about — I imagine the Prince's equerries will be there, keeping the hoi polloi at a distance." Mary's eyes had narrowed, as if examining the scene in her mind. "We're acquainted with Albert, and it would be odd if we were there but didn't greet him — his people will recognize us and not seek to prevent us from doing so. From what you say, it seems as if the best time to engage him — to encourage him to focus on the Throgmorton exhibit — will be as he finishes with the invention before. Whatever the number twenty-three exhibit is."

Ryder had shifted to study his wife. He caught her eye and cocked a brow at her. "You think to charm Albert into paying special attention to the Throgmorton exhibit."

Mary nodded decisively. "Exactly."

Rand straightened in his seat. "Actually, that might work out especially well." Across the table, he met William John's eyes. "I was wondering how to get the pressure up in time to demonstrate the full capacity of the engine." To the others, he said, "Once the engine is turned on — the coal ignited — it takes a few minutes for the steam pressure to build. But the organizers' rules state that we're not allowed to turn on the engine until the Prince is finished with the previous invention and turns our way." Rand looked at Mary, including Ryder with his gaze. "If you two step in the instant Albert's finished with number twenty-three, and chat, charm, and delay him, then William John can push the start button the instant Albert turns our way —"

"And by the time we release him, and he reaches you and William John, the steam carriage will be primed and ready for its demonstration." Mary grinned. "Consider it done."

Felicia grinned, too; it was clear that her soon-to-be sister-in-law was delighted to have carved out an active role for herself and her husband in their plans to present the Throgmorton steam carriage to best advantage.

"That will be perfect." Enthused, William John met Rand's eyes, eagerness in every line of his face. "If we have the pressure properly up, then if the Prince shows interest, we'll be able to take him for a short drive."

Rand, Felicia, Mary, and Ryder — the four of the company who had already experienced the thrill of driving the steam carriage or even being driven in it — fell silent as they considered how someone like Albert, with a known penchant for new inventions, would respond to such an experience, however curtailed . . .

"That," Rand said, his tone suggesting he was contemplating an unexpected windfall, "would set the seal on the steam carriage's success."

William John looked from one to the other. "Then let's do it — there's no reason we can't ask if he would like to go for a drive."

Everyone agreed.

"How long does the public showing go for?" Mary asked.

"Until six o'clock." Rand caught Ryder's eye, then glanced at the men. "At the end, it'll be left to us to remove the steam carriage and get it safely away."

That necessitated another round of discussion and planning.

Eventually, with the manner of their departure, steam carriage and all, from the

Town Hall decided, Shields said, "I've spoken with the innkeeper, just to confirm — when I was here earlier, he said we could use his coach house to store the steam carriage overnight as the doors have a lock. Seems there's no problem with that — I took a look, and the building will do well enough."

"The steam carriage will fit?" William John asked.

Shields nodded. "Plenty of room."

Regardless of any lock, Ryder and Rand set a roster for guarding the steam carriage over the following night.

With all decided and arranged as far as it could be, with an atmosphere of quiet confidence infusing the company, the men pushed back from the table and, with nods to their various employers, went off to find their beds. William John bade everyone a vague farewell and followed the men from the private room.

Ryder, Mary, Rand, and Felicia rose and followed the others more slowly.

With Felicia's arm tucked in his, as he and she followed Ryder and Mary up the stairs, Rand murmured, "I plan to survey the other inventions presented to determine if any are worthwhile investing in. Exhibitions such as this are often a good source of future projects" — he caught her eye — "and I would like you to assess them with me." He smiled. "I would appreciate picking your brains regarding any problems you see in the designs, and also what strengths you perceive in the concepts."

Felicia felt contentment well and wash through her. She inclined her head. "I'll be happy to oblige."

"Depending on the interest the steam carriage garners," Rand went on, "I might be able to make some time before the Prince approaches, but once Albert's finished with us and the greater part of the crowd's attention moves on with him, I should definitely have time to wander the other exhibits and investigate their potential."

She nodded as they stepped into the upper corridor and turned toward her room. That he valued her mind and her insights into inventions beyond the steam carriage could not have been clearer. "While you're busy," she said, "I can make a round of the exhibits myself and see what I can discern."

"Do." He squeezed her hand, then, as they paused outside her door, he looked to right and left along the currently deserted corridor. Then he met her eyes. "Should I go to my room and return later? Or . . . ?"

Her smile grew radiant. "No." She shifted

her fingers, gripped and tugged his hand. While it was reassuring that he valued her mind, to be wanted for her body was another delight. "We're affianced. You're mine, and I'm yours, and that's all there is to it."

His answering smile warmed her heart.

He reached around her and opened the door. She walked in and drew him with her.

Their lovemaking that night was a scintillating mixture of the tender and the torrid.

Tender in the way they started, with long, gentle kisses that stretched their senses and heralded a slow slide into rising passion; torrid in the final moments, when heat and hunger geysered and drove them, before passion exploded, their senses dissolved, and ecstasy claimed them.

Finally, with oblivion beckoning, they slumped to the sheets, their skins dewed, hers rosy with sated desire.

Their breathing ragged, they lay on their backs, side by side, and waited for the tumult of their hearts to subside.

Despite the tug of satiation, they were both, it seemed, as yet too keyed up to slide willingly into slumber.

After several minutes, Rand drew up the sheet. They settled beneath it, still lying shoulder to shoulder.

Felicia tilted her head, resting it on his shoulder. "We're nearly there, aren't we? It's all falling into place."

Beneath the sheet, his fingers found hers; gently, he stroked his thumb over the back of her hand. "Yes." He paused, then added, "In more ways than one." He felt her gaze brush his face and went on, "The moment tomorrow when the Prince views the steam carriage is shaping to be one of those fraught instances — those particular moments in time on which so very much depends."

Her fingers curled with his, and she snuggled closer. "The invention itself and all that flows from that. Your reputation with your investors, the outcome of your investment and theirs, William John's reputation, his future prospects, the prospects for me and our family, the future of the Hall and our household." She gripped his hand. "Far-reaching, indeed."

After a moment, he said, "I know the steam engine works — that it is a vast improvement over what existed previously. I know we've taken every possible step to keep it safe, so that it can be presented as a working invention to the Prince tomorrow. Yet . . ."

Her head moved on his shoulder as,

slowly, she nodded, then — softly, wryly — she huffed out a laugh. "It appears that's another trait we share." She looked up as he looked down. She searched his eyes, then her lips gently curved. "Neither of us, it seems, is at all comfortable taking things for granted and trusting to Fate."

He grunted, then let his head fall back and looked up at the ceiling. "Trusting to Fate is not my strength, especially not when so much is at stake."

"Realistically," she murmured, "this could still end in tears."

"Sadly, with inventions, there is always a risk they'll blow up in your face."

"In this case, as I well know, that's a literal prospect."

They fell silent, then he raised their linked hands and settled them in the center of his chest. "There's one thing we've found, one thing we've secured, that I hope that fraught moment tomorrow won't affect — won't change or alter — regardless of the outcome."

Her breath wafting warm and soft against his skin, she murmured, "You and me. And this. That's already ours, and no one and nothing — no turn of events, however catastrophic — can take it from us."

He raised her hand and pressed a kiss to

her knuckles. "Regardless of what happens, we go on together."

She nodded. "Together. Into whatever future awaits us, regardless of the vagaries of Fate."

He glanced down, but could only see her red-gold curls. "We haven't discussed our future."

"No — and both you and I would rather not. Not at this juncture, this moment of waiting to see what tomorrow brings, whether it be wild success or bitter disappointment." She paused, then, her voice gaining in confident certainty, went on, "We know our future is there. It won't disappear if we leave it unaddressed for another day, and I — and you — would rather that when we do eventually come to consider it, we can devote our full attention to it. To us, to defining what we want."

Her resolve, her agreement, dispersed his lingering uncertainty — his nebulous need to seize and hold and make sure of her above all else. Slowly, he nodded. "When this rather major distraction is over, we'll focus all our energies on defining our future."

"Done." She snuggled down, curling into his side. "Let's leave our personal discussion until the exhibition is over, and you and I have done everything we can to ensure our efforts reap the ultimate reward. Then we can turn to 'defining us' with utterly clear consciences."

He smiled, because in that — in needing to feel their duty properly done — he and she were also alike.

The exchange had settled them. Their way forward decided, their minds finally relaxed, along with their already lax limbs.

He drew her fingers to his lips once more and pressed a soft kiss to her knuckles. "To success," he whispered.

"To success," she breathed.

And they closed their eyes and let Morpheus take them.

FOURTEEN

Felicia had had no idea that viewing inventions had become such a popular pastime with the general public.

When she, Mary, and Ryder, along with Shields and the other guards, arrived at the Town Hall a few minutes before one o'clock, it was to discover an eye-openingly large crowd thronging the foyer before the exhibition hall's doors.

There were ladies in bonnets leaning on the arms of gentlemen attired for a day about town. There were merchants in their best suits, their wives sliding glances at other ladies' gowns, as well as many men Felicia took for tradesmen, in less well-fitting jackets and with many sporting flat caps. She spotted more than a few apprentices in their coats; along with everyone else, their expressions stated they were eager to get through the doors and look upon what lay inside.

"Good gracious!" Mary blew out a frustrated breath and came up on her toes to peer around. Then she tugged at Ryder's sleeve and pointed to the side. "There's a secondary door over there. Perhaps we can slip in."

Tending grim, Ryder obliged, and, with a glance commanding their men to follow, he escorted Felicia and Mary in the right direction. "I don't like this," Ryder stated. "Rand will need our men in place before these people, one and all, descend."

It transpired that Rand had had the same notion. As they approached the secondary door, it started to open.

From the other side, still out of their sight, some man squeaked, "Lord Cavanaugh — I must protest! Everyone is supposed to come through the main doors so that we may count heads."

"Indeed?" Rand's tone was even, yet chilling. "Am I to take it that the committee is prepared to assume full responsibility for any damage the crowd may do before the guards I have organized, who are somewhere in the foyer, reach our exhibit and get into place?"

An irascible mumble came in reply.

"I thought not." Rand hauled the door fully open.

"We're here." Ryder drew Mary and Felicia to one side and waved the men in. "Go and get into position."

Rand held the door open and pointed. "That way. You'll find the steam carriage and Mr. Throgmorton close to the end of the aisle."

The men ducked their heads and streamed past Rand and on down the hall. Felicia, Mary, and Ryder brought up the rear.

Just then, others outside noticed them vanishing into the hall. There were cries and people came running.

Rand slammed the door shut, and Ryder whirled to help him throw the heavy bolts.

Ignoring the thuds on the door and the muffled demands for it to be opened — that it was almost time — Rand turned to the official, now distinctly choleric and inclined to view them all severely. Coolly, Rand waved at Ryder and Mary. "The Marquess and Marchioness of Raventhorne."

The official goggled, then paled.

Felicia glanced at Ryder and Mary and struggled to swallow a laugh. She'd never seen either look so coldly and arrogantly aloof. They both looked down on the official — quite a feat for Mary given her lack of height — then Mary glanced at Rand. "I take it the inventions are farther along."

Dismissing the official with an extremely distant nod, Ryder placed his hand at the back of Mary's waist. "I believe that's correct, my dear. Shall we see?"

As they stepped toward the central aisle — and the officious official exhaled with poorly concealed relief — the clock in the Town Hall's tower chimed, tolling for one o'clock. To their left, other officials hauled open the main doors, and the crowd streamed in.

Just ahead of the first wave, Rand, with Felicia's hand tucked in his arm, followed by Ryder and Mary, swiftly strode down the aisle to where their men had taken up their positions in front of and flanking the Throgmorton Steam-Powered Horseless Carriage.

The four of them halted before the exhibit. Felicia took in the gleaming steam carriage, with William John, remarkably neat and wearing a spotless gray coat, standing proudly before it, and felt tears prickle. She blinked rapidly. She clutched Rand's hand; her gaze on the sight before her, she said, "Papa would have been so very proud."

She felt Rand's gaze on her face, then he ducked his head and murmured, "You should tell William John."

She swallowed the lump emotion had set in her throat, drew her hand from Rand's, stepped up to her brother, and did.

William John's face creased in a fond smile. He met her gaze, and for just a second, she glimpsed the big brother who had played with her in the workshop all those many years before.

Then two well-dressed gentlemen came forward, clearly wishing to speak with William John.

Felicia smiled at the pair and stepped back, releasing her brother to them; she supposed this was one of the major purposes of such an exhibition — to spread word of the invention far and wide.

She walked the few paces to where Rand, Ryder, and Mary stood a little to the side; the brothers, both tall enough to see over most heads, were apparently scrutinizing the security arrangements of other exhibitors.

"The cordons help," Rand said.

Felicia looked and saw that most exhibits had been cordoned off by thick gold-colored ropes suspended from metal stands.

Ryder humphed. "Looks like you were the only one able to get your guards in ahead of the crowd."

In front of many of the larger exhibits, guards were still pushing their way out of the body of the crowd and climbing over the golden ropes to take up their positions.

"Obviously," Mary said, "all inventors take the business of protecting their inventions seriously." She glanced inquiringly at Rand. "While I can understand the threats to the steam carriage, I hadn't realized the problem was widespread."

"It can be a cutthroat business," Rand replied. He'd been watching William John deal with the gentlemen who had approached, and who had now been joined by several others; Rand and their group were close enough to hear William John's confident explanation of the improvements made to Russell's design and the changes to the controls.

Felicia shifted closer to Rand and murmured, "He's in his element."

Rand smiled, then looked down at her. "If you'll wait here for a moment, I'll just have a word with him."

She nodded. Mary and Ryder were looking at the next invention in line. Felicia watched as the gentlemen who had been speaking with William John moved away, and Rand stepped up to William John. They spoke, then William John smiled a smile of transparent happiness and nodded — although the nod was delivered in her brother's usual vague way.

William John turned to another group of gentlemen, along with one lady, who were waiting to approach, and Rand returned to her side.

"He said he's happy to deal with all the inquiries for the next hour or so." Rand took her arm. "I thought we might take a quick look around, and then I'll return to spell William John."

Felicia laughed and slid her arm into Rand's. "We're talking of William John — he's in his version of heaven when speaking of his inventions and explaining how they work. He so rarely gets a chance to speak with an audience of interested people, I very much doubt you'll prevail on him to let you take over."

Rand acknowledged the comment with a wry smile. "There's no denying he's earned his moment here. If it weren't for him and his never-say-die pursuit of success, we'd never have got the steam carriage here. But I'll at least offer him the chance to take a break — whether he takes it or not can be his decision."

After they collected Ryder and Mary, who had been fascinatedly studying the printing machine that was the twenty-fifth exhibit, the four of them eased into the swelling crowd. As the bulk of the crowd seemed to be heading down the central aisle toward them — presumably following the numbers on the exhibits — they went in the other direction, crossing the wide central space to examine the inventions numbered twenty-six and on.

While Rand and Felicia dallied to more closely examine the latest steam-powered loom, Ryder and Mary continued up the line. Felicia asked several technical questions of the loom's inventor, much to that older gentleman's discomposure; that a lady would know to ask of valves and pressures thoroughly rattled him, and he struggled to answer.

Felicia wasn't impressed; as she moved away on Rand's arm, she murmured, "I hope you haven't put any money into that invention."

"No. I haven't." After a moment, he added, "There are too many decent steam-driven looms about already."

She humphed. "I doubt he's run his engine for longer than ten minutes. Fifteen, and I would expect it to blow a pipe or a gasket — his configuration suffers from the same problem the Throgmorton engine originally had."

The reason he hadn't invested in the steam-driven loom was because of the established competition — not because he'd known it wouldn't work.

The idea that had quietly wormed its way into his brain regarding one aspect of his and Felicia's joint future grew clearer, taking more definite shape.

They strolled on, pausing here and there to more closely question various inventors. Rand met and stopped to chat with several investors, mostly competitors of sorts. All congratulated him on his prescience in supporting the Throgmorton project at such an early stage; several inquired whether there might be a chance to buy in at some point. Rand smiled easily, said he would let them know, and left it at that. Now they'd had a chance to see the steam engine and consider its points, that more investors were declaring interest suggested that they, too, thought the Throgmorton Steam-Powered Horseless Carriage had a definite and lucrative future.

While he'd chatted with his peers, Felicia had drawn her hand from his sleeve and drifted to speak with a nervous young inventor whose very small exhibit was wedged between two much larger and showier machines. Hardly anyone seemed to have noticed the poor man, but Felicia appeared to be deeply immersed in the explanation the young inventor was proffering.

Drawing nearer, Rand saw that Felicia held a slim rod in her hand. A channel had been scored down its length and a stop-pered glass vessel fixed in the space. At the other end of the rod from the elegant metal stopper was a small piece of burnished metal. Rand halted beside Felicia, and as she lifted the rod to show him, he realized the metal addition was a very fine nib.

"Mr. Finlay" — Felicia nodded at the young man — "was just explaining that the pen works via a combination of gravity and capillary action. See?" She set the nib to a piece of paper the inventor had laid atop a traveling writing desk mounted on a pedes-tal and swiftly scribed numbers and letters, capital and lowercase. "It's remarkable — no more open pots of ink or splotches."

Rand looked at the young man. "I've seen pens like this in Paris. What makes yours different?"

Mr. Finlay leapt to explain. "If I could, miss?" Tenderly, he took the pen from Fe-licia, then, with a fingertip, directed Rand's attention to the detail of the stopper. "I've made changes to the seal to make it more airtight. I've also altered the vessel — it's really an annulus of glass with air in the central shaft. I discovered that makes the flow of ink more even. Then I've worked with the local steel mills to refashion the nib. This one gives a steady and even line and will outlast anything presently on the market."

Rand knew Birmingham foundries were setting themselves up as manufacturers of all sorts of steel products — from the largest and heaviest to the smallest and finest, apparently. Rand reached for the pen, and Finlay let him take it from his hands. Rand held the pen up at eye level, studying the stopper, then the glass vessel, then, in very close detail, he examined the nib. The work was unquestionably fine and quite different to what he'd seen in France.

He looked at Finlay. The man returned his regard hopefully; Rand judged him to be as honest and as earnest as the day was long. Rand handed the pen back to Finlay, then looked at Felicia and arched a brow.

She didn't smile, but her attention returned to the pen, her gaze almost covetous. "It seems a very fine piece of work. I can't think of any point of its design that could be bettered."

Finlay blinked at her, then, realizing she'd paid him a compliment, smiled shyly.

Rand reached for his card case. He extracted a card and handed it to Finlay.

The man took it, read it, and his eyes went

wide. He looked at Rand. "You're Cavan-augh?" He glanced again at the card, then looked up, patently stunned. "Lord Cavan-augh?"

Rand hid a smile; from the corner of his eye, he saw Felicia grin. "I am. And after the exhibition, I'd like you to come to London and demonstrate your pen to some other like-minded gentlemen. I'd like to explore what arrangements we might con-template to make the most of your inventive modifications."

"Oh yes — of course, my lord. I will be happy . . . well, *thrilled* to set up a dem-onstration in London." Finlay looked across the aisle and down the hall. "I heard you're backing the Throgmorton steam engine. I didn't think you'd be interested in" — he looked down at the pen, lying in his hand — "something so small."

Felicia put her hand on Finlay's arm. "Smaller inventions often make the biggest difference and just think of how much people write."

Finlay smiled back.

"One thing," Rand said. "If anyone else approaches you with a view to backing your pen, I and my syndicate would appreciate having the first opportunity to consider sup-porting your work."

"Absolutely, my lord — you have my word." Finlay looked at Rand's card.

"Send a letter to that address tomorrow," Rand advised, "detailing the scope of your work and where you can be contacted. I'm out of town for the next few days, so it may be a week or more before I'm there to read it, but you can expect to hear from me within a few weeks."

"Thank you, my lord." Finlay was clearly still in awe of his own luck.

Rand nodded, as did Felicia, and Finlay swept them a bow. As they moved away, Felicia smiled and looked up, meeting Rand's eyes. "You've made his day — his exhibition."

Rand quirked his brows. "It's perfectly possible he's made mine — well, at least looking beyond the steam carriage. Speaking of which" — he halted, letting the crowd part and flow around them — "I should get back and relieve William John."

Felicia tilted her head. "If you don't have need of me — and I'm sure William John won't — I rather think I'll wander farther and see what I can see."

Rand nodded. "By all means do." If it hadn't been for her, he would very likely have missed seeing Finlay. Even if he had noticed the man with his small and unprepossessing exhibit, as until now Rand hadn't seen much to interest him in the latest pens, he might not have ventured close enough to speak to the inventor and recognize the value of what he'd produced.

Unlike him, Felicia was coming to the field of inventions with an entirely open and highly educated inventive mind. He squeezed her hand, then released her. "Wander, study, and investigate — and let me know if you see anything you think I should look into."

She smiled and graciously inclined her head. "If you wish it, I will. Have fun with William John."

He chuckled, and they parted, she continuing up the line of inventions while he made his way across the aisle and back to where the Throgmorton steam carriage stood proudly displayed — with a long line of people waiting to ask questions of its inventor.

Rand grinned at the sight and made his way to William John's side. The Throgmorton steam engine was creating an even bigger stir than he'd hoped.

Clive Mayhew threaded his way through the crowd clogging the wide aisle of the exhibition hall. He moved slowly — carefully —

keeping his eyes peeled for any of the denizens of Throgmorton Hall. The crowd reassured him; as long as he remained alert, it was unlikely anyone from the Hall would spot him among the jostling throng. And if they did, he would have time to flee and plenty of other bodies for cover.

Besides, Clive doubted Miss Throgmorton or Mrs. Makepeace would have made the journey; of those Clive had met at the Hall, only Cavanaugh was likely to be there, and as Clive understood things, his lordship would almost certainly remain close to the Throgmorton invention, which Clive had learned was at the far end of the hall.

All Clive wished to do was find his uncle and tell old Horace that he had had enough. Regardless of his dire need of the ready, Clive was finished with his uncle's grubby schemes.

At that moment, Sir Horace Winthrop was parading up the exhibition hall, projecting his customary and — to his mind — entirely appropriate superior air. He was the most established leader of investing syndicates in London, and, as such, he was recognized by many and was determined to be accorded all due deference. He inclined his head to the two older inventors who, on seeing him eyeing their exhibit — one involving modifications to a horse-drawn plow — bowed low.

As they should. It was Sir Horace's prerogative to decide which of the owners of displayed inventions he would honor with an invitation to speak with him in his office in the City. Effectively, it was in his gift to decide which invention prospered and which sank without trace.

Given that it was widely known that he disapproved of the entire panoply of steam-powered inventions, stigmatizing them as entirely unnecessary, the inventors of such things didn't attempt to catch his eye; regardless, he passed their exhibits with his nose in the air — wordlessly declaring his view of their works.

On entering the hall, he'd made his way as quickly as his dignity permitted to view the Throgmorton exhibit — from a safe distance. Seeing it displayed in all its glory, he'd smiled to himself and made a mental note to congratulate his nephew on having the good sense to damage the steam engine in such a way that the failure would not be evident until they started the engine on the exhibition floor. How Throgmorton had managed to pass the assessors' inspection, Sir Horace had no idea, but, presumably, the engine was simply fired up to make sure it worked, and that was that.

He had little idea how the blessed things functioned and even less interest.

All that mattered was that the Throgmorton machine failed most spectacularly — and having it fail in front of Prince Albert was as spectacular a failure as Sir Horace could conceive.

He truly was thoroughly pleased with Clive.

On the thought, he saw his nephew easing his way through the crowd toward him.

Sir Horace halted and planted his cane before him. He stood in the middle of the central aisle, closer to the main doors than the rear of the hall; entirely pleased with his world, he ignored the annoyed looks as members of the public were forced to tack around him.

Clive reached him and halted before him. His nephew inclined his head respectfully. "Uncle. I hoped to find you here."

The boy looked rather stern, almost grim.

Sir Horace's nerves fluttered, and he glanced swiftly around. "What about the Throgmorton party? Is there any chance of them seeing you — us?"

"They're nowhere near, and I don't plan on remaining for long."

Sir Horace relaxed, and his earlier satisfaction bloomed anew. He returned his gaze to

Clive and smiled approvingly. "Excellent, my boy! I must congratulate you —"

"No."

Sir Horace blinked. Looking more closely at Clive's face, he realized that it was, indeed, grim resolution that was increasingly overtaking his nephew's expression.

"There's no reason for congratulations." Clive drew in a breath, straightened, and, from his more lofty height, looked censoriously down on Sir Horace. "The only reason I'm here is to tell you to your face that I want nothing whatever to do with your scheme. I've seen the Throgmorton steam carriage in action, and as far as I'm aware, it's working perfectly."

Sir Horace lost all ability to maintain his superior façade. Aghast, he stared at Clive. "Wh-what?"

"It's next to immoral — trying to hold back progress like that, and purely for your own ends, I have no doubt." Clive slid his hands into his pockets and cast a wary glance at the crowd around them. "I find it difficult to conceive of the degree of sheer selfishness that would prompt you to attempt to damage an invention of such promise, but regardless, I want no part of it. God knows how I'll find the money I need, but I'd rather do a bunk to the

Continent than prosper from a nasty, nefarious scheme like yours." Clive met Sir Horace's wide eyes. "You mistook me, Uncle — I'm not such a blackguard."

Sir Horace's reeling wits latched on to the critical point. "The steam carriage works? It hasn't been tampered with?"

"Yes. And no. As I said, as far as I'm aware, it's working perfectly."

Sir Horace's expression blanked as he stared disaster in the face. Only two days ago, he'd pooh-poohed the Throgmorton steam carriage to his most valuable investor, pouring scorn on all of Cavanaugh's projects as well as on the entire concept of horseless carriages . . . and now one of the damned devices was going to be demonstrated there, in front of the crème de la crème of the inventing world, Prince Albert included? With Cavanaugh smiling in triumph in the background? "No!" Sir Horace seized Clive's sleeve and focused on his nephew's face. "You don't understand. You *must* stop it!"

Clive's expression hardened. He detached Sir Horace's clutching fingers from his sleeve. "No, Uncle. I will not act for you in this."

Sir Horace opened his mouth —

Clive cut him off with a disgusted look

426

and "If you want it done, you'll have to stir your stumps and do it yourself." With a last hard look, Clive stated definitively, "I want nothing more to do with you or your schemes."

With that, Clive stepped past Sir Horace and disappeared into the crowd.

Sir Horace stood rooted to the spot, uncaring of the bodies jostling him as the crowd streamed past, as a vision of utter ruination — financial, reputational, and ultimately personal — took far-too-solid shape in his mind.

In seconds, he'd moved well beyond horrified. "I can't let this happen." The mutter sounded hollow and distant in his ears.

Devastation loomed, second by second drawing inexorably closer. Slowly, he swiveled and looked down the hall toward where the Throgmorton exhibit stood in all its glory. He couldn't see it; the crowds were now far too dense to see more than a few yards in any direction.

But he knew it was there.

Knew that if he was to have any chance of coming about, he would have to act now. The Prince would arrive shortly. There was really no way around it. He would have to do as Clive had said and attend to the matter himself.

How to do that — how to bring about the disastrous failure he'd envisioned for the Throgmorton steam engine — he didn't know, but he would have to try.

On the heels of that fainthearted resolution, a stir about the main doors had everyone turning that way. Sir Horace looked, too, and swallowed a groan. The Prince had arrived. Sir Horace's time — his moment of reckoning — was nigh.

Along with the rest of the crowd, Sir Horace stood unmoving, his gaze directed toward the main doors as the Prince was welcomed by the chairman of the organizing committee, then His Highness said a few words in his accented English.

By the time the resulting enthusiastic applause had faded and the Prince, surrounded by the fawning committee members, embarked on his progress down the hall, Sir Horace had found his backbone. He'd also managed to formulate a plan.

His first step had to be to gain access to the Throgmorton steam engine without being seen.

His earlier view of the Throgmorton display was blazoned on his brain. He hadn't missed the cordon of guards Cavanaugh had arranged in an arc before and to either side of the steam carriage.

Sir Horace's lips twisted in a sickly smile, and he made his way up the hall, pushing past the knot of people gathered about the Prince as Albert chatted with the first exhibitor. Finally, Sir Horace gained the main doors and stepped into the foyer. Although people were walking to and fro across the large, open space, no officials were stationed there anymore — they were all inside hovering about the Prince. Relieved — and taking it as a sign that Fate was on his side — Sir Horace drew in a breath, puffed out his chest, and walked to the right, to the service door set into the foyer paneling. On reaching it, he cast a last swift glance around, but no one was taking the slightest notice of him. He opened the door, walked through, and closed it behind him.

As he'd remembered from previous exhibitions there, the door gave onto a long corridor running the length of the hall. As the exhibition hall was frequently used to host large official dinners, it was necessary to give staff access to the hall from both sides.

Today, the corridor, dimly lit by widely spaced gaslights turned low, was not being used and was, therefore, helpfully deserted.

Sir Horace breathed a little easier. He removed his hat and set it down in a dim corner with his cane. Then he hurried down the long corridor. Doors were set into the wall every ten or so yards. He tried one door, most of the way down the corridor, but he wasn't far enough down the hall to glimpse the Throgmorton display. He shut that door and walked quickly on to the second-last door along the corridor. He halted before it, then, holding his breath, turned the knob and eased the panel open — just enough to put his eye to the gap and ascertain what lay beyond.

The Throgmorton steam carriage stood to the right of the door, one long side parallel to and two feet from the wall. Shifting and scanning farther, Sir Horace saw the backs of two guards; the men were standing on this side of the rope cordon with their hands behind their backs and their gazes trained on the shifting crowd pressing close on the other side of the rope. The Throgmorton display was plainly garnering a significant amount of attention from the public — yet more reason, had Sir Horace needed further convincing, to ensure that the steam carriage failed and failed definitively here and now.

Yet if he stepped out of the door, before he could crouch out of sight behind the contraption, he would — for a bare second

— be visible, not to the guards who were facing the other way but to those jostling and pressing as close as they could to study the steam carriage.

Sir Horace eyed the throng, which included young boys and groups of youths eagerly pointing and exclaiming. Sharp-eyed monsters who would think nothing of pointing him out to the guards —

A commotion sounded farther up the hall. Everyone — boys, youths, guards, and all — peered in that direction. Sir Horace realized the Prince had advanced down the line and something had happened with some invention he'd asked to see demonstrated . . .

The Prince was closer than Sir Horace had expected; there was no time to lose.

Sir Horace dragged in a breath, pushed through the door, and, leaving it to swing silently closed, scuttled on tiptoe three paces to his right — and sank to his haunches behind the Throgmorton steam carriage.

Breath bated, he waited — dreading to hear one of the guards coming to see who had slunk past . . . but there were no calls, no heavy footsteps. The steady, excited murmuring of the crowd continued unbroken.

Hardly daring to believe his luck, Sir Horace turned his somewhat frantic attention to what he took to be the engine compartment. Throgmorton had erected a metal housing over the top, but although there were panels closing in the sides, the one facing Sir Horace had plainly been designed to fold down if the knob securing it was released.

Holding his breath, Sir Horace reached up, twisted the knob, and slowly lowered the hinged panel toward him, until it rested on the lip of the housing that swept up to shield the upper rim of the front wheel.

Sir Horace peered into the workings of the engine — at a bewildering array of pipes and gears and God knew what else besides. He searched for a lever he might pull, or a knob, but although he spied several levers, they were attached to rods and couldn't be easily moved.

Now what? He knew nothing about engines — had never deigned to even listen to discussions about the bally things. *Think!*

Valves! He vaguely remembered that valves mattered. He peered this way and that and saw several. One was close enough to easily reach.

Feverishly, Sir Horace turned out his pockets — did he have any string?

He didn't. All he drew forth were bits of paper, coins, and two silk handkerchiefs . . .

Silk was strong, wasn't it? And these were of the finest quality silk. After stuffing the other items he'd unearthed back into his pockets, he shook out one handkerchief and, holding opposing corners, wound it into a short but very strong length. He turned back to the engine and quickly tied the silk over the valve in a way he hoped would stop the valve from working. From releasing. That was what valves did, he thought.

He paused and listened. Judging by the sounds from the crowd, the Prince was still several exhibits away.

Sir Horace looked down at the second silk handkerchief. Then he peered into the engine compartment, but none of the other valves were sufficiently accessible. Then he noticed the pipes leading back toward the rear of the carriage. He dropped to his knees and, with his head almost on the floor, followed the pipes back . . .

There! Another valve — a good-sized one close enough that if he lay on his back he could reach it.

Sir Horace carefully shut the side panel he'd opened, sealing away the sight of his tampering, then, dispensing with all dignity, he gritted his teeth, rolled onto his back, angled his shoulders under the contraption, and, with his second handkerchief, swiftly tied the second valve down tight.

He blew out a breath, then quickly wriggled out from under the carriage and clambered back to his previous crouch.

He edged toward the end of the carriage. The door he needed to reach was two yards away, with the entire distance in full sight of the crowd.

Clinging desperately to calm, he forced himself to wait — *wait* — until he heard the Prince exclaim.

He didn't hesitate but rose and walked swiftly — silently — to the door and, without even pausing to check that no one had seen him, he slipped behind the panel and closed it behind him.

In the dimness of the corridor, he waited to see if any hue and cry was raised. He was breathing stertorously; he hadn't realized until then.

His brow was damp. He reached into his pocket for his handkerchief . . .

Grimacing, he blotted his face with his sleeve, then, as no shouts had come from the other side of the door, Sir Horace turned and walked back up the corridor.

By the time he retrieved his hat and cane,

stepped onto the tiles of the foyer, and closed the corridor door behind him, he was starting to believe.

To think that he'd pulled it off — that he'd done what was necessary all by himself. He hadn't, after all, needed any help.

A slow tide of relief washed through him. He'd saved the day.

His day, at least.

Confidence rose in the wake of the thought that, now, all would be well. All would play out exactly as it ought, and he would return to London fully vindicated, with his position as the acknowledged leader of investment syndicates even more firmly entrenched. No one would dare question his assessments in the future.

He resettled his coat sleeves, then walked toward the exhibition hall. He had no intention of missing the glorious moment when the Throgmorton engine stalled and refused to run.

Increasingly assured, once more holding his head high, Sir Horace strode into the hall and joined the cluster of people gathered behind the Prince.

Members of the committee saw him and inclined their heads. Those of the crowd less well-connected nevertheless recognized his air of authority and shuffled aside, yielding to Sir Horace until he stood with several other worthies alongside the committee and close behind the Prince.

Thus installed in pride of place and in the perfect position to view the outcome of his actions, buoyed by a sense of righteousness in having struck a blow for his fellow countrymen — those like him with a deeper understanding, who knew beyond question that steam-powered vehicles should never be allowed on England's roads — Sir Horace, his aloof and superior façade once more in place, pretended to an interest in the exhibits as the Prince continued down the line, and waited to bear witness to the utter failure of the Throgmorton Steam-Powered Horseless Carriage.

After speaking with his uncle, Clive had intended to beat a retreat, but several exhibits caught his eye, and he got distracted.

Never before had he had a chance to examine mechanical devices, and after the tug he'd felt on setting eyes on the steam carriage, he was eager to see more; the machines' lines and the symmetry many possessed beneath an overlay of weaving pipes and tubes enthralled his artist's soul. The way the light played over the curved metal surfaces made his fingers twitch. He no longer had his satchel, but how he wished he had; he would have liked to take up the challenge of capturing the aura of the machines.

His fascination drew him down the hall. Although he remained alert, he didn't see Cavanaugh, then, to his surprise, he spotted Miss Throgmorton speaking to one of the exhibitors. She was asking questions and seemed quite animated. At the sight of her, Clive felt a very strong prod from his conscience. If he truly wanted absolution for his actions against the Throgmortons, then he owed Miss Throgmorton a fervent apology.

Cloaked by the crowd, he watched her for several minutes, then made up his mind. Before he quit the hall, he would apologize to her and seek her forgiveness, but to do that . . . He set his jaw, turned, and, without allowing himself time to think and balk, purposefully made his way farther down the hall. If he wished to prostrate himself before Miss Throgmorton, he first needed to make his peace with Cavanaugh.

Exactly what the relationship between the two was, Clive didn't know, yet given Cavanaugh's murderous expression when he'd last seen Clive, if Clive wanted to approach

Miss Throgmorton and live, he needed to explain himself to Cavanaugh.

Despite wishing to speak with the man, Clive approached cautiously. As he'd assumed, Cavanaugh was hovering within sight of the Throgmorton exhibit. Still screened by the crowd, Clive halted and seized the moment to rehearse what he wanted to say.

Cavanaugh was tracking the Prince's progress. His Highness was still several exhibits away from the steam carriage, but as he moved one exhibit closer, Cavanaugh raised his head and looked up the hall, then he moved into the shifting tide of bodies, unknowingly making his way toward where Clive was standing.

Guessing that Cavanaugh was on his way to summon Miss Throgmorton, Clive metaphorically girded his loins; when Cavanaugh drew level, Clive stepped into his path.

Rand jerked to a halt. Barely able to believe his eyes, he felt his jaw clench, his fists close.

Mayhew held up a hand. "Before you take a swing at me, please hear me out."

The man's nerve was breathtaking, but also intriguing, and, combined with his steady, direct regard, served to give Rand pause. After a second of staring at May-

438

hew's face — and recalling that someone must have hired the man — Rand stiffly inclined his head. "I'm fascinated to hear what you have to say."

Mayhew drew in a deep breath, then stated, "When my uncle asked me to interfere with the Throgmorton invention enough to ensure it wouldn't appear at this exhibition, I didn't understand what he was, in fact, asking me to do. I thought inventions and exhibitions such as this" — Mayhew glanced around — "were . . . well, more like games. Games played by men with the funds to tinker and dabble in such things — nothing serious at all." Mayhew glanced around again and his lips tightened. "Obviously, I was ridiculously naive, but this isn't an area in which I've previously been interested — I had nothing more than popular notions by which to judge."

Before Rand could ask who Mayhew's uncle was, Mayhew rolled on, "Then I got to Throgmorton Hall and met Miss Throgmorton and Mrs. Makepeace, and you, too, and none of you seemed silly and frivolous. You all seemed normal and, well, nice. Honest and welcoming — straightforward, sensible people. I started having second thoughts then. When I left the area the first time, I was debating whether I should continue, but then it seemed I had to, so I returned and tried to find some way to do what my uncle wanted." Mayhew moistened his lips and lowered his voice. "But then in the woods, when I was chasing Miss Throgmorton, I suddenly realized what I'd done — what sort of man I'd become, or rather, was on the cusp of becoming."

Mayhew met Rand's eyes; Mayhew's remorse was clear to see. "I didn't want to be that man. I ran from you both, but I also ran from what I almost became. I waited long enough to see the steam carriage drive away from the Hall — that was the first time I'd seen it. And instantly, I could understand why people get so excited by such things — by the promise they hold for advancements of all sorts."

Rand noted the spark that ignited in Mayhew's eyes, the eager lift in his voice, and recognized the signs.

"And now . . ." Mayhew paused, then lightly shrugged. "I've given you no cause to believe me, but I swear by all that's holy that I will never lend myself to such a scheme again." He hesitated, then rather diffidently added, "I would like to make my apologies to Miss Throgmorton, but I felt it would be wise to clear the air with you first."

That was undoubtedly true. And as well

as that statement, everything Mayhew had said had rung with sincerity. He was, at base, an honest man, seduced into acting — into attempting to act — outside his nature. So why . . . ? Rand fixed his gaze on Mayhew's face. "What hold did your uncle have over you?"

Mayhew shrugged again, and his gaze wandered over the crowd. "The usual."

"Debts?"

Mayhew tried to suppress a grimace. "Too many." Then he pressed his lips tight.

That brought them to the most critical question. "Who is your uncle?"

Mayhew met Rand's eyes. "Sir Horace Winthrop. Do you know him?"

Rand nearly laughed, although it wouldn't have been humorously. His lips thinning, he nodded. "Oh yes. We're acquainted."

"Ah." Mayhew glanced around. "Well, he's here somewhere."

So Rand had assumed. Despite his dislike of steam-powered machines, there were enough other inventions present to ensure Winthrop's attendance.

"The main reason I came," Mayhew continued, "was to tell old Horace that I hadn't damaged the steam carriage and wasn't going to. I told him if he wanted the thing sabotaged, he'd have to do it himself."

Rand stilled. A frisson of premonition slithered down his spine. "When did you speak with your uncle?"

Mayhew frowned. "I'm not sure . . . Twenty minutes ago, perhaps? It might have been half an hour." Mayhew glanced at Rand. What he saw in Rand's face made him draw his hands from his pockets and straighten. "Surely you don't think . . . ?"

"You told him to sabotage the engine himself." Rand turned to look over the heads at the Throgmorton exhibit.

"It was just a figure of speech." Mayhew looked, too.

"Perhaps." Rand started to push his way toward the exhibit. "But what if old Horace took it literally?"

"Would he?" Mayhew fell into step beside Rand. Together, they forced their way through the now-packed crowd — the Prince had just moved to view the invention next to the steam carriage.

After a moment of wondering if he was overreacting and deciding he didn't care, Rand replied, "If Winthrop was prepared to pay you to sabotage the engine, I believe we have to take it as read that he's willing to do just about anything to prevent the Throg-morton engine from working."

Mayhew huffed — in dismay, rather than

disagreement. Regardless, he didn't argue but helped Rand force his way through the crowd.

FIFTEEN

Rand reached the cordon and their guards. He cast a swift glance at the knot of people around the Prince. Luckily, Albert had asked for a demonstration of the steam-powered threshing machine, and the exhibitors were still stoking their boiler.

Remembering that William John was scheduled to fire the steam carriage's engine as soon as the Prince turned toward their exhibit, Rand stepped over the cordon, saying to the nearest guards, "Keep watching." He jerked a thumb at Mayhew as the artist made to follow. "It's all right — he's with me."

With Mayhew on his heels, Rand rounded the steam carriage.

He crouched, and Mayhew did the same.

"Winthrop couldn't have got within spitting distance of the other side of the engine." Rand reached for the knob that secured the side panel of the engine housing. "I can't imagine how he might have reached this side unseen, but . . ." He had to check. His instincts were pricking him like hedgehog quills; he couldn't ignore them.

He twisted the knob, and the catch released. Smoothly, he lowered the panel. With Mayhew looking over his shoulder, he peered into the engine compartment.

With his sharp artist's eyes, Mayhew spotted the anomaly first. "There." Reaching over Rand's shoulder, he pointed. "That looks like material — it shouldn't be there, should it?"

Rand looked and swore. "No." He reached for the white band holding down the pressure valve. He felt and found the knot, tried to unpick it, and realized that wouldn't be easy. "Damn — he's used his silk handkerchief. The knot's pulled tight."

Grimly, he worked at the knot, frantically trying to ease it apart; they didn't have much time . . . An unwelcome thought intruded. Over his shoulder, he murmured urgently to Mayhew, "Look further. This might not be all he did."

Rand shifted to the side to allow Mayhew to press closer and peer deeper into the engine compartment.

Telling himself the artist's eyes were keen,

Rand concentrated on freeing the valve they knew was stuck — one of the critical valves William John had added off the boiler to equalize the pressure . . .

"There's another one — looks like another handkerchief around one of those things."

"Valves," Rand gritted out. "Where?"

Mayhew pulled back from the compartment. "Farther from the engine. He must have reached it from underneath."

Rand gave Mayhew due credit; the artist didn't hesitate, but rolled onto his back and wriggled beneath the carriage's underbelly. "I can get this one."

Mayhew's words were indistinct. Rand raised his head and realized the noise from the crowd had grown. The Prince and his entourage must be on the point of moving on.

His jaw clenching, Rand ducked his head and worked feverishly to ease the knot, but everything he did only seemed to pull it tighter.

Distantly, he heard Mayhew swear about silken knots.

Then Mayhew asked, his words faint but clear, "Cavanaugh — what will happen if these valves are still tied down when the engine starts?"

Rand's jaw couldn't clench any tighter.

His eyes felt like they were burning, he was concentrating so fiercely on the silk band. "Nothing initially." His tone, strangely, sounded entirely even. "But then the boiler will explode."

"Explode?" Mayhew squeaked.

"Quite spectacularly." Rand was barely aware of what he was saying, so focused was he on the knot.

Then with a rustling of skirts and petticoats, Felicia crouched beside him. "What . . . ?" Her hand on his shoulder, her eyes had gone to the tie he was wrestling with. "Good God — is that silk?"

"Yes! And the damned knot has pulled tight." Rand was dimly aware her hand had gone from his shoulder; a glimpse from the corner of his eye showed she'd grabbed her reticule and was desperately hunting inside it. "I can't get this undone." Through gritted teeth, he ground out, "Go and tell William John to wait for my signal before starting —"

The coal igniter flared, flames whooshed, and the boiler rattled to life.

Rand cursed.

Then Mayhew called, "I've got it!"

He pushed out from under the carriage, triumphantly brandishing the white scrap like a flag.

Felicia spared him a shocked glance, then her features hardened, and she returned to ferreting in the depths of her reticule.

The tone of the engine changed as the pressure in the boiler built, but William John hadn't yet engaged the pistons and gears.

Without pausing in his desperate tugging at the silk band, Rand shot Mayhew a glance. "Get Miss Throgmorton out of here. Felicia — tell William John to shut the engine down and get everyone back." The steam engine was going to blow — and the Prince was mere yards away, along with Ryder, Mary, and a host of others Rand cared far too much about.

"Don't be daft." Felicia dropped her reticule and waved a pair of embroidery scissors. "Let me at it."

She pushed his shoulder to make him move aside, and despite every instinct screaming against it, Rand gave way.

The pitch of the engine continued to rise.

Felicia leaned in. "Keep holding the band taut. That's it."

A split second later, the band slid free.

The silk clutched in one hand, Rand fell back, sprawling to sit on the floor. Felicia overbalanced, toppled backward, and sat beside him.

Still crouching alongside the steam carriage, Mayhew looked at them with wide eyes. *Now what?* he mouthed.

Rand held up a staying hand. Both he and Felicia were listening intently to the sound of the engine.

Then Felicia grinned and turned to him. She reached for his arm and gripped hard. "The pressure's leveled off — it's going to be all right."

He stared at her face, then he raised a hand to her nape, pulled her face to his, and kissed her.

For one second, he allowed the violent need that owned him to hold sway, to take control of the kiss and ravage and plunder, then he pulled back.

Mayhew had averted his eyes, looking upward as if listening to William John, who was giving Prince Albert a lecture on the Throgmorton engine's finer points. The engine was now purring, a reassuringly benign and steady hum.

Felicia crawled back to the side of the carriage and carefully and silently closed the compartment Rand had opened.

Seconds later, they heard William John, closer now, open the engine's other side and then lift the cover over the engine's top to display the inner workings to Albert, who was predictably taking a very keen interest and asking relevant questions.

Rand took that as their cue to depart. He returned to a crouch and, using hand signals, directed Mayhew to shuffle to the rear of the carriage, then stand and walk out to the side. As, urging Felicia ahead of him, Rand moved to follow, he felt a draft, looked at the wall, and saw the door Winthrop must have used. Their guards hadn't fallen down on the job. Winthrop had slithered in like the snake he was.

After helping Felicia to her feet, Rand guided her and Mayhew to the end of the cordon on that side. Rand paused there to take stock. The crowd was too dense and pressed too closely against the cordon for them to have any chance of slipping into the throng. Luckily, Ryder and Mary had joined the Prince's party, and the pair now stood on the inside of the cordon, not far from William John, ready to support him if need be.

Rand drew Felicia's hand through his arm. Over his shoulder, he said to Mayhew, "Stick close." Then he led Felicia forward to join Ryder and Mary, which was where, according to their plan, they were supposed to be.

As Rand settled beside Ryder, without turning his head, Ryder inquired, "Where did you get to?"

"We've been nullifying our would-be saboteur's efforts." Rand sensed Ryder shoot a sharp glance at Mayhew and added, "Not him. He helped us."

"Which is something you will both need to explain to me later," Felicia muttered, glancing at Mayhew.

Rand raised her hand to his lips and kissed her fingers. "We will, but later. Definitely later."

William John had noticed Felicia's and Rand's arrival. He flashed them a relieved smile, but his recitation of the wonders of the improvements he and his father had made to the steam engine didn't falter. At Felicia's insistence, William John had somewhat grudgingly agreed to omit her name from the discussion; while Rand had understood Felicia's reasoning — the involvement of a female wouldn't be viewed in a positive light by the majority of those present — he'd also sympathized with William John and his dislike of being forced, by default, to accept credit for her work.

Perhaps that would change in the future, but for now, Rand agreed with Felicia's pragmatic stance.

So they stood and listened, and a slow but steady wave of relief and pride welled and rolled through him — through them. He read as much in Felicia's fine eyes as she glanced at him, the green misty with pride and rising joy.

William John had come into his own. His confidence in discussing the invention with the Prince, the committee members, and several other inventors who had pressed close was impressive; not once did he falter.

And when, with what was, for William John, a remarkably graceful gesture, he invited the Prince to step into the carriage for a drive down the hall, the excitement that gripped not just Albert but the entire audience was wonderful to behold.

After a moment of further discussion, Albert accepted.

William John spared a triumphant glance for Felicia and Rand, then turned back to show the Prince to the steps to climb up to the carriage's bench seat.

Thrilled and eager to witness such an event, the crowd was quite orderly in falling back to clear space for the carriage to turn out of its allotted spot and then roll up the hall.

Rand doubted he would ever again know a moment like this — the first time an invention he'd backed had been given such a clear stamp of approval from the monarchy. As he and Felicia, together with Ryder and Mary, stepped back with the rest of the onlookers, Rand felt the white silk band still wrapped around his fingers. Releasing Felicia's arm, he unraveled the remnants of the silk square.

It was monogrammed. For several seconds, Rand stared at the entwined HW. Then he tucked the handkerchief into his pocket and glanced over his shoulder. As he'd instructed, Mayhew had remained close. "I suggest," Rand said, "that with all attention on the steam carriage, now would be a good time to find your uncle and have a quiet word."

Mayhew arched a brow. "He would have waited to see what happened."

"Indeed. Let's catch him before he realizes nothing is going to mar the Prince's enjoyment and does a bunk."

Rand bent his head and whispered to Felicia, "Mayhew and I need to speak to the man who tried to get him to sabotage the engine. You need to stay here in case William John needs any support when he returns. We should be back soon after."

She shot him a look, one that stated she was torn, but in the end, she nodded. "All right. Just as long as you tell me all later."

He pressed a quick kiss to her temple. "I

promise."

"Do you need help?" Ryder murmured, his gaze fixed on the steam carriage.

Rand thought about it. "Not at this point."

Ryder nodded, and Rand turned to Mayhew. Rand tipped his head toward the main doors. "Come on. I would wager your uncle's still watching and waiting, and I believe he owes us all several boons for preventing the assassination of Prince Albert by his hand."

Mayhew blinked, then his eyes widened. "Good Lord! I hadn't thought of that."

Rand smiled grimly, yet predatory satisfaction glimmered in his eyes. "Indeed. I doubt Winthrop did, either, and, in this instance, his handkerchiefs are as good as a calling card."

They found Winthrop at the rear of the crowd, not far from the main doors. As they approached, he was scowling and rising up on his toes in an attempt to see what was happening over the intervening heads. His peeved expression stated very clearly that he was utterly perplexed as to why the engine — only just audible at this distance — was still running.

Rand approached from behind Winthrop and dropped a heavy hand on the older man's shoulder. "Winthrop."

Winthrop stiffened, then whirled. For a split second, his expression was aghast, but he immediately recovered, summoning a tight smile and drawing himself up in a vain attempt to look down his nose at Rand.

Rand simply waited.

Eventually forced to it, Winthrop inclined his head and managed a rather stilted bow. "Lord Cavanaugh."

As he straightened, Winthrop noticed who was standing by Rand's side, and his expression faltered. "What . . . ?" Then he swallowed and glared. "What are you doing here, boy?"

Clive smiled. "If you recall, we met earlier, Uncle."

Winthrop's color rose.

Before he could splutter at Clive, Rand drew Winthrop's silk handkerchief from his pocket. "I believe this is yours, Winthrop."

Winthrop stared at the handkerchief, focusing on the embroidered initials Rand held displayed. From tending puce, Winthrop's face paled to a pasty hue.

"Obviously, you forgot that your handkerchiefs were so distinctive." Rand returned the incriminating evidence to his pocket. "I'm sure you won't be surprised to know where we found it — and its mate. I doubt you could concoct a story that would explain that away."

Winthrop drew in a shuddering breath, then switched his choleric stare to his nephew. "You ungrateful pup! What have you done?"

"What Mayhew has done, Winthrop," Rand stated, "is to save you from the Tower and a very bad end."

Winthrop blinked. "What?"

"If Mayhew hadn't told me of your attempt at interfering with the Throgmorton invention, and I hadn't been prompted to check the engine, and in the very nick of time, assisted by Mayhew and Miss Throgmorton, managed to release the valves you'd tied down, then the engine would have exploded." Rand's voice hardened; his tone darkened. "Exploded, Winthrop, with the Prince and his advisors, and several other members of the nobility, standing beside it. For your information, the last time the Throgmorton engine exploded, the boiler ruptured — thick copper peeled back like a grape. The carnage . . . doesn't bear thinking about. So that's what your nephew has accomplished — by his redeeming actions, prompted by his better self, he saved others from death and you from being hanged, drawn, and quartered."

Winthrop's color had progressively worsened. He looked ill, his jaw slack. "I . . . I had no idea."

"Of course you didn't." Scorn rang in Rand's tone. "Your antipathy toward steam-powered inventions is well known — your ignorance of them can be inferred. Consequently, no one in the investment community or more generally will find our story at all hard to believe."

A spectrum of emotions flitted across Winthrop's face, horror, dismay, and panic among them. He shifted, then, apparently, realized there was nowhere for him to run. Nowhere Rand would allow him to hide.

Winthrop cleared his throat. "Wh-what do you want?" When Rand arched his brows, Winthrop clarified, "To . . . er, help you forget this incident." He glanced vaguely toward where the steam carriage, with William John behind the wheel and a delighted Albert perched beside him, was rolling smoothly up the hall toward the open doors. "The damned thing's a raging success. No harm done, and all's well that ends well, heh?"

Rand studied Winthrop long enough to make the older man shift uneasily and glance at Mayhew — as if gauging his chances of his nephew somehow stepping in and rescuing him.

"I think," Rand said, drawing Winthrop's gaze back to his face, "that the first thing you need to do is to show your gratitude to your nephew for his sterling service in protecting your health by paying all his debts. Every last one."

Stiffly, Winthrop nodded. "Of course." He shot a look at Mayhew. "You gave me the total, didn't you?"

His expression one of wonder, Mayhew slowly nodded. "Yes. That's all of them."

"When I return to London, I will send you a draft." Winthrop cleared his throat. "And perhaps, in the circumstances, I should add a stipend — a regular payment?"

Rand fought to hide a grin and inclined his head. "I think that would be most appropriate." Winthrop thought — possibly correctly — that such a payment would ensure no future mention of his misdeeds within his family.

Mayhew rose to the occasion and half bowed to his relative. "Thank you, Uncle. That would, indeed, be a kindness."

One all of them were well aware Winthrop could easily afford.

"Now," Rand said, "returning to the world of inventions, Winthrop, as this incident has demonstrated beyond question that you have not the first understanding of modern machines, I suggest it's time you admitted as much and retired from investing in this and associated fields."

Winthrop looked as if he was having trouble catching his breath. Rand arched a coolly censorious brow. "Don't you agree?"

Winthrop pressed his lips together, then jerkily nodded. "Yes, all right. I hate all this newfangled nonsense — the railways were bad enough." Glancing at Rand, his peevish gaze indicating he knew what Rand wanted of him, Winthrop continued, "I'll give it out that I'm retiring from all investments in machines of any kind. If any of my clients wish to invest in such projects, I'll steer them your way."

Rand suppressed a satisfied smile and inclined his head. "I believe we understand one another. I will, of course, be leaving a report on today's incident, along with the evidence" — he patted the pocket in which Winthrop's handkerchief resided — "with those I trust."

Winthrop's expression suggested he'd sucked a lemon, but he forced himself to stiffly bow. "Of course." Straightening, he continued, "If that concludes our business, my lord, I will bid you good day." Winthrop nodded sharply to Mayhew. "Clive."

Then Winthrop turned and, rather slowly, made for the main doors, edging around the crowds lining the central aisle, all excitedly watching the Throgmorton Steam-Powered Horseless Carriage being put through its paces.

Rand and Mayhew watched Winthrop go, then Mayhew looked rather wonderingly at Rand. "I say . . . well, there's nothing I can say but thank you." As Rand met his eyes, Mayhew spread his hands. "You could have thrown me to the dogs —"

"But I didn't." Rand studied the artist's open expression; he could understand why Felicia had trusted the man — there really wasn't any vein of villainy in him. "I didn't because you didn't have to stop and confess all to me. You could have come here, told Winthrop you'd decided not to do his bidding, and walked away with a clear conscience. No one could have blamed you for anything that transpired thereafter. But instead, you made the effort to come and clear your slate with me and the Throgmortons. If you hadn't, I would never have felt the need to check the engine one last time. And if you hadn't stuck with me and been there — and stayed and kept working even when it seemed the engine might explode — it might well have done so. We needed to get both those valves free, and without your help, we might not have succeeded." Rand tipped his head toward where cheering could be heard coming from the forecourt before the Town Hall. "And the Throgmortons and all those associated with them would have been devastated in more ways than one."

Rand studied Mayhew's face as the other man assimilated those facts. Finally, Mayhew frowned faintly and refocused on Rand's face. "Still, I did try . . ."

Rand couldn't help but smile; Mayhew truly was honest to the bone — in selecting him as his henchman, Winthrop had been blind. Rand turned toward where he'd left Felicia. "If you insist on making amends . . ."

Mayhew straightened and turned to walk beside him. "I do."

"Then having seen your sketches, I suggest you send a few of your perspectives of the Hall to Miss Throgmorton and Mrs. Makepeace as peace offerings, and we'll consider the matter settled and done."

Mayhew nodded eagerly. "I'll do that."

"And now" — Rand looked ahead to where the crowds were still thick around the Throgmorton exhibit — "you had better come with me, because at the end of this exceedingly eventful day, I suspect we'll have a significant amount of explaining to do."

Their eventful day had not yet ended. Rand and Mayhew rejoined Felicia, Mary, and Ryder beside the empty Throgmorton exhibit in time to watch Prince Albert, under William John's tutelage, drive the steam carriage down the center of the hall, back to its place in the lineup of inventions.

For the attentive and excited crowd, this would plainly be the highlight of their day.

For those associated with the Throgmorton steam carriage, it was a crowning achievement.

Nothing, simply nothing, could be better — could surpass the moment when William John showed Albert how to set the brake and turn off the engine, and with that done, the Prince looked up, beaming with undisguised delight.

The organizers gathered around, thrilled at the unexpected episode and delighted to support the Prince's approbation.

Her face wreathed in a smile of incandescent joy, Felicia watched William John deal with all the questions and congratulations with newfound confidence and authority. More than any other there, she could appreciate the vindication he had to be feeling, then he briefly looked her way, and his eyes shone with just that emotion, and, simultaneously, he and she nodded to each other, then William John returned to answering the questions and inquiries that were now coming thick and fast.

Felicia turned her attention to the crowd, observing the intrigued interest that now filled so many faces. When Rand shifted to better protect her from the surge of bodies, she gripped his arm and murmured, "I hope my father — and my mother, too — are looking down and seeing this."

Rand dipped his head, and she felt his lips lightly brush her temple. "The triumph of the Throgmortons?" he murmured.

She laughed. "Yes. Exactly that."

And that triumph reached far further, far deeper than the steam carriage. She was, finally, at one with her father and her brother. She'd reconnected with them in a way she had never thought she would. Now, she could accept them as they were — as inventors — because she'd finally found and embraced the inventor in herself.

That was the ultimate triumph here, the change that would give them — her, Rand, and William John — a solid base on which to build their futures. Their inevitably intertwined futures.

Rand had been the catalyst that had brought about the change that had allowed them to get to this moment and secure their triumph; he now was and would forever be an integral part of their whole.

Glancing at Rand, Felicia saw Mayhew standing on Rand's other side. After having seen Mayhew help Rand to free the valves, she no longer understood Mayhew's role.

Apparently sensing the questions on her tongue, Rand squeezed her hand where it lay on his sleeve and murmured, "We'll explain later, but Mayhew's on our side."

Across Rand, she met Mayhew's eyes. "You helped us."

He smiled rather shyly and bobbed a bow. "I can't say I wasn't a trifle flustered at one point, but I'm glad I was able to assist."

Clearly, there was a story behind Mayhew's actions, but as Albert reluctantly returned to his duties and moved on to view the next exhibit, and a horde of newspapermen, other inventors, and investors converged on William John, Felicia accepted that Rand was right; he had no time for explanations now.

Rand pressed her hand and unlinked their arms. "I need to help William John."

Felicia murmured encouragingly; her

brother was starting to look a trifle over-whelmed. She watched Rand push his way to William John's side. Almost immediately, William John's smile — a smile Felicia knew meant he was reliving his recent drive with the Prince no matter that he was answering people's questions — returned. Luckily, the newspapermen and the investors quickly recognized Rand as the more useful source and directed their queries to him, leaving William John to the other inventors, who were every bit as vague as he.

Ryder and Mary came to join Felicia; they had been speaking with Shields and the other guards, who had once again instituted a protective cordon about the steam carriage.

Felicia saw Ryder's outwardly easygoing yet inwardly suspicious gaze rest on Mayhew, who, now Rand had gone, was standing beside her. Rand may not have time to explain, but there was no reason Mayhew couldn't oblige. She turned to him. "Mr. Mayhew, perhaps you can explain what's been happening." Boldly, she took his arm and steered the artist away from the worst of the crowd.

Mary and Ryder moved with them, on Felicia's other side.

Mayhew looked rather nervously at Ryder.

"Ah . . ."

Releasing Mayhew, Felicia waved at Ryder and Mary. "Allow me to present the Marquess and Marchioness of Raventhorne, Lord Cavanaugh's brother and sister-in-law. You may speak freely before them."

Ryder rumbled, "We know of your attempts to sabotage the engine, culminating in your attempt to kidnap Miss Throgmorton." Ryder's lips curved in a gesture that was not a smile. "We're all quite keen to learn what, exactly, has been going on."

Mayhew studied Ryder for a moment and, apparently, decided the invitation to exonerate himself was not one to dismiss. Briefly, he met Felicia's eyes, then he drew in a breath and said, "I'm afraid I managed to get myself into quite horrendous debt. My principal creditor isn't one to balk at violence. And then my uncle contacted me, and —"

Along with Mary and Ryder, Felicia listened as Mayhew unburdened himself of what she judged was a comprehensive confession; certainly, he missed none of the events of which she was aware, and despite Ryder's looming presence, Mayhew made no attempt to gloss over his perfidy. That he'd been shaken to his senses by the incident in the wood and, subsequently, had recoiled from executing his uncle's plans rang true. He then explained what had happened earlier that afternoon, in the exhibition hall.

"So Winthrop took your offhand comment to heart and acted?" Mary asked.

Mayhew nodded. "I never imagined he would. I parted from him, then I saw Miss Throgmorton and Lord Cavanaugh and decided I couldn't just walk away without giving them the explanations I felt they were owed." He paused, then lightly shrugged. "His lordship thought it best to check the engine, and I went to see, too."

"I saw Rand and you slip behind the engine." Felicia looked at Ryder and Mary. "When I found them —" She succinctly described what had gone on in the fraught minutes leading up to the engine settling and performing as expected.

"So that was why the engine made that strange noise at the start," Mary said.

Felicia nodded. "The pressures were unable to equalize — not until both valves had been released."

Ryder thought for a moment, then nodded at Mayhew. "So you helped save the day. That's exoneration enough for me."

Mary and Felicia echoed, "And me."

"And," Felicia continued, "quite obviously, Rand has decided you're to be excused your transgressions."

Mayhew seemed to squirm. "As to that, his lordship and I confronted my uncle, and the upshot was that he — my uncle — will cover my debts as he promised and also pay me a stipend." Mayhew appeared not entirely comfortable with that result, but added, "My uncle also agreed to retire from this arena of investing — henceforth, he'll send any of his clients interested in investing in inventions to Lord Cavanaugh."

Ryder grinned. "It seems my brother has ensured that Winthrop pays appropriately for his sins." Ryder regarded Mayhew, then smiled. "I believe we can consider the incident dealt with and put it behind us."

Being of much the same opinion, Felicia nodded. She looked to where Rand and William John were still surrounded by the curious.

Mary slid her arm in Ryder's. "We're going to stroll some more — I want to take a look at that pen device Rand mentioned."

Felicia nodded. "I'll stay here in case they need relief."

With a smile and a nod, Ryder led his wife away.

Mayhew shifted. When Felicia glanced his way, he somewhat diffidently asked, "I wonder if I might take another look at the engine? I only caught the briefest glimpse before, and I was too tense to take proper notice."

She studied him for a moment and decided they owed him too great a debt not to let bygones go. With a smile, she tipped her head to the steam carriage. "Of course. Come on."

She led him past the cordon and a still-suspicious Shields — there would have to be more explanations later — and she and Mayhew walked around the steam carriage to the side away from the crowds. She opened the side flap to the engine compartment so Mayhew could crouch and look inside. Still explaining to other inventors, William John had the opposite flap as well as the top cover open, allowing light to stream in and illuminate the gleaming pipes and tubes, the heavy gears and cogs, and the silvery steel housing of the pistons.

Felicia looked at the engine and felt proprietorial pride bloom within her — something she'd never thought to feel over any invention.

Smiling at herself, she shifted her gaze to Mayhew and studied his expression as he gazed at the engine. She sensed the moment something took hold, and Mayhew caught his breath.

Unmoving, he stared as if committing the sight to memory, then, slowly, he straightened his legs and rose. He glanced at her. "Thank you." He hesitated for a second, then said, "Lord Cavanaugh suggested that to repay you and Mrs. Makepeace for your forbearance and understanding that I should present you with some of my sketches of the Hall — which I intend to do." He drew breath and, with rising enthusiasm in his voice, went on, "I would also like to do a series of sketches of the steam carriage and especially the engine as a gift." He caught her eye. "If you'll permit it?"

Felicia knew that William John and Rand would lodge registrations of the improvements made in assembling the Throgmorton engine, and a pictorial record of the work would certainly not go amiss. Slowly, she nodded. "That sounds like an excellent idea. We'll need to consult with my brother and his lordship, but once the steam carriage is back at the Hall, I'm sure we can arrange a viewing for you."

As the words left her lips — to be greeted with eager acceptance by Mayhew — Felicia was thinking of the quality of Mayhew's sketching and how that would translate if his subjects were inventions . . . All in all, she thought sketches of that sort might be a unique and valuable resource and getting first call on Mayhew's skill might prove to be a very good thing.

Mayhew's face had lit with enthusiasm. "If we can get the light just so —"

She let him ramble. From the other side of the carriage, she could hear William John talking, and Rand was still fielding questions from newspapermen and investors.

Ryder and Mary returned, joining her and Mayhew in the relatively uncrowded space behind the exhibit.

As she exchanged a smile with Mary, Felicia felt a sense of peaceful calm — a recognition of pending contentment — steal over her. They had done it — they'd succeeded in all they had come there hoping to achieve. After all the ups and downs, the near-disasters, and after staring down looming failure, they'd made their mark in a way none of them had even dared to dream.

Despite Winthrop's attempts at sabotage, everything had turned out resoundingly, amazingly, astonishingly well.

Twenty minutes later, the urgent interest in the Throgmorton steam carriage had abated to a level such that Rand felt able to leave

William John to handle the inquiries on his own.

After asking Shields for her direction, Rand found Felicia with Ryder, Mary, and Mayhew behind the steam carriage. When he insisted he needed to spend some time examining the other exhibits with Felicia, the other three waved them on, then fell in behind them, ambling and chatting in their wake.

They avoided the knot of people still gathered about the Prince, who had almost completed his circuit of the hall. As Rand steered Felicia toward the inventions Albert had examined before reaching the Throgmorton display, he heard Mary quizzing Mayhew. It appeared that, having understood that Mayhew was talented — both Felicia and Rand had mentioned the quality of his work — Mary had also realized that Mayhew was in need of a patron.

Rand glanced over his shoulder and met Ryder's gaze and was allowed to briefly glimpse an expression of long-suffering resignation. Grinning, Rand faced forward. Both he and Ryder knew where Mary was heading, but, all in all, there was no reason to rein her back.

Rand had his own female brain to pick; he guided Felicia to an invention he'd glimpsed earlier — a novel alteration to a printing press. "What do you think?" he asked.

She moved forward to examine the exhibit.

The inventor recognized Rand, but was quick enough to sense that Rand was waiting on Felicia's opinion; despite her being a lady, the inventor sidled closer and, when she pointed and asked questions, gave her his undivided attention.

Eventually, Felicia smiled and thanked the older man, then rejoined Rand.

She took his arm and surreptitiously pushed; he nodded to the inventor and led her on. Once they'd left the exhibit behind, he dipped his head and asked, "No?"

She shook her head. "I'm fairly certain the weight of the upper panel will very soon wear out the gears — there simply isn't enough support for moving that much weight. Ten passes — maybe as many as a hundred — then the gears will give and the upper plate will collapse onto the lower. That's not a commercial proposition."

Looking ahead, Rand smiled to himself, murmured in agreement, and led her on.

Somewhat to his surprise, she diverted to look at an invention he hadn't thought warranted their attention. It was still in the early stage of development and seemed to be a different sort of loom. He stuck to Felicia's side and, by listening to her questions and the inventor's eager answers, realized it was a knitting machine.

Felicia and the inventor went back and forth for some time. Eventually, Felicia thanked the man.

Rand nodded a farewell as Felicia retook his arm. Once they were strolling again, he asked, "Is that a project in which we should consider investing?"

Faintly puzzled, she glanced at him. "We?"

He met her gaze, but they'd drawn level with the crowd around the Prince and now was not the time. "I'll explain later, but there's a proposition I would like to put to you, one I hope you'll find attractive." He smiled. "A proposition other than marriage — or rather" — he hurriedly amended — "in addition to marriage."

"Oh?" She was intrigued.

Before she asked for more details, he waved at the displays across the hall. "At the moment, we're here, and so are all these inventors and inventions — we need to learn what we can, while we can."

She dipped her head in acknowledgment, despite her curiosity — or perhaps because of that — ready enough to fall in with that suggestion. As they wended their way across the aisle to the other side of the hall, she murmured, "To return to your earlier question, I do think the knitting machine is worth a closer look. He'll need to make changes to that assembly of pins, and the gears need a better degree of control, but I definitely believe it holds promise."

"If the results are what he claims, then there should be a market for both the invention and its product here and in other countries, too."

She inclined her head. "One would imagine so."

He'd already noted that she tended to evaluate inventions on the basis of whether they could be made to perform properly, rather than in terms of financial return. Luckily, the latter was something for which he possessed a knack. He steered her on to the next exhibit. "What about this one?"

Fifteen minutes later, the deeply resonant *bong* of a gong rang out over the exhibition hall.

Briskly, the organizers called the still-considerable crowd to attention, insisting the inventors come forward and gather in front of a small dais that had been pushed into place before the open main doors.

William John walked up from the end of

the hall. He grinned at Rand and Felicia, then took Felicia's other arm and dragged the pair of them with him. "Come on."

There wasn't time to remonstrate that William John was the true inventor — and Rand wasn't about to deny that Felicia fully deserved to go forward as well. He wasn't so sure of his place among those gathered to the fore, but this was not the moment to make a scene.

The venerable chairman of the committee — a member of the Royal Society who had officiated at such events for years — climbed onto the dais and, in ringing tones, announced, "His Highness, Prince Albert, has graciously consented to present our prestigious award of Most Promising Invention of the Year." The announcement caused a stir; the Prince's imprimatur would mean the award carried even more weight than it normally did. The chairman continued, extolling the illustrious history of the event and the award.

Before the audience grew restive, the chairman invited Albert to join him on the podium, along with another gentleman bearing the heavy silver statuette that signified the award. The chairman spoke briefly with Albert, then turned to the audience and announced, "Without more ado, the

unanimous selection of this year's commit-
tee to receive the award of Most Promising
Invention of the Year is the Throgmorton
Steam-Powered Horseless Carriage!"

Cheers and applause erupted from all
sides, even from the inventors surrounding
them.

William John turned to Felicia — he threw
his arms around her and hugged her hard.

Felicia laughed. She felt tears fill her eyes.

Still holding tight, William John whispered, "I wish Papa had lived to see this."

Felicia patted his back. "He didn't do this
— you did." She knew it was the truth,
knew how much of their father's original
design he'd — they'd — changed.

William John released her and met her
eyes. "I couldn't have done it without you."
He looked at the man beside her. "Without
you and Rand."

The organizers were urging William John
to come forward. With a huge smile split-
ting his face, he headed for the dais, towing
Felicia behind him. "Come on," he com-
manded, including Rand with his gaze.

On the dais, Albert stood holding the
statuette and smiling. When William John
stepped up, after a few well-chosen and
mercifully brief words, the Prince handed
William John the statuette.

With a reverent expression taking hold, William John accepted the award. The audience cheered, clapped, and whistled. After a moment, he faced the crowd, waited until they'd quieted, then said, "Inventors are generally solitary, but by the most amazing luck, I was blessed to have more help and support than most ever find." He glanced at Felicia, then reached out, caught her hand, and tugged her up beside him. "I had my sister, who knows more about concept and design than I ever will, to guide me past the inevitable hurdles" — his gaze moved to Rand, standing beside the dais — "and I had Lord Randolph Cavanaugh and his syndicate of investors — people who understand the vagaries of inventing — to smooth our way and keep us progressing over those hurdles to a successful end."

William John looked back at the crowd and raised the statuette high. "On behalf of the team who worked on making the Throgmorton Steam-Powered Horseless Carriage a success, I thank Prince Albert and the organizers for this recognition — and wish that, for all the other inventors here today, they find the right teams to support them so that they, too, achieve success."

The crowd roared. Everyone was smiling,

even the inventors passed over for the award.

Rand shook Albert's hand and those of the committee members. Then he turned to find Felicia and William John waiting, identical smiles wreathing their faces. Rand smiled back, spread his arms, and hugged them both.

Success, at long last, was theirs.

SIXTEEN

The celebrations lasted far into the night. It was close to midnight, and the publican was looking longingly at the stairs, when Ryder and Mary excused themselves and went up to their room.

William John, Shields, and the men who had been their guards — not counting the four presently standing guard about the barn housing the steam carriage — were still toasting a success William John had insisted be regarded as an all-inclusive team effort. Felicia caught Rand's eye, then looked toward the stairs.

He smiled, took her hand, rose, and drew her to her feet. To the others, he simply said, "Goodnight, all."

Felicia paused to add, "Don't forget we'll be leaving at nine o'clock sharp."

Several groans were the only replies, then the group went back to reliving the day's events.

Smiling, Felicia linked her arm with Rand's, and they made for the stairs.

They reached her room, and Rand followed her in. She shut the door and turned — to find herself drawn into his arms.

Leaning back against his hold, she looked into his face. The lamps had been turned down, but sufficient light streamed in from outside for her to see his expression. She trapped his eyes with hers, raised her hands and framed his face, and, with heartfelt sincerity, said, "Thank *you*. I haven't said that yet today, and I don't think William John's acknowledgment went far enough. Without you, we wouldn't be here — we would never have overcome the hurdles, much less reached such a glorious end." She hesitated, then, her eyes on his, went on, "More, I wouldn't have found myself — my true calling. And I wouldn't now feel so much closer to William John, and so much more reconciled to my father's ways." Her voice lowering, she said, "I know I have you to thank for that. If you hadn't come to the Hall and been willing to stay and work with us to see the invention through, we wouldn't be where we are."

Rand's smile was the definition of mellow, full of confident satisfaction. The same emotion rang in his voice as, after turning his

481

head and pressing a kiss to her right palm, he replied, "It truly was my pleasure — and all of what's followed, all our combined success, is my reward. All the reward I look for." He paused, then added, "*This* is the sweetest part of what I do and a large part of what attracts me to the challenge."

She slid her hands back, locked them at his nape, and tipped her head, studying him. "Succeeding — pulling it off."

No question, Rand noticed; she understood. "And speaking of such challenges — and pulling them off — as I mentioned, I have a proposition to place before you, one I wish to state at the outset is not in any way connected to my proposal of marriage." He continued to hold her before him, continued to meet her eyes. "If you don't think this proposition has merit — if it doesn't appeal to you — please don't feel obliged to agree. Your decision won't affect our marriage in any way."

She narrowed her eyes fractionally. "I think you had better make your proposal clear, my lord — and allow me to be the judge of how much impact it might have."

His lips twisted wryly. "Very well — it's simply this. Quite aside from marrying you, I want to bring you into the firm of Cavanaugh Investments as a full partner."

Her brows rose. "A partner? Doing what?"

"Working alongside me in evaluating inventions in which the various syndicates I manage might invest. I have a feel for things from a financial perspective, but you have a talent for sensing which inventions can be made to work efficiently and which are more likely to hit insurmountable obstacles. You can winnow the chaff from my grain. As partners, working as a team, our chances of success — and of avoiding failure — will be greatly increased."

Her eyes had widened. "You truly want me working beside you . . . openly?"

He nodded. "In the office, sitting alongside me while I meet with my investors." He couldn't help his smile. "You'll feature as my number one advantage over all other investment-syndicate managers, at least those focusing on inventions. Especially now the Throgmorton steam carriage has achieved such preeminent success."

Her gaze had grown unfocused as she envisaged the picture he was endeavoring to paint. "Together, we could steer funds toward those inventions most likely to result in new and better ways of doing things — producing things — society needs." She refocused on his eyes and smiled her warm, engaging smile. "This proposition of yours, husband-to-be, appears to have been quite thoroughly thought through — a most well-grounded and well-rounded proposal."

He smiled into her green eyes. "I thought so." After a second, he arched a brow. "Does that mean you'll accept?"

She tipped back her head and laughed. "Of course — how could I resist?"

He dipped his head to place a string of hot kisses down the sweet line of her throat. "I'm glad you can't. We'll make a remarkable team."

She righted her head and, moving into him, her gaze locking on his, softly said, "I never thought to have anything to do with inventions — not ever. But by your side . . . that's where life now calls me."

He held her gaze. "It's where you fit — by my side, working with me in every way."

"Yes." For a second, she held his gaze, letting him see her commitment to that — a commitment to match his own — then she stretched up on her toes and pressed her lips to his.

She kissed him, and he gathered her to him and kissed her back.

And as the moon and the stars shone upon them in silvery benediction, they gave themselves up to their private celebration. With minds and souls committed, wholeheartedly, they embraced all that linked them, surrendering with joy to the need, to the undeniable wanting. To the hunger and desire, to the passion that rose up and, in a fiery conflagration, erupted and drove them to the bed.

Onto sheets that tangled as they reached for each other and burned.

They came together in a rush of joy and incandescent pleasure, driven by a force too powerful to deny.

They seized and clutched and let the sensations grip and whip them on, up and on to the peak — then over to where soaring ecstasy seized them, broke and shattered them, and glory flooded in, until, at the last, oblivion ruled.

Later, much later, when he lifted from her, then settled beside her and drew the covers over their cooling limbs, when she turned to him, into his arms, he dropped a soft kiss to her temple and whispered, "Together in everything from now on."

Three days later, Rand and Felicia stood on the porch of Throgmorton Hall and waved Ryder and Mary and the men from Raventhorne on their way.

As the small troop passed out of sight down the drive, Felicia sighed. She glanced at Rand, standing beside her. She'd promised Mary and Ryder that she would accompany Rand on a visit to Raventhorne Abbey in a few weeks. In truth, she was looking forward to learning more about him and his family — about his life.

Flora, who had come out with them to wave their guests farewell, turned and walked toward the open door. "Do come in for tea later, my dears."

Rand glanced at Flora and smiled. "We will." He turned back to Felicia, took her hand, and drew her down the steps.

As she acquiesced and allowed him to lead her onto the lawn, in reply to her inquiring look, still smiling, he said, "It's time we discussed the details of our own crowning achievement."

She laughed. "You mean our wedding?"

"Indeed. Did I mention that Mary is — or was — a Cynster? If she's involved in any way — and trust me, she will be — then the words 'crowning achievement' will definitely apply."

Felicia smiled. Having now spent many hours in Mary's company, she could appreciate his point.

They'd strolled past the end of the terrace and onto the south lawn. From around the rear corner of the house came the sounds of

William John's and Clive Mayhew's voices. The steam carriage was presently angled on the paving outside the workshop, with its various panels removed to display the engine in all its glory. Clive was busy creating a range of sketches, some of which would eventually hang in the Hall and also in Rand's office in the City.

"That was an excellent idea of yours to put Clive on a retainer to do sketches of all the inventions we take under our wing." Rand met her eyes; his were laughing. "Aside from keeping him solvent, the retainer will ensure we can get him away from Mary when the need arises."

Felicia chuckled. "I'm not sure Clive realizes what's in store for him and his sketches, now that he's agreed to allow Mary to be his patroness."

Grinning, Rand nodded. "With her connections and her determination, she'll steer him to great heights. Given his talent, there's little doubt of that."

They strolled on in comfortable silence. After several minutes, Rand glanced at Felicia. "So to our big question. When shall it be?"

When she gave no answer, but, instead, met his gaze and arched her brows in invitation, he went on, "I would prefer it to be sooner rather than later, obviously. There are, however, formalities that are best observed — banns, for instance. I was thinking of late August."

She considered, then nodded. "Late August will suit, my lord."

Lips twitching, he inclined his head. "Having agreed on that — and on the need for banns — I assume you would prefer to be married here, from the Hall?"

She glanced at the house. "If you're agreeable. I've known the people here and in the village all my life — I would like to have our wedding in their midst, at St. Mary's."

He raised her hand and brushed a kiss across her knuckles. "That's as it should be. So a wedding at St. Mary's in Hampstead Norreys on" — he swiftly counted through the days — "I believe it would be August the twenty-sixth."

Lowering his arm, settling her hand in his, he met her gaze. "On to the next question — where should we live?"

She frowned. "Does it have to be in London?"

"In the main, no — I imagine we'll spend most of our days, those when we're not traveling to view exhibitions and such, in the country." He tipped his head and acknowledged, "We will need to live in London for short periods scattered through the year, but given how rarely Ryder and Mary use Raventhorne House — it's a massive old mansion in Mount Street — and I've always had rooms there, I suspect Mary will tell us that we'll be doing her and Ryder a favor by using that as our London base."

"All right." She met his eyes. "So where in the country should we live?"

"I thought," Rand said, trying to read her expression, "that as Raventhorne Abbey isn't far, we might look for a property between here and there."

Her answering smile set his mind at rest. "That would, indeed, offer the best of all worlds."

Although Flora had stated that she would remain at Throgmorton Hall and keep the household functioning, Rand knew Felicia would prefer to be within easy reach of her brother, and Rand himself thought that wise, not least given the likelihood of further joint inventions. He had a suspicion that, brilliant though William John undoubtedly was, he would always need his sister's mind to bring his ideas to their ultimate fruition.

"That's settled, then." Rand gripped Felicia's hand more firmly and looked ahead. "We'll start hunting for a likely property tomorrow."

She laughed, but didn't argue.

He glanced at her as she strolled beside him. There was a deep contentment inside him now that hadn't been there before; he'd never before felt on such an even keel, with his future, clear and unclouded, stretching ahead of him.

And he owed his newfound certainty, his inner peace, to her. He was beyond grateful he'd found her — the right wife, the perfect helpmate, the partner-in-life he hadn't had the faintest inkling could exist, much less that such an intelligent, independent lady was the bride he'd instinctively if unknowingly been searching for — the one lady in the whole world he needed to complete his life.

His life as he wanted to live it.

She offered him all he needed — she anchored him and gave him the necessary insights to imbue his chosen life of investing with a wider, deeper purpose, transforming it into a more fulfilling, long-term endeavor.

She was his future in every way.

With her walking by his side, her hand in his, he was . . . quietly joyous.

Felicia glanced at Rand's face, took in the softened lines and the aura of relaxed happiness that invested his expression, and felt the same emotion, powerful and strong, dwelling inside her. Filling her and pushing out all doubts. She looked ahead — not at the old oak but into the future. The future that lay all but tangibly before them. By his side, that future was one she would embrace with fervor — one she would seize and hold on to with all her heart.

But that future hadn't just accidentally found her — it had come to her courtesy of the nobleman pacing by her side, the knight in shining armor who had swept into her life and slayed dragons left and right, then opened her eyes and shown her who she truly was.

He'd released her true self to grow, then he'd taken her hand and encouraged her to be all she could be.

She was still riding the crest of that wave of newfound growth, buoyed high and on, into their future, and she had no plans to ever slide her fingers from his.

This is life.

This is love.

And it was glorious and wonderful and exciting beyond description — she would cling to this, to him, forever, and never, ever, let go.

EPILOGUE

Lord Christopher Cavanaugh reached the church just in time. On the southern edge of the village of Hampstead Norreys, the Church of St. Mary the Virgin, with its proud Norman tower, had — thank God — been easy to locate. After leaving his groom, Smiggs, to deal with the curricle, Kit found the reverend standing by the door; after shaking Kit's hand with some relief, the reverend directed him around the outside of the church toward the vestry, where, apparently, his brothers were waiting.

Striding down the side of the church, Kit felt something of the good reverend's relief. He'd overslept; if it hadn't been for Smiggs, Kit would still be snoring in his room at the inn in Newbury. While such a lapse might be excusable, given he'd landed in Bristol yesterday afternoon and had had to make a mad dash across the country, driving for as long as he'd been able to make out the road, if he hadn't made it in time, his brothers would never have let him hear the end of it. He'd reached Newbury too late to forge on, so had made a halt there, leaving covering the last ten or so miles to the village for this morning.

He'd driven those last ten miles like a madman, but he'd reached the church before the bride, and with time to join his brothers for Rand's last minutes of freedom.

Lips quirking, Kit reached for the latch of the door to the small room built off the north transept. Before he could grasp the iron ring, the door was hauled open, and his younger brother, Godfrey, looked out at him.

"It *is* you — I thought I recognized your footsteps. About time." Godfrey — who appeared to have grown another lanky half foot since Kit had last seen him, which had been only a few months before — impatiently waved Kit inside. "You're just in time."

"But I am in time," Kit stated, stepping into the small room and letting Godfrey — at twenty-five years old, four years Kit's junior — close the door behind him. "And that's what counts." Finding his two older brothers standing before him, Kit beamed. He nodded to Ryder, who, lazily amused, nodded back, then Kit turned to Rand, reached for his brother's hand, and, simultaneously, clapped him on the shoulder. "Well, old man, so the time has come."

As Rand shook Kit's hand, Rand's answering smile held a happiness — a contentment — Kit hadn't expected to see. He felt a jab somewhere in the region of his solar plexus; unbelievable though it seemed, apparently, Rand truly had found what Kit had long thought none of them — Rand, Kit, their sister, Eustacia, and Godfrey — would ever claim.

The sort of love Ryder, their half brother, had found with his Mary.

After what their mother, Lavinia — Ryder's stepmother — had put her own children, Rand especially, through, Kit had assumed none of them would ever be tempted by marriage. Although Lavinia had died nearly six years ago in a self-inflicted accident, her malignant influence lived on — or so Kit had thought.

When he'd received the letter informing him of Rand's impending nuptials, he'd assumed either Rand had fallen victim to the matchmakers — a possibility Kit had found difficult to believe — or, more likely, Rand had decided to contract some sort of comfortable marriage in order to put an end to the unrelenting onslaught of the aforementioned matchmakers.

Looking at Rand, at the shining expectation in his eyes, Kit realized his assumptions had been incorrect. With his Miss Throgmorton, Rand had found love.

"We'd thought you would meet us at the Abbey," Ryder drawled.

Raventhorne Abbey, the principal seat of the Marquess of Raventhorne, was their ancestral home and, presently, Ryder and Mary's principal residence, shared with their growing family. As the Abbey was only about three hours away, Rand's family had elected to gather there before traveling to Hampstead Norreys for the service. "I'd hoped to," Kit replied, then transferred his gaze to Rand. "But I was in Bermuda when your letter reached me — I had to race to get back in time. And then, of course, we ran into storms off the Bay of Biscay. Truth to tell, I'm just glad I got here at all."

Rand grinned. "So am I — if you hadn't arrived, the wedding party would have been unbalanced, and Mary and Stacie would have been exceedingly peeved."

"The pair of them have done most of the

organizing," Ryder explained, somewhat un-
necessarily as Kit was well acquainted with
his sister-in-law's and his sister's proclivi-
ties.

Rand's face softened. "Arranging social
events is not Felicia's forte."

"Indeed?" Kit leveled a mock-challenging
look at Rand. "It sounds as if I should be
doubly sorry I didn't get a chance to meet
Miss Throgmorton before she agreed to let
you put your ring on her finger."

Rand's eyes lit, and he laughed and shook
his head. "You wouldn't have stood a chance
— you know nothing about inventions."

Ryder was chuckling, too.

Kit looked from one to the other and
noticed Godfrey was doing the same. "You'll
have to fill us in on what inventions have to
do with anything later."

Rand grinned. Then the door leading into
the church opened, and the reverend looked
in. He beamed at them all, his gaze coming
to rest on Rand. "Lord Cavanaugh — it's
time."

Although the words should have sounded
like the knell of doom, Kit noted that
Rand's expectation — his joy — only
mounted. As the brothers filed into the
church, Kit pondered that; he was increas-

ingly curious to meet Rand's soon-to-be wife.

On the steps before the altar, they lined up beside Rand, with Ryder to Rand's right, Kit next to him, and Godfrey the last in the line. As they took their places, a wave of hushed feminine whispers rippled through the crowd. Kit straightened and, clasping his hands before him, exchanged a cynical look with Godfrey.

It wasn't often society saw the four brothers all together, displayed in such a way. Although Kit stood just over six feet tall in his stockinged feet, Ryder and Rand both had several inches on him, and over the last months, Godfrey had nearly caught up, although he was still an inch or so the shortest. While Godfrey had inherited the lean, lanky build of their maternal grandfather, Ryder, Rand, and Kit had been blessed with the broad shoulders and powerful, athletic physique of their father; having all four brothers in their perfectly tailored morning coats and dark-gray trousers lined up with their backs to the congregation was setting quite a few of the females — and not just the young ones — tittering.

In his mind's eye, Kit envisioned what the congregation saw. Viewed from the back, Rand, Ryder, and he were, in body, very similar, but the color of their hair instantly distinguished them one from the other. Although the way their hair grew and the styles they favored for their faintly wavy locks were similar, Rand had dark-brown hair, Ryder's mane was a tawny mixture of golds and brown, while Kit's hair was a rich mid brown. Godfrey had inherited their mother's shade — a dark brown with russet tints, a true auburn — a feature he shared with their sister, Stacie.

As if Kit thinking of Stacie had called her into being, the organist changed his tune to a processional wedding anthem, and together with his brothers, Kit turned and watched the bride's attendants walk up the aisle. Stacie led the way, a relaxed smile on her face suggesting she was glad to be there, although Kit had his doubts.

Possibly even more than Rand, Stacie had had her mind and certainly her view of marriage manipulated and impacted on by their mother and her doings. Stacie was already twenty-six years old and, to date, had shown no interest in marriage — and that wasn't an issue her brothers, or even Mary, bossy as she was, sought to push. Kit thought it very likely Stacie would never marry. That conclusion stemmed not so much from a judgment on any likely suitors as a suspicion that Stacie would never trust herself in such a union; she'd seen all too clearly what their mother had become.

He might be her brother, but Kit was also a man; as his gaze took in Stacie's artfully arranged dark-auburn hair and her figure stylishly gowned in pale-violet silk, he couldn't help but admit that his sister bade fair to being as voluptuously attractive as their mother had been.

As Lady Eustacia Cavanaugh, Stacie hailed from an ancient noble lineage and was well-dowered and well-connected. Kit cynically mused that the grandes dames had to be severely exercised over the prospect of such an eligible bride insisting on placing herself beyond their reach.

As Stacie neared the end of the nave, she met Rand's eyes, and her smile brightened with patent sincerity — then her gaze skated along the line of her brothers, fleetingly meeting each of their gazes. Kit allowed his lips to curve as his eyes met Stacie's, then as she turned to take her place along the bride's side of the steps, he looked up the aisle at the second bridesmaid.

The young lady who would, he realized, be his partner in much of what followed.

Gowned in the same pale-violet silk as Stacie, the unknown lady was tallish, slender

— distinctly willowy — with golden-blond hair piled in a neat knot on the top of her head. Her face was heart-shaped, her complexion pale with just a hint of color in her cheeks. Her forehead was wide above finely arched brown brows; her eyes were large and well-set beneath those brows, but Kit couldn't guess their color, and somewhat to his surprise, he discovered he wanted to know. His gaze lowered to her lips . . . and, for several heartbeats, lingered there. Perfectly sculpted in pale rose, the curves drew his gaze even when he tried to look away.

Following in Stacie's wake, the young lady's figure was nothing in comparison, yet . . .

Kit drew in a breath and shifted his gaze and his attention to the determined lines of the lady's nicely rounded chin. As she walked, she looked ahead, but, apparently, without focus, yet as she neared the steps, she smiled sweetly at Rand.

Kit waited, but she — whoever she was — didn't glance his way.

He felt vaguely cheated; she had to know that he would be her partner for the rest of the ceremony and the associated events.

Surreptitiously, he nudged Ryder. When Ryder cast him a sidelong glance, Kit murmured, "Who is she — the other brides-maid?"

As Mary, a delighted smile on her face, was presently walking down the aisle, "the other bridesmaid" could mean only one person.

"A Miss Sylvia Buckleberry — a distant cousin and childhood friend of Felicia's," Ryder murmured back.

Mary reached her place, then the music swelled, and the bride — an utterly radiant golden-haired young lady gowned in ivory silk — walked down the aisle on the arm of a gentleman Kit realized must be her brother, William John Throgmorton.

The brother halted before the altar and, with an insouciant grin, placed his sister's hand in Rand's.

Even though Ryder's bulk was between them, Kit would have sworn he literally felt Rand's and Miss Throgmorton's — Felicia's — joint happiness, an incandescent joy like a small sun casting its rays over everyone near.

As one, the bridal party faced the altar and, with the congregation, gave their attention to the reverend as he commenced the service.

Kit had stood beside Rand at Ryder's wedding; he knew the ropes. Having sensed the nature of the connection Rand and Felicia shared, Kit wasn't surprised by the clarity and sincerity that rang in their voices as they made their vows.

This, Kit inwardly acknowledged, was how marriage ought to be. He felt both glad and humbled that Rand had found his way to Felicia and had had the courage to embrace love and thus secure all it would bring them.

Kit knew himself well enough to admit that he also felt just a tad jealous. Not over Felicia herself, but over the future Rand now had a chance at creating with her.

On the one hand, he would dearly like such a chance himself, but, on the other hand, after all he'd learned of his mother and her doings — in actuality, far more than Rand, Stacie, or Godfrey had ever known, and a great deal more than Ryder had ever guessed — marriage was an entanglement he couldn't see himself ever risking.

Then the reverend pronounced Rand and Felicia man and wife, and they shared a kiss before God and the congregation. Kit found himself grinning, infected with the newlyweds' happiness as the pair drew apart, then, arm in arm, their faces glowing, led the bridal party up the aisle.

With a proud smile, Ryder offered his arm

to his marchioness. Mary took it, and they fell into step behind Rand and Felicia — slowed by the well-wishers on either side, all wanting to press their congratulations.

Kit duly paced to the center of the step and offered his arm to his enigmatic partner. "Miss Buckleberry." He watched, waiting to catch her eyes if, finally, she glanced at him.

She did, and he discovered her eyes were a soft violet blue — periwinkle blue.

Somewhat to his surprise, she met his gaze with a very direct, level look.

Before he could say anything more, she dipped her head crisply. "Lord Cavanaugh."

Then she placed her fingertips on his sleeve and stepped down — perforce, Kit moved with her.

As they took their place behind Ryder and Mary, Kit glanced sidelong at the confounding Miss Buckleberry, but even though he waited — and he was fairly certain she could feel his gaze — she didn't look his way again. Instead, she kept her gaze fixed forward, her chin high . . . almost as if her nose was, at least figuratively, in the air.

What?

Puzzled by the muted but distinct frostiness emanating from the lady by his side, Kit wracked his brain. Had he met her before? Was she miffed because he hadn't recognized her?

But no. He had an excellent memory for faces, and he'd take an oath he'd never seen hers before.

Buckleberry. The name rang not a single bell; he hadn't met her father or any brother, either.

They reached the front of the church, and, after Rand and Felicia had braved a storm of rice, everyone gathered in groups on the sloping lawns to chat while the carriages were brought around.

Miss Buckleberry drew her hand from Kit's sleeve the instant they stepped out of the church, but of necessity, she remained in the same group, more or less by Kit's side, although she largely ignored him in a perfectly polite way.

Rand and Felicia departed first in Rand's curricle, which had been bedecked with ribbons and rosettes. The crowd waved them off, then Ryder and Mary followed in Ryder's curricle. The Throgmorton brougham drew up next, with Kit's curricle following behind.

Kit studied Miss Buckleberry, then touched her arm. When she looked inquiringly at him, he waved toward his curricle.

She glanced at it, then, again, met his eyes with a direct — and faintly challenging —

look. "Thank you, my lord, but it's more appropriate that I travel with your sister in the brougham." She turned her perfectly polite and faintly smiling gaze on Godfrey. "I'm sure you and your brother have stories to share."

Kit stared at the confounding creature.

More appropriate?

What the devil did she mean by that?

After Felicia's cousin Flora had taken her seat, Kit, clinging to what was — where Miss Buckleberry was concerned — fast becoming a mask of civility, handed her into the brougham, then stood aside as Godfrey helped Stacie in and Felicia's brother followed.

Kit shut the brougham's door, then stalked to his curricle.

Godfrey followed and climbed up to the seat beside Kit.

After Smiggs swung up behind them, Kit shook the reins, and the pair of bays obediently stepped out in the brougham's wake.

As the curricle rolled behind the carriage, Kit rested his gaze moodily on the back of Miss Buckleberry's fair head. She had settled beside Flora on the forward-facing seat, which left him free to glare at her as much as he wished.

Godfrey leaned back in the curricle's seat.

"We — Ryder, Mary, Stacie, and I — are leaving for the Abbey after the breakfast. Are you planning on joining us?"

"That was my intention." Without shifting his gaze from its obsession, Kit added, "I could do with a few days of —" He broke off, then his lips twitched. "I was going to say *peace and quiet,* but with our nephews and niece racing about, I suspect there'll be precious little of that. Still . . ."

Godfrey nodded. "I know what you mean. A stay at the Abbey might not be restful, but it is comforting."

Struck by the fact that was true, Kit made no reply.

After several more seconds of staring, he gave up all thought of understanding Miss Buckleberry's incomprehensible attitude and glanced at Godfrey. "So what have you been up to?"

Godfrey shrugged. "This and that."

Recognizing the response as an invitation to pry, Kit obliged and learned that his little brother, courtesy of several friends, was spending a significant amount of time with a more arty circle.

"They're not Bohemian — I could introduce them to Mary without a qualm — but they do see things rather differently." Godfrey tilted his head consideringly. "I wouldn't say they're practically minded. Often, hauling them back to earth falls to me."

That was said with a self-deprecatory smile.

On glimpsing it, Kit smiled himself and drove on.

"That's the drive." Godfrey pointed to where the brougham was turning in between two gateposts. "It's rather a nice place — close to the village but quite private, what with these woods all around."

It transpired that they were to make use of that privacy — tables had been set up on a long, sloping lawn. After leaving the curricle with the various grooms in the forecourt, Kit and Godfrey were shown to their places as more of the guests from the church arrived.

Rand and Felicia had wanted a small wedding, but given their family, "small" still numbered more than fifty guests. Of course, judged against the last family wedding — Ryder and Mary's — fifty qualified as tiny.

A long table had been set up for the bridal party, just below the raised terrace and facing down the lawn toward the other tables. Accustomed to the way such things were done, Kit wasn't surprised to find himself seated between Mary and Miss Buckleberry.

As he claimed his seat, Miss Buckleberry was already deep in conversation with Miss Throgmorton's brother, who was seated on her other side, and Mary was chatting avidly to Rand, on her right.

Kit settled — and Mary turned to him and immediately quizzed him on his intentions after the breakfast. After assuring her that he would, indeed, be joining the family at the Abbey — which was definitely what she'd wanted to hear — he deftly turned the tables and asked her about her offspring. From experience, he knew that recounting their latest exploits would occupy Mary for quite some time, and so it proved.

The first toasts were made, the meal was served, and the event rolled on in customary fashion — and, finally, over a particularly good syllabub, Kit managed to seize a moment of Miss Buckleberry's time. He absolved Felicia's brother of monopolizing her attention; if anything, the shoe had been on the other foot.

As the laughter occasioned by the final toast — proposed by Ryder — faded, he fleetingly caught the lady's elusive eye. "I understand, Miss Buckleberry, that you've known my new sister-in-law for some time."

Rather than look at him, she poked at the syllabub, but consented to nod. "Indeed.

We met as infants and have been close friends ever since."

Kit waited, but she said nothing more. "So you often visited each other's homes?"

"When we were young children, yes. But after her mother's death, Felicia was more or less stuck here, managing the household, so I was the one who visited."

"Do you live far afield?"

"My father has a living not far from Bath."

Aha. She was a clergyman's daughter. Perhaps that was what was behind her prickliness.

They were interrupted by the staff clearing the empty plates, then Miss Buckleberry pushed back her chair. "If you'll excuse me, I must speak with Cousin Flora."

Kit summoned a meaningless smile, rose, and drew back her chair for her.

With the faintest inclination of her head, she headed to where Flora sat at the end of one of the other tables.

Other guests were getting to their feet and mingling in groups.

Kit stepped back into the shadow of the terrace. With his hands in his pockets, he stared, faintly frowning, at the confounding Miss Buckleberry.

From her words and also from what he'd seen, he judged her to be of much the same age as Felicia, who Rand had told him was twenty-four.

No green girl. No silly, flighty flibbertigibbet.

Miss Buckleberry's attitude to him had nothing to do with nerves. If anything, he sensed hers were quite steely.

No. For some unfathomable reason, Miss Buckleberry was deliberately giving him the cold shoulder.

Kit wasn't accustomed to inspiring such a reaction in the breasts of young ladies. Generally speaking, they were effusively attentive, very ready to return his smiles and chatter to him with eager enthusiasm for however long he deigned to make himself available.

Not Miss Buckleberry.

Ryder, with Rand at his elbow, strolled up, interrupting Kit's cogitations.

"So," Ryder drawled, "did you succeed in securing what you went to Bermuda to get?"

Kit had discussed his plans with his half brother; from their earliest years, Ryder had always been the one Rand, Kit, and Godfrey had turned to for advice and to sound out their ideas. Shifting his gaze to Ryder's face, Kit nodded. "Yes. Cobworth has agreed to return to England and build for me." He paused, then added, "I'm thinking of setting up in Bristol, rather than somewhere on the south coast. There's so much ship-building going on in Bristol at the moment, any trade or materials we'll need will be there, at our fingertips."

Ryder arched his brows, his expression considering. "That might well be wise, especially given you want to build larger yachts, rather than just sloops to run across the Channel."

Rand added, "That will also be a point of distinction between you and other yacht-builders — not just the location of your works but that you'll have access to different craftsmen. And that's not something to sneer at."

"No, indeed. Hence my chasing Cobworth. And," Kit continued, "there's also the fact that the town council are likely to be encouraging — they want more jobs, and an enterprise such as I'm proposing will deliver that."

The three of them settled to go over Kit's plans. Ryder's business acumen and Rand's background in raising capital gave Kit plenty of support on which to draw. While they talked, Kit saw Godfrey and Stacie chatting with several other young ladies farther down the lawn — then Miss Buckleberry joined the group, smiling and chatting, relaxed and assured, and not at all buttoned-up, aloof, and reserved, as she had been through every second she'd spent with Kit.

A string quartet had set up on the terrace, and the soothing strains of an orchestral air floated out over the three brothers' heads.

Then Mary bustled up. She threw Ryder and Kit a meaningful look, but it was Rand's hand she caught. "Come along. It's time."

Rand sent a look heavenward, but he was smiling as he allowed himself to be towed away.

Mystified, Kit asked, "What was that look — Mary's — about?"

Ryder dropped a hand on Kit's shoulder. "Apparently, just because we're out on the lawn, doesn't mean we get to skip the bridal waltz."

"Oh — I see." Kit's gaze fixed on Miss Buckleberry as she laughed gaily at something Godfrey had said. "I'd better go and claim my partner, then."

Ryder made a sound of agreement and ambled off in his wife's wake.

Smiling intently, Kit walked across the lawn. The fact that Ryder — who, despite his lazy air, inevitably noticed damned near everything — hadn't commented on Miss

Buckleberry's frostiness suggested that, although the lady's attitude to Kit was glaringly obvious to him, her façade of easygoing politeness had been good enough to screen it from everyone else.

He circled the group she was still chatting with — the one including Stacie and Godfrey — and quietly came up behind her. The lawn was thick; she didn't hear him approach.

At that moment, Mary, up on the terrace, clapped her hands, and when everyone looked her way, she asked the gathered guests to stand ready for the bridal waltz.

Immediately, the violins swelled, and Rand stepped out with Felicia in his arms, and they revolved across the lawn.

If anyone had entertained any doubt that theirs was a love match, the glow in Felicia's face, the simple pride in Rand's expression, and the open devotion with which, their gazes locked, each regarded the other, oblivious to the onlookers all around, would have slain it.

Stacie and the other young ladies in the group sighed as Rand and Felicia whirled past.

Curious, Kit leaned to the side and checked, but Miss Buckleberry did not sigh. She was too absorbed scanning those standing on the other side of the lawn.

Behind her, Kit grinned — a touch evilly.

Then Stacie grasped Godfrey's sleeve. "The bridal party is supposed to join them on the second circuit. We should step out after Kit and Miss Buckleberry . . ." Stacie glanced at Miss Buckleberry and saw Kit behind her. Stacie smiled at Kit. "There you are, brother mine."

Miss Buckleberry whipped around. Her eyes were wide when they collided with Kit's.

She hadn't known about the bridal waltz — she'd assumed it wouldn't be held on the lawn.

For one instant, those truths were easy to read in the violet blue, then she drew breath, her lashes lowered, hiding her lovely eyes, and her expression smoothed from . . . What had he seen in it? Shock, yes, and something akin to horror — but why?

But she was safe behind her aloof, reserved shield again. With a little dip of her head, she murmured, "Well met, my lord." She glanced at Rand and Felicia — and at Ryder and Mary as they stepped out in the newlyweds' wake. Without looking at Kit, Miss Buckleberry held out her hand. "Shall we, my lord?"

Kit didn't bother replying — not with

words. He closed his hand about her fingers
— felt them tremble, but the reaction was
so swiftly stilled he wasn't sure, in the next
moment, that he'd felt any such thing.
Smoothly, he drew her into his arms, then
stepped out and expertly steered them so
they fell into line, revolving in Ryder and
Mary's wake.

From the corner of his eye, he glimpsed
Stacie and Godfrey joining the group.
Another circuit, and all the other guests
inclined to do so would join them.

Kit bided his time, very aware that although he was holding her in prescribed
fashion and not so much as half an inch
closer, Miss Buckleberry's spine was rigid,
her back beneath his hand stiff as a board.
He had no idea how she managed it, but
despite her rigid state, she performed the
dance with commendable grace.

Throughout, her gaze remained fixed past
his left ear.

As the rest of the company joined in and
the sound of laughter and conversations
rose around them, he transferred his gaze
fully to his patently reluctant partner's face
and said, "Miss Buckleberry, I greatly fear
that our paths have crossed before, and I
must have — somehow, in some fashion —

515

stepped on your toes. Literally or figuratively."

Her lips tightened, and she threw him a glance so swift he wasn't able to snare it. "Why do you imagine that, my lord? I assure you we've never met before."

"I believe you must be mistaken, and I have, indeed, at some time, done something quite grave to earn your displeasure." This time, when — puzzled — she glanced at him, he caught and trapped her gaze. "How else am I to account for your chilly, not to say frigid, behavior toward me?"

Several seconds passed. He felt sure she would disclaim and turn his probing aside with a flustered disavowal.

Instead, she surprised him. Her eyes fearlessly meeting his, her gaze as ever direct and uncompromising, she drew breath and evenly said, "My reason is simple enough, my lord. I've heard of your reputation, I know it to be well deserved, and I have no wish whatever to feature as another of your conquests, intentional or otherwise."

For two revolutions, he held her gaze. Then, his eyes narrowing, he softly said, "I wasn't aware you stood in any danger of falling at my feet, Miss Buckleberry. Was I mistaken?"

The flare of temper that lit her eyes turned

them a deeper violet. Her chin rose a notch, but her voice was cool as she replied, "What an exceedingly arrogant presumption, my lord."

The music ceased. Their feet slowed of their own accord. But Kit, lost in the tangle of whatever this was between them, didn't immediately let her go.

Her chin set, and she stepped back, tugging her fingers from his grasp and forcing him to lower his arms.

She drew herself up, icicles positively dripping from her as she inclined her head to him. "Good day, my lord."

Kit stood unmoving and watched her walk — with outward serenity — away from him.

During the rest of the wedding breakfast, he didn't get another chance to approach her — not that he tried. He knew quite well what his reputation in society was, but was it his fault that young ladies dreamed and fantasized about things he never even spoke of, much less promised?

He could, of course, have informed her that his intentional conquests were always thoroughly aware that marriage was not on offer; aside from all else, his intentional conquests were invariably already wed.

By her own admission, they hadn't previously met, so what the devil had she been about, flinging his reputation in his face like that? She'd pokered up on him before he'd so much as smiled at her.

Miss Buckleberry, he concluded, was touched in her upper works.

He waltzed with Felicia, who he found delightful, warm, and easy to talk with — nothing like her closest friend. Relaxing — he wasn't losing his touch — he told Felicia several stories of Rand's exploits when they'd been children, just to keep his brother on his toes.

Mary and Stacie both claimed him for waltzes, then he set himself to beguile Flora into taking a slow turn with him.

By the time the sun started to slide down the western sky and the guests drifted toward the forecourt, where the carriages were waiting, he'd largely managed to blot Miss Buckleberry from his mind.

The first to depart were the newly-weds. Rand had told Kit that he and Felicia were going to spend the next months in the house they'd recently bought near the village of Wickham Heath, roughly midway between the Abbey and Throgmorton Hall.

Kit had promised to call in after his stay at the Abbey.

The entire company of guests and all the household gathered to wave Rand and Felicia off. Then came the usual fuss as the party bound for the Abbey sorted themselves into carriages and tendered thanks and farewells.

Just before he climbed into his curricle, Kit glanced around, but Miss Buckleberry was no longer in the forecourt.

Deciding that was probably just as well — he had no idea what he would have said to her if she'd been there — he climbed up, took the reins, and, with Godfrey once more beside him and Smiggs up behind, he gave the bays the office, and the curricle rolled smoothly down the drive.

Just before they were engulfed by the woods lining the drive, Kit glanced back at the house.

His gaze went directly to a window on the first floor — to the golden-haired lady standing there, watching him drive away.

His gut tightened. Premonition swept over him.

Shrugging off the sensation, he faced forward and set the horses to a faster pace.

Miss Sylvia Buckleberry was the sort of irritating, judgmental female he might, in other circumstances, have been tempted to subtly pursue, purely to rattle her in payment for her hoity dismissal, but the reality

was that he would, very likely, never set eyes
on her again.

ABOUT THE AUTHOR

#1 *New York Times* bestselling author **Stephanie Laurens** began writing as an escape from the dry world of professional science, a hobby that quickly became a career. Her novels set in Regency England have captivated readers around the globe, making her one of the romance world's most beloved and popular authors.